the
Present

By Geanna Culbertson

North Carolina

Published in the United States by BQB Publishing
(an imprint of Boutique of Quality Books Publishing Company, Inc.)
www.bqbpublishing.com

978-1-952782-33-6 (p)
978-1-952782-34-3 (e)

Library of Congress Control Number: 2021946497

Book design by Robin Krauss, www.bookformatters.com
Cover concept by Geanna Culbertson
Cover design by Ellis Dixon, www.ellisdixon.com
First editor: Pearlie Tan
Second editor: Olivia Swenson

Explore the fantastical books in
The Crisanta Knight Series

Looking for more magical shenanigans, epic adventure, and heartwarming heroic journeys?

Geanna's new guardian angel series releases April 2022 Visit www.GeannaCulbertson.com to learn more.

Dedication

This book, like everything I shall ever accomplish, is dedicated to my mom and dad. You are my heroes, my coaches, and my best friends. I am thankful for you every day for more reasons than there are words in this book.

Special Thanks

Terri Leidich & BQB Publishing
The greatest publisher in the history of the universe.

Gallien Culbertson
The person I can always count on for support and guidance.

Veronica Reynosa
The friend who I didn't know I needed and I could not be
more grateful to have found.

Alexa Carter
The girl who will always be one of the first people
who believed in my books.

Pearlie Tan, Olivia Swenson, & Ellis Dixon
The women who make me better, and who I couldn't
do this without.

Mr. Charles Dickens
The man who wrote the wonderful, inspiring, compelling classic
that has inspired countless storytellers to write grand, and
also deeply-moving holiday adventures, and that has inspired
countless people to try and change for the better as they
let Christmas Spirit into their hearts.

*I also want to thank Julie Bromley, Ian Culbertson, The Fine
Family, Bree Wernicke, // TECHYSCOUTS, the Girl Scouts
organization, Girls on the Run, Claire Bretzke, and all the other
wonderful people who have supported my writing so actively, and
my many fans who I hope to continue to amaze, enthrall,
and surprise in the future.*

Bonus Dedication

This book is dedicated to all people, of all ages, with glimmers of Christmas Spirit in their hearts all year round.

The world holds a lot of bad—heartbreak, anger, disappointment, cruelty—and sometimes it can feel discouraging because people can suck. HOWEVER, the world is also full of TONS of good—love, compassion, triumph, kindness, hope—and people can be awesome!

I think it may be easy to let the first half of the preceding paragraph make you cynical, but all around the world there are people who lean into the latter and choose to live in the glow of optimism. People who choose to be their best selves, treat others well, and strive to make the world an increasingly merry and bright place.

This book is for you! Thank you for spreading joy, wonder, and goodwill toward humankind every month of the year, not just in tune with a holiday. Thank you for letting your lights shine bright even in the darkest of times like lanterns in the winter night. And thank you for bringing your own kind of magic into the world!

1

"Lights. Lights! Can somebody get the lights?"

The fireworks-shaped chandeliers dangling from the ballroom ceiling dimmed, reminding me of stars muted by haze. Choked brilliance.

"Thank you, Louise," Specter One said from the stage, where he stood in front of a huge white screen.

Louise Banks nodded and took her seat at table ten with the other Ghosts of Christmas Past. Like all the round banquet tables in the room, it was draped with a crimson tablecloth that hung to the floor.

Specter One fiddled with his remote, aiming at different parts of the screen while clicking, trying to get his slideshow presentation started. His wavy whitish-blonde hair shimmered in the spotlights pointed at the stage, emphasizing the frosty silver streaks swirled with the rest of his locks like the brush strokes of a Van Gogh painting. Golden glitter sparkled across his cheekbones, and a gold Christmas tree brooch engraved with *#1* was pinned to the lapel of his crisp white suit. The whole look read like an old-timey ballroom dancer.

"After giving this presentation every November for hundreds of years, you would think he would finally have a handle on it," my friend Bismaad Hansra whispered to me. "Or at least run a tech rehearsal."

Despite the shadows of the auditorium, Bismaad's knee-length, metallic gold Anarkali dress glimmered. The sparkle of her dark eyes and endearing smile outdid it though. My friend moved one of her long double braids behind her shoulder as she reached for her goblet. I thought it remarkable how even in low lighting, the truly striking still shined. With that level of Bollywood beauty, it surprised me that Bismaad never married when she was alive. Maybe she would have if gifted more time.

As for me? I doubted it.

I scratched the nails of my left hand against the palm of my right—a nervous habit. I imagined it was akin to what humans felt when they squeezed stress balls, only in my case feeling the moderate pressure against my skin centered me because it made me *feel* in general. Being a ghost was a strange thing—cold as ice, no aging, no heartbeat. The touch of my own normal skin was comforting because it reminded me of the humanity I'd left behind. Without constantly looking in a mirror, it was the best way to remind myself I was more than a wisp of misplaced death.

I gazed around at my colleagues in the dimness. Close to one hundred of us gathered on this same date and time every year. This form of afterlife may have been odd, but the ghosts in our department still looked human, not like the spooky mascots of Halloween. That brought me comfort too. And it helped keep me from going insane.

"Specter One has been having technical difficulties before we even *had* technology," I quipped from the side of my mouth, reaching around my goblet for a roll from the breadbasket.

We wouldn't be served entrees until halfway through our boss's presentation, and I was getting hungry. With surgical precision, like a dog gutting a squeaker from a toy, I removed the soft white center from the roll, set the hollowed-out crust on my plate, and used my knife to pick up a pat of butter.

"During my first decade here," I continued as I buttered, "he used huge scrolls as visual aids. He couldn't get them to stay up on the wall. They kept falling and rolling up."

Bismaad giggled, but Allan Cantes shot me a look from across our table. "*Shhh.*"

"The presentation hasn't even started, Allan." I glared at him, then shifted in my seat so the turtledove ice sculpture centerpiece blocked the view between us.

"Okay, here we go!" Specter One said from the front as the projector flickered and the screen showed the first slide. On a muted red background framed by garlands, our department name and motto appeared:

C.C.D.
CHRISTMAS CAROL DEPARTMENT
We'll Make You Merry or Die Trying
Just Kidding—We're Already Dead!

"Welcome back, all Past, Present, and Future spirits," Specter One bellowed with enthusiasm. "I hope you enjoyed your slumber and are excited to get started on a new holiday season. To begin, I just want to acknowledge that I know the last decade has been a challenging one. We've had more Scrooge nominees than ever, and with natural disasters, corrupt governments, and 2020, the world has been a bit . . . shaky lately."

"*Poop show,*" coughed someone in the audience.

Several ghosts laughed. Specter One did not.

"*Nevertheless,*" he continued. "These troubling times are no excuse to not try your hardest. In fact, in our line of work, increased difficulty in the world is a call to action to give the season even more effort. We can do this, everyone. Humanity is worth saving! All it takes is a little elbow grease and a reminder of how good people can be. To get you in the spirit—pun most definitely intended—please enjoy this brief Pro-Human Slideshow set to the charming 'Best Song Ever' by last decade's musical darlings, One Direction."

"That's not a Christmas song," Bismaad whispered, eyebrows furrowed.

I shrugged. "Maybe he's branching out."

Specter One clicked his remote. A montage of images and short clips began, set to the beat of the peppy pop number. Soldiers coming home from war and reuniting with their dogs, people handing out food to the homeless, new schools being opened in impoverished areas, a woman taking off her shirt to save a baby koala during a forest fire, a teenager helping an old woman cross the street . . .

After a minute of heartwarming propaganda, the slideshow ended to the tune of my colleagues' impassioned applause. Some clapped extra loudly—spirits who'd been extra moved.

"She didn't even hesitate. The shirt came right off!" A Ghost of Christmas Past at the adjacent table exclaimed—wailing but with no tears, like a broken sprinkler head of emotion. A coworker patted her on the back.

I rolled my eyes as I swallowed the last of my roll. The video was moving, but it was nothing I hadn't seen before.

"What's the matter, Frost?" Bismaad asked over the fading applause, her chandelier-shaped earrings hanging toward me as she leaned in.

"He's been showing us slideshows like that for almost twenty years," I whispered. "All that good humans do is great, but does it really make up for all the bad that goes on down there?"

"On that note," Specter One practically sang, "it's time to talk about this year's assignments. You may now open your cards."

My eyes shifted to the scarlet envelope centered on my place setting. I stared at the golden wax seal imprinted with the CCD logo, then took a deep breath.

Here we go.

I broke the seal on my envelope at the same time as everyone else and pulled out a thick notecard. The card was printed in beautiful calligraphy and decorated with hand-painted bells and holly.

TEAM PRANCER – JAY NICHOLS
Past: Brandon Gleeson
Present: Frost Mason
Future: Midori Oguri

"Crud," I muttered.

Bismaad glanced at me and I showed her my card. "I got Midori. I haven't worked with her before, but I've seen her around the department. Her whole silent staring thing gives me the creeps."

Bismaad shrugged. "How scary can she be?"

Our gazes drifted across the ballroom to where Midori sat with a group of Ghosts of Christmas Future. The elderly Japanese woman was *presently* staring at me.

I darted my gaze away.

"Any ghost that makes *other ghosts* feel uncomfortable left scary in the rearview mirror a long time ago," I said.

"And now, as your salads are served . . ." Specter One announced, "we will begin a brief introduction to this year's Scrooges. I hope you like the green goddess dressing! Spoiler alert, there are sugar plums mixed in!"

The double doors leading to the kitchens opened and a procession of kitchen elves came through with loaded carts.

Specter One clicked to the next slide, which featured the same background and the words: "*SCROOGE OVERVIEWS*".

I didn't see why it was necessary to have this fancy presentation every year. Each team had its own Scrooge, and later today Specter One would provide us with our own files for our assignments. I knew some ghosts liked to collaborate outside of their teams to get feedback or workshop a difficult case. But I'd never felt a need to do that. Coming together for this kind of pomp and circumstance should have been optional. I would've preferred to be in my office right now reading info on Jay alone instead of sitting in a ballroom breaking bread with my coworkers. Even if it was good bread . . . I glanced at the basket and took another piece.

"For the newer spirits here," Specter One readdressed us, "I realize what we do has a lot of fantastical footnotes, but always remember that those are mere toppings—sprinkles, nuts, and cookie crumbs. The core of what we do, the ice cream, is simple. Every Christmas, the North Pole picks a number of people on Earth who have lost their way and, unless they correct their paths, will cause massive negative ripples on humanity. These are our Scrooges. In your teams of three, you will create a 'Christmas Carol' experience that will push your assigned humans to realize the error of their ways, repent, and reform. If done right, your teams will reignite the goodness in our Scrooges' hearts, motivate them to embrace the Spirit of Christmas, and get them back on the right path."

Specter One strode confidently across the stage, staring out at the audience. "We've had record nominations from the North Pole, and I have no doubt you all will perform wonderfully. Now, without further ado, let's begin with Team Fruit Cake."

I munched on my salad, half-heartedly listening to the descriptions of each Scrooge. It must've been rough for the

North Pole to narrow down the number of jerks on Earth who could use reforming. We worked in teams of three, and while there wasn't a cap for how many spirits could join the CCD, a ghost had to meet some pretty specific qualifications to end up in this place. As such, our workforce rarely reached triple digits.

Entrees came out during the explanation of the sixteenth Scrooge—rosemary roasted chicken with buttery potatoes and peas.

"I have to say," Bismaad remarked under her breath, leaning closer to me. "Although it took me a few years to get used to being dead, being able to eat without gaining weight definitely lessens the blow."

I smirked. Bismaad had only died a few decades ago. Her youth in the CCD game allowed her an optimism that had started to fizzle for me around my fiftieth year. A spirit with a lot of spirit, it was no wonder that her name stood for "utter bliss" in Punjabi.

"Next, Team Prancer," Specter One said. I sat up straighter and put my fork down, paying full attention. Specter One didn't go deeply into detail on any of the humans. He didn't even bring up the darker parts of their character and histories, which is what set them on our radar in the first place. This was like a general, upbeat introduction that—*again*—I could have just as well absorbed in a memo versus socializing here with other people. That being said, I wasn't one to openly show my distaste for the elements of my job I didn't like. At work, I kept my personal feelings where they belonged, inside.

"Jay Nichols is thirty-three years old, born and raised in Los Angeles," Specter One began. He changed slides and I got my first look at my target for the holiday season.

Jay was a handsome man—moderately dark skin, long eyelashes for a guy, clean and sleek low fade haircut with waves. His eyes were intense and held a shine like a glass ornament caught in a peripheral glow.

"In college, Jay studied political science," Specter One continued. "After graduation, he accepted a position in a congressman's office, then later a senator's. From there he was elected to city council and started to get more attention. Recognized for his charisma and commitment to building strong communities, Jay was put on the shortlist for rising political stars in his late twenties and recently announced his intention to run for governor of California next year. He has two children, a ten-year-old son named Kingsley and a six-year-old daughter named Kamie. His ex-wife Celia remarried a couple years ago. Jay's top dislikes include freeway traffic, red apples, and flowery perfume. His favorite things are dogs, Billy Joel music, strong coffee, and hugs from his children."

"*Aww*," cooed several spirits.

With my elbow propped on the table and chin in hand, I studied Jay's face.

Specter One paused and took a glance himself. Then he turned to the audience and, despite the spotlights in his gaze, it felt like he somehow knew exactly where I was sitting and looked straight at me. I experienced a flutter of discomfort. His irises were like ice cubes—no shade of their own, instead reflecting whatever color of light hit them. Sometimes it made you feel like they could see through you and into your mind and soul.

"This is an important one," my boss said sternly, keeping his eyes focused in my direction. "Should Jay win this election, he not only will have the fate of a state in his grip, the role would start a domino effect for the remainder of his incredibly successful career."

My boss finally broke the eye contact and glanced around the audience. "Moving on, Team Snowman . . ."

"Your fellow is choice handsome," Bismaad commented, reaching for the pepper grinder. "I can't believe I got *another* old CEO. Stocks, bonds, quarterly reports—ugh, kill me now."

"Too late," I replied.

"*Shh*," Allan said across the table.

"Allan, I swear to St. Nick—"

"Are you finished?" A kitchen elf had appeared by my elbow, purple wisps of hair flailing out from under her white toque.

"Um, no not yet," I said, spearing a piece of chicken with my fork to prove it. Once the elf left, I reverted my eyes back to Allan, pointed at him, then cut my hand across my throat. I wasn't taking his shortbread today.

The Scrooge Overviews went on for another twenty minutes. When the clock had finally migrated to noon, Specter One wrapped up his presentation.

"All right, spirits, that's everyone for this year. Per usual, your offices have been stocked with files and film reels compiled by the North Pole to give you a more in-depth understanding of your targets. However, I always encourage you to do your own additional research on what makes them tick. On that note, Ghosts of Christmas Present, it's Thanksgiving week, so you will begin infiltrating your assignments' lives on Monday. Your undercover instructions will be in your offices as well. And now . . ." He clapped his hands and rubbed them together, eyes sparkling. "Before we break, it's that magical time when we honor the CCD ghosts celebrating their centennial. Ty Watanabe, Bill James, and Frost Mason, come on up here!"

A spotlight burst into brilliance above me and I resisted the urge to shade my eyes. I had been expecting the announcement but still felt awkward as I stood amid the applause. The skirt of my floor-length, emerald velvet dress hovered just above the carpet as I strode through the shadowy ballroom. The bustles and ruffles may have seemed cumbersome to others, but I was fond of their form. On Earth, ghosts from my department tended to wear modern attire. Here in our home base we preferred to remain in clothes from the time periods when we were alive. I dressed in high-waisted dresses from the early 1900s. Bismaad died in the 1980s and her colorful, glam style never disappointed. Allan—mistletool that he was—always looked dapper in a tailored suit and tie combo reflective of a 1960s executive.

As I climbed the steps to the stage, elves flung glitter and tinsel at me in celebratory fashion the same way mortals threw rice at weddings. I nodded to Ty and Bill as they joined me. Together we turned as two kitchen elves wheeled out a massive sheet cake rimmed with lit sparkler candles. Green icing on the top declared: *Happy 100th Soul Served!*

"Once Ty, Bill, and Frost have completed this year's assignments, they are free to leave the CCD and pursue the next afterlife path of their choosing," our boss proclaimed. "So let's wish them a happy last Christmas with us and the best of fortune on their final missions!"

The spirits cheered. I stared out at the darkened faces in the ballroom. I couldn't believe I'd been doing this for a hundred years . . .

"Lulu, will you cut the cake please?" Specter One said to a kitchen elf with dimples as deep as canyons. He pivoted to the crowd. "It's peppermint bark flavored! Vegan cookies are in the back for our spirits with special dietary preferences."

"Whoo!" someone shouted from the crowd.

Specter One pivoted to our trio; for a moment his joviality was replaced by seriousness. "Good luck, you three. I hope you enjoy your last chance to affect humanity. Don't screw it up."

Kind of an ironic warning considering that it was our Scrooges who usually screwed things up—before *and after* we got there.

I opened my mouth to reply, but someone tapped my leg. I glanced down at Lulu's smiling face as she offered me a slice of cake. I took it and thanked her, then followed Ty's lead and left the stage. Specter One readdressed the gathering.

"Table one, come forward and get your cake. After retrieving your dessert, please meet with your teams at the designated areas marked across the room to begin talking strategy. Spirits up, everyone! I have faith that this December will be the most magical season yet. Remember, the night is always darkest before the dawn!"

"Isn't that a line from a Batman movie?" a deep voice called.

"I'm trying to branch outside of Christmas references, Ricardo," Specter One said with a touch of sass. "Can someone turn the lights back on?"

A second later full luminescence returned—the fireworks chandeliers glowing at max capacity. I waved to Bismaad with my cake plate and fork in hand and migrated to the part of the room where a *TEAM PRANCER* sign had been taped to the wall.

Midori already waited there, wrapped in a shawl that hung away from her body due to a slight hunch in her back. Her long silvery hair had been woven into a braid that fell over her left shoulder. As I approached, I felt pity for the Scrooges she was assigned each year. The tiny old woman—no taller than 4'10" and at least eighty—could intimidate without saying a word. In fact, I'd never heard her say a word in all the years I'd been here.

"Hello, Midori," I said.

She nodded, eyes never leaving mine. Their darkness put the shade of my chocolaty peppermint bark cake to shame.

"Well, well, well, Frost Mason, happy to get such an old ghost on my team." I turned as Brandon Gleeson joined us. The nine-year-old redhead had more freckles on his cheeks than there were visible stars in the sky over the Grand Canyon. This was only his second year at the CCD but my instant first impression was that he had a healthy dose of confidence.

He stuck out his hand. "Put 'er there."

I shook his hand. So did Midori.

"Now then," Brandon said, taking charge, "I want to address the reindeer in the room. Even though this is my first official Scrooging, I've got some big ideas. For starters, I think we should employ the kill box approach with our target."

"Kill box approach?" I repeated.

"Been a while since you read the department literature, Frost? Chapter Eight in the CCD guidebook. Once you infiltrate the target's life, you find a way to lure him into an escape-proof confront-your-demons scenario during Christmas crunch time, then BAMO! Midori and I hit him hard from both sides with blasts from the past and future. I'm thinking we pour nostalgia and fear on him like rain in Vancouver. Midori's got the chops. Right, old M?"

Midori blinked.

I set my slice of cake on the closest table, bent to be at eye level with my young, over-enthusiastic colleague, and put a hand on the shoulder of his polo t-shirt.

"Brandon, your excitement is . . . inspiring. But why don't we talk specifics like the kill box approach later? I have found that the best way to start Scrooge prep is to go straight to the source and find out exactly why the North Pole picked our guy. All Ghosts of Christmas Present do this eventually, but I like to do it as a jumping off point. The three of us can do individual research with our respective resources and powers, then meet to compare notes in a few days. The best Christmas Carol scenarios happen when all three ghosts work as a team and form a plan based on as much *and as many kinds* of research as possible. Trust me. I've been doing this a long time."

"Yeah, but in training I read up on all the ghosts who've been here more than seventy-five years. Isn't your long-term success rate barely above forty percent?"

He said it so plainly—not like he was trying to insult me, but as simple fact. That made it more cutting somehow.

I lowered my hand from his shoulder and straightened. Midori studied me mercilessly and I didn't blame her.

What Brandon said was accurate. Less than half of the Scrooges I'd helped reform had *stayed* reformed. The matter had been a growing fissure in my soul for decades, so this kid pointing out the dismal truth wasn't revelatory or anything, but it definitely wasn't helpful. In order for me to concentrate on my job I had to bury the feelings associated with my disappointment. For years now I had resorted to treating my job and my view of the CCD like a pill someone gave to their dog—hiding it in enough deli meat (or in my case, outward Christmas Spirit and job focus) so I could choke it down and get through this.

"My advice, Brandon . . ." I said, squashing some feelings that had been stirred. "Don't concentrate on the numbers while you're here. They give you perspective. Trust me, that's not a gift you want to unwrap."

"Thank you again, everyone!" Specter One called from the stage, suddenly claiming our attention. "Please be on time for Saturday's first seasonal Employee Training Seminars. Happy Holiday Haunting!"

I turned my focus back to my team. "Research first," I said firmly. "We'll meet after our seminars on Saturday."

"But—" Brandon started.

I held up a hand and he fell silent. Although I looked like

someone in her late twenties, I had been around *a lot* longer. A century and a quarter was more than enough time to learn exactly what kind of look to give kids to get them to not question you.

"I am a Present Ghost, Brandon. Present Ghosts are always the team leaders and the architects of Christmas Carol scenarios. Go do your research. Then we'll work together. In the meantime, I'm heading to the North Pole."

"And then he was all, *Your success rate is barely over forty percent.*"
I stirred the candy cane in my hot chocolate with a touch of
agitation, but care—the mahogany desk I sat on would not
appreciate any splashes.

Tiny cries of "Whee!" and "Wahoo!" sounded from the
battery-operated model winter carnival built on a table to my
left. I glared at the small villagers riding hand-painted sleds
down a plastic hill.

"Was he wrong?" Paul asked.

He was crouched on the floor across the room and didn't look
up from the red tricycle he'd been fixing. On the wall above him
hung a large family portrait. His dad and mom—Santa and Mrs.
Claus—stood in the center, arms around their kids Margo and
Paul. An avalanche of silver tinsel surrounded them, and they
wore kooky polar bear sweaters and Santa hats with twinkly
rainbow lights.

"No, it's true." I frowned. "But even ghosts with the highest
success rates are scarcely at fifty percent. The sad fact is that
people who go through the full—face your past, present, and
future—Scrooging experience commit to changing when they're
caught up in the December moment. But once the aphrodisiac
of the holidays fades, most people return to their old ways. They
become UnScrooged, as it were."

"You can't hold that against them," Paul said, taking a smaller
wrench from the pocket of his loose red overalls. "Earth is hard.

The Naughty List gets longer every year, but you don't see my dad losing heart. Neither should you."

"It's not the same thing. The North Pole focuses on the big picture. Your dad isn't personally invested in any particular individual on Earth like I am. Trust me, when you dedicate yourself to helping a specific person become better, and they promise they will change but then backtrack . . . It breaks your heart."

Paul glanced up. The thirty-five-year-old son of Santa Claus may have had some magic up his sleeves, but he was human. I'd known him since he was a baby. I'd known his father since *he* was a baby. And I'd met his grandfather as a toddler. Paul was alive; he would age and one day pass away, having lived a full life. Unlike me.

The young Claus stood and came to sit next to me on the desk. He and his father had the same twinkling eyes, wide nose, and thick eyebrows, but the similarities ended there. Paul's hair was dusty brown, and his jawline was square and without facial hair. Also, whereas the Big Guy had a bowl-full-of-jelly belly, Paul's biceps and abs would make a Christmas tree angel cry.

"Frost, I say this with all the compassion in the world: a lot of people suck. If being awesome were easy, everyone would do it. Human beings rarely change permanently—however they all have the potential. That very fact makes trying to help them worthwhile. That's why my ancestors created the CCD. That's why we need people like you."

"Ghosts," I corrected. "We are not people. I haven't been a person for a long time."

And that wasn't only because I died. It was because I'd had my faith in humanity stomped on too many times over the last century to feel alive.

I took another swig of hot chocolate, then set the mug down on the snowman-shaped coaster. "I hear you have new elves working at the N&N. Care to walk me over and introduce me? If you're busy I can go by myself."

"Nah. I'll go. You're in one of your moods and that means I should do the talking. Can't let cranky spirit rub off on North Pole folk. No one wants to see a depressed elf. That's why we don't serve eggnog in the break room anymore."

Paul offered me a hand up, grabbed his coat from a hook by the door, and we exited his office. The smell of gingerbread and the sounds of a busy factory filled the fourth level of Santa's Workshop. I glanced over the railing to the production floors below. Garlands and bows draped across every railing; silver bells decked every door handle.

While some elves dashed around from station to station, others worked seated on ergonomically designed gumdrop chairs. They hammered wheels on toy cars, manned conveyor belts, sewed buttons onto bears, tested remote control gadgetry.

Aside from the lanterns, twinkle lights, and wall sconces shaped like gingerbread men, an enormous stained-glass mural of a gingerbread village inlaid in the ceiling cast a rainbow glow over the whole production.

Suddenly, a train whistle sounded. On level two, a curly-haired elf with a clipboard shouted, "Union-mandated break! Hot cocoa and cookies in the common room. Chop chop!"

"When did the elves unionize?" I asked Paul as we climbed aboard one of the glass-walled elevators.

"You know how I borrowed your top 150 movie list last December?"

I nodded.

"I started a weekly movie night for the elves a few months ago. The first week of November they watched *The Pajama Game* and it's been trending on Tinsel for weeks now." He took the phone out of his pocket, tapped on the mistletoe icon that represented the Tinsel app, and held up the screen. The app's slogan at the top read "*Turning the Yuletide on the Most Pressing Issues.*"

"Ugh. Social media." I rolled my eyes.

"I know, right? The elves already get breaks every hour," Paul said. "And when they 'unionized,' they didn't actually ask for anything. So I think this is just a phase. Last month they watched *Cool Runnings* and did nothing but bobsled for two weeks. Now they're totally over it."

The elevator stopped and we exited the factory among a bustle of elves. Paul's coat was thick to shield him from the North Pole cold. I needed no such thing. Ghosts thrived in winter, the icier the better. We made our way down the sparkly cobblestone path through the snow.

The Claus operation lit up every part of my periphery with glimmering buildings. A few penguins wearing scarves and beanies with pompoms waddled past. Elves on break sat on benches drinking cocoa or played in the snow. Farther off, two elves in aprons chased a couple of baby polar bears that had denim pants hanging from their mouths.

Paul and I crossed a small bridge and approached a two-story townhouse. Icicles hung from the edge of the roof like tiny stalactites. Luminescent candies decorated the walls. Snow caked the windows and main door. The sign over the front read *Naughty & Nice Department.*

"Knock, knock," Paul said as he opened the door.

Inside, five elves perked up. "Paul!" they chorused in glee.

Every inch of wall space was lined with books or stuffed with scrolls. In the center of the room, one unfathomably long scroll spilled over the table and ran across the space, curling like a roller coaster, swerving in and out of rooms, and laying over any piece of furniture in its way. The elves were stationed at different parts of the scroll, inspecting it with magnifying glasses.

"Are Betty, Troy, Phil, and Nona upstairs?" Paul asked.

"Yep," said an elf with an afro. He looked around, then scampered over to Paul and held up a hand to the side of his mouth, feigning the telling of a secret. "The upstairs elves clock out at three o'clock these days. They don't have much to do now that they've made their Scrooge selections." He shook his head. "They *say* they're still working, but truth is, they don't start on next year's preliminary choices until January. They'll spend the next month playing chocolate milk drinking games while they bet on ping pong and the NBA."

Paul folded his arms. "You're the list supervisor, Moe. Why don't you say something to them?"

Moe's eyes shot wide. "And start a conflict? Goodness, no! Nona bakes my favorite strawberry pies. Troy is teaching me Portuguese. And Betty, Phil, and I are on the same igloo building team."

"Well, it's your call," Paul said as we began to ascend the spiral staircase in the center of the room. As our steps took us to higher vantage points of the room, I marveled how holly bulged out of every nook and cranny a decorator could get to. Over a dozen live turtledoves rested on perches hanging from the ceiling, canoodling in pairs.

"Afternoon, Nona," Paul said to an elf with pigtails when we mounted the final stair. "I'd like to introduce you to Frost Mason of the CCD."

Nona—who had been upside down on a couch reading *Holly Happenings Magazine*—did a flip off the seat and landed on her feet. "Oh, hello there! We were wondering when we'd get our first ghost visit."

"Frost is always the first one," called an elf from another room. He stuck his head through the doorway. "Hey, Frost."

"Troy." I saluted. "Nice buzz cut."

He winked and disappeared.

"Can she see the Scrooge info on Jay Nichols please?" Paul said to Nona.

"Of course!" Nona scurried past the ping pong table where two other elves were enjoying a game. The bells on her floppy shoes jingled all the way. She climbed onto a stepping stool to reach a high shelf of an ornate bookcase, then pulled out a hefty volume.

Nona hopped down to ground level in a single bound and presented Paul and me with the cerulean colored book, which featured a large silver "N" on the cover. I took it. A pair of bookmarks stuck out from the top. "Jay Nichols is the second bookmark," she explained. "Nice to meet you by the way, Frost."

I smiled. "The feeling is mutual."

I flipped to the section with Jay's name in cursive font. Then I paused. Scrooging more than one journalist in my century at the CCD taught me to always ask the most obvious question when you found a credible source. "Before I start reading," I said to Nona, "Tell me. Why this guy? What makes Jay Nichols so special?"

"Well, he has the power to influence a whole generation," Nona said, bouncing on her toes. "He's a rising—"

"Political star, I know," I interjected. "I mean, why has he reached a point in his life where he needs the CCD's intervention now?"

She paused. Thought. Then held up her hand. "In short, three things." She counted off on her fingers. "Resentment toward his family. Disorganized priorities. Fear of rejection."

I nodded. Sounded like a typical Scrooge. Those first two anyway were very common reasons people ended up on our radar. "Thank you. Mind if I borrow this book for a few days?"

"Well . . ."

Paul gave Nona a nod.

"We usually prefer CCD ghosts read the books here," Nona replied. "But for a friend of Paul's . . . Just bring it back by Wednesday. Margo does inventory every Thursday morning."

Paul rolled his eyes. "My OCD younger sister would have the reindeer organized alphabetically if the song didn't already specify the order."

I put the book in my bag and thanked Nona, then waved to the other elves as we departed the Naughty & Nice Department. We walked back through the winter wonderland until we came upon a low-roofed, unmarked building.

I looked at Paul. Snow had started to fall from the azure sky—the flakes sticking to our hair and clothes. "Good luck, Frost," he said sincerely.

"I don't need luck, Paul. This job has a formula. I've done it ninety-nine times; I can do it again with Jay."

"I don't mean good luck with Jay," Paul said. He gave me a concerned look. "I've known you my entire life, Frost. You went from my babysitter to one of my best friends. I feel like every year you seem a little less . . . spirited. I don't like seeing you lose your sparkle."

"Sparkle is for tinsel and ornaments. Most of mankind manages without it. So can I." I smiled sadly. "I'll see you when I bring the book back."

"Want to have pancakes at Short Stack when you do?" Paul asked hopefully. "The elves have invented an apple cider recipe this year."

"Tasty offer, but maybe another time. It's going to be a busy week."

I turned and entered the building. The lobby was an expanse of marble floor with the building's name written across it in gold lettering:

Crazy, Magical, Interdimensional Travel Depot

Four silver elevators, two on each side (one of which was a larger freight elevator) were the only things in the room. The *realm-evators*. A strand of glittering garland framed each one.

My heels clicked across the space and I pressed the down arrow then waited, thinking about Paul. I appreciated his concern but spirit wasn't necessary to exist. And I didn't need to believe wholeheartedly in what the CCD was doing to help them do it. That altruism started to evaporate ages ago and it hadn't affected my performance because people don't need to like their jobs to be good at their jobs. As long as I kept my feelings hidden and put on a nice show, everything was fine. Scrooging was like a movie—emotion, special effects, dramatic conclusion. Another assignment, another production. The plot and main characters were always predictable.

One set of doors opened. Inside, the realm-evator panel had half a dozen chocolate bar sized buttons, all of which required ID or a key to use. I swiped my CCD ID over the reader and pressed the button labeled "*Christmas Carol Department,*" right between the "*Earth*" button and key-required "*Portalscape*" button, whatever that was.

The scanner flashed green and the doors slid closed. The realm-evator shook like a malfunctioning massage chair.

FLASH.

Following a burst of Caribbean blue light, the doors opened and I was back in my ghostly realm. The CCD wasn't just a work environment—it was a world. Ghosts of Christmas Present spent the majority of their time on Earth in December, trailing our Scrooges, but our home base was here with our Past and Future colleagues. This place was a weird slice of the afterlife that certain souls were sent to. In addition to office space, conference and ballrooms, and a huge cafeteria, there were dorms, a library, screening rooms, and so much more. Plus, the North Pole was only a quick realm-evator ride away.

I stepped out. Unlike the relatively plain realm-evator lobby of the North Pole, ours was ornate. A floor of shimmering crystal fragments supported two dozen pillars—spaced out with no clear pattern. The high ceiling hosted a glorious assortment of gold and silver bells dangling from a snowflake skylight

I paused at the pine adjacent to my realm-evator. The lobby was shaped like an equilateral triangle, a massive Christmas tree in each of the three corners. One held a star at the top inscribed with the word "*Past*," another was labeled "*Present*," and the third "*Future*." Despite this difference, the trees featured identical striking décor. Each pine was adorned solely with crystal ball ornaments. The baubles pulsed with the faintest aura of light, like fireflies taking their last breaths.

Fascinating things.

I strode between the columns, meaning to pass the lobby's centerpiece without a glance, but my steps slowed and I couldn't help looking into the icy eyes of Charles Dickens. My favorite author, and the man best known for chronicling how our department worked, had been immortalized here in a detailed ice sculpture. Within the ice, enchanted lights glowed and changed colors.

I stopped for a moment in front of the statute. At his feet, a frosted silver plaque bore a quote from his classic *A Christmas Carol*:

"I will honour Christmas in my heart, and try to keep it all the year. I will live in the Past, the Present, and the Future. The Spirits of all Three shall strive within me. I will not shut out the lessons that they teach." – Charles Dickens

I sighed. It was a lovely sentiment; unfortunately, most humans forgot its message as easily as a person turned a page in a book.

When I first began working for the CCD, I couldn't read those words without my soul glowing a little brighter, like a candle flame regrouping after a breeze. Now the quote had become a steak without seasoning, a cupcake without frosting, a cookie without crunch.

I still believed in *Christmas*, and in the value of what the ghosts and I were trying to accomplish. It was people that I had lost faith in. They talked a good game, and once you got through to them, they were receptive to lessons of humanity. Sadly, despite their intentions, the majority couldn't help but relapse, returning to who they were before they tried to change because that version of themselves was easier and familiar, whereas changing demanded something of you every day.

It's like, the other ghosts and I could open a door to a new life for them, one that would save their souls from withering and destroying their potential for good, love, and decency. But our Scrooges had a bad habit of letting that door shut again. We were the brick propping the door ajar, and without us most people didn't seem to have the strength to keep it open on their own. So what was the point of us? We were a bandage to problem people; we hardly ever healed them permanently. That's why my job and the department's purpose didn't fill me with optimism anymore. Too frequently they were a valiant waste of effort.

I left Dickens and the lobby and trekked down the maze of corridors to my office, the same one I'd had since I arrived in the afterlife. When a ghost awakened in the CCD, we got the welcome speech from Specter One, the welcome packet, a dorm, an office, and then "Best of luck with the next century" well wishes.

I spotted my den and went for the ornate bronze handle. Outside my door, a silver nameplate read:

Frost Elise Mason
Born 1891

The second I entered, my slumbering Westie terrier barked and sat up in his checkered basket. He scurried over, tail wagging.

"Hello, Marley." I bent to pat him on the head affectionately before heading to my desk.

I liked my office. The window faced a snowy mountain range. My bookshelf and desk were antique, plucked from my era with the kind of detailed craftsmanship modern furniture passed over. The thick lavender carpet complemented the violet sofa, and my fireplace across the room was pure white marble.

As Specter One had promised, files and several canisters of film reels about Jay Nichols waited on my desk. Midori and Brandon would have files in their offices too, and they would have their own investigations to make into Jay's past and future, but the reels were just for me. Ghosts of Christmas Present couldn't travel through time like they could, so Specter One and the North Pole compiled these as add-ons for our research.

Beside the resources, I also found a folder with a note from Specter One:

"Frost, this is Brandon's first year with a Scrooge assignment, so keep an eye on him. Here's a little background about his time on Earth to give you perspective."

Hm. I'd give that a read later.

I moved all my folders to the coffee table between the sofa and fireplace, then unpacked my book from the North Pole and placed it there too. A decent amount of information in the book would be redundant with the files, but the Naughty & Nice elves tended to expand on details in their own books, sometimes even writing side notes as they narrowed down their Scrooge selections.

I walked over to the marble fireplace, grabbed a matchbook, and struck a light. I hesitated a moment as the glow of the flame flickered in the reflection of the silver engraving over the mantle. It read: "*Face All Plans Unafraid.*"

I tossed the match into the fireplace.

As the hearth roared to life like I sometimes wished I could, I grabbed a fluffy shawl from a wooden coat hook in the corner. I wasn't cold. I was never cold. The internal temperature of the CCD was kept in the low twenties on the Fahrenheit scale, which ghosts preferred. The shawl, like the fire, were out of habit. They added atmospherics of calm and Christmas, which helped me study.

Marley watched me—tail wagging and expression eager. I patted the seat beside me. "Come on, boy." He barked happily and leapt onto the cushion, curling into a contented ball at my side.

I smiled fondly at the creature, giving him a scratch behind the ear before picking up the North Pole book. The orange glow of the flames illuminated the text as I flipped back to my Scrooge. My finger traced his calligraphied name.

"Okay, Jay Nichols. Who are you?"

3

Ten-year-old me peeked out from the storage closet. The last of the people shuffled from the lobby into the theater—a blur of corseted dresses, floor-length skirts, crisp suits, and feathered hats. I ducked back inside, then squatted with my ear pressed to the door, waiting for silence.

The sound of excited chatter started to die down, then evaporated entirely. Another peek revealed an empty lobby. I scampered to the main theater doors and peered in. The unmistakable sound of the projector whirring to life told me my window of opportunity had arrived. The theater was dark, and the audience captivated. I had my distraction.

With stealth and skill for disappearing I'd honed for years, I slipped inside and up a short stairwell to the mezzanine. By the railing near thick velvet curtains, I found a suitable place to lay low. I crouched and sat with my legs folded, barely taking up any space.

The moving picture mesmerized me immediately. It was a new one just premiered last month. So far 1901 had been like any other year for me—a lot of scraping by and wishing for things I'd never have—but I had discovered and fallen in love with these silent moving pictures, and I was definitely not going to miss this one. It was called *Scrooge, or Marley's Ghost*. The nuns at the orphanage read us *A Christmas Carol* by Charles Dickens every week during the holiday season, and I loved it. To be watching the story play before my eyes was as thrilling as it was fascinating. The ability to tell a story through visuals that mass crowds could enjoy together at the same time took art, skill, and a very specific kind of magic.

A ghost called Marley was being used as a storytelling vehicle in the stead of the Ghosts of Past, Present, and Christmases yet to come. I gasped along with the rest of the audience when Marley's face appeared on the doorknocker. What a trick!

I clutched my knees to my chest, absorbing the tale I knew so well unfold in this new medium. Dickens' tale had always made me feel warm and fuzzy inside—my soul ablaze with spirit and hope each time I experienced it. My lips curled into an optimistic smile as one black-and-white scene dissolved into the next.

If Scrooge could change, then anyone could. That's why I treasured this story so much. It was nice to know that people, given the right push, could be better. They could come back for the ones they love and make amends . . .

KNOCK. KNOCK.

I glanced around in panic. The distant thudding somehow made the entire theater shake. Everything melted to the same muted shades of black and white that displayed on the screen. The shaking continued and then—

"Frost! Frost, are you in there?"

Adult *ghost* me opened her eyes.

Where am I?

I yawned sleepily and sat up, my neck stiff from having been tilted off to the side as I dozed in my seat. I'd fallen asleep in one of the CCD's screening rooms. I rubbed my eyes and stretched back to life, well, afterlife I should say.

Ghosts couldn't dream anything new; sleep only allowed us to relive our past. It was no surprise that my spectral mind had transported me to that memory. A black-and-white film showing key moments of Jay's life continued playing on the screen in front of me. Unlike in 1901, these reels had sound, but I'd lowered the volume last night as I'd gotten sleepy.

It was funny. The world had evolved so much in the last century; I was certain Specter One could have arranged some sort of interdimensional Wi-Fi signal for a holiday streaming service, or even a DVD collection that would allow us to watch these clips of our Scrooges' lives like movies. However, there were some aspects of our job that he and Santa said should remain rooted in "a simpler time" as they called it. Though by my memory, no time in history had ever been simple.

I'd spent the past few days diving deep into Jay Nichols's life. These films helped break up the monotony of reading paperwork as I looked for patterns and connections that would help me understand what made this guy tick, and formulate initial plans for best approaches to his Scrooging experience.

Midori and Brandon would have done their own research and magical investigation with their powers in anticipation of our meeting today. I genuinely thought it was vital that we worked separately in intervals like this. It allowed each of us to bring unique contributions and perspectives to the table when we met up. As their leader, it was my duty to sift through everything and find the strongest threads for us to pull, the ones most likely to unravel Jay so we could weave him back together better than before.

"Frost?" A stream of light skewered the room as Bismaad entered from the door behind me. She'd been the one knocking. Today she wore a checkered print saree with teal embellishments that matched the teal hair ties at the ends of her long double braids.

"You missed breakfast, so I thought you might have fallen asleep in here again." She settled in the seat next to me and gestured at the reel. "What is it about these screening rooms that mellows you out?"

I shrugged, sitting up straighter. "Moving pictures were my escape when I was on Earth. For a certain amount of time you can forget your reality and experience someone else's. I guess no matter how many years solidify between adulthood and childhood, the things that matter most always resonate."

"Which is why the Ghosts of Christmas Past and Future have it way easier than we do," Bismaad mused. "Being a Present Ghost is such a mega responsibility. We have to guide the Scrooges through their journeys and have way more magical powers to balance."

She leaned back in her chair and diverted her eyes to the screen, tilting her chin toward it. "So what are we watching?"

"It's a montage of every election Jay Nichols has ever lost," I explained, eyes falling back to the flickering footage I'd watched so many times now. The reel had been playing on loop since yesterday "This guy has been running for elected positions since he was six. Not because he wanted power or a title, but because he is full of ideas and wants to make a difference. Unfortunately, for fourteen years, he never won a single race."

I gestured at the screen as the scene shifted to thirteen-year-old Jay standing outside a middle school auditorium. He stood to one side of the double doors as students filed in. He passed out little pamphlets, talking to the kids about fixing water fountains and organizing lunch lines for better traffic flow. Meanwhile, a frizzy-haired girl on the other side of the doors handed out massive chocolate bars—the kind that only the biggest mansions would distribute on Halloween. The students were far more interested in what she was offering.

Jay glowered at her, but the girl was too busy handing out candy to notice.

The scene changed to Jay sitting in a leather chair across a desk from a balding man. The name plaque on the man's desk read "*Principal Flack.*"

"It's not fair that she won," Jay protested. "She gave everyone free candy. I can't compete with that. There should be a rule about candidates having a budget to campaign with."

"Calm down, Mr. Nichols. It's just a student government election. I'm sure you'll find another club to occupy your time."

The film reel moved on to high-school-age Jay standing frozen in a school hallway, listening to the PA system. Two friends waited next to him, faces worried.

"And this year's vice president . . . Miguel Sanchez!"

Jay hung his head in defeat. One friend put a hand on his shoulder. "You gave it a good fight, man. But the dude is more popular. Nice, smart guys like you don't stand a chance."

I sighed and stood up, moving for the back of the screening room.

"It goes on like that for a while," I told Bismaad as I turned off the projector and flicked on the house lights. "The first time Jay ever ran for something it was first grade class representative. That loss was the beginning of the rejection that would plague him throughout his life. Every year he tried to get into one or more positions where he could enact positive change and make a difference. He made attempts to be everything from Secretary Treasurer of his middle school choir to editor-in-chief of his high school newspaper. By my count, he lost fifty-six elections from elementary school through college."

I took out the film reel, carefully loading it back in its case.

"I can't believe he kept trying . . ." Bismaad said in amazement. "You'd think a person would break at some point and give up."

I nodded. "Jay's definitely more persistent than the average Scrooge."

"So did he ever win an election?"

"His junior year of college," I replied. "But if you ask me, I think that win actually broke him more than any of his losses."

"Why do you say that?"

I checked my watch—CCD issued with rose gold rim, ornate ticking hands, and a glittering snowflake at the center. "Our Employee Training Seminar starts in ten minutes. We better go. I'll tell you about it later."

I placed the reels back in my bag and Bismaad followed me out. We strode across the skybridge connecting this tall tower of the CCD with the adjacent building. She and I filed into the lecture hall a minute before noon. It was already packed with Present Ghosts so we claimed seats at the back.

A teenage ghost in a jean jacket distributed the day's handout to our row. We each took one and passed the stack on. I unfolded the desk attachment on my chair and unpacked my notebook, a candy cane shaped pen, and an aluminum can of *Cocoa on the Gogo™*, courtesy of the vending machine outside.

"Welcome, Ghosts of Christmas Present, to your first training seminar of the season," a voice boomed from the front.

The tall woman had light brown skin and smooth black hair fashioned in a sharp bob. A Christmas tree brooch with a *#9* on it was pinned to her mulberry lapel. The shine of her elaborate sparkly eye make-up was almost plain in comparison to the Olympic-bronze-medal glitter swept across her cheekbones. This sparkly physical trait was the mark of all the Senior Specters, the CCD's management staff.

"For those of you who don't know me, I am Specter Nine. I will be running your weekly classes this season to help you blend in with the modern era while you're infiltrating your targets' lives, and help you prep for the best possible Scrooging. Let's begin." She pivoted and wrote the title of today's seminar on the chalkboard: "*Modern Slang.*"

I glanced down at the handout in front of me. It was a long list of words followed by their definitions.

"We shall start with term number one used in a sentence," said Specter Nine. "Say it with me: *That outfit is fire.*"

Everyone in the room repeated the phrase in a monotone.

"*That outfit is fire.*"

"And those are the proper and improper uses of the word 'snatched'," Specter Nine said, underlining the term on the chalkboard.

A tiny Santa suddenly popped out from the cuckoo clock on the left wall and began dancing as holiday music played.

Specter Nine lowered her chalk. "Your homework for the week is to use each new word in a sentence. Extra credit if you can list five examples of people 'throwing shade' at each other. Dismissed."

The sounds of rustling papers and zipping bags filled the room as everyone packed up. These seminars were long but extremely helpful. If not for them, most of us would stick out like sore thumbs on Earth. Our Senior Specter instructors taught us not only about modern Earth culture, but also shaped us into modern beings. The majority of the girl I was in the early twentieth century had been left behind long ago; I was a contemporary, independent ghost of the twenty-first century and proud of it.

"I think I'm going to bejewel 'That is so extra' on one of my sarees," Bismaad said to me as we gathered the last of our belongings. "Do you want to come with me to the North Pole Crafting Cottage? Maybe have lunch afterward?"

"Can't. I have my first meeting with Brandon and Midori."

"Frost!" I turned to see Griselda approaching us. "Did Bismaad tell you about our accents study group?"

"I was about to," Bismaad said. She turned to me. "I know you don't need it this year, but do you want to join our study group in a few hours as we prep for the different countries our Scrooges are in? We bring snacks and run fun improv scenarios."

"You've been here the longest and Scrooged on all seven continents," Griselda chimed in. "The less experienced ghosts would definitely benefit from your expertise. I hear you do an awesome New Zealand accent."

"I'm sorry. Thank you for the invitation, but my job priorities come first and I'd rather not waste time on side activities that don't directly pertain to that. I hope you understand."

"Oh, okay," Griselda replied sadly. "I understand."

Bismaad gave me a hopeful look. "Maybe we can hang out later?"

"Maybe," I said, inching toward the door. "I really have to run though. Have fun at the Crafting Cottage. Happy hot glue gunning."

I waved goodbye to the girls and made my way to the CCD library. It was a magnificent round space with pillars separating the spiral walkway and study rooms. The marble majesty reminded me of Napoleon's tomb. I'd had two Scrooges in Paris in the latter half of last century and that—*the building, not the man*—had left an impression on me. What a way to be buried. Unlike my own plain gravestone in California . . .

I moved down the walkway. Naturally the library had a much bigger Christmas emphasis than Napoleon's tomb. Spotlights illuminated Christmas trees in alcoves, each tree decorated with golden ornaments, garlands, bows, and tiny harps. Every inch of wall space was carved with elaborate moldings of wintery scenes.

Crystal candelabras wrapped in holly decorated the shared study tables in the main section.

My heeled boots beneath my floor-length indigo dress clicked along the marble floor, creating a soft echo. I approached Study Room 1, the Partridge Room—spotting my teammates through the glass on the door. Inside, Midori sat silently in an erect armchair, staring straight ahead. Brandon lounged with one leg over the armrest of his seat, playing a handheld videogame. A sparkly purple pear with a bite missing rested on the table next to him. It looked like it'd been taken from the glowing candleholder at the center of the table, decorated with pine boughs and purple and green pears. Despite the fact that they looked like they'd been rolled in glitter, evidently they were edible.

Complementing the centerpiece, depictions of partridges and pear trees covered the walls.

"Good afternoon," I said upon entering. I hesitated at the chair closest to the door, which would place me opposite Midori, then shifted to the spot beside Brandon. I couldn't deal with her Jedi-level eye contact focused straight at me through the meeting.

"I hope your research on our Scrooge was as productive as mine was," I continued. I folded my hands on the table. "So tell me, what are your initial reactions to Jay?"

Brandon scowled at his game as it made a series of sad bleeps. He set the device down and drew a disorganized bundle of colorful notecards from his backpack. "Okay, hold on . . ." He started to lay the different colors in piles, but had a little trouble separating some due to a misplaced wad of gum that'd gotten stuck in between them.

"Alrighty," he said, finishing his sorting. "Out the gate, for my three visits to Jay's past Christmases that we incorporate into his Scrooging, I'm thinking I'll do one when he was a kid, one involving that lady Celia he was married to for a while, and the third could be to when he won his first election in college."

"Taking him to see his childhood is a must," I agreed. "That's a best practice for every Scrooging—nothing gets people choked up like seeing themselves at their most innocent. As for Celia, I want to meet her in person before we expand on how to involve her. I don't think the election thing is the best angle though."

"Why not?" Brandon frowned. "The guy lost a gazillion elections. Remembering his first win should inspire him with hope. If he's going down a dark path, reminding him that good ol' fashioned, honest persistence eventually pays off is an awesome lesson."

"I don't argue that," I said. "However, that's not the lesson he learned in that election."

"I read his files," Brandon protested. "He won. After so many losses, nothing should've made him happier."

"Yes, Brandon, but you're not seeing the full picture."

Brandon huffed. "Frost, I'm in charge of the past. This should be my call. Maybe you're not seeing *that* picture." The small boy had gone from cool and confident to, well, frosty.

I sighed internally but didn't let his testiness affect me past that. I had been new once. This job was a ton to process with a lot at stake. I didn't blame him for getting defensive in response to his ideas being questioned. When you had the soul of a human being riding on your shoulders, you wanted others to fully believe you knew what you were doing.

That being said, Brandon was at the beginning of his journey and it was important that he learned this job had many different moving parts that required attending. I would shepherd that. He wasn't my first new recruit I'd been obliged to mentor, so I could be patient with him. It took a great deal more than a snippy nine-year-old to get me riled up. I hadn't lost my cool with anyone in decades. Even all my past Scrooges—selfish, cruel, shortsighted people that they were—never got under my skin.

I adjusted tone to address Brandon calmly. "I know this is your first year participating in a Scrooging mission, Brandon, but you need to remember that part of the job means seeing all the angles. I can't visit the past like you can, so that does make you the most powerful of us where that aspect of Jay's journey is concerned, just as Midori is the most powerful of us where Jay's future is concerned. But since you have dozens of Decembers to scan through, Specter One provides Ghosts of Christmas Present with film reels of key moments throughout our Scrooge's life so we can help Ghosts of Christmas Past navigate all those memories. It's like you are the one with the boat and sailing skill, but Jay's past is a vast ocean and I have the compass."

Brandon blinked at me. Anger faded from his face, but confusion and doubt still lurked.

"I think you need to see one of the clips I watched yesterday," I said. "It will have more of an impact if we view it in person though. Can you take me and Midori back?" He of course could take us back, but asking was much more polite than demanding.

"Okay . . ." Brandon said. "I assume this magical memory was something that happened in December? I can only travel to events that happened around Christmas, so if this involved an epic Fourth of July, that's not in my wheelhouse."

A second internal sigh. "I know, Brandon, this isn't my first rodeo. It's a moment from mid December thirteen years ago. Based on your comments, I'm guessing you only *read* about Jay's first successful election; you didn't visit that part of his past yet."

"You're right. I didn't . . ." Brandon's haughty demeanor gave way to embarrassment. "It's a lot of past to go through, you know?"

"I know," I said supportively. "Come on. Let's do this together." I offered him my hand.

After a second, he huffed. "Just make sure to concentrate hard on the destination. Lose focus for even a second and we could end up anywhere or anywhen." He gave me and Midori each one of his squishy little boy hands.

Why is he sticky?

Brandon began to glow with evocative blue light that enveloped the three of us. I closed my eyes and thought about a specific scene from the film reel last night—the one I believed may have caused a major ripple in the fabric of Jay's soul.

Energy seeped through my body. What felt like a bubble of air burst inside me and I gasped, opening my eyes. We now stood on the messy, smelly upstairs landing of a two-story house. Numbered bedroom doors lined the corridor. A few of them held wreaths. A ratty garland had been tied to the banister of the staircase. Mistletoe hung over the front door below.

I let go of Brandon's hand. He, Midori, and I remained coated in the blue color of the kid's magic, but we'd become partially translucent.

A rowdy group of college boys with Greek letters painted on their chests raced by and phased through us, chanting "WIN-TER BREAK! WINTER BREAK!"

There was a door directly across from us. It was barely open a crack, but the murmur of several voices leaked out. That's when I saw a college-aged Jay climbing the steps behind us, carrying a stack of books. At the top of the stairs he started to head right, but then paused on the landing with us. The voices caught his attention too.

This was my first close-up of our Scrooge. His eyes were tired but alert. His face was unmarked by wrinkles or worry lines.

Jay cautiously drifted closer, coming to hover by the door. I nodded to Midori and Brandon and we phased through the walls into the room Jay eavesdropped on. Within we found four fraternity boys. Two lounged on the bed, one on the floor, another on a beanbag chair.

"So, we're in agreement then?" asked a guy with spiky blond hair sitting on the beanbag. "We'll give the presidency to Abed and then Eric can have the Fraternity Relations position."

"You sure the house won't ask questions?" asked a skinny boy. "Eric won the presidential vote by a solid number. A lot of guys picked him."

"They didn't see the votes so they don't know that, and they trust the system, so why would they be suspicious?" Spiky Blond responded.

"Okay," said a deeply tanned boy. "Assuming we lock in that decision, that only leaves the VP slot and the Social Chair job. We need to count those votes."

"The votes don't matter at this point," interjected Spiky Blond. "Jay only ran for the VP slot while Teddy ran for that and Social Chair. Just give Jay VP, make Teddy Social, and we have our newly elected board."

"What's going on here?" Jay pushed the door open, confused and upset.

The guys almost jumped out of their skins. One kid even fell off the bed. If Jay hadn't been so concerned, it may have been comical.

A dark-haired boy in shorts stood up quickly. "Jay, man." He shut the door behind him. "You weren't supposed to hear that."

"I wasn't supposed to hear that the council we approved to count our house's election votes doesn't actually count them?" Jay replied angrily.

"It's not that simple, Jay," said Dark Hair. "Fraternity houses survive based on member count, and we get more members by being popular. To make that happen, we have to make sure that the people who are the face of this place reflect the best image."

"What's wrong with Eric being president?" Jay argued. "He's a great guy."

"*He is*," replied Tan Boy. "He's super nice, smart, and reliable. But Eric is also a chubby white guy who likes Model UN and the campus horticultural society. Abed is a basketball star who the sorority girls go nuts for, his diversity makes our house look good, and he's got friends in campus media. In terms of best representing a fraternity, the latter gets the job done."

"And what about me?" Jay asked. "You're just going to *give* me the VP spot?"

"You're perfect for it, Jay," replied Spiky Blond. "You know that you are. And it's not like we're denying Teddy anything—he gets a great position and so do you. Everyone's happy."

Jay furrowed his brows, upset and . . . maybe sad?

"We gave speeches," he said after a moment. "We laid out our plans for the future. We went through the motions."

"And all that stuff is great for appearance's sake," replied Dark Hair, putting his hand on Jay's shoulder. "But trust us, we know what's best here. Now do you want the VP spot or not?"

Jay stood pensively for a long beat, his fingers clenched around his books.

Then he nodded.

I signaled for Brandon and Midori to follow me out and we phased through the wall. On the landing, Brandon began to glow brightly and provided us with his hands. We took hold and a moment later we were back in the study room, our bodies tangible once more.

"So he cheated," Brandon summarized, picking up a notecard and crumbling it into a ball. He tossed it backward and it bounced into a trashcan like a basketball.

I shook my head. "We don't know if he won or lost fairly, but he went along with the result because it gave him something he'd wanted for a long time. Had he forced them to count the votes, he legitimately could've lost. Like he'd lost dozens of times before. The outcome became more important than the means. So you see, I—"

"I'm sorry," Brandon said abruptly.

I blinked at him. "Why?"

"I kind of got in your face at the welcome banquet *and* a few minutes ago. It's my first Scrooging assignment and I wanted to prove myself. I came in figuring I could see stuff you couldn't, both in terms of my powers and bringing a fresh perspective to the table. But you know exactly what you're doing. It only took you a few days to find one of this guy's key turning points."

"I call them breaking points," I corrected. "Because they're the moments in people's lives that break them—what sets them on darker paths and leads them to becoming disheartened, cynical Scrooges. We all start as pure snow; something on Earth has to make us dirty. Understanding the breaking points that sully a soul is vital if we are going to cleanse it."

I reached into my bag and took out my notebook, then paused. "And thank you for the apology. I wouldn't say I know *exactly* what I'm doing, but after all this time in the afterlife, I've learned that humans are predictable, and I've developed a formula for this job as a result."

"Is it a secret formula?" Brandon joked.

I smirked. "No. And the set up is pretty simple. I shadow our assignment in some position that allows me to get close to him. I observe firsthand what a jerk he is and how much people hate him. Seeing exactly how far-gone he is will help me give you two feedback that hones what parts of his past and future to research, and what trips to the present I'll include in my Scrooging."

I shifted to address both my teammates together, taking a final glance at to-do lists I had written in my notebook. "I spoke to an elf named Nona who told me that one of the reasons they picked Jay was because of his relationship with rejection. We should explore what he's willing to do to avoid feeling that kind of hurt again. A person's morality and logic can warp unintentionally to avoid pain. Midori . . ."

I reluctantly met the gaze of the elderly ghost. "Can you run scenarios for what various futures would look like for Jay with avoidance of rejection as the main variable?"

Midori gave a single nod.

"Great." I adjusted in my seat. "Brandon, you and I will keep rejection in mind as we do our research too, but Nona told me Jay's other issues were resentment toward family and disorganized priorities. So this week, I'd recommend thoroughly researching Jay's Christmases before the age of ten so we can form preliminary decisions about what pieces of his childhood to use for the Scrooging. I'll make learning about Celia and his kids a priority goal for my understanding of the present."

"Sounds like a good plan, chief," Brandon said.

I nodded as I stowed my notebook then put the strap of my bag over my shoulder and stood. "Once I deploy to Earth, my weekday schedule will be tricky, but I'll book this study room for us every weekend for the rest of the season so we can touch base. I'll also let you know whenever I have time to come back to the CCD on a weekday. All on board?"

"Yep, let's save a soul!" Brandon pumped a fist in the air.

"Let's try to, anyway," I responded with far less enthusiasm. "Midori?"

She gave another nod.

"Okay then." My stomach grumbled loudly, causing Brandon and Midori to stare. I hastily grabbed one of the sparkly pears.

"Meeting adjourned." I took a bite and headed out.

"Who's next?"

All Ghosts of Christmas Present were gathered in our realm-evator lobby for equipment pick up before our deployment to Earth. I stepped up to the lace-dressed table where Specter Three and Specter Four were seated. The former, who had peach glitter glistening on her cheekbones, gave me a discerning look.

"Frost, don't you ever get tired of taking that thing with you on assignment? Isn't it distracting?" She nodded toward Marley, cradled in the crook of my arm.

"Marley isn't a *thing*, Specter Three. Not to me. He behaves himself. Anyway, having a pet is one of the better parts of being human. If I get to pretend to be one for a month on Earth, why not make the most of it?"

Marley yapped as if in agreement, jingling the tiny pair of silver bells hanging from his ruffled maroon collar.

"You are a strange ghost, Frost Mason," mused Specter Three. She checked off my name on her clipboard and picked up a dark green phone from the neat stack beside her. "Here is your phone. Stay in contact with your team. Keep your notifications on. You know the drill. And now for your annual donation."

An elf lifted a weighty brick of ice onto the table. Familiar with the routine, I placed my hand upon it and transferred a single spark of magical blue energy into the ice.

"You Specters have been requiring this of us for decades. I'm retiring this year; maybe you'd like to finally tell me what this donation is for?" I asked pointedly.

"Next," Specter Three said, waving me off. The elf picked up my magic-charged brick and hoisted it over to a cart loaded with blocks my colleagues had already enchanted.

I gave the load a second glance before moving on. I liked having all the information. Working an afterlife job where success hinged on research meant this trait had become thoroughly integrated into my core. Unfortunately, Specter One and his Senior Specter staff weren't always forthcoming. They told you things that you needed to know, not what you wanted to know. I wasn't fond of that, but after a hundred years I'd gotten used to this annoyingly vague aspect of their leadership.

Another of my Present Ghost colleagues who'd been in line behind me stepped up to the table and I scooted over to Specter Four. He was much friendlier—a smile so bright and white it looked like he brushed his teeth with stars and gargled with moon glow.

"Your Fa-La-La-La Fashion Pod, Miss Mason," he said, placing a sparkling gift in my palm. It resembled a chestnut with a long wax end like a candle.

"Now, time for everyone's favorite tool of the trade. Would you like a bracelet or key ring this year?"

"Bracelet, please."

I held out my arm and he fastened a silver charm bracelet next to my watch. The CCD accessory came with nine basic charms. The other Present Ghosts and I would get additional, more powerful magic charms later in December.

"Thank you, Specter Four." I jangled the bracelet and stashed my phone and pod in the outer pocket of my satchel. Marley and I migrated away from the table. Many of my coworkers were mingling on the other side of the room. A few smiled and gestured for me to join them, but after a respectful wave, I went to hang out alone in the corner to mentally prepare for the coming journey. Bismaad, however, found me anyway.

"This is my first time being assigned to a Scrooge in England," she remarked, giving Marley an affectionate pat. "I'm a tad nervous. You've had five assignments over there, right? Any advice?"

A small shiver of repressed memory tremored up my spine. Three out of those five assignments had become UnScrooged in later years. Collin Whitmore, Mary Kauffman, and Todd Birch. They had forgotten the people they promised to be, but I hadn't. I never forgot any of them, or how much it hurt when I realized my work with them had been for nothing.

I swallowed the bitterness and smiled at Bismaad. "They drive on the left side of the road. A lot of places put cream in their eggs. Make sure you understand the money or they'll know you don't belong." Then I smiled. "And visit Kew Gardens if you're near West London. They go all out at Christmas."

"Lovely. I thank you for the recommendations," Bismaad said, surprising me with her practiced British accent.

"All right, Ghosts of Christmas Present!" Specter One clapped his hands together at the front of the room. "Who's ready to change someone's life?"

Temporarily anyway.

"Follow your infiltration instructions to the letter and you'll land a role in your targets' lives. Apartments and homes are ready for you in your base cities. As usual, your teleportation station is found within the bathroom. Be as subtle as you can with your comings and goings, and never allow anyone into your dwelling. As many of your roles involve full-time jobs, I encourage you to sleep on Earth as often as possible and communicate with your teams via phone rather than in person."

"Nothing says goodwill toward mankind like a good cell signal," I whispered to Bismaad. She snickered.

"Happy Holiday Haunting, everyone!" said Specter One. "Please begin transport."

Bismaad and I lined up in front of a realm-evator. The ornaments on the lobby's three pines seemed to glow more brightly. Marley wagged his tail.

When it was Bismaad's turn, she squeezed my arm before stepping into the lift and swiping her ID badge. Her smile was warm and eyes determined. She winked as the doors closed. A flash ensued, followed by the sound of sleigh bells. When the doors opened again, Bismaad was gone.

Marley and I entered the realm-evator next. I scanned my ID, pressed the Earth button, and watched the doors shut as I pocketed my card.

I hate this part.

Unlike rides between the CCD and the North Pole, traveling to Earth was a bit jarring. I'd never completely gotten used to it.

The number 12 displayed on a screen above the button panel. The realm-evator started to rapidly descend as that number dropped: *11, 10, 9 . . .*

I took a deep breath and pet Marley to keep him calm. The sides of the elevator lit up with lightning streaks of red and green. The laugher of children and the deep toll of church bells echoed around us. Golden rings of light flickered on the ceiling.

The lift fell faster, rumbling as we descended—*8, 7, 6, 5, 4, 3, 2*, and . . .

A shimmering number *1* appeared on screen as the realm-evator came to an abrupt halt. I stumbled a second and put a hand up against one of the walls for stability.

"Welcome back to Earth, Miss Mason," said an automated voice coming from the scanner. The realm-evator doors slid open, revealing another simple white door. I twisted the knob and discovered my new home for the next month. Behind me, the transport twinkled and closed its own doors. It would remain there for the rest of the month for my return trips to the CCD. I closed the "bathroom" door that concealed my magical way home and strode out on the wood flooring. At first glance, I was pleased. It was a spacious loft-style apartment with big bay windows that threw gray light over everything, making the white linen bed glow with angelic haze. Only temptations of the sky were visible through the windows—the metal and glass hallmarks of urban planning took up most of the view.

Marley wiggled so I set him down. He immediately scuttered off to explore.

Behind me, a single red bow hung over the front door. On the wall beside it was a magic thermostat that always came with our Earth dwellings; it read 28 degrees. Ghosts could deal with whatever climate we were assigned to just fine—*it's not like I was going to melt stepping outside in the Southern California weather*—but the colder it was, the more relaxed and recharged we felt, so icy temperatures were ideal while we slept or regrouped in our domains.

Light fixtures dangling from the high ceiling twinkled like turkey-sized sparklers. In the chrome-dominant kitchen to my right, candles decorated shelves and garlands hung from counters and cabinets. To the left, a white sofa draped with a scarlet blanket sat next to a flocked Christmas tree. I went up to it and poked my reflection on one of the silver ornament balls. Since my death, I had never gone a full day without seeing a Christmas tree; yet in the last century I'd never actually decorated one myself. I thought that was sad.

"Woof! Woof!"

In the kitchen, Marley had pressed his front paws against the window and was staring down at the cars on the street two floors below. I placed my palm against the glass and looked out with him.

Los Angeles.

It had been decades since I'd been back. This was once my city. I was born here. I had died here. So much was different, and yet the hallmarks of the place seemed the same. I knew better than to believe it would *feel* the same though.

"LA at Christmas. Traffic glistening once again," I mused. Then I noticed a massive silver clock on the wall and was pulled from my reverie. It was a quarter to seven in the morning.

Sugar plum! I need to get changed!

The only other door in the apartment, aside from the exit, was tucked in an alcove behind the kitchen. I opened it. Nothing inside but a broom, which I took out and leaned against the wall. I drew the Fa-La-La-La Fashion Pod out of my bag, hurried to the stove, and lit the wax end. Sparks began flying. Although I had compared this thing to a candle earlier, it was more akin to a stick of dynamite.

I launched the sweet-smelling grenade into the closet and slammed the door. A moment later, the door expanded like a bubble—as if the closet were burping. A cloud of creamy smoke that smelled of cookies wafted out from beneath the frame. I opened the door to reveal the innards of the closet had been converted into a fully mirrored box. Even the inside of the door was one large looking glass.

I stepped into the shower-sized chamber and shut the door. Christmas tunes performed by pan flutes and guitars in a Peruvian style emanated from invisible speakers like elevator music. The perimeter of the floor had a strand of tiny bulbs that created dreamlike uplighting. As soon as I lifted my ID card to a reader on the wall, the digital pad scanned me from hair to heel with a judgmental crimson light.

Then I waited. My frosty blue irises, which I imagined had inspired my namesake, were big and empty in the reflection of the mirror. Per usual, my brown hair was pulled into a conservative updo with a braid on each side looped around a bun at the back.

Glistening particles best described as stardust began to fall from the ceiling and stuck to me like lint. The particles shone brighter and brighter until a fantastic flash consumed me.

When I opened my eyes, I beheld my transformation. My hair remained in its updo, but everything else had changed. I now wore a stylish black coat—not too thick; this was California after all—over a cherry-colored, long-sleeve blouse tucked into a dark forest green pencil skirt. Black pumps matched the black leather briefcase that my satchel had morphed into.

As I stepped out of my magical closet, I checked if my bag still retained all its things—files, keys, phone, miscellaneous office supplies, and wallet. Yup, it was all there. I pulled out a blue folder before zipping everything up.

"Be good, Marley," I called. "I have a job to get."

I brusquely exited my apartment. When I set foot outside, I felt off balance for a moment. I loved Los Angeles when I was alive, but since ghosts didn't get to choose their assignments, I'd only been here a few times in the last hundred years. Like the other ghosts, I'd had to disconnect myself from considering where I once lived as *my home*. It was the healthiest thing.

The whir of honking cars, the bustling foot traffic, the gleaming sun against the buildings . . . I took a deep breath and then shook my head firmly. *No.* I'd laid my connection to this place to rest a long time ago and I doubted it could be resurrected any more than I could.

I began my stride down the sidewalk, not met with a single smile from the people passing by. I was not surprised. It may have been Christmastime, but it was still the Monday morning after a major holiday.

I checked my watch and flipped open my folder to reference a map, looking between it and the environment to triangulate my position as I walked.

Okay, there's S. Grand Avenue. Take a right.

I glanced up from the map just in time to leap back as a black sedan made a sharp right without checking for pedestrians crossing. I made a sound like *"Eeep!"* The driver didn't even notice.

I took a deep breath and stood still for a minute. My nerves felt shot. Had I still possessed a functioning heart, it would have been racing.

Déjà vu still works after a century, I guess.

Eventually I forced myself to find my center and continue on my way, keeping my eyes up this time, lest I get hit by another car. My nerves were still kind of jittery, so to distract myself I ran through facts and names pertaining to my new job in my head.

According to my files, Jay had a campaign manager who basically handled his whole life. I was going to be taking on the role of their general assistant. However, based on the description of the girl who'd previously occupied this position, the term general lackey would have been more appropriate. I was basically just supposed to do whatever and go wherever Jay and his campaign manager ordered, come when called, follow them around in case they needed anything from a reservation at a restaurant to a tissue for a runny nose. *How glamorous.*

It was nothing new. Our undercover jobs were frequently lackluster, made all the worse by thankless, cruel, belittling bosses. Ugh. Scrooges were the worst.

Finally I reached my destination. Once inside the sky-reaching metal building, I stepped into an elevator—the regular kind. The doors closed. Before selecting a button I took a long, calming inhale and exhale, pushing my personal feelings about the CCD as far down as they would go so they wouldn't disturb me for the rest of my assignment.

I was a pro at concealing my disenchantment when on duty. Despite my doubts about how much our ghostly work mattered, I'd successfully Scrooged every one of my predictable, cynical assignments because I could detach myself and embody my Christmas role as easily as an actor did a part in a movie. Now, once again, it was time to put on a good show. My final show.

I pressed the button for the fifth floor and stuffed my blue folder in my bag. As the lift ascended, I glanced at my charm bracelet and its nine basic charms—the coffee cup, the snowflake, the heart, the bug, the banana, the ear, the cage, the brain, and the fork. The coffee charm caught my eye.

Always make a strong first impression.

I snapped my fingers. *POOF!* With a spray of sparkles, a hot to-go cup magically appeared in my hand. The coffee charm on my bracelet disintegrated into golden glitter.

These charms didn't come with their own magic. Ghosts of Christmas Present utilized our powers to activate them. My CCD watch flashed briefly in accordance, noting the small amount of magic I'd just used.

The doors slid open with a *DING!* and I strode into a thriving workspace. Men and women at desks typed away on computers or spoke on phones. People darted back and forth with clipboards or calendars. Posters and banners with Jay Nichols's face were plastered all over the walls. I hadn't seen an office this raring after Thanksgiving since the '80s on Wall Street.

The space had a fairly open floor plan. A short staircase across the room led to a raised section with two glass-front offices and a conference room on each side. That's when I spotted him. Jay Nichols walked from a conference room toward one of the offices, speaking tensely to an Asian woman in a violet blazer. I headed up the stairs after them.

"Trina can't just leave, Annie," Jay protested loudly. "She's been our assistant for months." He entered the office and sat on the edge of the desk. The woman leaned against the open doorway.

"I'm sorry, Jay. She won an all-expense-paid Christmas holiday to Switzerland. She felt it was a once-in-a-lifetime opportunity."

"Why would she even enter that kind of competition when she knew how many events we have this month?" Jay exclaimed.

"It's my understanding that it was a random raffle or something—"

I knocked twice on the doorframe to get their attention. The Asian woman turned around and glared at me. "I'm sorry, can I help you? We're in the middle of a meeting."

"Actually, I can help you," I replied, entering the office. "My name is Frost Mason. Your assistant Trina Anders called the temp agency before she departed for Switzerland. I have been briefed on your schedule and I am here to fill in until Christmas. I can literally do anything she did for you. You're Jay's campaign manager, Annie Jung, right?" I pulled out a red file from my briefcase and handed it to her. "My resume and references."

She looked at me suspiciously and took the folder. As she flipped through it, I met Jay's eyes. Bismaad was objectively right; he was handsome. He'd grown into his height since college and filled out in muscle mass. Unlike the young version of him I'd seen with Midori and Brandon though, this man had crow's feet around the eyes, wrinkles forming in his forehead, and a tightness in his jawline that suggested he ground his teeth while he slept.

Hm. I may only be posing as his assistant, but maybe I should make him an appointment with a TMJ specialist . . .

"It says here you have been a temp assistant to three senators and a congresswoman within the last year," Annie said in disbelief.

"Their direct office numbers are listed. Feel free to give them a call for personal recommendations." I pivoted and handed Jay the to-go cup. "In the meantime, this is for you. Three shots, two sugars, and a lot of cinnamon. Exactly how you like it."

Jay warily accepted the cup and took a sip. His frustrated face softened in surprise. "Perfect. Surprisingly perfect." He glanced at Annie. "We're in a bind. If she says Trina briefed her, then we can try her out for a week. Not like we have much of a choice."

"Fine," Annie said. "I *will* be calling all your references though." She glanced at Jay. "Jaffrey plays dirty; I wouldn't put it past her to send a spy in here."

I subdued a grin. I always got a kick out of imagining Specter Seven at his desk in the CCD—monitoring a team of elves working a phone bank like an old-timey telethon. The slew of impressions and voices needed to answer our magically redirected "reference calls" from Earth must've been hilarious to behold.

Annie stuck out her hand. I extended mine and she shook it aggressively.

"We move fast around here; keep up or get out. We're too close in the polls with Jaffrey to allow anything to mess with our flow. And if you *are* working for her, I'll find out." She dropped my hand. "Follow me. I'll show you to Trina's old desk."

"I was actually hoping to talk with Jay for a—"

"It's *Mr. Nichols* to you and he has a speech to go over. Come with me. Now." Annie beckoned for me to follow as she exited the office. I glanced back at Jay but obeyed.

Deep breaths, Frost.

"Sit," Annie instructed when we reached a desk at the foot of the stairs. I did so and took in my underwhelming workstation. It held a basic computer, stapler, and a landline phone. Annie kept my resume folder tucked under her arm and texted with one hand on her cell as she addressed me.

"If Trina briefed you properly, you know we have a ribbon-cutting ceremony in two hours, an interview with the *LA Times* at three o'clock, and a cocktail party with potential backers from the Restaurant Owners' Association at six. You can't be trusted with anything important right now, so just go help the interns make collection calls until we have to go." She extended a black polished, manicured finger at a group of twenty-somethings gathered in the left corner of the office.

"Actually, I can help with more than—"

"Nope." Annie held her finger in front of my face. "Do exactly as I say. The car is picking us up in eighty minutes. You will stay at my side for the events today, but no interfering and no questions. If you don't disappoint, we can see what else you can assist with tomorrow."

Annie strutted away, still tapping on her phone. I fingered the banana charm on my bracelet.

Nope. Not the right time.

With patience and the mental reminder that this was my last Christmas season on Earth, I went to join the interns.

"Hi, everyone. Who needs help?"

The adjective I would use to best describe Christmas: *persistent*.

If there was one thing I never stopped admiring about the holiday—no matter where you were in the world—it found a way to shine through. Here in the land of palm trees and concrete paths, jammed freeways and blue skies, eternal seventy-degree days and grown men in shorts, all it took was a touch of glitzy December decor to bring you back to the season.

I hustled across the plaza carrying a pair of massive scissors that weighed more than Marley. Despite their awkward weight and the fast pace of our walk, I still appreciated the holiday spirit brought out by long, golden strands of tinsel wrapped around lampposts and the plaza's Christmas tree constructed entirely of poinsettia plants. Those touches alone made the area feel magical.

Jay's two bodyguards, Rocco and Lucas, led our group—followed by Jay, Annie, and me. A few other bodyguards flanked our sides, fielding back reporters.

We approached a stage set up in front of a three-story building. An impressive ribbon wrapped the handles of the front doors. A sign at the front declared it the *"Los Angeles Women's Center"*. There was a crowd of maybe two hundred people surrounding the stage. It was difficult to gauge the exact number with all the cameras and mics invading our personal space.

"Jay! What is your reaction to Farah Jaffrey's latest accusation of your history with the congresswoman?" a reporter shouted, shoving her microphone forward.

"Any thoughts on the new unemployment numbers released for the county?" another reporter asked.

"Members of the Diverse Leaders Association claim you're not doing enough for your own community. Any response?"

That last question seemed to faze Jay, who'd kept his eyes forward until now. He paused and turned his head—brow creased—and opened his mouth to respond, but Annie cut him off with the speed of an alley cat and the assertiveness of a brown bear protecting her cub. She addressed the reporters while simultaneously herding Jay up the stairs to the stage.

"Mr. Nichols will not be taking questions at this time. We

have a press conference tomorrow. In the meantime, please direct your focus to the purpose of this event."

Jay's bodyguards moved him to center stage, marked by a podium with a mic. He shook hands with a small group of people gathered there. I hastened up the steps with Annie. She directed me over to the side where we waited behind a curtain framing the stage. Several bodyguards situated themselves there as well.

"On behalf of the community, I want to thank Mr. Nichols for being with us today," announced a plump Hispanic gentleman into the microphone, voice carrying over the plaza and crowd. "As we enter the Christmas season, a lot of us focus on gifts. But there is no better gift than one that will keep on giving and fostering positive change for the future. Mr. Nichols's participation on the board of this project was instrumental in getting it approved and built so quickly. Everyone, please join me in giving him a round of applause."

The assembly clapped and hooted. I would have joined the applause had my hands not been full with the aforementioned crazy-giant scissors.

"Thank you, Dominic," Jay said, trading spots with the man who had introduced him.

Jay cleared his throat and placed both palms on the podium.

"I am honored to be here today and appreciate the warm welcome. I have, and will continue to gladly donate anything I can to support this center. It is important to me because the people in this city are important to me. I know we've been hit hard in recent years, but the great thing that drove people to migrate to California hundreds of years ago is still what makes us strong today. Gold. I'm not talking about the metal that Americans dug from the ground or panned for in rivers. I'm talking about the gold that is in each of us—our potential. We are a state of dreamers, doers, builders, thinkers, and fighters. We have the work ethic to expand and reach for new heights, and the courageous creativity to impact our country and the world. In spite of the ways state government has faltered over the years, California has still been our country's highest grossing economy overall and has even reached the distinction of being the fifth largest economy in the entire world. If we can do that, *as is*, imagine what our state would be like if it was governed by someone who truly cares about you. Imagine what we can achieve together if we *worked* together, and the people in charge listened to the people they pledged to serve. That is what I promise you. Since I was a kid, I have worked to build a better life for myself, and I can commit to making sure that the people I govern will always have a fair shot at the same."

The crowd roared with enthusiasm. I looked out at the sea of spectators. It was amazing to see genuine belief and spirit beaming from these people like bright lanterns on a cold winter night. They really believed in him. That was . . . weird. People usually loathed or feared Scrooges. In fact, they always did because Scrooges were notoriously unlikable people.

I shook my head. I was probably overthinking it. It'd been a long time since I was assigned a politician. However, from what I recalled, most were two-faced creatures. This compelling version of Jay had to be an act—a convincing persona for the voters— and behind closed doors his true corrupt, cruel nature would reveal itself. He likely didn't have anything to do with that speech and there was some professional writer back in his office churning out uplifting talking points for all his events.

"Now, without further delay . . ." Jay gestured to me backstage and I hurried forward to hand him the supersized scissors. He stepped down from the stage and moved in front of the ribbon-wrapped doors.

"I give you all the Los Angeles Women's Center. A safe and inclusive shelter to provide services that support women and children on their journeys out of difficult situations and into stability and security. May it stand here to support our community for many years to come." He cut the massive ribbon and more cheering ensued.

A couple of volunteers in red shirts opened the main doors to the building and people started filing in. Jay remained out front, shaking hands with folks and flashing endearing smiles.

"So how many staff writers do you have back at the office crafting Jay's speeches?" I whispered to Annie.

"None unfortunately. Jay writes all his speeches himself."

My brow rose. "Seriously?"

"I know," she huffed. "I keep telling him we need to hire professionals. I counted at least three syntax mistakes in there, but he refuses so we have to work with whatever speeches he comes up with, even if they do leave a lot to be desired, like this one."

"I thought it was . . . nice," I commented, still in shock that those were *Jay's* words, not someone else's.

"Nice doesn't win elections." Annie replied. She redirected her eyes to Jay and went to join him. She whispered something in his ear before they both moved inside.

I followed diligently as Jay mingled under Annie's careful guidance, shadowed by the bodyguards. My Scrooge met with reporters, volunteers, and event bigwigs—confidently shaking hands, kissing babies, and answering questions.

"Sometimes people hit a bad break in life and need help to move forward. I'm glad this place can give women in our community an opportunity to do that," he replied to a reporter.

After a while of this, I began to get bored and claustrophobic in the packed welcome foyer. In need of a breather, I wandered into the main room where festivities had been set up. A table of snacks and treats, a hot cocoa stand, game booths in carnival style, and a craft station surrounded a bare Christmas tree.

Under supervision of adults, children were making paper chains, painting ornaments, and stringing popcorn for it. I smiled and sat down among them.

"What are you painting?" I asked a young girl busy working a paintbrush over some construction paper.

"It's a snowman," she said. "But I'm giving him four arms so he can fight winter crime from every angle."

"Very practical," I mused.

"Excuse me?" Someone tapped my shoulder. I turned to face a girl in her early twenties looking down at me. "You work with Mr. Nichols, right?"

"I do," I said as I stood up.

"Can you thank him for me? I can't get near enough to do it myself, but the center gave me a job in social media outreach and they're letting me live here. At Christmas, most shelters get really full. This place is giving my son and me a chance at a better future, and I just want to let Mr. Nichols know that . . . I mean, I get I'm just one person, but tell him Nia says thanks. Please. He's made a difference to me."

"I'd be glad to." I put my hand on her shoulder. "And I can't think of anything that matters more than making a difference to one person."

She smiled before moving away. I glanced toward the foyer. The cluster of people who'd surrounded Jay for interviews and statements had broken apart. Where had my charge gotten off to? I journeyed into the foyer and spotted Annie's violet blazer disappearing through a door at the end of a connecting hall. Where Annie went, Jay went. I made my way over and pressed my ear to the door. The voices inside were muffled.

There was a staircase a few feet over. I ducked under where no one could see me. Then I closed my eyes and concentrated. My form turned transparent blue. I came out from my hiding place in the nick of time for a couple of children to run through me. None of us felt anything—it was like wind meeting wind. Whereas Brandon could make himself and his passengers ghostly invisible and intangible in the past, I could do so in the present. I phased past the door Annie had gone through and joined the meeting. I found her, Jay, and three men gathered around a small conference table. Jay stood and was pacing though; he appeared confused and upset.

"One year, tops," a slender man was saying, mouth in a firm line within his beard.

"I thought the fundraising we did was enough for three years," Jay argued.

Annie shook her head. "That fundraising was for the Jay Nichols Community Relief Fund. We've allocated a third of that to this project since it's so important to you, but the rest has to go toward your expenses for next year. Even with all your supporters and backers, it's not enough to carry us right now. We have to campaign across the entire state, Jay. Every dollar counts considering we have to contend with Jaffrey's personal fortune."

"But that's a misuse of the money that people donated," Jay protested.

"Not really," Annie reasoned. "If you're elected, you will be able to help countless communities. You can't help anyone if you aren't anyone who matters."

"Miss Jung is right," said another man with an elongated face like a horse. "This center will stay afloat with your contributions for a year and that's plenty. Plus, you've given it great publicity. Now you have to move on and let this place sink or swim without you. It's not a part of the big picture. Your big picture."

Jay sighed, putting his hands in his pockets. "I spearheaded the fundraising for this place. What if they can't sustain the momentum without me? If we don't provide the support we promised, it could shut down and be a supermarket by next year. These people have no idea that they could be celebrating their first and last Christmas here."

Annie's steely expression did not waver. "Win the election, Jay. If Jaffrey gets into power, we'll all sink. You are the greater good—someone who actually cares enough to *do* good. Don't let yourself and your constituents down by sacrificing your shot for small, one-off charity projects like this."

A knock came at the door. The man from the stage entered the room. "Sorry to interrupt, but we'd love to get some pictures of Jay in front of the tree with the kids."

"Of course, Dominic." Annie nodded with a saccharine smile.

"Just give me a minute," Jay said. He glanced at the others in the meeting. "Go on. I'll meet you out there." His team obliged and got up to leave, Annie reluctantly.

When they'd left, Jay paced another moment. Then he sat and leaned back in one of the office chairs. He let out a frustrated exhale. I walked over and observed him curiously.

The conflict in his eyes surprised me. Usually when I worked with Scrooges, they had a complete lack of awareness that what they were doing and how they were living was wrong. Whoever they'd been in brighter days was gone and forgotten. Scrooges were the protagonists of Christmas Carol experiences but, prior to our intervention, in their own lives they were the villains. And villains didn't inspire people, argue on behalf of the meek, or feel internal conflict about the morals of their choices. They were too lost in their own selfish desires and cynical perspectives to care about anyone else.

Strangely, Jay wasn't giving me that impression. It was only my first day with him, so maybe I was mistaken. But from what I could tell thus far, he wasn't lost. He hadn't forgotten the person he used to be. That man was still there; he was just . . . struggling.

I tilted my head, processing the idea.

Could that be right? Could Jay be different than the men and women I'd been assigned before? I studied him as he studied the ceiling—not quite sure what to make of this Scrooge.

"Let's get down to brass tacks," said the reporter. She had a huge, fluffy hairstyle that I imagined provided solid insulation against the elements. Even more impressive, she'd managed to prevent even a single fleck of dust or dirt from landing on her snow-white pantsuit. Did she cover herself in bubble wrap this morning to keep her outfit pristine for this interview?

"With it being the holiday season, our readers want to know more about your childhood and your family," the reporter continued. She and Jay sat in twin gray armchairs facing each other within her office of the news building. Annie and I stood by the door. Jay's campaign manager could've given watchdogs pointers. Focus radiated off of her at all times.

"After your father abandoned your mother when you were seven, she raised you and your sisters as a single parent until you were nine, when she married your stepfather, Raymond. Tell me what it was like to have him replace your father."

Jay's brow pinched taut. "My father didn't abandon my mother. She had personal issues that drove them apart. He visited me and my sisters when he could after that, but it was awkward for him once my mother remarried. My father tried to maintain a relationship with us until he was killed in a traffic accident when I was twelve. Raymond never replaced him."

"Mmm, I see. Can you tell me more about these *issues* that your mother had?" the reporter asked. "Were they similar to the problems you had with your ex-wife Celia?"

"Every couple is different. We all hope for the best when we commit to each other, but love doesn't always sustain. People disappoint you."

"Your ex-wife remarried two years ago. Would you say that you visit your children more or less frequently than your father visited you?"

"I travel a lot with campaigning, but I try to stay as close to my kids as I can," Jay responded flatly. "This job has a lot of responsibilities, so it can be difficult."

"Will you be spending Christmas with them?" the reporter asked.

"I would like to."

"And what about your mother and siblings? Any Christmas plans with them?"

"Not at this time. I haven't spent Christmas with them in many years. They have their own lives and I have mine. I wish them well, but we're not close."

"Any particular reason?"

"We grew apart. It happens in a lot of families I'm sure."

The reporter sighed. "Jay, you're not giving me much here. I'm not going to be able to run this story without more . . . meat. Tell me about some of your family's Christmas traditions. Maybe something you did when you were young that you continue doing with your children?"

Jay considered. "Cookies," he said finally. "I made cookies with my parents when I was young. We always baked some to enjoy during the week leading up to the holiday. Then on Christmas Eve, we made more to put out for Santa. Every year we tried a new recipe to mix things up so Santa wouldn't get bored with our offerings."

I smiled.

The reporter did too. "That's lovely. And do you make cookies with your kids too?"

"We used to. I was terrible at it, but Celia is a baker so my kids are happier now that she's taken the helm."

"Anything else? I spoke with your sister Monica and she mentioned a red apple tradition. Can you tell me more about that?"

That piqued my interest. Specter One had said red apples were one of the things that Jay hated the most.

Jay's jaw tensed as he dismissed the subject. "Oh, that was a tradition in my family a long time ago. My sisters were never that into it, so I'm surprised if they picked up the habit again. It's nothing your readers would be interested in though—I can't imagine stories about produce sell many periodicals."

Annie stepped forward, intervening. "We have time for one more question."

The reporter nodded. "Okay, how about the most basic question. What do you want for Christmas, Jay Nichols?"

The question seemed to cause Jay pause. After a moment he looked at the reporter with sincerity. "Time," he said. "It's probably what every person would ask for if it was a gift that could be given. I'd love more time to spend with my kids, and more time to spend connecting with the different people in this amazing state I hope to someday govern."

Jay stood, buttoned his suit jacket, and shook the reporter's hand. "Thank you. Feel free to phone my office if you have clarification questions." He gave the reporter a nod and then promptly headed for the door. Ten minutes later, we were back in our SUV with tinted windows, merging into street traffic. The back of the car had been laid out like a limo—two long shared seats with multiple seatbelts facing each other.

A divider separated us from the front seats, giving us privacy from Rocco and Lucas. Annie and Jay sat next to each other; she was showing him something on her phone. I sat opposite them. I pulled my agenda book from my bag. We were returning to our office now, and tonight we had that cocktail reception with the Restaurant Owners' Association. I would need to go home and change before that.

I glanced at Jay, his face concentrating on whatever Annie showed him. So much intensity on his face. Seemed like a good time for an interruption.

"When was the last Christmas you baked cookies with your kids?"

Jay looked up and blinked at me. "What?"

"You told that reporter you used to do it. How long ago was the last time?"

"Frost," Annie interjected. "When is your deadline?"

"My deadline?"

"For the article you're writing. I assume you're a reporter, otherwise why would you think it's your place to ask Mr. Nichols personal questions?"

Her cutting look perturbed me, but part of my CCD job was keeping whatever Earth job my cover came with. That was vital, as it allowed me the proximity and access to get to know my Scrooge better. Given the low-level roles we were usually assigned, that involved taking a lot of cranberry sauce—*my substitute for the curse word most people would use in this case.*

I took a cleansing breath. Overqualified or not, I had to maintain this assistant job no matter what. I wouldn't do that if I told Annie where to shove her sarcasm.

Mistletool.

"Sorry," I said.

Jay gave me a more sympathetic look than expected before Annie recaptured his attention. As they talked, I perused the charms on my bracelet, enticed to activate one.

I didn't though. The remaining eight had to last me several weeks, which meant I had to be selective with my magical moments, no matter how tempted I felt.

Our evening event was being held in an Italian restaurant. The North Pole would fully approve of the festive décor. Wreaths riddled with pinecones and bows hung from the walls and doorways. Tall tables were elegantly draped with red tablecloths trimmed with sparkly emblems. Each centerpiece was a Christmas tree shaped tower of frosted beignets. The waiters and waitresses wore elf costumes, fake pointy ears included.

Always knowing exactly how to outfit me, the magic closet created by my Fa-La-La-La Fashion Pod had garbed me in a dark green lace dress with an illusion neckline. Jay's tie was the same color as my frock. Annie wore an onyx number with a conservative slit by the left leg.

"Remember, the goal tonight is maximum impact," Annie said to Jay as we walked in. "Smile. Get them to like you. Charm them into trusting you. You're Jay Nichols—a man of the people. You get it, and you get them."

"Thanks for reminding me, Annie," Jay said with a touch of sarcasm. "What would I do without you?"

At my tiny huff of amusement, Annie whirled to face me.

"Frost, your predecessor was a whiz with names. If she didn't know someone, she got the info ASAP. Were you exaggerating when you said you can literally do anything Trina could do, or can you handle this?"

"Don't worry, Annie. I have everything under control. Trust me."

"Trust has to be earned, Frost. But this is a good time to earn it. Stay close. If I give you a signal, you have one minute to provide quick background on whoever Jay is about to talk to. Got it?"

My smile was confident, even a bit devious. "Absolutely."

When Jay and Annie turned to start greeting guests, I snapped my fingers and the brain charm on my bracelet dissolved into glitter. My watch flashed a moment in response.

I had to say, while making Annie happy was not my main goal, I did enjoy the surprise on her face as I shined during the meet-and-greet that followed. The knowledge charm I'd used gave me instant information on anyone I locked eyes with. Like the dream assistant to any high-ranking society type, I whispered names, dates, and fun facts into Jay's and Annie's ears as they mingled with different restaurant owners. I even had time to snag the occasional appetizer off a passing tray between introductions.

As the evening progressed, I was struck by Jay's chameleon adaptability. He worked the room like a nominee for homecoming king. It was impressive, although a tad unsettling. He listened patiently to the problems and concerns people voiced and seemed to always know the right thing to say to ease their worries and secure their confidence. That wasn't necessarily a bad thing, but I lost count of just how many promises Jay pledged during the merry mingling montage.

He was speaking with a man who owned a chain of sandwich shops when a confident voice caused his shoulders to tense.

"Jay, what a nice surprise."

We all turned.

"Farah," Jay said. "Why do I feel like I'm the only one being surprised? What are you doing here?"

Farah Jaffrey was an elegant woman of Middle Eastern descent. Her dark hair was long, loosely curled, and highlighted with honey blonde. She looked glamorous in her scarlet, cap-sleeved dress, holding a sparkly black clutch in her manicured hand.

"I was invited, Jay," Farah replied. "My family and I are investors in several restaurants downtown." She leaned around Jay and spoke to the man he'd been talking to.

"Mr. Kudrow, how are you this evening? I hear your granddaughter Marcy just finished her first semester of culinary school. You must be so proud."

"She did, it's so nice of you to remember," the man gushed. "Marcy is extremely talented. I know she would love to work in one of your restaurants someday."

"My restaurant development teams are always looking for interns in their kitchens," Farah responded. "Let's talk." She smiled at Jay. "Excuse us, won't you."

Mr. Kudrow shook Jay's hand and let Farah guide him away. When she'd gone, Jay turned to Annie. "Did you know she was going to be here?"

"Of course not, but you're fine; we simply need to work faster. For the rest of the night, skip any lengthy, in-depth conversations and only use our general talking points to move through the crowds quickly. Assure each person you talk to that you can get them what they want, then move on to the next one."

"Can you really blanket guarantee that?" I asked. "Every business is different. If you're going to aid anyone here, you probably have to do a lot more work on understanding their needs before you make those promises. I think really talking to these people is a good way to learn what they actually need help with versus going through them like a speed dating exercise."

Annie glared at me. "Frost, you've been doing well so far, but leave the strategizing to people who have clocked in more than one full workday on this team."

"She may not be wrong, Annie," Jay interjected. "I feel like I've been pretty fast and loose with my assurances tonight already. Maybe for the rest of the reception I should keep trying to get to know these people better and explain to them my general pro small business platform. Then we can discuss the specifics of their needs and how I can assist them afterward."

"*Afterward* being the optimal word, Jay. There won't be one if these people feel more confident Jaffrey and her resources can get them something you can't. They need to know you have the intention of satisfying their needs. Intentions are promises with wiggle room we can work around later."

"I don't know, Annie . . ."

Farah and several men exchanged a loud laugh in the corner. Then she shook hands with one of them.

Annie gestured for Jay to come with her to the wooden staircase in the corner, but motioned for me not to follow. In fact, she gave me a very clear "*Stay*" as she held up her hand like I was a needy dog.

While the two of them conversed, I glanced around for a place to go ghost. The event was crowded, and the bathrooms were on the opposite side of the room. By the time I found a place to hide and returned I would've lost out on whatever secret Annie was telling.

I glanced at my charm bracelet.

Dang it, I'm going to have to use another one.

I snapped my fingers and the ear charm evaporated into

glitter. A wireless gold ear pod appeared in my hand. I stuck it in my ear as my watch flashed. Despite the socializing people moving between us, I kept my eyes glued on Jay across the room. Annie stood close to him, her back to the party.

"Jay, you need to stop fighting me on these things. My advice is for your benefit. I'm excellent at winning elections. *You're not.* That's why Friedman's hired me to work with you. I know your history and you need to trust me. If you waste time constantly trying to cross every *t* and dot every *i*, we're never going to make enough noise to stand a chance. You *will* lose. The world will move on and that strong heart and mind inside you will be as wasted in adulthood as they were when you were a kid and no one gave you a chance. Do you want that? Do you want manipulative people like Farah to call the shots forever, or do you want to do what's necessary to finally have the platform to enact the change you always hoped to accomplish?"

A beat passed.

Then Jay nodded. "Fine, Annie. I get it. You win."

"No, Jay. *You'll* win. That is the point. Nothing else matters until we make that happen."

I sat on the sofa in my loft. The lights on my Christmas tree twinkled as I pet Marley with one hand and scrolled through an Earth web page on my CCD phone with the other. The phone worked like a regular cell, plus a few extra magical applications.

Suddenly my "Jingle Bells" ringtone began to play and Bismaad's profile picture filled the screen. She was calling me on SpaceTime. I accepted.

"Good morning!" she bellowed with her British accent—fully committed to the role.

"Same to you," I replied. "Though I should mention it's night here."

"Right, right. Continental time differences." She pushed up the glasses on her nose.

"What's with the glasses?"

"My Fa-La-La-La Fashion Pod keeps dressing me with them. Evidently, it's part of my look. What are you up to?"

"Researching new movies and their showtimes at the local theater," I said. "With my workload at Jay's office I think I can see at least two a week while I'm here."

"You and your movies." Bismaad shook her head. "We get to be on Earth one month a year, and you'd rather spend that time in a dark room watching other people make stories than creating some of your own."

"Bismaad, we weren't all party girls like you in our day. We have different tastes. Let's leave it at that."

My friend shrugged. "It's your afterlife, babe. Do what you want. Anyway, I'm on my way to the office. How did your first day go?"

"Honestly, it was strange. To my recollection, I don't think I've encountered a Scrooge like Jay. The humans we're assigned are usually far-gone jerks who wouldn't alter course without us. Jay seems to be . . ." I searched for the words. "Resisting on his own."

I bit my lip as I thought about it. "Today could've been an outlier—*it probably was an outlier and he'll show his harsher side soon enough*—but as is, he's not giving off the villainous vibe I've come to expect. It's throwing me. This job has a formula because the subject matter is predictable. What if Jay . . . isn't?"

"Wouldn't that make the assignment more fun?"

"I'm not here for fun, Bismaad." I frowned, thinking back

over my interactions with Jay. "He's another box to check. I just need to get a better understanding of him in order to do that."

"You should post about it on Tinsel," she suggested. "I know you're not a big social media person, but I find it can spark inspiration to see what the other Present Ghosts are up to. You can share your situation too. Maybe ask for feedback?"

"Pass."

"At least skim our group page. I'm telling you, it's helps to see you're not alone."

I sighed. "Fine. I'll check it out and post an emoji or something to make you happy."

"Promise?"

"Yes, yes." I huffed. "Though I doubt any of our coworkers have dealt with a campaign manager as obnoxious as the one blocking me from Jay. If I'm going to put this whole 'is he different' theory to rest, I need a better read on the guy and she keeps getting in the way of me talking to him."

"Are you going to pay him an invisible visit to spy on him instead?"

"Maybe later in the week. Right now, I want to get to know him in person, if I can find a way."

"Is that as efficient?"

"He lives alone, so I am not sure how much help spying on him will be."

She shrugged. "You're the more experienced of us. Do what your gut tells you. And speaking of gut," she winked, "you know what card to play if his manager keeps blocking you."

"Yeah. I do. I hate doing it but . . . she's kind of the worst." I sighed. "Good luck today."

"Thanks! Cheerio!"

We ended our call and I opened the Tinsel app. I scrolled through updates from my ghostly colleagues in the main feed.

Allan had posted a picture of his target at a winter carnival. Griselda commented that her elderly Scrooge had intentionally run over her foot with his motorized scooter. Michael's latest post was just a series of hashtags—*#michiganvibes #humbug #momoneymoproblems #betterlakethannever*

Eventually, I opened my own page. My last post had been from two years ago.

Ugh. What was I even supposed to say? I wasn't about to ask any of the other ghosts for opinions on my case or suggestions for the *possible* anomaly that was Jay Nichols. It was not in my nature to reach out. I'd been a solo act for a long time and I'd made peace with that. Alone was not always an adjective of sorrow; it was one of security for those of us who knew the pain of severed connections.

I tapped my finger on my chin as I thought about my status update. Then finally typed.

"FEELING FROSTY"

Snowflake emoji. Devious emoji. Bug emoji. Thinking emoji.

Dream memories were no different than regular memories; the older you got, the foggier your younger recollections became. I was grateful for that. The haze was like antiseptic on a wound, numbing the pain a bit and keeping it from poisoning you.

Like every evening, my ghostly mind visited the past. Tonight my sleeping consciousness grasped at my earliest memories of childhood, but settings were a blur and people were shadows.

From the vantage point of a crib I saw two silhouettes looking down at me. A flash consumed my view and then I was a toddler, looking up at someone holding my hand. The sun in the background ringed the man's head. He smiled at me. I think he had blue eyes like mine, and dimples. Exact details past that were difficult to make out, but the warmth I felt in his hand and in his expression were clear. Another flash and I was at a door. I didn't know how young I was, but my eye line didn't make it past the handle.

There was yelling in the background. I turned and saw the man and a woman arguing. Their features, again, were hazy, and their arguing a loud garble. The man grabbed a jacket from a chair and went for the door, but before reaching it he turned back and crouched before me. He took my chin in his hand. His frosty eyes seemed to glow; then other parts of him did too—the red on his shirt, the metal on his watch, the black of his shoes. After a moment the man let me go and stood. He went for the door and walked out.

"Frost! Frost!"

I turned around. The dream had changed. Suddenly I was a teenager.

Wyatt Glass jogged over a busy sidewalk to reach me, holding onto his hat so it wouldn't fly off. It was old and tattered like his gray tweed jacket—a hand-me-down from his brother—but the navy strip along the side matched his tie and pocket handkerchief. You didn't need money to have style.

He caught up with me, impish grin shining. I didn't know if all sixteen-year-old boys looked like they were up to mischief, but he certainly did. Or maybe I just felt that way because I was a naturally suspicious sixteen-year-old girl.

Wyatt looked down at the bags of groceries I was carrying. "Do you need help?"

"No. The orphanage is only a couple of blocks away. I have to hustle though. Sister Jocelyn was very specific about what time Christmas Eve dinner needs to be ready."

"Oh, okay. Well, if you finish dinner early, maybe you can meet me at the Christmas dance at the Racket Room tonight? I'd be glad to cover your entrance fee."

I fidgeted. "I don't know, Wyatt. Parties are not my forte."

"Talking to pretty girls isn't my forte either, but it's Christmastime and I got up the nerve to face my fear." From the inside pocket of his jacket, he pulled out a humble bouquet of holly and thistle, tied with a red ribbon, and offered it to me. "Maybe you will too."

I stared at the bouquet and then awkwardly glanced at the grocery bags in my hands.

"Oh." Wyatt cringed. "Here." He delicately stuck the bouquet within the brim of one bag so it was poking out.

"Um. Thank you, Wyatt. I . . . have to go now. Merry Christmas."

I made my way back to St. Francis's orphanage. Being poor may have been inconvenient in most respects, but it certainly built calf strength.

Upon opening the door, I side-stepped as a stream of girls ran by playing tag. Chatter, giggles, and creaking floorboards echoed from different parts of the house.

A pair of younger girls straggled away from the pack dashing past me and hugged my legs on either side.

"Frost!" exclaimed Doloris, a tiny girl missing a front tooth. "Sister Jocelyn said you went out and got ingredients for a special dinner."

I patted her on the head. "I sure did. It's not a feast, but it will warm your soul. Quality over quantity, girls—something to always strive for."

"Will you read us stories later?" asked Bridgette, the second little lady.

I cupped her chin in my hand. "Of course I will, Bridge."

"Will you do it now?"

"I can't," I said. "Right now, my holiday spirit is so strong that if I don't distract myself with hard work in the kitchen, my body will light up like a tree angel and I'll glow brighter and brighter until I burst into a puddle of pudding."

"Eww," the little girls chorused before running off laughing. I smiled and headed for the kitchen.

The rest of the day and night blurred into a slew of memories cut together like a movie montage. I cooked with the nuns. I helped serve girls in the dining hall. I worked at the homeless shelter distributing baked goods we'd prepared. I came back late and assisted the nuns and older girls in washing dishes and cleaning. Then I ate leftovers alone in front of the fire. By the time midnight struck, I was seated at the windowsill in the smaller girls' dormitory with an open book in my hands, surrounded by sleepy young things.

Charles Dickens's *A Christmas Carol* was as familiar in my grasp as a child's security blanket. When I was very young, the holidays were hard for me. I used to sit on this windowsill or hide in some corner of the orphanage to cry—wishing for things and people I didn't have. I found solace in stories; whenever any of the older girls would read to us, I sat front and center, glad to be transported to some other world and life. *A Christmas Carol* was my favorite. Listening to Sister Jocelyn read it every year filled up the cavern in my chest with hope. It built a belief in holiday magic and promised me that with proper motivation people could learn to be different. They could repent, improve, and be the people we wanted them to be.

Once I learned to read, I devoured more Dickens tales and countless other authors' works on my own. And when I got older, Sister Jocelyn passed the torch of this Christmas tradition on to me. I loved keeping it alive, both for myself and the other girls. Though none of them looked particularly alive right now . . .

The small people were utterly tuckered out. Some lay on their beds clutching stuffed animals. Others had passed out on the floor around me atop piles of pillows and blankets. Bridgette had fallen captive to dreams and rested on my lap while Doloris lay beside me, yawning like a kitten clinging to consciousness. As they drifted, I gazed at my book.

The lantern lights of the dormitory had been dimmed, but the moon radiated through the window. I had no trouble seeing the old words printed in the text. I fingered through the pages, admiring the language, pausing every so often to appreciate a particular passage.

"Read more, Frost . . ." Bridgette mumbled, pawing at my lap.

I smoothed her hair and continued reading aloud in a whisper. *"'It is required of every man,' the Ghost returned, 'that the spirit within him should walk abroad among his fellow-men, and travel far and wide; and if that spirit goes not forth in life, it is condemned to do so after death . . .'"*

JINGLE! JINGLE! JINGLE!

The alarm on my phone went off and I blinked awake. My apartment gleamed with sunny light.

Goodness. Sometimes my dream memories were so clear and developed that my mind got tricked. For a moment, that all felt so real . . .

I rubbed my eyes and scooched up to a seated position. Fair golden haze spilled over me from the bay windows. The light made Marley glow like a furry angel at the foot of my bed.

I threw the covers aside and drifted to the glass by the kitchen, gazing out at the California morning. I'd decided to approach my second day on Earth with optimism, but little did I know that this day, and the rest of the week, would end up feeling like one long movie montage. A movie with a confusedly mixed genre.

The Christmas trees, wreaths, and garlands that framed our settings reminded me of a holiday film, but the constant rallies, press photography, and handshaking mirrored the whirlwind of a political drama.

Through it all, I honed in on Jay. My focal point. My purpose. The many distractions and people preventing us from connecting didn't stop me from perceiving idiosyncrasies about him. Though my Scrooge's handsome grin graced his face whenever cameras or spectators were nearby, it faded behind the shadow of a curtain or in the car—the seemingly charismatic man falling into shadow as well. Despite Annie keeping me at a distance, I also noticed how stern he became when she talked to him in private. And on more than a handful of occasions I saw Jay on the phone in some corner, agitated.

Unfortunately, that was the depth of what I was able to glean from my post afar. When we were on the move for the day's events, it was nearly impossible to go ghost and spy on Jay. We were in the public spotlight or in meetings constantly. Worse, Annie gave me larger work responsibilities each day, none of which involved more access to Jay. I needed to interact with him one-on-one if I was going to get to know him well enough to craft a successful Scrooging, let alone confirm or deny my curiosity about his true character, but Annie was always by his side. She left me no choice.

I didn't like doing this to people, but drastic measures would have to be taken if I was going to get anywhere with this assignment.

By Thursday, I was ready to delete the thinking emoji on my Tinsel status update and take bolder action.

"Look at this spread!" one of the interns exclaimed as my co-workers crowded around the breakroom table. A magnificent feast of holiday treats had been delivered—panettone, towers of red and green macaroons, bowls of chocolate drizzled popcorn, snowman-shaped cookies. I watched them attack the sugar like finches fed on breadcrumbs.

My bracelet was down another charm—the fork charm, which materialized any snacks of my choosing. I raised my wrist a moment as my colleagues migrated around the table excitedly. With a smooth, upward flick of my finger across the face of my CCD watch, the numbers and hands vanished and all that was left was a glow and percentage reading. The reading indicated 95%

and the haunting blue light filled up a corresponding amount of the watch face.

Ghosts in the CCD had a certain quantity of magic in their tanks for each holiday season. I hadn't used much with the last four charms; they'd been harnessed for small tasks. But I was about to do something a bit bigger.

"Who sent it?" asked Davis, one of the collection callers.

"It's from the head of the Restaurant Owners' Association," I lied, glancing at Annie. "I already called to thank them."

"Hm." Annie wrapped a single sugar cookie in a napkin and trotted off.

I moved a safe distance from the famished, frenzied workers and snapped my fingers. The bug charm on my bracelet glimmered away. My watch flashed in response and I checked it. The glow had decreased a more notable chunk this time. Ghosts of Christmas Present could pour more magic into our charms for a grander effect. I'd just gone down to 85%. I'd given this charm *a lot* of juice.

Friday I entered Jay's office with his coffee.

"Good morning, Mr. Nichols. Where's Annie?" I asked, though I already knew the answer. "She always beats me to these daily rundown meetings."

"Annie called ten minutes ago," Jay said. "She's sick. Like *Apocalypse Now* sick. I didn't get into the details with her, but she's never missed work before, so this flu bug of hers must be really intense."

Poor, Annie. Even though I didn't like her, I still felt bad. It had to be done though.

"Think you can take the reins today, Frost?"

"Absolutely. I have your itinerary right here. We can go over it, and then we need to leave for a meeting with the city's Recreation and Parks Department in twenty minutes. Also, I have this."

I reached into my bag and pulled out a small Christmas tree tchotchke, which I placed on the corner of Jay's desk. The knickknack was designed like a bobblehead so the top part wiggled when I set it down.

"What's that?"

"A Christmas tree. It's December and seeing your *American Psycho*–styled office every day was starting to bum me out. It can't be good for your psyche either. You're welcome."

Jay stared at me. "Okay . . . Fine. I guess." He flicked the Christmas tree with a finger and watched it bobble. "Let's just—" The phone on his desk rang. He looked at the caller ID and gestured for me to exit.

As I stepped out, my CCD phone sang too. I fished it from the pocket of my black dress, which I wore over dark green tights today.

It was a text from Specter One!

"*Meet me in my office Sunday at noon. We need to discuss your future plans.*"

I raised my eyebrows so high they probably touched my hairline.

What does he mean, my future—

"Frost?" Jay called.

"Coming." I darted inside and tried not to think about Specter One's message. I dealt with the present, after all. The future had not been on the table for me in a hundred years.

"That tree has gone up every year for decades," Jay said, dismayed. "For at least my entire life."

We sat in a conference room with navy carpet and a well-polished wooden table. Ten members of the Recreation and Parks Department joined us. Jay typically played it cool, so the emotional response this topic elicited got my attention. It mattered to him.

"It's been going up my entire life as well," said the department director, a white-bearded man named Lou. He could've passed for one of Santa's cousins. Lou nodded to the image of the Christmas tree on the slideshow. It looked to be over thirty feet tall and was decorated with peach and red ornaments. Matching wavy ribbons cascaded down the sides of the tree from the top to the bottom, reminding me of stripes stemming from the tip of a bigtop circus tent.

"Unfortunately, we just cannot afford the expense this year," Lou went on. He gestured to his assistant in a yellow cardigan, who held a polka dot clipboard.

"Tree prices have gone up twenty percent," she said. "Plaza management is tired of putting in the extra hours and cost for installing and decorating the tree, along with decorating the plaza. And of course, there was last year's incident."

"What happened?" Jay asked.

"Perhaps 'incident' is misleading," Lou said, eyeing his assistant. "It was several things, actually. A few teenagers were apprehended tagging the tree. Twice. And one evening, plaza security caught a couple engaging in . . . indecent behavior behind the tree."

Disgust formed in my throat like a hairball in a tabby's windpipe. "You're not serious?"

Everyone looked at me.

"What?" I said. "I know human beings can be terrible at times, but is nothing sacred? It's a *Christmas tree*." An awkwardly silent moment passed. My good sense returned and I shrank in my chair with a touch of embarrassment from having spoken out of turn so passionately. I'd just been so shocked. I regained my composure and sat up straighter then glanced at Jay. "Sorry."

"Don't be," he said, giving me a sincere look. "You're not wrong. I feel the same way."

The genuine understanding in his eyes surprised and confused me.

There it was again—another inconsistency, another gleaming light that differentiated Jay from my previous assignments. I had served as an assistant to countless Scrooges. It was a common cover because Scrooges were often important big shots. Previous occasions where I'd spoken out at a meeting with those targets hadn't ended well.

As the lead ghost on a Christmas Carol journey, I was supposed to push my Scrooge's buttons to get him or her to evolve when we were alone, but I was never supposed to interfere or speak out in mixed company. Unfortunately, in my early CCD days I had not been as strong in the keep-my-mouth-shut department. That was a time in my life when I cared too much about these people, a time when I didn't realize caring about my Scrooges on a personal versus professional level was an easy way to get hurt later on when they let me down.

Back then, when I got overly involved in a public setting, my Scrooges would let me have it—reprimanding me fiercely and often cruelly. It was mean, but expected. Scrooges weren't known for showing kindness or compassion to underlings, and they certainly never cared about Christmas. Jay didn't seem mad at all though—super weird. And he appeared truly invested in this Christmas tree situation.

"Please continue," Jay said to Lou.

"Yes, well . . ." The director cleared his throat. "With the increased cost, overtime pay, and the expense for extra security to protect the tree, that puts the department at least $8,000 over budget. We can't justify the expenditure."

"I understand that, but the tree lighting ceremony is a cornerstone of this community," Jay said. "*My* old community. Isn't there another way?"

"Actually, we were hoping you might be able to help," Lou said. "We have a few fundraising drives scheduled for next week at different parks across Los Angeles. Wholesome family holiday fun to raise money for local charities. Friday specifically is geared toward raising money for community programs. We know you're busy, but as a beloved leader in our community, it would be huge if you came to Friday's event. Maybe give a speech and help out at the different booths, blast about it on social media. You could generate a big buzz for us and hopefully raise some extra funds to save the tree. What do you think?"

"My team can definitely help with publicity," Jay replied. "Send my assistant Frost the details and I'll personally work with our media department to promote your events next week. In terms of being there in person, that's going to be tough. My schedule is tight."

Lou nodded. "These are all-day events, so maybe you can squeeze us in?"

"I'll try my best," Jay said, giving him a sympathetic but sincere smile. "Hopefully my assistant and I can work something out. We'll crunch my calendar and get back to you soon." He looked at his watch. "Now if that's all, I have to get going."

"Thank you for your time, Mr. Nichols," Lou said as the men shook hands. "We appreciate you taking an interest in the coming year's budget and activities, and helping with the fundraiser."

Jay shook a few more hands, Lou's assistant gave me several documents from her clipboard, then in five minutes we were back in our SUV. The engine revved and we were on to our next destination, Christmas music playing quietly from the speakers in the background.

"So I was thinking," I said, flipping open my agenda book. "You have several school visits next Friday, but you're done by three o'clock, so if we move your dinner with . . ." I read the time block on the calendar, "Friedman's Election Consulting to the following week, you can definitely attend the Parks fundraiser. You can probably make it there by four, depending on traffic, and have a few hours to participate like Lou wants."

"Huh? Oh, Frost, don't worry about that."

I blinked. "What do you mean?"

"The Friedman's dinner is important. Annie wouldn't advise that I move it. And honestly, any time I'm not scheduled to be at an event in the next couple of weeks, I should be working on my speech and talking points for the debate with Farah on Christmas Eve. With all the buzz on the rivalry and close polling between us, this broadcast will drastically set the stage for the election year ahead."

I nodded slowly. "I understand that's important . . . But I thought you cared about the tree? Why did you give the Parks Department the idea that you may be able to make it if you never had any intention to do so?"

"I do care about the tree, it's just not as essential as the other things on my plate. And I said what I did because straight rejection is disagreeable. No one wants to hear *no*. The appearance of trying can placate a lot of people and disappointment."

"Sounds like a fancy way of saying that it's easier to lie than tell the truth."

Jay shrugged. "Well, isn't it?"

I closed my agenda book. "So was it a truth or a lie that

you'd have our team blast the Parks Department events on social media?"

"Neither. That was a good intention. If you and the team can spare the time to get something out without interfering with your current schedules and responsibilities, I fully support it."

"Will you *'personally work with'* us?" I asked, quoting his pledge in the meeting.

He pulled out his phone and started texting. "You're my assistant, Frost. I'm sure you can handle it."

I sighed. "Whatever you say, Mr. Nichols."

I massaged my temples. The cheery Christmas music was annoying me now; it clashed too much with Jay's behavior. I made a move to turn it off on the console, but Jay held up a hand. "Wait, I love this song. Billy Joel holiday mixes are hardly ever on the radio."

My focus sharpened. Specter One had mentioned Billy Joel music was one of Jay's favorite things. "I can't say I ever really listened to his music," I replied.

"What?" Jay's mouth fell open. For the first time since we'd met, his excited smile seemed genuine, almost childlike. Not scripted or strategized.

"You don't know 'Uptown Girl'? 'Only the Good Die Young'? 'We Didn't Start the Fire'?"

I blinked at him. "Sorry. Not in my wheelhouse."

"What *do* you listen to?"

"Honestly, I feel like the only music I listen to is Christmas music."

Not a lot of options given my place of employment.

"Really? That's . . . different. I have to make you a playlist sometime. Any person who works for me needs a proper appreciation for musical culture. Music is to the soul what cream is to coffee—it makes it richer and sweeter. That's what my dad used to say. He loved Billy Joel."

Just the opening I needed. "Your *dad* dad? Or your stepdad?"

Jay's enthusiasm dwindled considerably.

Fascinating.

"I never called my stepdad Dad, so yes, my *Dad* was a musician. He wanted to make it as a recording artist. You know how I told the reporter that story about making cookies? When my parents were still together, he would get out his record player to blast music while we baked."

"You didn't tell the reporter that."

"I'm not big on sharing personal details with the press." He looked at me curiously. "To be frank, I'm not sure what compelled me to tell you."

"I've been told I have a face for secrets. It's my blue eyes— they're large and accepting like a Siberian Husky."

Jay leaned forward to study me. "That is a specific yet accurate description." He nodded and sat back. "Anyway, winter dog eyes aside, I'd appreciate it if you didn't spread the word. Annie thinks it's best not to play it fast and loose with my personal life. The fewer details the world has about you, the fewer ways the press can spin them into fake news that brings you down."

"I wish I could argue that, but I have been around enough important people in my seasons to know you're right. Your holiday secrets are safe with me, Mr. Nichols. Assistant's honor."

"Thank you. And you can call me Jay if you want. Annie can be a bit intense."

"I appreciate that. The name Nichols makes me think of St. Nicholas, and that makes me think of Santa whenever I look at you."

He huffed with amusement. "Atypical train of thought, but if you want to picture a suave, handsome black man as Santa, who am I to stop you."

I smirked. "Someone's confident."

He smirked a bit too and listed off on his fingers. "Confidence, articulation, and staying cool under pressure—these are the key ingredients to a successful politician's career."

"I think you forgot endless hand-shaking, matching ties with pocket squares, and moral ambiguity."

"Those factors come with time. The last one only if you forget the reason why you got into the game in the first place."

"Isn't referring to democracy as a game a sign that a person has already forgotten?"

Jay stiffened slightly and he stared at me from across the car. "Don't take everything so seriously, Frost. It's just an expression."

"So is every smile a leader paints on his face when he makes a promise. Should we not take those expressions seriously either? You certainly give plenty of them when you make assurances to people that you're not sure you can follow through on."

Jay's stare turned into a glare. The camaraderie had gone. "Frost, you're my assistant, not my life coach. How about you stick with your job description and I'll stick with mine? You've only known me for a few days, and I don't appreciate the judgment radiating from you."

"Fine. I apologize if I overstepped," I said—not actually sorry and my tone not really conveying it either. "Can I assist you with anything else?"

The car came to a stop in front of a restaurant; a handful of photographers waited outside. A moment later, Jay's bodyguard Rocco came around the side of the vehicle.

"Just use every spare moment to make sure things are all set for the school tours next week. There's a lot that can go wrong with such a tight schedule."

"That's the spirit," I said sarcastically.

Jay shot me a look as his bodyguard opened the door.

Pictures started snapping and I watched as my Scrooge activated his camera-ready smile. He strode out, the paparazzi parting like the Red Sea.

6

"I hope you don't have any plans for the weekend, Marley, because we're going to the movies." I scooped up my precious pet and bopped him on the nose. "If anyone at the theater asks, you're my emotional support animal, which we both know is true."

The lights of my apartment glistened in the reflection of the darkened windows. I couldn't have been happier to be off duty. The phrase TGIF certainly meant a lot when you spent your week with cranky political folk while trying to understand the making of the man employing you. Getting rid of Annie was a good call, but today's experiences with Jay had only puzzled me more. The man seemed to have multiple personalities. His fluxing behavior continued to vex me. It was like I was going after a target in a funhouse full of mirrors. One week in, and I couldn't tell which Jay I should be focusing on. That scared me.

Perhaps a mental break from the subject would help.

I kissed my dog before setting him down. "Let me get changed, boy, and then we're getting the holly out of here. I'll just let the team know we're coming back to the CCD late tonight."

I pulled out my phone and saw a notification from Tinsel. Bismaad had tagged me in a post on the Ghosts of Christmas Present group page. I swiped my phone open and read the post.

"Drinks with the toy vehicle elves at the North Pole to celebrate the first week of December. The Nutcracker — 8:00pm. Come in your 'work clothes'. Prize for best look. BYOB."

I bit my lip. I didn't really feel like going to a party. I wanted some solo decompression time. But tagging me was Bismaad's not so subtle hint that she expected me to go. I'd blown her off on several occasions since the start of the season and it was about time we hung out. I looked at Marley. "What do you think, boy? Do I ignore the invite or see the movie another time?"

Marley rolled onto his back.

"All right, fine. Change of plans," I said, my conscience getting the better of me. "Time to be social."

Marley whined.

I sighed. "Yeah, my feelings exactly."

The Nutcracker was the North Pole's prime tavern for merriment. Just past Penguin Park and through Toffee Pudding Tunnel, the establishment was at the bottom of a pure ice basin, accessible only by ski lift gondola. I always worried about Marley slipping and breaking something down there, so I left him at the CCD.

Twelve-foot-tall nutcrackers with gold pants and white hair stood on each side of the tavern entrance. The door they guarded was intricately inlaid with rainbow-stained glass. I stepped inside the establishment and nodded a greeting to the elf standing on a stool behind a podium. "May we take your coat?" she asked.

Before I could respond, a toy helicopter with outstretched mechanical arms darted in and began pulling my coat off my shoulders.

"Uh, thank you." I relaxed to allow the helicopter to do its job, then proceeded into the tavern. It was packed. And chaotic. The toy vehicle elves were a throw-caution-to-the-wind bunch, and they brought their work home with them. I had to watch my step as tiny remote control cars zoomed across the floor and elves riding in miniature electric vehicles whizzed around the stools and tables.

"Incoming!"

I ducked to evade another helicopter carrying a plate of snacks in each mechanical arm.

Across the tavern ghosts from the CCD danced, chatted, and cavorted by the piano. Through the crowds I saw it was Allan who was jamming away on the keys. He sang as well, to the delighted wonderment of others. I caught his eye and his smile fell. I turned away in a hurry and ran into Lorette and Lindsey, two newer ghosts; I think they were only in their fourth season.

"Frost! How'd your first week go?" Lorette asked. She was a plump ghost with a heavy French accent.

"Um, fine."

"We saw your post on Tinsel and wanted to let you know that after drinks tonight we're having an afterparty where a bunch of us are going to share stories about how we used our charms this week. You want in? It should be fun, and also inspirational if you're looking for new ideas for your man. Jay, right?"

Unlike the ghosts who'd been my colleagues for decades, Lorette and Lindsey didn't know me well enough to realize that group workshopping our assignments was not my thing.

"Thank you, but I think I have a handle on it." I spotted Bismaad seated on a green velvet stool at the bar. "Excuse me, ladies." I made my way over, ducking when a toy drone zoomed a little too low. I slid into the stool beside my friend and grinned, giving a theatrical gesture.

"TA-DA!"

"You made it!" Bismaad exclaimed, still using her British accent. My friend wore an emerald-colored pantsuit with thick-framed glasses perched on her nose.

"Your post made it sound more like an order than an option. Plus, I could use a drink with a friend. It's been a long week." I signaled to the Yeti in a plaid vest and bowtie behind the bar. "Nigel, can I get a Dark Forest—extra marsh?"

The Yeti, who'd worked here longer than I'd been around, made a gargling screech that sounded like "ARGRADARGH!" and nodded. He thumped over to the elaborate beverage machine built into the back wall. Constructed by Italian elves in the 1860s, a series of shimmering copper, bronze, and gold pipes connected to five different hot cocoa machines. The Nutcracker was exclusively a *hot cocoa* bar, and the snack menu consisted of cookies, cakes, and churros. Elves needed sugar the way normal humans required water.

Nigel worked various levers on the machine, and a dark chocolate liquid poured into a mug. He twisted a knob, releasing an avalanche of snowflake-shaped marshmallows. A few twists of nozzles for syrup, and lastly a tiny porthole opened and spewed out chocolate sprinkles like confetti.

The Yeti passed me the drink and I clinked my mug with Bismaad's. "By the way, the toast word tonight is Scrooge," she whispered, hand to the side of her mouth.

I sipped my beverage. It coated my insides like a hug. Ghosts loved the cold, but warm treats like this didn't bother us. Maybe sugar—in all its forms—was good for the soul.

A waiter elf with a mustache that looked like it had been designed by ribbon curlers from the wrapping department flounced over and held up a tray. "Complimentary cake pop?"

Bismaad and I each took a stick.

"I don't think you're going to win our work clothes costume contest," Bismaad commented, pointing at my black dress and dark green tights combo. "You look so hot they should change your name from Frost to Steam. It's not at all silly like my work gear."

"You look . . . nice," I commented.

"I look like the librarian who stole Christmas," she said. "But the pods know how to dress us so we fit in. At least I'm playing a receptionist this season. Lulu is an air traffic controller." She pointed at one of our colleagues across the tavern. "And Allan is a butler."

"Geez." I gazed at Allan's black suit uniform with white gloves and bow tie. He still sat at the piano. "That's some old-fashioned Scrooge stuff."

"Scrooge!" Bismaad bellowed loudly. She pulled a ribbon of silver sleigh bells from her pocket and waved it above her head.

"SCROOGE!" every patron in the tavern echoed, doing the same. The place rang with jingles. A bit delayed, I took out a ribbon of bells from my dress pocket and shook them too. Then we all drank from our beverages.

Bismaad was beaming. "I love Bring Your Own Bells parties. It really adds to the cheer."

My phone sang. I took it from my pocket and frowned. "It's a text from my boss, Annie. I used the flu bug charm so I could get closer to Jay, but she's still sending me orders and updates every hour."

I read the text aloud. "*Frost, I expect a full report of today's events emailed to me by midnight. There are no weekends off in our business.*"

"Maybe you should have Scrooged *her*," Bismaad said.

The ghost beside her heard the comment. "SCROOGE!"

Furious bell ringing and unified drinking ensued.

I wiped my mouth. "Our department helps people who can still be saved. Granted, we don't usually save them for the long term, but the point is those people have a shot even if they blow it later. Annie doesn't seem like someone who can be saved."

"What about Jay?" Bismaad asked. "Any luck with him since we talked?"

"There's more to the story with his father than I initially

suspected. I'm curious to see what Brandon has come up with when I meet with my team tomorrow. And next week should be interesting. We're visiting different schools and one of them is the elementary school that Jay's kids attend. I think that will provide a lot of insight."

"Family is the source of a person's greatest strengths and neuroses," Bismaad commented wisely. She took a sip. "I read that on a throw pillow once."

"Good thing we never had any *real* family on Earth then— fewer neuroses."

My phone jingled. I checked it and rolled my eyes. "Annie again." I didn't answer, set the cell to vibrate, and pocketed it. "Tell me about how your assignment is going."

Bismaad dabbed her mouth with a napkin. "Well, on Monday my guy's doctor told him he shouldn't have caffeine anymore because it's bad for his blood pressure, so he reacted by banning the consumption of all coffee within his company."

I raised my eyebrows and opened my mouth to speak, but then my phone buzzed voraciously. Bismaad glanced at my tremoring pocket; I tried to wave it off. "Continue."

"Well, the gent is lucky someone hasn't sued him."

"He is lucky someone hasn't tried to kill him," I replied, taking a sip. "I—"

Once again my phone went off, vibrating my dress like a tiny earthquake. I whipped out the cell and sighed. "I think I'm going to go. I won't be any fun with my mind on Annie's tasks as well as my own." I handed Nigel my CCD badge. He swiped it to close out my tab.

"But you just got here," Bismaad protested. "There's a carol karaoke contest starting soon, and earlier I went and found the other ghosts who've been assigned politicians this year. I spoke to them and they love the idea of collaborating on shared strategy.

If you're open to it that is? I know unless you're forced team-ups aren't your flavor, but it may help you with Jay."

"You didn't have to do that, Bismaad," I said, equally appreciative of her efforts to assist me and irritated by her intervention. "Tell them I said thank you, but I can figure this out alone."

"You know you don't have to, right?"

I blinked twice. Nigel handed me back my ID and I pocketed it. "See you at the seminar tomorrow, Bismaad." I held up my mug in reverence to her. "Unless I get Scrooged by Annie before then."

"SCROOGE!" everyone bellowed.

Bells rang and a final swill of hot cocoa glided down my throat.

"Mommy, why has Daddy been gone so long? When is he coming back?"

It was strange how within the confines of your dreams you could feel so disconnected from yourself. This memory—this tiny, undefined version of me—was foreign to the woman I had become over the years. I hadn't been that little girl in such a long time and yet, as I looked through her eyes at the hazy image of my mother, I felt touches of the hope she held back then.

My mother came over to the couch where I was situated. "I don't think your daddy is coming back, Frost . . ." she said sadly, sitting down beside me and stroking my hair. So much of her was in shadow—only brief gleams of color and light accentuating her cheekbones, eyes, and long brown hair. It fell past her shoulders, illuminated by the bright sunrays coming through the window behind her.

"We are alone, dear. In this world we always are alone and have to be strong."

I hadn't understood the words at the time. My mother stroked my hair some more; her touch and the bright light absorbed in her locks pacified and mesmerized me. Before I knew it, that light expanded like a flash and we were walking down a busy street.

My mother held my hand. Much like in my memory of my father doing so, I was filled with warmth, but when I looked up I could not make out her face. This moment was just too long ago . . . She may as well have been a ghost herself.

In the spotty distortion of old recollection, my mother walked me up some stairs to the entrance of a building. "Mommy, where are we?"

"This is my friend Jocelyn's house. I need you to go inside and find her. Tell her your mother dropped you off and that I need her to look after you for a while."

"When will you be back, Mommy?"

"Soon, sweetheart. I promise. You'll barely notice I'm gone." The woman knelt in front of me and stroked my hair. She put a note in my hand. "Give this to her. And, Frost, remember—you can be strong alone."

She kissed my forehead. "Go now."

I hesitantly reached for the doorknob and twisted it. Then I glanced back and something changed. While the world hazed around us in the memory, for that moment, my mother's face became perfectly clear. Every detail—the exact colors of her eyes, the curves of her face. It was as crisp a vision as you could wish for.

"Go on, Frost." My mother waved me forward. "I'll be back before you know it."

I turned and entered the building, no idea what I was walking into . . .

"And now for our last topic of the day!"

Adult, ghost me blinked hard, snapped out of my daze by Specter Nine's voice.

How long had I been mentally drifting?

The dream memories that bombarded me last night had been so vivid and unsettling that they kept pulling me into a trance as I relived them.

It'd been difficult to concentrate all morning. Normally I shook off my nightly recollections easily, but these had bothered me. Seated next to Bismaad in my Saturday Seminar, I felt like they were an anchor trying to drag me down.

"Let's talk about the new magic charms available this year," Specter Nine continued. She clicked her remote and the slideshow changed to an image of four charms.

"As many of you have realized, the twenty-first century is a progressively tech-filled environment. This can make getting your Scrooges' attention difficult, and avoiding detection equally tiresome. Which brings us to the four updated charms that will be available to you Christmas week."

Specter Nine pointed a delicate finger (decked with glittery fuchsia nail polish) at the different charms.

"The lightning bolt charm causes blackouts, electrical malfunctions, and power surges. Our frying pan charm will fry any piece of technology you choose. The satellite dish charm jams phone signals. And of course, my personal favorite, the TV charm will allow you to possess technology in any way you choose. Allan actually inspired the idea. Last season his Scrooge was a make-up artist for horror films."

Specter Nine gestured at Allan, who turned to address the

rest of the class. "The guy made me watch *The Ring* a half dozen times."

Yikes. That's definitely not a Christmas movie.

"We have a limited number of charms available," Specter Nine continued, "so each of you can select a maximum of twelve charms for Christmas week, in addition to whatever you have left from your basic set. Plan accordingly, and make sure to get to the equipment room early on D-Day to ensure you get the kind and quantity you want. Okay, that's all for today, everyone. Enjoy the rest of your weekend."

I closed my notebook and packed my bag. It was time to meet with my team. I waved to Bismaad and arrived at the Partridge Room at the same time as Brandon. Midori was already inside reading. There was no title on the weathered navy cover of the book she held.

"How did your first week go?" Brandon asked, holding the door open for me in a gentlemanly fashion.

"A bit awkward," I replied as we took our seats. I nodded in greeting to Midori.

"I was hoping to talk to you about Jay's father, Brandon. I know the facts from my Scrooge files. Jay's mom was an accountant and his dad a musician. Once they divorced, Jay lived with his mom and sisters. I've noticed when he speaks, Jay has a lot of fondness for his dad, but he seems really cold where the rest of his family is concerned. Have your visits to Christmases past shown you anything revealing about their relationships, particularly where Jay's dad is concerned? I can't find any giant red flags in the research."

"There's definitely tension," Brandon said sadly, pulling out his files. "I can't confirm the specifics yet, but I get the idea that Jay's dad didn't visit frequently after his parents divorced. He did come by every Christmas Eve with red apples though."

"Red apples . . ." I thought aloud.

"Uh-huh," Brandon said. "Jay's dad, Marlon, is from a part of Central America where red apples are a luxury. Around the holidays, parents save to buy the fruit for their kids, kind of like what Christmas oranges are for other cultures. Marlon continued that tradition with his family—always bringing each of his kids a red apple."

"So why the trauma?" I asked.

"Do you want to see?"

The warily way Brandon said it told me this wasn't going to be a pleasant memory.

It was easy to dislike Scrooges. They were jaded, self-centered sourpusses. But the truth about such people, which was easy to overlook, was that they'd turned out that way for a reason. And that reason was usually some form of pain. Disappointment, loss, struggle—each had a way of warping a person. In other words, what the unburdened often didn't appreciate was that many hearts didn't turn hard on their own. Something had to fossilize them. Seeing those causes over the years, seeing the reasons behind why my Scrooges had gone down their dark paths . . . *that* was never easy. It was necessary to understand someone though.

"What do you think, Midori?" I glanced at our other teammate.

She nodded and outstretched her hand to Brandon. Internal sigh—one of these days I was going to get that woman to say something.

Brandon took each of us in his hold and we faded to blue energy. The next thing I knew, we were standing in the living room of an apartment. Jay, barely six years old, wore a tiny red tie and played with a plastic truck in front of an artificial silver tree. There was a plate of cookies on the floor he'd clearly been munching on. His twin younger sisters crawled around in a playpen beside him.

The home was small. Paperwork sat piled on shelves and tables. Toys lay about the floor. Two baskets of laundry were stacked in the corner. Unopened mail spilled out of a tray on a coffee table. Despite the mess, the small fake Christmas tree, various wreaths, and plastic nativity next to the mail made the place feel festive.

Brandon released our hands and we strode into the space. Loud music blasted from a record player—Billy Joel; I recognized the voice from the car ride with Jay. The music filled the apartment, but did not completely cover up the muffled arguing from the next room.

It suddenly cut off, and a woman strode into the living room. She had short hair and wore a forced smile and a splotched apron over her dress.

"Jay, baby, you can put that truck away now. It's dinnertime," she said.

A handsome man with a mustache and thick eyebrows emerged from the kitchen behind her. Jay's father. The frown on his face changed as he turned off the record player and squatted in front of young Jay. His grin looked a lot like Jay's campaign smile. Marlon held out a shiny red apple to his son.

"You won't be able to distract him with those when he's older," the woman said.

"I don't know about that, Sandra. It's all about presentation. Isn't it, kid?" Marlon affectionately rubbed Jay's head then reached under the tree and pulled out a lumpy package.

"Marlon, not before dinner." Sandra sighed. "He will only have one gift left now."

It was too late; the little boy was already tearing off the paper to reveal a baseball mitt. Marlon tossed the apple into the mitt and Jay's expression filled with wonder.

Brandon reached out for our hands. Spectral glow consumed

my team as he transported us to another Christmas scene. This time we stood outside a one-story house. Happy strands of Christmas lights framed the roof and garage.

Brandon gestured for us to follow him. We phased through the front door and into a festive living room full of people—a pair of girls around six years old, a toddler with curly hair and khaki pants that were too big for him, an elderly couple, a woman holding a baby. Everyone seemed to be having a good time. However, Jay was missing.

His mother Sandra emerged. Her hairstyle was the same, but her expression was completely different. The woman's smile shone brighter than the bulbs outside.

"Dinner will be ready in fifteen minutes," she announced.

A man appeared behind her and kissed her cheek. It wasn't Marlon. This man was taller, clean shaven, darker in skin, and wore a forest green cardigan. Jay's stepfather, Raymond.

"Girls," Sandra said to the twins. "Where is your brother?"

"Pouting in his room," one of the girls replied.

"He says we're stupid and he doesn't want to play with us anymore," the other added.

Sandra and Raymond exchanged a look. Then Raymond clapped his hands to distract the girls. "Come on, ladies. Let's wash up for dinner. Santa doesn't like sticky children." He raised his arms and chased the giggling girls around the living room and into the bathroom.

Sandra checked her watch and frowned before making her way through the house. We followed her until she entered a bedroom. Ten-year-old Jay was on his bed sullenly reading *The Swiss Family Robinson* by Johann Wyss.

"Jay, he's an hour late. I think you may need to accept that your father—"

"He's coming," Jay said, not looking up from his book. "He

always comes on Christmas Eve. He's probably just late because his feelings are hurt."

Sandra sighed. "Jay, I know you're mad at your sisters for not wanting to go, but you can't hold it against them. They want to spend Christmas Eve here with their whole family, and their Christmas tree, and presents, and things that are familiar."

"*Dad* is familiar," Jay responded, shutting his book and sitting up. "And they'd be more used to him if he didn't only have to see us in short bursts."

"That's his choice, Jay. Your father is welcome to spend time with you, anytime. I even invited him to Christmas dinner with us here. You can't be angry at everyone else because he turned that down."

Jay stood crossly. "What choice does he have? You really expect Dad to sit with us and have a good time while Mr. Cardigan out there carves the turkey and Felicia and Monica call him Dad too?"

Sandra's tone did not heighten with emotion like her son's did. Instead, she spoke more gently—calm and understanding radiating from her like an invisible aura. "Jay, it's okay for your sisters to love both Raymond and your father. Hearts aren't apartment buildings; people don't have to move out in order to make room for new tenants." Sandra reached over to touch Jay's face tenderly, but the doorbell rang.

Jay grabbed his backpack from the floor and dashed from his room. My team and I, and Sandra, hustled to keep up, arriving just as Raymond opened the front door. Marlon stood on the welcome mat.

"Raymond," he said.

"Merry Christmas, Marlon."

"Dad!" Jay called. He ran forward and flung his arms around his father. Marlon was taken aback by the show of emotion, but hugged his son before pulling a red apple from the plastic market bag he carried. Jay jogged back a few steps, hands up for a catch. Marlon obliged and lobbed the fruit to his son, though in my opinion his heart didn't seem in it. Jay didn't notice. He just smiled, shooting a see-I-told-you-so look back at his mother.

Felicia and Monica arrived at the doorway. "Daddy!" They hugged him and he patted them modestly on the heads as if they were dogs instead of daughters.

"Are you sure you can't stay for dinner, Daddy?" asked one of the twins.

I think that was Monica.

"I'm sorry. Not tonight. But maybe I'll see you next weekend." He reached into his bag and withdrew red apples for them too. The twins pouted as they took the fruit. Then Marlon pulled out a wrapped gift from the bag for each girl and their attitudes changed.

"Thank you!" they said in unison.

"Merry Christmas, girls." Marlon smiled at his daughters. He turned to Jay. "Let's go, kid." Marlon nodded at his ex-wife. "Merry Christmas, Sandra."

He put a hand on Jay's shoulder, and they headed down the driveway toward his truck. Sandra, Raymond, and the twins watched them go from the doorway—huddled together, faces touched with sadness.

Brandon offered his hands to me and Midori again. After another flash, we found ourselves in front of the same house; however the twinkle lights were gold instead of rainbow and the house was blue instead of peach. The whole block looked slightly different. We entered Jay's home and based on the changed ages, I realized we'd jumped forward in time a couple of years. I looked around. While Jay's family sat at the dinner table eating, talking, and laughing, Jay lay on the couch in the living room, this time reading *Lord of the Flies* by William Golding. His backpack was on the rug beside him, and he kept glancing at the clock on the wall.

Sandra glanced over worriedly. She left dinner and came to perch on the coffee table in front of Jay. "Are you sure you don't want to eat something? Just until your father arrives."

"Pass, Mom. Dad called half an hour ago from the grocery store. He should be here any minute and I want to be ready to go."

She stroked his head, eyes full of love and sadness. "Okay, baby. Do you want me to wait with you?"

Jay shook his head and swatted her away, eyes already back on the book. Sandra returned to the dinner table and leaned in to whisper to Raymond.

I exchanged a look with Brandon.

Oh no.

Brandon gripped our hands, his eyes glowed, and the scene around us sped up—people moving rapidly like someone was hitting fast forward on a remote control. The hands of the clock whipped around until they pointed at half past nine. Then Brandon let us go. The house phone rang as time flow returned to normal. Sandra left the table where the family was feasting on cookies to answer it. When she caught a glimpse at the caller ID, she scowled.

"Marlon, I hope you have a good excuse for—Oh, I'm sorry, who is this?" She listened, then her face sank. She gasped, glancing at Jay and the twins on the couch.

Brandon took my hand and Midori's one more time. With a magical burst, we returned to the study room in the CCD library.

"I didn't want you to see any more," he said, kind of shaken. "It's too sad."

"I knew Jay's dad died in a traffic accident when he was

twelve," I said. "And my files told me it was on Christmas Eve. But the apples . . ." I gulped.

"His truck was t-boned at an intersection after he left the store where he bought the apples for his kids," Brandon said. "I think Jay has always blamed himself. His sisters weren't into the apple tradition, which means his dad theoretically wouldn't have been on that road if not for him."

I took a deep breath. I hated car accident cases.

Feelings tried to travel up from where I kept them locked down. I shook my head, cleared my throat, and thought out loud as I suppressed them. "Jay's dad didn't seem like the greatest guy in the world, but whatever kind of person or father he was doesn't matter to Jay. First off, the kid clearly already thought the world of him. Second, if you blame yourself for someone's death, you're not going to reflect back and think too hard about that person's flaws. In fact, you'll probably mythize them, burying anything that contradicts that idealized image. To us, Marlon didn't seem like anything special in those memories, but he is cemented in Jay's mind as the perfect father; his brain has never let him consider otherwise."

I glanced around the table. Midori's eyes shone with sympathy and thoughtfulness that spoke volumes. I held her gaze for a moment and for the first time understood the meaning her irises broadcast which her mouth did not.

That moved me.

Maybe there was more to this ghost than I gave her credit for. Maybe she drew her wisdom from listening and watching. Not all ghosts shared the same approach to Scrooging, after all. Brandon was nine, and new, so I'd been giving him special consideration. But Midori was a part of this team too, and perhaps I should've been approaching her quiet, reserved style with the same level of attention and acceptance that I showed his outspoken, bold one.

"Something to reflect on, I suppose . . ." I released a weighty exhale. "Anyway, I'd already picked up from Jay that he doesn't like his stepfather, but I think I understand that situation better now having seen some of his resentment in person. So thank you, Brandon."

I rapped my fingers on the table, deep in thought. "Jay's ex-wife Celia remarried two years ago. We could be looking at a classic history-repeats-itself scenario. Marlon put distance between him and his family because of Raymond. Jay could be doing the same thing because of Celia's new husband . . ." I flipped through my files. "Eddie. He's an executive at a lucrative advertising firm."

"You could be right," Brandon said. "In recent Christmases I've checked, Jay collects his kids in the afternoon from Celia and Eddie's house. He doesn't even go inside."

I pursed my lips. "Have you found anything that shows what kind of issues Celia or Sandra may have had that led to their divorces? Jay touched on that in an interview this week, but my files don't mention anything. Just the facts—the years the women got married, the years they got divorced, etcetera."

"Nope," Brandon said. "But people tend to behave themselves more at Christmas when kids are present. If they had problems, maybe both couples tried to keep a lid on them when the holidays came knocking. I wish I could check a different season for you, and that our files on Jay's relatives weren't so vague. I know this is my first official year, but is that normal?"

I nodded. "Unfortunately. The elves that prep the Scrooge list only have so much magic. They are able to glean certain specifics about the Scrooge nominees, and can glimpse an overall picture, but they're not all-powerful. Their magic is like a fishing net— they catch some big stuff, but finer things, the details in our case, slip through. It's up to us to fill in the blanks. You're doing great though, Brandon. We'll figure it out."

I hesitated, then reached out and patted his arm. It surprised him as much as it surprised me. I always maintained good working relationships with my fellow ghosts, but I wouldn't say I'd ever had personal relationships with any of them except for Bismaad. I didn't see a point to connecting with my colleagues that way. We were here to do a job, not make spectral friends.

That being said . . . I found myself becoming endeared by Brandon. Between what I knew about him from the file Specter One had given me, and the time I'd spent with the kid, I don't know, I guess I liked him. And I felt for him too.

"I would suggest looking at different angles," I advised Brandon. "As a Ghost of Christmas Past, you don't need to concentrate only on the Scrooge. You can use your powers to explore Christmas from the perspectives of the people closest to your target as well."

"I know . . ." Brandon said, wringing his hands. "But it takes *a lot* more magic and focus. I've been afraid to try it out. What if I can't do it? What if I can do it, lose focus, and end up stuck in the past for days?"

I smiled sympathetically. "You'll be fine, Brandon. Magic is mostly confidence. I have faith in you. Try it out this week. Take it slow, but don't put it off too long. It's important for us to know more about what went on behind the scenes when Jay wasn't in the room. Start with that first scene you just took us to. You showed us Jay in the apartment living room, but not what was going on with his parents in the kitchen before they entered. I bet finding out why they were arguing will provide us with telling information that helps fill in some of those missing details."

I turned my attention to my other teammate. "What about you, Midori? How did your week go? Any luck running those future scenarios with rejection as the main factor?"

She nodded.

"Okay. Do you want to . . . share anything?"

She slid her navy book into the middle of the table. Hesitantly, I picked up the text and started flipping through the pages. It was a logbook. After reading for a minute, my eyes widened. I glanced up, finding Midori's gaze over the book.

"*Really?*"

She nodded.

"Hello, Wyatt . . ."

I stopped on the street when I ran into my admirer arm in arm with another girl. She was pretty enough. Her bronze hair was held back in a fluffy bun. Her slender figure was accentuated by a pink silk dress trimmed at the sleeves and hemmed with white lace.

"Oh, hello, Frost." His face—smiling when he'd come around the corner—had become unsettled, like a pond with a stone thrown into it. Awkwardness rippled from his mouth to his eyes. He glanced at the lady beside him. "May I present Abigail Wakeman."

"How do you do?" Abigail said, pleasantly enough.

"Hello," I replied. I glanced again at their linked arms then up at Wyatt.

"Abigail and I met at the Christmas dance last week," he explained.

I felt a thickness in my throat like I had swallowed a large spoonful of cough medicine.

"Oh."

It was all I could say, but no poet could have argued there was a better word to encompass the flatness of how I felt.

"I'm sorry I missed it," I said, clearing my throat.

Wyatt's expression saddened ever so slightly. "Why did you?"

Why did I?

A dozen reasons came to mind—I was helping the nuns at the orphanage, some of the younger kids seemed sad and I wanted to spend Christmas Eve with them because I knew what they were going through, I didn't have anything to wear, I didn't feel like going out that late, my feet hurt from so many chores . . .

They were all excuses. I was self-aware enough to know the main reason I hadn't gone was that it would mean something to someone. I'd had amicable relationships with plenty of girls and nuns at the orphanage, but I'd never felt truly loved, or loved someone in return. I conducted my life like it was not connected with anyone else's because it wasn't. I'd never known any other way since the moment that shadow of a memory who was my father and the ice cold woman who was my mother had made it clear this was my fate.

It was for the best I didn't remember the former clearly, that only the outlines of my father's face remained in my recollection. It was hard enough remembering my mother. Having traces of her linger in my memory had made it much harder to move on.

I did though. After years of struggle I'd come to terms with the fact that they both had left me and I was alone. And I was fine with that. I wasn't going to try and undo that clarity.

It takes a while for a person to make peace with existing as a party of one. But it was only once I knew my parents would not return that I felt any peace. Accepting being on my own became my way forward and I had no desire to be dragged backward. As noted, it took a long time to get to this place and I was good here. I was in control—choosing this path for myself. The idea of sacrificing my comfortable solitude and endure the risk of inviting someone closer only to have them disappoint me, *leave me* . . . it was not a chance I was willing to afford myself.

Ignorance was bliss as certainly as caring was an incitement to break you.

"I had other plans," I lied. Then I nodded to the pair of them. "Well, enjoy the rest of your afternoon . . ."

The dream memory ended as my alarm went off.

I stared up at the ceiling of my CCD dorm room, and then sat up gradually. My loft in LA was certainly more luxurious, but I was fond of this space that had been mine since the beginning of my afterlife.

All ghosts had private, modest living quarters here. The hibernaculum was certainly an upgrade from the dormitory I'd shared with dozens of girls at St. Francis's. I remembered the lack of personal space well. That may have been over a hundred years ago, but being an orphan stayed part of a person's identity no matter how much time passed between you and the publicly funded brick building that used to keep you. I viewed that as a good thing—it meant you always appreciated the places and possessions you had. Even if you were a ghost.

I didn't own many things—some books and trinkets, old tech, a few long-skirt, long-sleeve dresses. Marley had a basket on one side of the room. The corkboard over my bed held a few snapshots of me with Bismaad and me with Paul from the last couple decades. The aspect of the room that most showed my personality was the collection of movie posters. Some were modern; others were antiquated renderings of classics premiered many years ago. The release dates didn't matter; I had been around to see all of them in person.

My eyes flicked to my bed. Feeling sentimental—very not me—I reached under the frame and withdrew my special keepsake box, that which held the most precious items in my possession. I ran my hand across the smooth wooden lid. I would take this with me on my next journey to Earth, keep it under my bed there. Maybe take a trip down memory lane one of these evenings. I tiptoed across the wooden floor to put the box in my bag.

Marley didn't stir in his plush basket. Once the box was stored, I paused by my dorm's frosted window. I tried to see outside, however the ice was too thick. I pulled the window open. Sharp wind hit my face, but I couldn't feel the below-freezing cold that came with it. I leaned against the small sill. Endless snowbanks continued to the horizon. I knew that nothing lay beyond them. Death was the only escape from Earth. The only escape from death was time served. And my time was just about up.

I had mixed feelings about my meeting with Specter One today. As my retirement approached, the question that lingered in the back of every CCD ghost's mind, but the Senior Specters never answered, was resurging—What was after the afterlife?

I guess I was about to find out.

Heedful of the time, I changed into one of my fancier early 1900s dresses. It was bulkier than what I wore on Earth, but it felt like wearing a piece of my old self, so worth the extra weight. Lace trimmed the sleeves and high collar, a black ribbon cinched the waist, and fake pearl buttons ran along the sides of the sleeves.

With my dog at my heel, I made my way from the Ghosts of Christmas Present dormitory to the offices of the Senior Specters. All CCD buildings were connected so we didn't have to set foot in the harsh tundra, but constant grand windows and skylights meant you never forgot the eternal winter outside.

Marley followed me obediently, only getting sidetracked occasionally when he wanted to smell something or greet other ghosts that walked by. He was a lot more of a people person than I was. Most of the ghosts were nice to him, and he started more conversations than I liked to have. It was to be expected though. I was the only ghost at the CCD with a dog, or a pet of any sort.

There weren't rules against it; it just had never happened before. Specter One, thankfully, allowed Marley to stay. The dog had been a gift to me, after all.

I arrived at the elevator to Specter One's office two minutes late. Annie would have fired me for the crime against punctuality. Ghosts like me couldn't be fired. Still, Specter One had always possessed an air of mystery about him that inspired us to not question what he *was* capable of.

It was odd to work for someone I knew so little about. He was like Santa Claus in a lot of ways—a mystical, magical Christmas being that had always simply been there.

By all accounts, Specter One no more had a beginning than he had an end. He did his job without question. His eyes twinkled with secrets and wisdom. And while he ran this big, complicated holiday ecosystem, his purpose was simple: help put a bit more good into the world.

I pressed the buzzer of the intercom next to the elevator.

"Come on up, Frost," Specter One's voice responded through the speaker.

The white door slid open and Marley and I stepped into an elevator of pure ice. My nails gently raked my palm with a touch of unease as I ascended.

This marked only my fourth visit to Specter One's office in the last hundred years. The first was after my death when he gave me the full introduction to this weird slice of the afterlife. Given what we'd spoken about on my second and third visits, I was a bit on edge. Again, I *assumed* it was to discuss the details of my retirement, which he didn't share with ghosts before their time came. However, I understood enough about this enchanted world to know that assumptions and presumptions were not to be relied upon.

The elevator stopped right in the center of Specter One's

office, my view of the room distorted by the ice. The door slid open and Marley and I exited.

I'd Scrooged a decent number of executives and CEOs in my time; their offices were always a grand extension of their power and position. Specter One's was like that. But while humans displayed wealth and prominence with things—leather furniture, gold ornamentations, beautiful tchotchkes—Specter One's office spoke volumes with minimalism.

There was nothing in here but a desk and a couple of seats. The room itself did all the talking. The office was a perfect cylinder with a ceiling shaped like an upside-down ice cream cone. From the uppermost point dangled an ice chandelier that would've made Elsa envious. All the light came from the curved ice walls that had globes of glowing energy embedded into them. They changed colors like Christmas bulbs. Thankfully, the floor was steel, not ice—equally cold and unforgiving, but you wouldn't slip and dislocate a shoulder.

The elevator sank out of sight and the floor sealed up where it had been. Marley yapped in surprise.

"Hello, Frost. Marley," Specter One said.

Marley scampered over to the ice desk my boss stood beside. It was bare except for a translucent, honeydew-sized orb on a pedestal, reminding me of a fortuneteller's crystal ball. He patted my dog and then gestured for me to take a seat on the ice bench facing his desk. I did so and folded my hands together.

"How is your Scrooging of Jay Nichols going?" my boss asked. "I know he is a unique target."

He was. And I was still trying to figure out to what extent. Could Specter One tell I was perplexed? That Jay was throwing me for a loop.

I tilted my head trying to get a read on my boss's mood, but it was impossible. I'd always found Specter One to be a fascinating character. He was both casual and formal. He seemed so nice, but there was this stay-alert vibe in my mind whenever he spoke. His friendliness came across in jokes and occasional sass. But from the *other* times I'd ended up in his office, I knew he could be extremely stern.

Overall the man—the ghost—whatever he was, kept you off balance. Kept you in wonder. He was powerful and ancient, and treated us the way a scoutmaster treated his troop: with guidance, patience, and encouragement. And yet, there was this ever-present element of distrust between us because he wasn't forthcoming on request.

I normally hid my feelings on the matter, but I *hated* that.

It was fundamentally absurd that a ghost like me had to complete one hundred years of work before learning what retirement reward came next. He and the other Senior Specters never answered questions they didn't believe we need concern ourselves with.

And so, like a kid who knew there was more to the story when adults answered a question with "Don't worry about it," my unease about my boss remained for the same reason. I knew there was more to the story with him, and this place, and I'd been blindsided with reveals about both in the past. Who knew how many huge reveals still awaited in my future?

Specter One sat down opposite me in a solid white marble chair behind his desk. His quaffed hair was a lot higher today. Was it magic or some brand of ghostly hair gel?

"It's going fine, sir," I responded. Marley rested at my feet. "Jay is unique, as you say, but I have things under control."

"That's good." His cold eyes penetrated my very soul. "Every year I worry that your—shall we say—pessimistic outlook on the CCD will get in the way of your job. But you have surprised us for decades by completing your Scroogings in record time. It will be a shame to see you go at the end of this season." He straightened, breaking his piercing stare. "Which brings me to the reason for your visit today. I wanted to discuss your future. Once a ghost in our agency completes one hundred years of service, they have the option to leave. Do you know what that means?"

"I was never a particularly religious person, but I assume that means an afterlife full of lyres and angels instead of Christmas trees and elves?"

"I couldn't speak to that if I wanted to." He'd said it plainly but Specter One's eyes shone with excitement. "The truth is, a successful departure from here is far more interesting."

My boss folded his hands on the desk and our eyes met. "You remember the reason you are here, don't you?"

A lump formed in my throat—goopy and hard to choke down like an oyster.

"Of course I do. We're all here for the same reason. We had great capacity to love while alive, but our hearts wasted that gift. At the time of our deaths on Earth, we didn't have any meaningful connections to anyone, alive or dead. So when we passed on, we were directed to the CCD because there wasn't, and never would be, anyone waiting for us in the traditional afterlife."

"Precisely," Specter One said. "When Santa Claus Twelve used his magic to create the CCD, he knew he needed good souls to operate it. However, good souls deserve the bounties of blessed afterlife and, more importantly, deserve to be reunited with loved ones on the other side. Conversely, with souls like you and your colleagues, it would be sad to send you somewhere for eternity with no one there who truly matters to you *and* no one who you truly matter to. So your souls get redirected here. For a hundred years, you can use your unused hearts to care about your Scrooges enough to help them become better people. When that's done, you are rewarded."

"With a different afterlife?"

"With *life.*" Specter One waved his hand over the orb and it shimmered, creating a sparkly cloud around us. The spectral fog began to display flickering images like a mystic film reel. I saw babies being swaddled and handed to gushing new mothers, toddlers taking first steps toward open-armed parents, teenagers holding hands, young adults hugging at graduations, couples kissing at weddings, old people dancing and laughing . . .

The lump pressed harder on the walls of my throat, and I felt like doing something I didn't know my body remembered how to do. I felt like crying.

I cleared my throat as the sequence of loving images continued to play.

"Why are you showing me this?"

"To show you what you missed out on, and what a good soul like you deserves," said Specter One gently. "We know that many Scrooges return to their old ways, but that is not your fault, nor is it the fault of any ghost here. Human beings are flexible, but like most things that can stretch, there is always that pull to return to original form. The Senior Specters and North Pole CCD regulators don't hold that against you. When successfully Scrooged targets reach the Christmas Eve deadline, we can see for that moment that you really did change them. It is evident and unquestionable. They have become better; they have been saved *because of you.*"

While I made strong efforts to hide my true feelings from my Scrooges and teammates—really everyone except for Bismaad and Paul on occasion—I wasn't going to lie to Specter One. I just couldn't. Especially not about something that cut me so deeply.

"Sir, with respect, that praise is undeserved. If you consider the long term, we have not saved that many people. And is it really considered change if it doesn't last? Surely you know how many of my Scrooges have returned to their old ways despite all the effort my teams and I have put into giving them a second chance?"

Specter One watched me calmly. "I am aware, Frost. And I am not disheartened. Show me your GA."

I cringed. "Do I have to?"

"Please."

With a sigh I drew out my phone and activated my least favorite app—Merry Meter.

The app tracked Scrooges based on the amount of Christmas Spirit in their hearts—you know, that intangible warmth of soul that imbued people with a desire to change and be better, restored hope for humanity, reawakened optimism, and created a deep, fundamental need to spread goodwill toward mankind. Every CCD phone had the app built in, which meant every CCD ghost knew when another of their Scrooges became UnScrooged.

"Bah humbug!" muttered a cranky automated voice as the app opened.

I pulled up the General Analytics view and hit the "*Share Screen*" button. The data—red and green line graphs, pie charts with percentages, and a detailed bar graph—jumped from my phone and took the form of a hologram display next to us. On the main graph, the red plot points of my lost Scrooges for the last century notably outnumbered the green points of Scrooges who remained changed. It was a cold, factual look at my teams' failed impact on humanity. I raked my nails against my palm anxiously. I knew things were bad, but being honest with yourself and seeing your failures laid out in front of you in graph form were two uncomfortably different things.

Specter One strolled in front of the data and took a gander. "Frost, you're doing fine. These results are similar to most ghosts who've been with the CCD for many years."

The emotions that I kept on ice pretty much all of the time suddenly spiked to burning hot, melting the walls that allowed me to make peace with my CCD existence—do my job without feeling invested, run a team without getting riled up by coworkers, become involved in people's lives on Earth without developing attachments to them.

"Fine is *not* the word I would use, Specter One. People are becoming harder to help. Long-term results aren't what they used to be. Even with your reasoning and understanding, it's difficult for me to take your compliments seriously. Honestly, that kind of feel-good brushoff actually stings more because *I* don't feel like I did my job. And sometimes . . . I doubt our jobs are even worth doing."

I sat back, embarrassed and unable to meet Specter One's eyes. It'd been a while since that emotional part of me had come out. I powered off my Merry Meter app and the floating facts and figures vanished. "I'm sorry," I said. "That kind of outburst isn't me."

"I disagree," Specter One said pensively, coming to lean against his desk in front of me. "Frost, you've always been more headstrong than other spirits. I know you try to hide it, and I respect how you've done so for the greater good of this department for decades. But the cool demeanor you present to others doesn't fool me. You are at your core a passionate person, and that is why the lost Scrooges affect you. If you really were as aloof as you try to seem, you would not be so bothered by these losses."

I fidgeted in my chair. Specter One's icy irises were translucent and yet—more than ever before—at this moment I felt sure he saw through *me*.

I didn't want him to be right. I didn't like that emotion seemed to be slipping through recently, that I'd been a little more . . . riled up since my return to Earth. Something about my assignment this year. Jay broke pattern; I suppose that was causing me to break pattern too. It was distracting and I was upset that I'd let myself *feel* so much, let alone in front of someone else.

My shoulders slumped with humility and I sighed. "I'd rather be the detached version of myself though. She gets the job done. So please don't see me any other way."

Specter one stared at me for a pause. Then nodded.

"Very well. Then I am addressing the 'detached version' of Frost Mason when I say this, and I hope she listens. *You can't overthink the lost Scrooges.* The world keeps turning and we keep going. Worrying too much about past jobs is not a part of your role. If those people waste our agency's aid by reverting to old ways later, it's not a reflection of how well you were able to touch their souls at the time. And you have touched so many souls, Frost. That is why you deserve a reward that makes you feel like this." He gestured at the heartwarming images still flickering around us in the mist.

"To change a heart and save a soul is the most impressive and magical thing anyone can do. It requires understanding, commitment, and selflessness. Souls who are able to do that a hundred times deserve to feel all the love they missed out on Earth. Which is why when you successfully retire from here, we offer you another chance. Only, we take the chance out of it by letting you select the specifics."

I blinked twice then tilted my head. "I don't follow."

"Our agency lies somewhere between Eternity and the North Pole. In that enchanted space, we can tinker with the allocation of souls in transition, like yours. When you've selflessly saved one hundred people, your soul will have naturally accrued enough magical energy that—with a little help from us Senior Specters and Santa—it can be inserted into a new body. And we can choose the life that goes with it. Do you want to be born into a family with many siblings? Perhaps a well-off family in terms of financial means and prominence? Maybe you'd like to be an adored only child or have plenty of grandparents to fawn over you. Be born in Los Angeles like you were originally, or somewhere more exotic like Paris or Tokyo? With the unbroken chain of magic you collected from one hundred saved souls, anything you want, any scenario you can imagine, is possible."

I was so shocked I felt like a snowman: frozen in position. Specter One had just offered me—

"A do-over," I said in awe.

He nodded. "I have already spoken to Ty Watanabe and Bill James and explained the same thing. You all are on your one hundredth soul so the stakes have never been higher. The only way you can return to Earth with a new life is if you get this last mission right. Hence my original question—*How is it going with Jay Nichols?*"

7

"Raise your hand if you want to make the world a better place!" Jay raised his own hand enthusiastically over his head as he looked at the students gathered in the elementary school library.

Cheap silver and green garlands swooped around the short bookshelves and back windows. Cutouts of Santa, snowmen, and reindeer were taped to the walls and shelves. A tree even Charlie Brown would have second thoughts about sat on the librarian's desk, but I gave it points for the impressive number of ornaments its branches somehow supported.

Around fifty students between first and fifth grade sat in lime-green plastic chairs squeezed around tables. A pile of blank paper and a handful of pens had been placed in the center of each one. Teachers and librarians stood at the back of the room, along with a few members of the media that had shown up to do a story on Jay's school tour.

"That's what I like to see," Jay said as most of the kids in the library raised their hands. Then my Scrooge noticed a young boy with a soup bowl haircut who hadn't lifted his hand. Jay wandered over to the table where the child sat. "And what about you, what's your name?"

"Joey."

"Don't you want to change the world, Joey?"

"My dad says no one ever really changes," the kid replied. He wiped his nose with the back of his hand. "It's too hard. That's why you gotta be smart and just look out for number one. Like LeBron or Thomas Edison."

Jay paused a moment, then knelt next to the boy. "Joey, if you could be anything at all when you grow up, what would it be?"

"Um . . . An MVP hockey player. With all my teeth. And six dogs."

"That's my kind of dream." Jay frowned thoughtfully. "But don't you think it will be hard to do all those things?"

"Super hard."

"But you still want them, right? You're still going to try?"

"Well, yeah."

"I'll let you in on a secret." Jay stood and turned to address the whole library. "When I was your age, my greatest dream was to grow up to be president and improve people's lives. *And have six dogs.*" He gave Joey a wink. "I knew it would be hard. I'm way older now and it's still a big, hard, almost impossible dream. But you know what? I haven't given up because I know that anything worth having is worth working your hardest for. I know that the first step to making a dream come true is having the courage to pursue it. And more than anything, even if something has a one-in-a-billion chance, there is no reason why any of you can't be that one."

Jay took a sheet of paper and a pen from the center of the table and passed it to Joey. He squatted down so he was at the kid's eye level again. "Will you sign it for me? That way someday when you're a world-famous MVP hockey player, I'll be ahead of everybody else and already have your autograph."

"Can I use the green pen instead of the blue one?" Joey asked excitedly.

"Of course."

Joey left a large John Hancock on the paper. Jay accepted

the autograph appreciatively then tucked it in the pocket of his blazer.

"Thank you, Joey." He pivoted to address the entire group again. "No matter how big or scary or unlikely a dream, it is still possible. A lot of people don't change, like Joey said, but that doesn't mean they can't. That doesn't mean *you* can't. And it's tough to really make a difference in the world, but that doesn't mean it's not possible either. We're all capable of being better and making things better. So I want all of you to grab a piece of paper and write down two things: your own personal dream for what you want to be when you grow up, and one part of the world you'd like to see get better. Then share those things with the other kids at your table. We'll read a few aloud in five minutes."

The kids started scribbling. Jay joined me by the science fiction section and took a drink from a bottle of water. I tried not to stare at him but it was difficult. Jay fundamentally astounded, intrigued, and confused me. At moments like this I found it difficult to believe that he and Ebenezer Scrooge would even move in the same circles, let alone deserve the same fate.

Who was this guy?

I cleared my tight throat, willing the emotion away. It was annoyingly fluttering inside of me again. "Jay, that was great. You're so good with these kids. So encouraging."

"Thanks." He fastened the cap on his bottle. "I'm not a hundred percent sure that I feel right about all the grand claims, but they're too young to be cynical. That comes later so why not prevent the condition as long as possible."

I tilted my head. Now came the confusion as my brain got dizzy from another recalculation of his character. "You don't believe the stuff you were saying?"

"I do on my good days, but you know how it is. It's like how it's easy to be in an upbeat mood in the morning until someone cuts you off in traffic. I still believe in my dreams, but some days they feel way more impossible than others because it's not just effort that goes into accomplishing them right? There's also timing, other people's actions, luck." He sighed. I noticed his grip clench on the water bottle a bit. "Regardless, I wish someone had encouraged me more like this when I was a kid. I feel like a lot of the things I've achieved have been in spite of people, not because of people. You know what I mean?"

Before I could reply, a reporter with a microphone beckoned to Jay.

"Give me a minute," he said. He followed the reporter into the adjoining hallway. When he'd gone, my phone jingled. Loudly.

Several kids looked at me. "Sorry," I said. I quickly snagged the phone from my coat pocket. A text from Bismaad.

"How's it going in sunny LA? So jealous. Blimey it's gray over here!"

I smirked and began to text back. *Jay keeps surprising me. Sometimes I think he's a difficult case; other times I forget why he's even a Scrooge—"*

A high-pitched harrumph made me look up. The elderly librarian, decked out in a frilly snowflake sweater, stood beside me with her hand outstretched. "No phones on in the library is a rule for kids *and* adults, Miss Mason."

"*Oooooh*," some of the kids heckled. Hushed giggles ran through the library.

"But I—" The librarian took the phone from my hand and stuffed it in her pocket.

Did that just happen? I'm like a hundred and thirty years old!

"Something wrong?" Jay whispered, seeing the surprise on my face as he rejoined me.

"I just got scolded by a librarian."

"You probably had it coming."

I paused and looked at him. He gave me a quick grin.

His ribbing was unexpected. I released a short gasp of a laugh, which earned me a *shhh* from a precocious seven-year-old in a monkey sweater.

I crossed my arms over my chest indignantly. "Well, tyrannical librarians may take my tech, but I still have the old-fashioned way of telling time." I raised my wristwatch. "We need to leave for your next school presentation in ten minutes. It's your last one for the day."

"I'm looking forward to it. This next school is where my kids go. My daughter Kamie is in first grade and my son Kingsley is in fifth." He looked out at the students, many of which had started whispering to one another. "Better get back out there. Don't get into any more trouble."

I rolled my eyes, but smirked.

After Jay completed his talk, we sped to the next school (or the Los Angeles version of speeding where you accelerate for ten seconds before hitting the brakes).

"I'm guessing Annie arranged for Kamie's and Kingsley's classes to attend today?" I said as I finished texting Bismaad.

He nodded. "Even in no man's land with this flu bug, she's sending me texts and emails."

"Because she doesn't trust me."

"Oh, one hundred percent," he said with a grin.

We stared at each other for a second. Then we both laughed.

Jay shook his head after a moment. "*Anyway*, Annie actually had to call last week to ensure that Kamie and Kingsley's teachers would bring their classes. The schools promoted my visit as an optional guest speaker event. Teachers could either have their kids go to recess or come see me. Evidently some educators see more value in swing sets and jungle gyms."

"I mean swing sets are pretty great."

"Your vote of confidence means the world to me."

"Who says you have it?" I gave him a smirk of my own. He mirrored that.

I took out my agenda book and flipped to today's page. "I noticed Annie booked a time slot twice as long as the others for this visit. Something to do with your kids also?"

He nodded. "Kamie and Kingsley each have one more class after my presentation, and I asked their teachers' permission to sit in so I could spend some 'scheduled family time' with them. That's what Annie calls it anyway."

"*Oh*, that's what SFT stands for," I said. "I saw that abbreviation in Annie's calendar but thought it was another association you're meeting with or a vitamin supplement."

He chuckled. "A vitamin supplement?"

"Annie's calendar is crazy detailed. She even specifies what time you should take your zinc and vitamin C." I accidentally rolled my eyes. "The woman is relentless, and probably needs a hobby. Or a pet."

"She gets the job done. And speaking of getting the job done." Jay reached into a compartment next to his seat and pulled out a CD in a plastic case. "I made this for you. It's a playlist of the best Billy Joel songs. Holiday editions included."

I took the gift and gawked at it. "I'm shocked."

He shrugged, not meeting my eyes. "It only took me a few minutes."

"No, I'm shocked you still use CDs. I feel like every time I move on to my next assignment the world has shifted dramatically. It's kind of nice to see tech from an era I thought people were already forgetting."

"You spend a lot of time going from job to job?"

"Yeah. I do." I rapped my fingers on the armrest, choosing my words carefully. "My whole existence revolves around whatever my current job is. It's kind of a sad life because if I ever look around, I feel like the world has continued evolving while I'm trapped on loop . . ."

I stopped.

What was that?

Did I just share something personal with someone I hadn't known a week?

I cleared my throat. "Anyway. Thank you for the CD. It's been a long time since someone gave me a gift."

"You're welcome. Please don't return the favor with a mix of your favorite songs. If all you listen to is Christmas music, then my stereo might kill itself by March."

"Now say your line."

He blinked.

"My line?"

I smiled wickedly. "Bah humbug."

We were ten minutes behind schedule when we arrived at the elementary school.

And I thought traffic was bad here in the 1920s . . .

All the kids were already seated at tables in the auditorium, paper and writing utensils at each one. The principal shook my Scrooge's hand and guided him to the front of the room, introducing him straightaway then passing him the mic without further delay.

As Jay proceeded with his opening, I noticed him scanning the crowd as he spoke. I could tell when he found who he was looking for. Jay's already sunny performer face brightened. From my standing area at the back with a slew of other adults, I followed his line of sight and saw a tiny girl near the front with hair in a pair of puffball pigtails. Kamie. She waved at him grandly when his eyes fell on her. Kingsley was harder to find, but I spotted the kid when Jay's smile increased as he looked to the far left of the auditorium. The kid had the same haircut as Jay.

When Jay was done, the energy from his pep talk still palpable in the air, teachers started herding the kids toward their last classes for the day. Kamie scurried to the front; Kingsley made his way there too, but more slowly—hands in his pockets.

"Daddy!" Kamie ran into Jay's arms, her puffy pink coat smushing against him.

"Hello, Kamie." Jay scooped her up. "Hi, son." He put his free arm around Kingsley and the two exchanged a side hug.

I weaved through the crowd to join the trio as Jay set Kamie down. "Kids, this is my new assistant. Her name is Frost."

"Like the snowman?" Kamie asked.

"That's Frosty," Kingsley corrected.

"But if you place an old top hat upon my head, I promise to dance around." I winked at Kamie and she giggled.

"Dad, are you still coming to sit in on our classes?" Kingsley asked.

"That's the plan," he responded.

"You and Mommy can both come!" said Kamie, taking Jay by the hand and pointing across the room.

"Wait, what?" Jay looked up. "Oh cr—"

"—hristmas carols," I cut him off.

Celia, Jay's ex-wife, was making her way through the auditorium toward us.

"Mom wanted to come see your speech today," Kingsley said.

"Did she now?" The joy was gone from Jay's face.

"Hello, Jay," Celia said.

"Celia."

Jay's ex-wife was a lovely slender woman with straightened hair to her mid back. While her earrings and watch were modest, her diamond ring was some serious ice—and that's coming from a woman literally named Frost. When she stopped next to us, I detected a distinctive scent shrouding her.

Flowery perfume . . .

One of the things Jay hates the most.

OH. It's because of HER.

"Hello," Celia greeted me.

"Hi, I'm Frost Mason. Jay's new assistant."

We shook hands. "Pleasure." She fixed her gaze on Jay. "Before you run off, can we speak in private please? There's something I need to talk to you about."

"Celia, I don't really—"

"Jay, it's important."

"Fine. Kids, get to class. Your mom and I are going to talk for a minute."

"Don't take too long, Dad," Kingsley said. "We're learning about the Bill of Rights in history today. You love that stuff."

"I do. So pay attention and take as many notes as those delegates did when they were figuring it out." Jay patted Kingsley on the head. "I'll try to make it as soon as I can."

"I'll save you a good paintbrush in art class, Daddy," Kamie said. She looked at her mother. "Mommy, is Eddie here too? I can get him a paintbrush."

"No, sweetie. He's working. He said to say hi and that he'll see you both at dinner."

Jay rolled his eyes. The kids didn't see, but Celia and I did.

Celia motioned for Jay to follow her.

"I'll be back, Frost," Jay told me.

The two of them exited into the hallway. I had to think fast.

There were still people around, so I rapidly scaled the stairs to the auditorium's stage and ducked behind the curtains to go ghost. Once consumed in my spectral blue haze, I darted after my target.

He and Celia weren't in the hall anymore. I phased my head through different doors checking rooms until I found them in an empty class.

"—don't answer any of my calls," Celia was saying as I entered. "So I came here in person."

"Fine. What's this giant issue that couldn't wait?"

"Christmas Eve."

Jay huffed—annoyed certainly, but his face also held guilt. "I know that last year I was a bit late to get the kids, but this year will be different. Mainly because I'm not going to make promises I can't keep. That's the night of the debate, and that's at nine. I have the gala beforehand, so maybe I could pick them up for an early dinner, then drop them off around—"

"Jay, stop." Celia held up a hand. "Monica reached out to me a couple of weeks ago."

"*My sister* Monica?"

"Yes, Jay. She and I have spent time together in the last year. I have spent time with Felicia and your mother too. We have gotten together for birthdays, lunches, park playdates—"

Jay suddenly slammed his hand against the wall. It made me jump in my spectral skin.

"What gives you the right?" he demanded.

Celia stood her ground. "How about the fact that they are Kamie and Kingsley's aunts and grandmother?"

Jay began to pace. "Why am I just hearing about this now?"

"The same reason that I had to plan a sneak attack at an elementary school to have an adult conversation with you. When people let you down you punish them by pushing away."

Celia released an exasperated sigh. "Look, I don't have any

immediate family I can share with the kids. So I thought it would be good for Kamie and Kingsley to get to know their cousins on your side and expand their family circle past you, me, and Eddie. Which is really just me and Eddie since every time your poll numbers go up, your visitations with the kids go down."

Jay stopped pacing to face her. "At least I'm here. At least whenever I do spend time with the kids, they always get the best of me and my full attention. You can't say the same about your past presence in their lives."

Celia crossed her arms. Her voice was sad now, and her eyes hurt. "When are you going to let this go?"

His eyes bore into her, merciless. "You didn't steal my sweater, Celia. You drove me away and broke up our family the same way my mom's drinking drove my dad away and broke us apart. I'm glad you got better, but when you left for a year to rehab, you abandoned me and I had to look after our kids by myself. That's not something a person can forgive."

"And why not?" Celia asked carefully, almost desperate. She approached Jay slowly. "I know I did some bad things. I hurt you, the kids, and other good people, and I am truly sorry for that, but I have changed. I'm not the person I was four years ago. I've tried to make amends to you so many times, but we can't move forward if you don't accept them. Accept me. Please, Jay."

Jay stared at her for a long beat. "I honestly don't know if I can ever do that, Celia. Just because my mom felt bad for laying waste to our family didn't mean the ruins got restored. The same goes for you."

The softness left Celia's face. In its place a coldness descended that seemed harder than ice or even steel. "You're right. But I'd rather not sit and sulk in the ruins like you. You're a lonely man, Jay. And one day you'll be *all alone* if you don't learn to forgive the past so you can create a better future. Your mother and sisters did, and they, Raymond, and Ray Jr. have been a happy family for decades. I did, and now I have Eddie and the kids, and we are happy. You can be a part of that. Which brings me back to Christmas Eve."

She took a deep breath, then put her hands on her hips—complete conviction, no cracks in power. "The kids asked if we could spend Christmas Eve with the whole family. Your mother is hosting a dinner at her house, like I know she always does even though we never went when we were married. All the kids' aunts, uncles, grandparents, and cousins will be there. Eddie and I are taking Kamie and Kingsley."

Jay's expression looked like someone had told him his dog had been shot. The hurt and horror were unmistakable. He sat on the edge of the teacher's desk. "You mean you're taking them away from me. How could you do this to me, Celia?"

"Jay, I'm not doing anything to you." Celia went over to Jay, leaning against the desk next to him. "Like I said, this was the kids' idea; evidently a quiet dinner with you followed by presents and TV in your condo wasn't that much fun last year. Besides that, we want you to come with us. The kids, me and Eddie, your sisters, your mother and Raymond—"

"Because that's just how I want to spend the holiday." Anger beat out the hurt in Jay and he shot to his feet. "Seeing how my family doesn't even remember that my father existed and watching how my own kids are replacing me too."

"Jay, that's not—"

"I have to go. I have a meeting downtown this afternoon and this unplanned talk ate up my time here. Tell the kids I said goodbye." He headed up an aisle of desks toward the door.

Celia took a few steps after him. "You said you'd come by their classes. They're going to be disappointed, Jay."

"Not if you're there. Put Eddie on a video call to say hi. They won't even notice I'm gone." He reached for the handle.

"Jay!" Celia grabbed his arm. "At least take this." She handed him a folded paper from her purse. "I wrote down the different holiday events the kids and our family have scheduled for Christmas week. Eddie and I will be there, but if you could make it to any of them . . ."

Her voice trailed off. Jay hesitated, then took the sheet and stormed out. I hustled after him in my ghostly work heels.

"Frost," Jay called upon entering the auditorium. I raced up the stage, dove behind the curtain, and transformed.

"Yes?" I stumbled out.

The resentment on his face faded slightly to surprise. "What are you doing up there?"

"Um . . ." I glanced around and threw the curtain aside. "Preparing to make a grand entrance?"

"Well, we're making a grand exit. Let's go."

"Are you sure? Because your next meeting isn't for a couple of hours. You can still—"

"Frost."

"Yes?"

"We're going."

I looked at him sadly. "Okay."

8

"*This* is exactly what I needed," I said to Paul.

I sat on the straw covered wooden floor of the North Pole's baby reindeer barn. Reindeer came in a variety of colors, but in this winter wonderland where the reindeer were magical, those colors signified their unique powers.

All North Pole reindeer had super strength, speed, and stamina, but dark brown reindeer were able to fly, light brown reindeer could distort time, and white reindeer had the power of invisibility. Once the reindeer reached adulthood, their powers were fully mature and they could harness them to greater extents, which allowed them to assist Santa. The Big Guy's sleigh team was a mix of all three breeds. When hitched to the sleigh on Christmas Eve for gift delivery, the invisibility reindeer cloaked the entire envoy, the light brown reindeer caused time to flux so they could travel around the world more efficiently, and the dark brown reindeer lifted everyone into the sky.

Baby reindeer, however, had no such control over their magic.

A light brown reindeer sat in my lap. His antlers were just starting to come in and they looked like pretzel sticks. I stroked his head, watching other little creatures gallivant and experiment with their powers. Two flying reindeer floated ahead, kicking their tiny hooves in the air to orient themselves. A couple elves were playing fetch with three white reindeer—golden horn stubs just showing. Every few seconds, one creature would flicker and vanish, then reappear somewhere else. A dark brown baby levitating nearby suddenly sneezed and shot back three feet into a pile of hay. The youngster popped his head out of the hay. He was a small, fluffy, chocolate thing with small ears and enormous, confused eyes that seemed to perpetually say: "*I'm a baby!*"

"This is probably my favorite place in the North Pole," I told the young Claus.

Paul wagged a carrot, trying to lure a flying reindeer closer to him. "It is a hidden gem for sure. The CCD ghosts who come hang out here during their downtime are drawn to flashier things, like the taverns, penguin ice sports, polar bear rides, and activity centers like the Crafting Cottage or Hot Cocoa Yoga. Visiting the barn isn't usually the first place on their minds."

"Suckers," I mused. "Baby animals do wonders for the spirit. I haven't stopped smiling since I came in here."

"I'm glad you're feeling better," Paul said. I knew he was studying me, but I focused on my reindeer. "You seemed really spooked when you arrived. Even for a ghost. And you hardly ever leave Earth on a weekday."

"It was a weird Tuesday . . ." I continued to pet the reindeer in my lap, but more absentmindedly. "Spending time with Jay is like being on a seesaw—one minute you're up and the next you're down."

I huffed. What *was* this guy's deal?

"Maybe it's the nature of his career," I thought aloud, trying to find any reason to satisfy me. "I haven't worked with a politician in a few decades. Am I just out of touch? Are all politicians today this complicated?"

Paul shrugged. "I can't say from firsthand experience. The North Pole doesn't have government; we only answer to the higher powers of magic, wonder, and cookies. But if it makes you feel any better, based on the Naughty & Nice List—complicated or not—I think you got one of the good ones. Most political folk can't be saved; they're in too deep. Yours sounds like he still has an active heart and soul struggling to stay alive. What did Brandon and Midori have to say when you checked in with them?"

I had touched base with my team before coming to the North Pole. They hadn't helped to lift my spirit. "Brandon took my advice from last week and by exploring different past perspectives, he'd already discovered what I did about Sandra and Celia today. Midori verified that on their current paths, both women never go back to their old ways. Which means what Celia said to Jay was true. They changed. They healed themselves."

"Well, that's good isn't it?"

A floating reindeer finally made its way to Paul, who handed over the carrot and patted the creature on the head. "Good, Comet Twenty-Seven. Nice, baby reindeer."

"Yes," I said. "But it doesn't help our assignment. I told the team our final Scrooging plan shouldn't highlight holiday moments specifically related to Celia and Sandra's past issues. Since Brandon, Midori, and I can each only take Jay on three visits, emphasizing any pain generated by his mother or ex-wife's mistakes seems like a waste of a magic journey."

"Why? The visits are supposed to help your Scrooge confront his greatest emotional issues."

"I don't think anger about Celia's and Sandra's mistakes, or fear about whether they will backtrack have anything to do with Jay's problems with the women in the present. If you ask me, Jay refusing to forgive Celia and his mom has more to do with not wanting to accept the reality of how his life changed—i.e. the additions of Raymond and Eddie, and the shifts in his family as a result. He feels like his mom ousted his dad from his life and that Celia is setting up the same situation with his kids now."

I sighed and rolled my head back in frustration. "Jay is way more unpredictable than any assignment I've had and that's messing with my usual approach to this job. The guy is nice, and smart, and funny, but he's also driving me nuts. Partly *because* of those very non-Scrooge qualities, and partly because it's difficult to watch a Scrooge who still has goodness in him get weighed down by so much bad. For all his talk about change at these schools, he's really letting resentment and misguided notions about family loyalties stop him from—yikes!"

A white reindeer had suddenly appeared an inch from my face. His black eyes had swirls of gold dancing around them like sun energy escaping the perimeter of an eclipse.

"Can I be honest with you?" Paul righted a baby reindeer that was floating upside down. "I think you may be getting too invested in this guy. You've always looked at Scrooges pragmatically. I've never seen you get so . . . riled up about one. Except for that zoo owner with the stuffed narwhal."

"Ugh, I *hated* him. I'm still shocked that he, of all Scrooges, didn't revert back. *Yet*, that is . . ." I shook my head. "Anyway, your worry is not needed, Paul. If I seem extra invested it's probably just because he is my last Scrooge and I can't screw this up. Just because I've never failed a CCD mission before doesn't mean I couldn't now. And if I don't succeed, then I don't get another chance on Earth."

I had told Paul what CCD ghost retirement entailed, but that I would only get another chance if I had the magic energy from an unbroken chain of a hundred saved souls.

"So what happens if you do fail?"

"I don't know. I've been at the CCD a century and I have no memory of any ghosts ever failing a Scrooge assignment. Our souls are here, after all, because we are supposed to be perfect for this work."

"Did you ask Specter One?

"I did. Many years ago I asked what would happen if we botched a job, and he told me failure is handled on a case-by-case basis. I reiterated the question in our retirement meeting, and true to form he was cryptic, telling me not to concern myself with 'North Pole Proprietary Info'."

"He and my dad are big on only-if-you-need-to-know policy," Paul said. "The elves in our patent department have more trade secrets hidden up their sleeves than Houdini. I didn't even know about how ghost retirement worked until you told me. Should you have done that?"

"*Well*, Specter One told me to keep the matter secret, but you're Santa's son and Bismaad sort of wrenched it out of me. I'm sure it's fine. It's not like I posted it on Tinsel."

Paul helped the same reindeer that'd turned upside down again, then he moved to lean against the barn wall. "If your retirement magic has to come from an unbroken chain of saved Scrooges, maybe failing means you go back to square one and do a hundred more."

My mouth tightened into a grimace. "That would be such a bummer. I can't imagine anything worse than doing this for another century."

I hadn't realized what I said would affect Paul, let alone sadden him.

He looked at me—eyes wide in disbelief at first, then brows lowering with some confusion and concern. "Has it really been that bad?"

He gestured at the adorable reindeer floating, disappearing, and jumping around us. "There are magical creatures, winter sports, desserts available at all hours of the day. Don't you like our enchanted realms? Don't you like *the people* you've gotten to know in these enchanted realms?" Paul shook his head and sighed. "I want you to be happy and succeed, Frost, but more years with you as a friend doesn't sound bad to me. You do get that I would miss you once you're gone, right?"

There was vulnerability in his eyes—a soft contrast to the hard lines of his jaw and frown. I lifted the baby reindeer from my lap and set him on his own feet before standing and dusting off my dress. I leaned against the wall beside the young Claus.

"Paul," I said caringly. "I've enjoyed our time together, as I enjoyed my time with your father, grandfather, and great grandfather over the past hundred years. But existing this way is a study in eternal melancholy. Every holiday season spent observing life on Earth reminds me of how I was robbed of mine. Pair that with the fact that friends like you keep leaving me in time's dust as you grow up, age, and die, *and* the demoralizing truth that a lot of people we help throw their fresh starts out the window, and I feel like my frozen heart is always breaking."

Paul's grimace matched mine from a minute ago. "When you put it that way, working at the CCD sounds awful."

"Not awful, just sad . . ."

Quiet settled between us until Paul looked at me anew.

"I want you to know, Frost—whether this is the last season I see you, or we spend many more together, I'll never grow old enough to forget you."

"I hope that's true," I said, emotions bubbling beneath my icy surface again. "But if you did, I'd forgive you."

On an impulse, I leaned my head against his arm and we stood in silence, watching the elves chase baby reindeer in a game of what looked like flying-invisible-freeze-tag. After a few seconds though, I righted myself and shook off the vulnerability. Paul was a friend like Bismaad was a friend. They'd gotten past more of my walls than anyone else had in a long time, and I was fond of our relationships. But I knew better than to let my connection and attachment to them develop too strongly. We had fun, we'd shared memories, we confided in each other on occasion. But even after all these years I still kept them at a distance, never letting them too close for too long. One way or another, people always would leave you. I didn't want to get hurt again.

Paul seemed to sense my aloofness returning and opted for a change of subject and an upbeat tone. He journeyed a few paces, then bent down to pet a white reindeer. "So once you're done at the CCD, what do you think you'll ask Specter One to send you back as?"

I was grateful for the new topic and tilted my head for a moment as I thought on it. "I think I want a few siblings. Not too many that I'd get lost in the shuffle, but enough so you could always talk to someone. Like two or three—brothers and sisters. I'd want to have both my parents in the picture, both sets of grandparents . . . and like six dogs."

"Sounds like a full house," Paul mused.

"Growing up in an orphanage, I was used to being around a lot people, but I still felt alone," I replied, coming over to pet the reindeer. "There's a difference between a full house and a full heart."

Paul nodded. "Well, wherever you end up, maybe my dad and I can visit you some Christmas in the future? I'll leave your presents under the tree myself."

"That'd be nice," I said wistfully. "Though you're overlooking two things. To start, I wouldn't remember you."

"I'd remember you, though, and it'd make me happy to see you happy, even if you didn't recognize me. What's the second thing?"

I smiled. "You're assuming I'd be on the Nice list. I got scolded by a librarian today. I've clearly got potential for mischief."

Twenty-three-year-old me stared up at the flickering screen that bathed my memory in entrancing light as the film played. Though I could only afford the cheapest ticket in the house—a spot on a wooden bench in the upper section—I felt like I had a seat in the finest balcony. A young man sat beside me. David Varot.

"Frost?" He leaned over.

I shushed him. "After," I whispered.

When the happy ending faded to black, the house lights came on and people started filing out. It was a bit of journey to leave; this theater was built to hold a capacity of 2,000 people. I didn't mind the prolonged exit though; it allowed me time to appreciate the structure's ecstatic beauty.

This new extravagance in the heart of downtown Los Angeles was abundant in ivory and gendarme blue décor, highlighted with gold accent points. As we made our way out, I admired the embellished proscenium arch and the marble floor of the lobby. Bronze frames on the walls advertised upcoming features, all of which I hoped to see.

David held the door open for me and we reacquainted ourselves with the sunny day. I glanced back at the building. Outside, the theater was no less handsome. A pattern of cream brick, glazed mat tile, and color-decorated polychrome tile supported the sign that declared the theater *The Orpheum*.

"Frost." David bid for my attention. His hair was chocolate and wavy like an old-fashioned storybook prince. His nose was round while his chin was sharp. "Can we speak seriously about something that has been weighing on me?"

I nodded and gestured to a nearby bench under one of the adjacent store awnings. We made our way over. As always, the sidewalks were thriving with people, the streets zoomed with traffic, and parked vehicles occupied every inch of curb space. A friendly dog and its owner passed by as I was sitting down. I got distracted petting the first and smiling at the latter and thus was caught off guard when David suddenly took one of my hands in his. The intimate action in public made me uncomfortable, but I restrained myself from immediately pulling away out of politeness.

"Frost, you and I have been spending some nice time together over the last few months," David began.

"We have a lot in common," I replied. "We like the same books, foods, movies—though I do wish you would focus more at the theater. It is disrespectful to the art form to not give it your full attention, David. And this astounding theater is a haven for stories like no other. I didn't mean to be rude to you inside, but since I can only afford to see the occasional daylight picture, I wanted to be fully present. You understand, don't you?"

"I do. And I'm sorry. I just have something I need to say, and I felt I could not contain it any longer." He took a deep breath. "Ever since we met, I have developed strong affections for you. Those feelings grow each time we see each other, and I dare say I think I am falling in love with you, Frost."

I gulped. The sun seemed hotter now.

"You have never referred to me as anything but a friend though, and my parents are pushing me to marry soon. So I must ask, is that something you're . . . interested in?"

I studied my shoe. "Maybe eventually."

"Isn't *eventually* a bit of a gamble?" David said gently. "I intend no offense, but you are already twenty-three years old. Why not marry me, a man who is interested in you right here and now? I have a promising job and could take care of you. I come from a good family that, given time, I could convince to accept your background. If you open yourself up more and truly let me in, I believe you could grow to love me too and we could build a life together."

In his eyes, I knew he meant what he said—every bit of it. That didn't matter though. I knew better.

"David . . ." I gingerly took my hand from his hold. "I do care about you. A great deal in fact. But I don't want anyone to take care of me. I don't want to have to convince anyone to accept my lack of a pedigree; I am not ashamed of where I come from because it made me strong and self-reliant and compassionate. And perhaps I could grow to love you like you suggest, but I don't want the threat of aging and the fear of being alone to force my hand. If what you want from me is a leap of faith—choose becoming an *us* over continuing to be a separate *you* and *me*—I can't give that to you."

I didn't tell him more. I didn't tell him that it wasn't in my nature to truly let anyone in because I'd faced too many goodbyes. Maybe with *enough* time I could change, but I couldn't force that. I couldn't risk the heartbreak of changing right here and right now for someone who I wasn't entirely certain about.

David looked hurt and sad, but also I daresay slightly unsurprised. "I am sorry to hear that." He stood and tipped his hat to me. "I hope you understand that I will have to find someone else. Someone willing to take a chance on me."

"I understand," I said, meeting his eyes.

He walked away. As his figure moved farther down the sidewalk, his silhouette became dark while the whir of traffic turned into a hazy blur of cars, civilians, and noise. Sounds and colors mixed together until they were a mash of subconscious and I woke up.

It was difficult to open my eyes. I felt the weight of the

memory and the late hour I'd returned to my loft last night. Not even Marley stirred at the foot of my bed when I slid out.

I checked the clock on the wall—five o'clock in the morning. I'd awoken before my alarm went off.

I went to the kitchen and poured myself a glass of milk from the fridge. My phone was on the counter, blinking. I must have forgotten to turn it off silent when I left the North Pole. I picked it up and my eyes widened with panic to discover a dozen new texts from Jay and Annie.

The first one from Annie got straight to the point: "*Book signing event rescheduled to 10:00 AM. Be at office by six.*"

I spit out my milk.

Cinnamon Wicks!

I put the phone down and darted for my magical fashion closet.

"So you wrote a book," I mused. I sat in the car with Jay, turning the paperback over in my hand: *Jay Nichols—The Long Road*. It was maybe two hundred and fifty pages. The uninspired photo on the front cover featured him in a suit sitting in a wooden chair.

"Why didn't I know this?" I thought aloud.

The discovery had really thrown me for a loop. If Jay was a writer that definitely should have shown up in the research files from Specter One and the North Pole.

"Maybe you're not very good at your job," Jay suggested. "You're not very good at answering your phone."

"I said I was—"

"I'm joking." He held up a hand. "Anyway, technically I didn't write it. When Friedman's Election Consulting approached me a year ago about running for governor and paired me with Annie, they recommended I release a book to talk about my journey. You know—overcoming adversity, emphasizing diversity in government, my plans for a brighter tomorrow, that kind of stuff. They hired this ghost writer woman who followed me around for a month to do research."

"Ha!" I barked a laugh before I could help myself.

Jay gave me a quizzical look.

"I, uh, thought the term was funny. Ghost writer. A woman who followed you around for a month researching you. Never mind, inside joke with, um, someone."

I cleared my throat and focused on the book again. Well, that explained why this wasn't in my files at least; the only thing Jay did to contribute to writing this book was exist. It did introduce a new question though.

"I'm surprised you'd have a book like this. I thought you weren't big on sharing personal details?"

He shrugged. "I'm not. Not where messy emotions are concerned anyway. Everything in there is hard fact free of feelings, so I'm fine. It's my history, but tailored to paint a certain image. To be honest, I'm more excited about the book signing than the book. We're going to one of the largest independent bookstores in the world. Part of my campaign is to protect local businesses like this—keeping chains from destroying them, rent control, manageable property taxes. This is the third location this store has been in and it's one of downtown's best treasures."

The car pulled over and he pointed out the window at a red neon sign: *The Last Bookstore*. Jay's bodyguard opened the door. My boss stepped onto the sidewalk then surprisingly turned back to offer me a hand. I accepted. My outfit today came with a pair of candy cane patterned stilettos.

Inside, the shop was much larger than I would have imagined. It must have been over 20,000 square feet. Innumerable shelves were spaced among white pillars, ridged like Corinthian columns and thick as redwoods. Hundreds of people browsed through thousands of volumes. The variety of vibrant texts must have represented every color in existence—a pure rainbow of bound prose that stretched on and on.

How a place so vast could still feel so quaint was a kind of magic in itself. I gazed around in a daze, taking it all in.

Several bookstore staffers came to speak with Jay. Posters featuring the cover of his novel were plastered around the main entry. There was already a line of people leading to a table framed by the same posters across the room.

With Jay occupied, my soul compelled me to explore. I wandered the rows of shelves that twisted and turned. It was a labyrinth of literature—a paradise of stories you could gladly get lost in. And I did, until Jay found me. I rotated to find him behind me in the stacks, smiling.

"You love books." He said it as a statement, not a question. It must have been all too evident on my face.

"I love stories," I replied. "Books were my first love. Movies stole my heart when I was a kid. They're a means for a writer's imagination to be transformed into something anyone can see, that can reach many people at once. At their core, great movies are simply great stories turned up to the highest impact level."

Jay nodded thoughtfully. "That's the perfect way to put it. I love books and movies too. I couldn't pick my favorite movie, but my favorite book is *The Catcher in the Rye*."

"That's predictable," I replied.

"Predictable?"

"That's every angsty boy's favorite classic book."

Jay rolled his eyes. "Like you're any less transparent. I bet I can guess your favorite classic. It's *A Christmas Carol*, isn't it?"

I was dumbfounded. "How did you know?"

"You said you mainly listen to Christmas music, your ringtone is 'Jingle Bells', and your outfits always incorporate red or green."

"Mr. Nichols." The manager came over to us. "We're ready for you. Please follow me."

"Fans await," Jay said to me. "You're on top of rescheduling the school visit from this morning, right?"

"Um, yes," I said, shaking off my stupor. "We can make it up tomorrow. The principal asked me to call her back at their lunch break."

"Good work." He patted my arm and left me alone, if you didn't count the hundreds of book bindings walling me in.

I heard applause and headed toward the front of the store. Jay was seated at the signing table, beckoning the first attendee forward—a gushing middle-aged woman with a thick headband and a crossbody bag. He gave her one of his crowd-melting grins, which set the woman atwitter with blushing and nervous hair twirling.

I was beginning to identify the different smiles that Jay used for different occasions. As bright, confident, and encouraging as the one he used for public appearances was, I didn't care for it. It was nothing like the one he'd just shown me in the stacks when there weren't any cameras or voters around. His real smile held vague excitement, a touch of cockiness, and was full of warmth. I liked it.

It made me smile too.

My phone jingled.

Probably Annie with a dozen more marching orders.

I would be tempted to let the cell die if it wasn't magically charged for eternity. Phone networks would go to war for this kind of tech. Personally, I preferred the days of telegrams, but those days were as dead as I was.

I checked my phone and my expression puckered like an angry Sour Patch Kid. The Merry Meter app had sent me an UnScrooged notification. I swiped it open and the app made its usual "Bah humbug!" sound effect. I read the details of my notification.

Another one of my former Scrooges had fallen back to her old ways—her Christmas Spirit regressed to what it was before our ghostly intervention. In other words, that warm and fuzzy feeling that filled her heart with hope, optimism, and a desire to change, be better, and spread goodwill toward humanity *had vanished.*

"Lucy Dukaine?!" I gasped. If possible, my frozen heart felt even colder.

I had actually grown to like that woman. I'd even related to her on some levels. Ten years ago, I had reconnected Lucy with her estranged daughter and grandkids and helped her make peace with the neglect and emotional torment she'd endured as a child. How could she return to her old ways? Where had I gone wrong with my design for her Scrooging?

Or maybe I should ask where the universe had gone wrong with its design for *people?*

I shook my head, the blues setting in.

Didn't Lucy realize how few of us got second chances, let alone magically engineered ones? Didn't any of my Scrooges care that a whole team worked hard to help them evolve? Did these people even *want* to change?

While Ghosts of Christmas Present oversaw Scroogings, in my opinion Ghosts of Christmas Future packed the strongest punch. All movies based on our Christmas Carol activities confirmed that. It's why we saved the future for our finale; our visits there showed Scrooges dismal fates of their own making that were full of disappointment, sadness, regret, and loneliness.

If I had seen my future when I was alive—this state as an immortal ghostly servant to people who took you for granted—I'd like to think I would have changed *my ways* for good . . .

"And we're done!" Jay said, joining me at the back of the school auditorium. He smiled as he waved at the kids filing out.

His enthusiasm startled me out of my depressed mental drifting. "Hm? Oh, yes. You're all done for the day in terms of events. We can go back to the office to work on your talking points for the morning show next week. I also told the media team I'd help them prepare the promos for the Parks Department."

Jay raised an eyebrow as he stared at me. "Something's wrong."

I checked my phone in a panic. "Did another event get moved? Do we have something else today?"

"No, not with me. With you. There's something wrong. Where's that feisty-but-chipper, partridge-in-a-pear-tree vibe you usually give off?"

"First off, partridges are actually jerks. Second, I could try one of your Cheshire Cat campaign smiles if this face doesn't please you." I tilted my head back and gave an obnoxiously large grin before sucking it back in and frowning at him.

"Sir?" interrupted one of Jay's bodyguards. "Lucas is pulling the car around."

"Thanks, Rocco," Jay said. The three of us began making our way to the front of the school, but Jay kept his focus on me.

"Personal problems?" he asked.

"Something like that," I said.

"How bad?"

"Have you ever seen *Home Alone 4*?"

Jay made a face like a kid eating broccoli ice cream. "Ugh, I watched three minutes of it by accident once. It's like the

Quantum of Solace of the Christmas world. I try to forget it exists. You're feeling *that* bad right now? Geez, I'm sorry."

The SUV pulled up to the curb and Rocco opened the door for me. I climbed in, but Jay hung back to whisper something to Rocco before getting in.

"Plotting something?" I asked as Jay buckled up.

"How did you know?"

"Should I ask about what?"

"I'd prefer if you didn't."

"Fine by me." I wasn't in the mood for a conversation about work or anything else. Getting that UnScrooged notification had really soured my mood and poked another tiny hole in the inflatable bounce house that was my own Christmas Spirit. It'd been deflating for some time, and every additional prick just let more air out. It was a fortunate thing that this would likely be my final year at the CCD; I didn't think I could go on holding myself up—pretending for people like Jay that I wholeheartedly believed in all this.

We drove and my mind wandered. After a while though, I noticed we had turned onto *S. Broadway.* "We're going the wrong direction for the office," I said, eyeing Jay. "What's going on?"

"I asked Rocco if we could take a detour before heading back."

"Don't you have work to do? I have work to do."

"Yes, and yes. But I want to show you something. Look, we're just about there." He lowered the window and pointed outside. I leaned forward.

It was a movie theater. An old-fashioned kind, not one of the big chain places. The car pulled over and Jay beat his bodyguard to the punch and opened the door, helping me out. I was hit with déjà vu.

S. Broadway.

I gazed up at the large vertical signs on either side of the building. The name was different, the structure was updated, but this was definitely the same place.

"The Orpheum," I whispered in awe.

Jay crooked an eyebrow. "Yeah, that's what it was called when it opened in 1911. It's changed owners and names many times since then. Now it's called the Palace."

"I can't believe it's still here."

"Same," Jay replied, gazing up at the building beside me. "But just like that bookstore, the Palace is a piece of LA history, and keeping it alive is good for us in ways beyond profit. I want to help places like this stay in business once I'm in a position to really make an impact." He glanced at me. "Do you want to go inside?"

I nodded, still staring at the building.

Jay motioned for me to wait as he went to talk with the man at the ticket counter. I stood on the curb, absorbed with wonder until a car horn blared behind me. Every hair on my skin erected and I retreated several feet onto the sidewalk, pressing my back safely against the building.

Jay returned with an excited smile, but when he saw me with my hand held to my chest, concern clouded his expression. "Are you okay?"

I inhaled steadily and averted my eyes from the road. "Fine." I cleared my throat. "So what's the word?"

"The ticket guy is going to let us have a look around."

"No ticket?"

"He recognized my name."

"Well, *excuse me*?" I said with sass, mock fanning my face. "I guess I'm in the presence of a celebrity."

He cracked a grin then glanced at his bodyguards. "Give us five minutes."

We ventured into the Palace. So much had been remodeled,

but the core of the theater felt the same. It was like me—shiny and new on the surface, but inside thrived the ghostly essence of something from another time.

Jay opened the doors of the main auditorium. It was dark, a modern movie playing on the screen.

"The Palace is showing reruns of Christmas classics all month," he whispered.

I carefully stepped in and my eyes adjusted to the limited lighting. The theater had been redesigned with less seating but more comfortable options. Except for the benches. The cheap seats that I could afford a hundred years ago remained in back but looked like they were just for historical conservancy purposes now. The people watching the current matinée were gathered in mezzanines and seats closer to the front. I gazed around, lost in time.

After a while, Jay put his hand on my arm and tapped his watch. We made our way back to the lobby. Once there, I paused.

"Jay. Why did you bring me here?"

"You said you love movies. I do too. Like books, they sweep you away to another place that makes more sense and promises satisfying payoffs in exchange for the pain that main characters endure. Only, movies are quick outlets. Perfect two-hour escapes. This is my favorite theater in the city. In another life, when I was feeling stressed, I'd buy a cheap afternoon ticket and see whatever was showing by myself. I thought you may like it here."

"That's the only reason?"

He paused before responding. "I thought you may need it too. I know what it's like to have a rough workday combined with a rough personal day. Sometimes you just need a distraction, or a reminder of what makes you happy."

I gave Jay a long, hard look then finally released a breath as a weighty realization fully settled into me. One I had not thought possible until now. And one that I had been fighting to accept since I met this man.

"You're not a bad person, Jay."

He tilted his head. "Thanks. You're not so bad yourself." The SUV honked outside. "Come on. We have to go."

I took a final gaze at the building, nearly as ancient as I was and yet still standing, restored into something new. It gave me hope that this would be me soon. Reborn in the modern era for another chance at success.

"He's not a bad person," I told Bismaad via SpaceTime. Wrapped in a maroon robe with Marley beside me, I sat settled on my apartment's couch. In the background I had the TV tuned to a channel that solely played an image of a crackling fireplace, sounds and all.

The twenty-first century was hilarious, ridiculous, and amazing.

"That has to be why I've felt so oddly invested in Jay," I continued. "He's not just unpredictable; he's different than the others. Jay may be cold at times, and push his family away, but he's very much aware of, and cares about others. He proved that to me today."

"That is certainly unusual," Bismaad agreed, maintaining her accent. She was bundled up in a mint hoodie and preparing breakfast in her own apartment across the pond. "My bloke—who is back on caffeine by the way—threw a coffee at me yesterday and it *was not* iced."

I nodded. "Now that sounds about right. Specter One doesn't bring it up in our orientation, but the people we're trying to help always treat us like crud. More beverages have been thrown at me than apps have been invented. It's part of the deal—doors slammed in our faces, mean and belittling comments, the works. I've had none of that from Jay though."

"Maybe because he's not there yet," Bismaad suggested.

"How do you mean?"

Bismaad moved farther from the screen as she stirred something sizzling in a pan on her stove. "Well, normally we arrive when people have already gone down a bad path and need to be brought back to goodness. Maybe Jay hasn't made the choices that will destroy his Christmas Spirit and turn him into a full Scrooge yet. I bet the Naughty & Nice list red flagged him because you have a chance to save him *before* that happens versus the typical after. I had a case like that fifteen years ago. I got a teenage girl whose decisions about colleges and boyfriends would've turned her into a Scrooge. But the CCD intervened, our ghosts worked their plan, and we saved her before she became one of those far-gone twits. It's a rare kind of case, but it looks like that's what you're dealing with for this Scrooge. Cheers to you; it seems you got a good one for your final assignment."

"Yeah, he's a good one . . ." I said, gazing out at LA's glittering towers to my left.

"Want to go for drinks at The Nutcracker on Friday?" Bismaad asked, turning off her stove.

Again?

"Um . . ."

"I'll take that vague stutter as a yes. Oh, and because I know you only check social media if I push you, you need to RSVP to an invite on our Tinsel group page. Next Saturday, the Ghosts of Christmas Present are having a holiday party and potluck to go off into the Christmas countdown with a bang. Kooky Christmas sweaters is the theme, and there's a sign-up sheet for what food you want to bring."

"A potluck party? The night before D-Day? I don't know. There are other things I should probably be doing—strategizing with my team, last minute scenario drills, my Earth job."

"Just think about it. *Please.* I'm organizing, and it's going to be so extra."

"Fine. I'll consider it. And nice use of the new vocab. Now I have to get to sleep. Before I go though, I recommend keeping an extra blouse in your briefcase. I've found it helps with the more dramatic, beverage-tossing Scrooges like the one you have."

"Ooh. Hot tip. Thanks, babe. Good night!"

I yawned and turned off my fake fire and the other lights in the loft, leaving only a string of dimmed Christmas lights and those firework-shaped fantastic fixtures above sparkling in the darkness. Marley leapt from the couch and followed me. The second I got into bed, he plopped himself in his basket. I loved that little dog, programmed to move in sync with me perfectly.

I lay down and gazed up at the ceiling.

"Fade to black," I whispered aloud as my eyelids closed.

"Frost! Frost Mason! Young lady, where are you?"

Seven-year-old me scampered through the halls of St. Francis's orphanage then slid into the crook beneath a staircase, hugging my knees to my chest. My eyes and ears were alert and I remained perfectly still. Regrettably, Sister Jocelyn found me.

"There you are." She knelt by the stairs. "Frost, please come out. Mr. and Mrs. Kitridge are a lovely couple. They would really like to talk with you."

"They want to adopt me," I said with bitterness.

"Most little girls here would be excited about that."

"Most girls here don't have a mother coming back for them."

"Dear . . ." Sister Jocelyn tried to put a hand on my shoulder but I scooched away. She sighed. "Frost, your mother left you here almost three years ago. I am not one to speak against hope and faith, but I am sorry, dear, I do not think she is coming back."

My heart welled with doubt, but I shook my head with conviction. "No. She loves me. She wouldn't just leave me. I mean, I know my father did, but . . ." I shook my head again then locked eyes with Sister Jocelyn. "I am not going with the Kitridges, Sister. Introduce them to another girl. I am going to wait for my mother. I can't believe that both my parents would abandon me. It just . . . it just isn't possible."

I stood and pushed by her, running as fast as I could.

The hall of the orphanage blurred around me—shadows growing larger like monstrous beanstalks trying to break through the roof. The path itself seemed to shake as my worn shoes hit the floor with one small thud after another.

I felt panic, anxiety, unease. The sound of strong wind buffeting my windows stirred me from my dream memory, but like with the most clawing nightmares, I couldn't seem to break free. I tossed and turned, half-awake, face plowing harder into my pillow.

My subconscious subsumed me again. I was twelve, walking the streets of an outdoor market in downtown Los Angeles. Some of the nuns had taken us with them as they did their grocery shopping for the week. I looked about with curiosity at all the fruits and vegetables, colors shimmering together in my memory.

In the present, I could feel my hands tighten around the covers of my bed, but my dream of the past played on, not letting me escape.

Young me turned and then I saw her. A certain haze of color like a halo followed a woman with brown hair and a fancy burnt orange dress, matching hat, and silk gloves. Like a moth pursuing a light in the night, I was compelled to follow the woman. I slipped away from the nuns and began to bob and weave through the Angelinos. The woman was getting farther away, but her glow allowed me to track her through the increasingly hazy dreamscape.

I cut around a vendor carrying a crate of carrots, and that's when I caught up with her. Ten feet away, separated by only the passersby of the bustling market, *stood my mother.*

I couldn't believe it. Her face, eyes, and hair matched the one clear memory of her I still held to. My face enlivened and I started to race toward her, but then, just as abruptly, I stopped.

A man—a tall man with a tailored suit pushing a baby carriage—tapped my mother on the shoulder. She turned and smiled; I guess she'd been looking for him. For them. My mother gave the man a quick kiss and reached into the baby carriage to caress the face of the infant inside. I stood frozen as my mother linked arms with the man and the two continued on through the market pushing the carriage.

Every other soul in Los Angeles seemed to freeze and the entirety of my background turned black and white like an old movie. In the background—*Bang . . . Bang . . . BANG!*

"BLAWGH!" I finally managed to gasp awake.

Being dead meant I couldn't exhibit a racing heart or break into a cold sweat like other people who suffered nightmares. But my hands felt stiff from clutching the covers and my hair floofed around me in a tangled mess.

I glanced around the dark apartment. My Christmas lights twinkled meekly like extinguishing stars. More banging drew my attention to the windows. The harsh wind I'd heard in my nightmares was real and pummeling the glass. LA was intense like that; steady weather most of the time, but now and then from fall to winter the infamous Santa Ana winds blew mercilessly across Southern California.

I grunted and rubbed the side of my head with my hand.

Only being able to dream your memories meant it was always a risk you might dig up ones you'd prefer to forget. I hadn't had this one in decades. I kept it buried too deep. My soul hurt from re-experiencing it now—that day when I realized my mother had left me behind and found a new life. The day when I first fully accepted I *was*, in fact, alone and I should never let people get too close to me again. If I chose to be alone for myself going forward, I was safe. No one could let me down if they never got near enough to really matter.

Emotions that I'd frozen decades ago thrashed inside me. I refused to let them win. It was simpler to forget the past, forget feelings that nearly destroyed you. I had to focus on work and my goals; any pain that distracted me from that had to be distanced.

I clutched my knees against my chest like seven-year-old me used to do and listened to the winds beat my window. *BANG. BANG . . . BANG.*

"Way to go, everyone! The results have been fantastic today." I high-fived a few members of our social media team at the office.

It'd been one heck of a day. By the time the last bite of my breakfast had been swallowed, I'd successfully shoved all feelings from last night in the basement of my soul and was able to come to work with the classic Yay-Christmas-Spirit attitude that my job as Jay's ghostly savior required. Dream memories were just pieces of the past after all; I was a being engineered for the present.

I'd even gotten to the office super early to make sure my coworkers had everything they needed to run social media blasts for Parks' event tomorrow, in addition to their regularly scheduled duties. I'd been monitoring the results all day as Jay and I completed his school visits. It looked like we'd received huge impressions.

I congratulated a few more people then trotted up the steps to Jay's office to share the good news. However, I hesitated when I saw him through the glass of the door. He was sitting at his desk with his head in his hands. Concern fluttered inside me. He'd seemed to be getting progressively more tired throughout the day—countless speeches and handshakes would do that—but this seemed different. I started to retreat when he looked up. He waved for me to enter.

I cautiously journeyed in.

"What is it, Frost?"

"I, uh, wanted to tell you that the posts about the Parks Department have gotten a terrific response. If you decided to go tomorrow and we publicized that, I know we could get a—"

"I told you I'm not going to that, Frost."

Time to push. "I thought you may have a change of heart. I hoped you would anyway. To save that Christmas tree."

"I haven't. Sorry if that disappoints you. There are more important things to consider than trees and traditions right now."

I raked my nails against my palm with unease. "Did something happen? I know you have had an intense week, but you seem . . . angrier than when we got back a few minutes ago."

"I had a couple of voicemails from my sisters and one from my mother," he said, sounding lifeless.

"Is that a bad thing?"

"That's not the word I would use." He shook his head. "*Why am I telling you about this?* Just please go and confirm the final details for the last of the school visits. Call and move tomorrow's Friedman's dinner back half an hour. Have one of the interns pick up my dry cleaning. And get me an outline of the ways the social media team is publicizing my appearance on the morning show next week."

"Yes, Jay."

I returned to my desk and started flipping through my agenda book, then I paused. My eyes lingered on the contact details for Friedman's Election Consulting. The sounds of the bustling office seemed to shrink behind me as my brain fought with my soul over an idea.

The internal arguing continued at the base of my conscience for the rest of the day into the night. Literally. Hours later, as I stood in my loft's kitchen—twilight flooding the windows and police sirens ringing below from somewhere nearby—I rapped my fingers on the countertop. Two objects sat in front of me: my phone and my agenda book open to the page with the information for Jay's dinner tomorrow. I still hadn't called to delay it. I had to act soon; Friedman's offices closed in ten minutes. I reached for the phone, then hesitated again.

My head knew what to do. I always led with that. Doing so was easy when your heart had literally stopped beating a hundred years ago. But I . . .

Ugh. I hadn't broken a rule at the CCD in like half a century.

I glanced down at Marley. "What should I do, boy?"

He looked up, wagged his tail, and yapped.

"You seem pretty sure of yourself."

I groaned and rolled my head back in frustration.

Then I sighed. "You know what," I thought aloud. "I'm pretty sure of myself too."

I picked up my phone.

As we pulled away after our final school event, I nervously watched the kids filing out the doors, giddy about their Friday afternoon ahead. I envied them. I had gone rogue last night in relation to both my jobs. And I was about to see how it played out.

We drove along in silence for a while. Then exactly what happened to me on Wednesday happened to Jay. He looked around and realized we weren't where we were supposed to be.

"Frost, did I miss something? Shouldn't we be back at the office by now? I don't have a lot of time before I have to leave for my dinner with Friedman's."

"Your Friedman's dinner has been rescheduled," I said. "When I called to move it back as you requested, they told me they actually wanted to cancel due to a conflict. You're meeting with them next Thursday."

"Really?" Jay said in disbelief. "This dinner has been on the calendar for a month. Did they say why?"

"Holiday plans," I replied. "Something important came up. You don't pay me to pry."

"Okay then . . . so the reason we're not on the normal route back to the office is?"

"Because now you have time to spend the afternoon at the Parks' event."

"Frost, *I told you I'm too busy,*" he said, eyes narrowed. "If I don't have to attend this dinner, I should concentrate on the million other things on my plate." He turned to knock on the divider between us and the front. "Rocco—"

"It's too late," I said.

Jay twisted around to look at me.

"I had the social media team blast that you're going to be at the event to help raise money for community projects, including the 'Save the Holiday Spirit' fund for protecting that tree."

"What?"

"You can't back out of it now without generating a wave of bad press. The city is expecting you. And we're almost there." I pointed out the window at the rides, tents, giant inflatable St. Nicks, and plastic snowmen coming into view. Our car began slowing as we met the line of vehicles waiting to park.

Rocco lowered the divider. "Did you need something, sir?"

Jay looked at me.

I gestured at the group of Parks Department volunteers approaching our vehicle. They wore matching red t-shirts, Santa hats, and eager smiles.

"I texted them that we're here and gave our car description so they'd come greet us straightaway. They're going to take you on a walking tour of the event, followed by a meet-and-greet, and a speech on the main stage—nothing over ten minutes; you can just use an iteration of one of the school talks you gave this week. Then you can pitch in at different booths."

Jay was so livid he was speechless. It was how he had looked when Celia told him her Christmas Eve plans. I'd expected that and held firm eye contact with him, unwavering.

"It's fine, Rocco," Jay said over his shoulder, keeping his gaze locked with mine. "Park the car. Lucas and I will go with the volunteers."

"Very good, sir."

The divider closed. Jay looked at me harshly. "I take it my bodyguards, the volunteers, everyone thinks I'm doing this of my own free will?"

"Correct. You *should* be doing this of your own free will. One of your biggest passions is protecting communities and local interests. You told me so yourself when you showed me the bookstore and the theater. This fits with your MO. If you really mean what you say, that is."

The door opened before he could respond, and Jay was greeted by a bunch of enthusiastic volunteers. He could've given Sandra Bullock a lesson in congeniality as he shook hands and allowed people to usher him into the park. Lucas closed the door behind me and I followed at a reserved distance, really hoping this would go well.

It went well!

Actually, it went amazingly! Every booth Jay worked at spiked in sales and attendance. He posed for countless pictures with supporters and volunteers. The media that turned out thanks to Jay's social media blasts captured a lot of fantastic footage. And Jay's speech was flawless—he'd already given so many that, as I suspected, he was well-versed and naturally charismatic enough to pull one off on the fly.

It was getting close to six and the lights of the event had flickered on, making the park feel like a winter wonderland. A winter wonderland without any real snow, but it was a good effort for SoCal.

"Thank you so much for being here, Mr. Nichols," said Lou, the Parks Department director with the Santa-styled white beard. "You truly made a difference today, and your community appreciates it."

"You're very welcome. I was happy to do it," Jay said.

I smiled proudly as I watched him finish making the rounds. Five minutes later we were in the SUV and taking off again. I thought everything was fine; however the moment the door shut, Jay's smile fell.

"I told Rocco to take me to the office. From there, I've ordered him to drive you straight home. I'll have one of the interns ship you any personal belongings you left at your desk."

I blinked twice before I processed what he said. "What?"

"You work for me, Frost. You had no right to change my dinner, let alone one that I specifically told you was important. I talked to a contact at Friedman's. He told me you called to postpone the dinner at *my* request because I had a time-sensitive obligation. You lied in order to get me to do what you think is best. That's not your place. You're an assistant."

"*Which means I'm supposed to assist you,*" I argued passionately. "I told you earlier in the week that you're not a bad guy, and I truly believe that, but your noble intentions won't matter if they get buried under bad choices. I intervened and everything worked out great. You made a difference here; you made people happy and you did it by following through on the platforms you care about. Isn't that a good thing?"

A long silence hung between us before Jay spoke the last three words he'd utter to me in the car.

"Frost. You're fired."

"I am so stupid." I cradled my head in my arms on the bar counter, seated between Paul and Bismaad. The Nutcracker was ablaze with the giddy Friday night crowd, but I felt like I'd been punched by a polar bear.

"I wouldn't say stupid, maybe naïvely bold." Paul patted my head. "It's not crazy to think Jay would forgive you once he saw how people reacted to him being at the event."

I looked up and pushed escaped strands of hair out of my eyes. "No, I mean I'm stupid for even interfering at all. My CCD job on Earth is to observe, study, and research Scrooges so that my team can craft the best Christmas Carol experience. I'm not supposed to meddle with their lives and influence their choices. I am in so much trouble."

"What happened the last time a ghost did something like this?" Bismaad asked.

"I don't think it's ever happened," I admitted. "In my hundred years, I've heard of a few ghosts who crossed ethical lines . . ."

Myself included.

I cleared my throat. "But no Ghost of Christmas Present has ever lost the undercover position he or she was assigned. How am I supposed to keep studying Jay up close and filling in the holes to his story if I can't get anywhere near him?"

I sighed and pushed my empty cocoa mug away, signaling the Yeti bartender. "Another please, Nigel."

"GARGGHRAARGH!" the Yeti responded.

"What do you mean you're cutting me off?" I retorted angrily.

"RAARRRGHRAAAR!"

"Three cocoas is *not* above my sugar tolerance limit."

"DRAARGH!'"

"Fine," I huffed. "I'll do one with nonfat milk and no whipped cream, happy?"

"ARGH!"

Nigel got to work on my beverage as I pivoted in my stool and leaned back against the bar. It wasn't as full in the tavern tonight as last week and I was glad. The last thing I needed was for more of my colleagues to see me moping.

Unfortunately, the ghost most likely to bug me waltzed in. "Two nights out in one season, Frost? That's a lot for you," Allan said, trying to provoke me. "What's the occasion?"

"I just felt like relaxing, Allan," I replied, face deadpan.

"The stress of your Centennial Scrooge getting to you? Don't tell me Miss All About The Job is having problems."

"It's nothing I can't handle."

"If you need any tips, follow me on Tinsel. I post daily motivations and ideas for best ways to deal with difficult assignments."

"Thanks, I'll keep that in mind," I snapped.

"ARGHRARRGHH!" Nigel passed me my cocoa.

I took a sip then put down the mug with a puckered face. The reduced sugar content was obvious.

"You know what?" I said to Paul and Bismaad, standing. "I'm leaving. I want to be alone right now." I gave Nigel my ID, which he scanned, then went to get my coat from the elf at the hostess stand.

"Frost, wait!" Bismaad called.

I pushed through the stained-glass door. Icy particles collided with my face as I was met by a bitter, gusting wind. Dangerously heavy snowfall made visibility a lot lower than usual. I had to hold a hand up to cover my eyes and see through the veil of frozen tundra. I could barely make out the ski lift that took patrons out of the tavern's ice chasm to the snowy surface level.

"Frost!" Paul called out, catching up with me. "I think you should go talk to Specter One. If he doesn't already know what you did, he will soon. You should beat him to the punch and confront the matter directly, be honest about it. There may be less consequences that way."

"What is he going to do, kill me?" I rolled my eyes.

"Listen to me, there's more to it than that."

"There's always more to it," I retorted. "Live for yourself unattached to others, get sentenced to a century as a ghost. Save a soul every Christmas, it's just a matter of time until they go bad again. Try and help someone before they even become a Scrooge, and they fire you. Life, afterlife, it's all one big monkey's paw and I'm sick of it."

I spun back toward the incoming ski lift just as a snap of wind surged behind me.

My heel caught on a patch of ice.

I gasped, slipped, and fell.

It was brisk for an LA day, even in winter.

I exited The Orpheum theatre, feeling content. I loved seeing movies all year around, but it felt extra special to do it around the holidays.

When I'd aged out of the orphanage a decade ago, the nuns had sent me on my way. I couldn't say I was heartbroken about that; I'd seen it coming and I'd never let myself connect too deeply with anyone there in accord with that. Since then, I'd devoted myself entirely to work. I had a lovely job at a bookshop and had made a comfortable life for myself. It was easy to afford nice things and luxuries like movies when you worked nonstop—no relationships to distract or absorb you. Being alone was a safe move from an emotional and financial standpoint.

As I filed along the bustling streets with the others leaving the movie house, a cute pointer dog stopped to sniff my dress. I patted him on the head as I waited to cross the street.

LA traffic had become even more hectic in the last few years. A decade ago, public transit had been the norm with the yellow cars of the Los Angeles Railway and red cars of the Pacific Electric Railway. With the passing of the Federal Road Act in 1916, those modes of transportation were now fighting for their lives among a slew of jitneys charging a nickel for a ride and the surge of privately owned automobiles.

The moment to cross arrived. I vigilantly kept alert—looking left and right in case any drivers or bicyclists weren't paying attention. When I stepped onto the sidewalk on the other side, panicked yells had me turning around. The pointer I'd petted had darted three quarters of the way across the street before stopping to sniff the steam coming out of a partially open sewer hole, oblivious to the oncoming traffic and his owner's calls.

There were too many vehicles zooming by on the far side of the street for the owner to pursue his pet. Meanwhile, a trolley was coming straight at the dog just ten feet from me. I made a break for it. I hastened off the curb, grabbed the dog's leash, and pulled him to safety.

Success!

The creature secure, I waited until it was safe to traverse the traffic again and returned to the opposite side of the street, presenting the man with his dog.

"Thank you so much!" he exclaimed.

"You're welcome," I replied. I pet the dog on the head a final time. "Be good now."

I glanced around—all clear—and stepped off the sidewalk to cross again. I was eight feet onto the road when out of nowhere a bicycle whizzed by and knocked into me. I stumbled to a knee and hand, heart thumping wildly. Pivoting in the direction of the cyclist, I started to stand. "Hey! Watch where you're going!"

Honking from the opposite direction caused me to turn. The last thing I saw was the plate-sized headlights of a black jitney barreling toward me.

GASP!

I awakened only to have icy water overpower my senses. I shot up and my head burst through frigid waters.

"Frost. Hey, Frost?"

It was Paul's voice, but I was too shocked to respond. I sat, clothes and all, in a solid ice tub filled to the brim with water and glowing ice cubes. It was like a therapeutic ice bath Tom Brady might use to recover from a football game, only more mystical.

Water dripped from my hair down my forehead and cheeks. I wiped my face and reoriented myself—not cold, just surprised. I was in an . . . igloo? Paul and Bismaad stood on either side of me. The ice cubes in the tub clinked as I sat up more. Something tugged on my scalp. Reaching up, I felt a few wires with electrodes attached to my head. They must've been magic otherwise they would've electrocuted me underwater.

The wires connected to a blinking machine with a screen that monitored my vitals, currently being checked by a penguin with a stethoscope. Elves in doctor scrubs and nurse outfits bustled about, each with small sapphires growing out of their cheeks like million-dollar moles. Some worked with sparkly blue goo and what looked like a tank of liquid nitrogen. The hazard symbol on the side of the canister—taller than they were—was framed with boughs of holly.

This place seemed so familiar, but my head was too blurry to place the memory.

"Where am I?" I asked.

"One of the North Pole's infirmary igloos," Paul replied. "Specifically, 'Ghost Repair.' The dead get their energy from the cold. Hence how comfortable you feel at the North Pole and the CCD, whereas most humans would freeze after a few days."

"*Right . . .*" My head felt groggy and I squinted. "But the bathtub? The ice cubes?"

"We have systems in place in case a ghost ever needs a boost of magical, icy energy. See, even though your forms seem solid, your bodies are more like holograms—disturbances can interfere with their ability to sustain themselves. While you can't get killed as a ghost, if you harm your vessel, you'll go offline."

I clutched my aching head. One of the nurse elves offered me a glowing candy cane. I hesitated, but she insisted.

Bismaad frowned at Paul. "You make us sound like machines. How badly can we be damaged?"

"It's not about being damaged."

Everyone in the room pivoted at the booming voice. Santa Claus himself stood in the arched entrance of the igloo. The man's rosy cheeks complemented his red corduroy work overalls. His black leather boots were the same material as his gloves. The snow wished it was as white as his beard.

"Santa!" Bismaad's mouth dropped. A second later she recovered and dashed over. "I'm so excited to meet you! I mean, I've heard you speak at the CCD, but I've always wanted to meet you one-on-one because you're, well—and I'm, well—hi, I'm Bismaad. Huge fan."

He smiled at her warmly and put a big gloved hand on her

shoulder. "Hello, Bismaad. I know exactly who you are and I'm excited to meet you too."

He strode over to me and pushed the glasses up on his nose. "Frost, I heard you had an accident. Are you okay?"

"I'll be fine, Ni—Santa," I said, trying to find something in the room to look at besides his concerned face. "You didn't have to come and check on me. You're beyond busy."

"I am. I haven't even shared a proper meal with Paul or his sister in two weeks, and they're my children. But just because you and I haven't spent a lot of time together in the last couple of decades doesn't mean I don't still care about you, Frost. There was a time when we were quite close after all."

Bismaad looked from Santa to me. "You were?"

"So what were you saying about being damaged?" I asked Santa, avoiding the subject.

He sighed. "You can't be damaged because your bodies aren't real. Your souls are pure energy. That energy is generated from the good you bring to the world—your successful Scroogings— and is boosted by the cold."

"But some of our coworkers have been sent to South America, Africa, and so on. Frost here got assigned to sunny California," Bismaad responded. "And we drink hot cocoa *constantly*. I've wondered about this for a while, and now my curiosity has reached its peak. If we're as fragile as your igloo infirmary makes us out to be, isn't all that bad for us?"

"After almost a year of recharging at the CCD in the iciest—and most magical—environment possible, your energy is enhanced enough to allow you to roam any climate on Earth for all of December," Santa explained. "Returning to the CCD and North Pole provides energy refuels along the way. Because of this, you're also not going to combust from drinking a cup of soup, let alone cocoa, which, if you look at the latest medical research, is actually proven to help life expectancy—"

"Dad?" Paul interrupted.

"Right. The point: hot beverages and places aren't an issue. But if something violently disrupts your state—like this accident—your soul starts to flicker. It takes a lot of my magic to stabilize you, and the special ice fragments being used to restore you now are infused with that." He gestured at the glittering cubes. I looked down at them, then at Santa and Paul. Both had a serious expression.

"Is that such a bad thing?" Bismaad asked, noticing their wariness too.

"Dad's magic—the magic in our family—isn't infinite," Paul explained. "It comes from the amount of people on Earth who believe in him, and that powers the whole existence of the North Pole. The dead are meant to stay dead, and what the CCD does is a fragile enterprise. While the cold helps preserve you, the magical energy you incur with your Scroogings is the *only* thing keeping you here. But barely. Even little things like a nasty fall can break your hold on this world."

"Well, geez, guys," Bismaad exclaimed. "Why isn't that in the ghost guidebook? There should definitely be a section in the welcome pamphlet that says: 'Caution—If you slip you may cease to exist. *Ho ho ho* and good luck out there.'"

"My ancestors and the Senior Specters decided not to tell you the extent of your fragility," Santa admitted. "They agreed it would get in the way of you doing your jobs if you were always worried about self-preservation. I only found out when my father retired and promoted me to Santa. I told Paul recently because he has been hounding me with questions about your pending retirement, Frost."

The nurse elf who'd given me the candy cane came over and pushed on my arm, urging me to keep licking. I put the candy in my mouth, and she curtsied to Santa before going back to her station. Questions bubbled to my brim like an overflowing soda.

"I only hit my head. How much magic did you use to bring me back?"

"It doesn't matter," Santa said.

"It does matter," I insisted.

"Our toy production is going to be delayed three days behind schedule and the shield around our realm has been reduced by fifteen percent for the rest of the season."

I gasped. "For a bonk to my skull?"

Santa and Paul nodded.

"I'm really sorry," I said. "I was being emotional and I got distracted. I am extremely grateful, but I can't believe you wasted your magic and put the North Pole's schedule and shield at risk for me. I'm just one ghost."

Anything that could make Santa's eyes stop sparkling was not to be belittled. He looked me over with genuine concern and some sadness. I found it difficult to hold his gaze. Santa was not just an elderly, mystical Christmas legend to me. He was the child I'd once known as little Nicholas who I'd gone sledding and built snowman with. He'd grown into my friend Nick who I rode reindeer and watched Christmas movies with. Finally he had become this: old St. Nick. Time had changed him as it had changed his father before that. Years kept evolving his face and phase in life whereas mine stayed the same.

"I care for you, Frost," Santa said. "Just as my kids, my father, and my grandfather have cared for you. I wasn't going to just leave you to fade away. That being said, I did what I could today, but please proceed with caution. Every one of us in the CCD and the North Pole can run out of magic and time one way or another. Focus and finish out the season. Then you can have what you've long wished for. What I wish for you."

I groaned, remembering in a rush what had driven me to the distraction that caused my slip on the ice. "If that's even possible after I screwed things up with my job."

"About that . . ." Paul said, taking my CCD phone out of his pocket and handing it to me. "This may be magic tech, but your elfin carrier policy won't replace it if you drown it in a vat of magic-infused ice."

The phone had one new notification— a text from Jay.

"*I'm sorry. Call me back.*"

"Why am I so nervous?" I asked Marley as I paced around my dorm at the CCD.

Marley wasn't paying attention; he was waging some sort of war with a reindeer-shaped squeaky toy.

I rolled my shoulders back and selected Jay's number in my phone. It rang three times before he answered.

"Frost."

"Hi, Jay."

"You got my message."

"I did. I was . . . surprised."

"*Frost?*" Jay's voice sounded faint and distant.

I moved to stand near the window. "Jay, can you hear me?"

"Yeah. The signal is a little weak. Where are you?"

"I'm . . . out of area."

"Oh."

There was a long pause.

"You were right," Jay finally said. "The positive publicity hasn't stopped coming in about my involvement with the Parks' event. I'm trending on social media with #notalltalk and #nicholsforSoCal. Several news channels did a feature on it tonight. And I just spoke with Lou. We raised enough money to save the tree and support a large number of community programs in the new year. His department is grateful to me, but it's you they should be thanking."

"Mmhmm," I said.

Lengthy silence number two.

"You knew what was best, even if I couldn't see it," Jay ultimately admitted. "I am still upset with you for going behind my back, and if you do it again, I'll really fire you. But . . . I'd like you to come back to the office on Monday."

WHOO! Job saved!

I flung my hands in the air and danced with joy for a second. Marley stared at me.

"Frost?"

"Okay," I said, reining it in.

"Okay," Jay replied. "Oh, but I should tell you, Annie thinks she will be back by mid-week, so brace yourself. She's a lot less forgiving than I am. When she called asking what happened with the Friedman's dinner and I told her what you did, she wanted to have you blackballed in the political circuit."

I rolled my eyes at Marley. "I'll try not to let it keep me up at night."

And pause three . . .

"So I'll see you Monday?" Jay said.

"Yes."

"Things are going to be different this time, Frost. You know that, right?"

"Oh, you can count on it, Jay. That's just what I was thinking."

10

"Sample questions for Wednesday's morning show interview?" Jay asked. I stood in front of his desk with my checklist.

"In your inbox."

"Signed copies of my book sent to news outlets and reviewers?"

"Messengered out an hour ago."

"Friedman's dinner?"

"Confirmed for Thursday at six o'clock."

Jay laced his hands behind his head and leaned back in his chair. "Fantastic. Now what was it that you wanted to propose to me? I'm impressed that you're actually going to ask my opinion rather than tricking me into something."

I raised my eyebrows.

"Too soon?" he asked.

"You didn't take the last donut in the box, Jay. You fired me."

"You deserved what I did."

"I could say the same to you ... *but anyway.*" I cleared my throat. Maybe Paul was right; Jay did rile me up. "The Parks Department reached out to me this morning. Given your involvement last week, they were hoping you would do the honors at the tree lighting they have scheduled for Tuesday night. With Christmas approaching, they're aiming for a fast turnaround. They're picking up the tree today and will be paying the plaza's management staff overtime to decorate it tomorrow."

"Well, that's dumb," Jay thought out loud. "Plenty of people love that tree as much as I do. If this is for the community, why not invite the community to decorate it? We had great success promoting the event last week, right? Why not ask volunteers to come down and participate? It could be fun."

"Jay"—I lowered my notebook—"*that's an excellent idea.* I'll top you one too. I could talk to Lou about turning the decorating into a whole event. We could have a cocoa bar, music playing in the plaza, maybe an onsite Santa to visit with the kids."

"Fine. Make sure the interns mail out the last of my Christmas cards today, *and then* you can work on this." Jay picked up a pen and began writing something in his own notebook as he continued speaking. "I think it's an awesome idea and we don't have anything scheduled for Tuesday night so you can tell Lou I'll do the tree lighting."

"Okay, but under one condition."

Jay stopped writing and glanced at me. "Condition? Frost, this was your idea."

"Sure was, but if I'm going to do all this extra work, I have something to ask. It's not even for my benefit, but yours."

He sighed. "What is it?"

"Invite your kids to the tree lighting."

Jay's eyes narrowed. "Frost, my kids aren't any of your business. In fact, let me make something abundantly clear." He came around his desk to stand barely a foot away and glared down at me with severity. "Your job does not involve interfering in my life."

I was unfazed. In fact, I crossed my arms and leaned in.

"*Believe me,* I realize that. I'm not accustomed to this kind of on-the-job meddling. It goes against my training, and I could get in immense trouble, yet I'm doing it anyway. Do you know why? Because it's the right thing. I'm invested in you, Jay. I shouldn't be. I'm not completely sure why, but what can I say? I guess you're my exception."

GEANNA CULBERTSON   181

Jay's expression softened. He studied me. After a moment, the Scrooge turned away and went back to sit behind his desk. "I've fired assistants for way less, but I guess you're my exception too. I don't understand why either."

"Because it's the right thing?" I asked.

"Or because between losing my first assistant to a surprise vacation and my manager to the flu, I can't afford to send you packing."

"Save the sugar for my employee review," I said dryly. "Now, do you want to call your kids, or should I?"

"Frost."

"Yeah?"

"Get out."

"Aye, aye, sir." I mock saluted.

It was a wondrous sight.

Holiday cheer had not felt whole to me for many years. That's just what happened when you learned that the catch with the "the season of miracles" is that seasons change. And as such, those miraculous feelings in people aren't the truth; they're a temporary state of grace. But as I watched dozens of bright-eyed volunteers take part in decorating the tall tree in the center of the plaza, my soul rose like a soufflé in the oven and the cynical thoughts that sometimes snuck up on me were silenced in favor of the hope that drove me when I first started this job.

I swayed to the Christmas music playing from plaza speakers as I ensured there were still plenty of toppings at the hot cocoa stand. Jay had sent me to oversee things alone for a few hours before the tree lighting. I couldn't have been happier with the assignment. My spirit hadn't felt this strong in a while.

The sun would be going down soon and the final touches

were going up. "A little to the left!" I called, waving to the crane operator who had donated his machinery and time as he positioned the star on top of the tree. "Left! Left! Up! Perfect!" I gave him the thumbs up.

"Where do you think this should go?" a five-year-old girl in an orange vest asked me, holding up a bauble.

"How about here?" I said, strutting over to the tree and pointing at a bare branch. "Let me help you." I picked her up so she could attach the ornament herself.

"Thanks!" she said as I set her down.

The twinkle lights around the lampposts and storefronts in the plaza powered on as the clock struck five o'clock. Lou from the Parks Department came over to stand next to me and admire the tree. "Everything looks great, Frost. How are you feeling?"

"I hope it's not too on the nose if I say merry," I replied. "If you can believe it, in all my years I can't remember ever helping decorate a Christmas tree. This was a win-win situation."

"You can say that again," Lou replied. "The community got a two-for-one thanks to your ideas—the tree lighting and the act of coming together to create something beautiful. That's real Christmas Spirit. And as a bonus, we saved a ton of money not paying people to do the work for us. All thanks to you and Jay."

"Glad we could help," I replied. "I'm grateful that Jay has such a wide reach on social media. To get so many volunteers with a twenty-four-hour notice is impressive."

"The guy is likeable," Lou said. "I know we're a year out, but I'm going to vote for him. That Farah woman rubs me the wrong way."

"I don't know enough about her to take a stance. I only know Jay, and he has . . . potential."

"Frost!"

Speak of the politician.

"It's him!" one of the volunteers shouted. People swarmed Jay with excitement. He happily shook hands and chatted amicably, looking individuals in the eye and smiling warmly as he moved through the crowd.

"Everything looks amazing," he said, joining Lou and me. "Thank you for letting me be a part of this, Lou. To be honest, when I was a kid, I always wanted to hit the big red button that turned this thing on."

"Today, my good man, you will live that dream," Lou said with a chuckle.

"Actually, maybe not." Jay's gaze focused on something past me. He tilted his chin to indicate where I should look. Coming toward us were Kamie and Kingsley. Celia and another man— Eddie, I presumed—walked behind them.

"Daddy!" Kamie ran to Jay; Kingsley followed. Jay embraced them and then with a hand on each of their shoulders readdressed Lou. "I was hoping my kids could turn on the tree."

Kamie's and Kingsley's faces lit up. "Really?" they said in unison.

"Of course," Lou replied. "We'll do it at five fifteen on the dot. Come over to the stage when you're ready. Looks like the news crew is here; I gotta get them sorted." He patted my arm and started herding the volunteers. "Come on, people. Grab your cocoa and whip out your phones; it's almost time!"

Celia and the man reached us. "Hello, Jay. Hello, Frost. This is my husband, Eddie."

"Nice to meet you," Eddie said, shaking my hand. The guy wore thick glasses a lot like Bismaad's, though his probably had a prescription. His mustache was tasteful and his purple sweater worked well with the collared shirt he had on underneath.

"Thanks for inviting us, Jay," Eddie said.

"I invited the kids, Eddie," Jay replied. "I offered to send my car for them."

The estranged adults stared at each other. My skin crawled with discomfort. "Egads, this is awkward," I blurted.

They looked at me.

Kingsley snickered.

"Shall we go light a Christmas tree?" I suggested, throwing a thumb in the direction of the stage.

"Whoo!" Kingsley punched his fist in the air. I wasn't sure if it was enthusiasm or sarcasm, but he clearly felt weird about his parents' face-off too and seemed glad I'd broken the tension.

Kamie took my hand. It was super adorable and I didn't shy away from it. Despite my disinclination to letting people in general close, I'd always had a soft spot for kids; it was all my time at the orphanage. I felt protective of their innocence and found being around their optimism invigorating and uplifting, especially considering I had so little left. The longer you stayed alive the harder it was to keep that spark going.

The two of us waved for the others in our party to follow. We made our way to the stage as Lou addressed the assembled crowd. "Thank you to all the volunteers for your hard work. The lights on this tree may only last the month, but moments like this—when we come together for nothing more than a desire to spread joy—last in our hearts forever. Let's thank the man that helped raise the funds to make this possible; please welcome gubernatorial candidate Jay Nichols and his family!"

Everyone clapped, including Celia and Eddie. Jay led Kamie and Kingsley onto the stage where Lou waited with the control box for the lights of the tree—one ridiculously huge red button, as hoped.

"On three," Jay told his kids. "One, two, three!"

The trio slammed their hands down on the button and the Christmas tree powered to its celestial form—a beaming creation of light, ribbon, ornament, and tinsel.

The crowd cheered and I experienced that soufflé-of-the-soul feeling again.

Celia leaned closer to me. "How is it going with Jay?" she asked genuinely.

I turned. "It's fine," I replied.

"I'm sorry if my appearance at the school the other day threw him off," Celia said. "I only wanted to speak with him personally. Had I known Annie was sick, I would have come to the office. That little woman never lets me anywhere near Jay. I don't know if that's her agenda or his though."

"I can guess," Eddie said.

"Mommy!" Kamie and Kingsley appeared beside us.

I glanced back. Jay was speaking to a reporter while spectators filmed on their phones and took flashing pics.

"Dad got busy," Kingsley said, reading my mind.

"I'm sure he'll be back with you soon," I said.

Kingsley shook his head. "Doubtful. We asked him if he wanted to come to dinner with us and Mom and Eddie, and he got all distant saying he was too busy. He jumped at the interview like it was a life vest."

"He gets all mad just because we want everyone to be together." Kamie sniffed. "I don't understand. He liked us a minute ago when we were lighting the tree."

"Oh, honey, your dad likes you. He loves you," Celia tried. "He just . . . has trouble getting away from his responsibilities. But we're all really proud of him, aren't we?"

The kids nodded.

Celia turned to me. "Frost, please tell Jay we're heading out. And tell him I'll need an answer about Christmas Eve."

"All right," I said.

The group turned to leave, but Kamie stopped and walked up to me. "We're baking cookies as a family on Friday after school at our house," she said. "You're Daddy's special helper. Maybe you can get him to come?"

I bent to look her in the eye. "I'll try my best."

"That's what Dad always says," Kingsley muttered.

The family strode away from the plaza. Jay didn't even notice. Or maybe he was trying not to. After all, he'd driven them away.

For the rest of the evening, the contrasting image of Jay's wide campaign smile and the disappointed faces of his kids remained at the forefront of my brain. It haunted me enough to motivate a late-night visit to Jay's condo. A spectral visit anyway.

At quarter past eleven, I used my powers to beam to my Scrooge's private dwelling.

In addition to the magic I utilized to activate my charm bracelet, my "present" powers allowed me to teleport Jay to any three moments currently happening in the present—wherever and whoever they involved. That use of my power was for the final Scrooging, like Brandon and Midori's respective trips to the past and future. However, my colleagues and I could use our magic in other ways leading up to Christmas week. My powers, for example, were designed to easily teleport me anywhere in the present where my Scrooge currently was, *and* teleport back to my magical home base (i.e. my loft).

When I arrived in Jay's condo, he was in his kitchen—tie loosened, inspecting the innards of a mostly empty fridge. In my ghostly blue form he couldn't see or hear me.

I'd come on a mission, but found myself compelled to snoop for a minute. The place was relatively tidy and uninspired—no Christmas decorations. A simple black leather couch and pewter coffee table faced the TV. Jay's kitchen cabinets were stocked with different cereals and protein powders.

The first room down the hall was an extra bedroom furnished with bunk beds (the bottom one girlie with a flower comforter and the top bunk more boyish with a dinosaur comforter). Gym equipment and storage boxes filled three corners of the room. Not a good sign, but it checked out with what I knew about Jay's relationship with his kids.

I moved on, then stopped in my tracks upon entering Jay's large home office. It had the most personality of any room in his home. Floor-to-ceiling shelving on two walls was devoted to books and records. The rest of the wall space was decorated with vintage movie posters, several of which I had hanging in my dorm at the CCD. I wandered over and ran my ghostly hand across one of the posters in a daze. The guy had good taste. I gave him bonus points for being cultured, but negative points for the complete lack of Christmas décor.

I proceeded to his master bedroom, then to the closet.

"Holy holiday, that's a lot of suits and ties," I muttered.

It took me a while of poking around, but eventually I found the blazer Jay had been wearing the day we visited Kamie and Kingsley's school.

Even in my intangible and invisible ghost state, if I concentrated on an object I could pick it up. Then I could spread my powers to coat it the same way that Brandon extended his magic over people when he wanted to take others to the past with him.

I found the Christmas week schedule Celia had given Jay stuffed in his blazer pocket. I spread my magic over the document and held it tight. Suddenly I heard music coming up the hall. I drifted back to the living room. Jay had poured himself a glass of milk in a bourbon tumbler and turned on the record player in the corner. I didn't know the song, but I thought I recognized the voice from that car ride the other day. My Scrooge sat on his couch—listening to Billy Joel and drinking his glass of milk while staring off into space the way most stressed adults would absentmindedly drink whiskey.

Transfixed, I wandered closer and studied the aftermath of a man who was wearing himself out. The smiling politician's mask he'd displayed at the tree lighting was gone and I got a good look at his tired eyes. He seemed so sad. And it made me sad to watch him.

I shook my head curtly and stepped back.

I didn't want to be any more unprofessionally invested in him than I already was. Since I'd gotten what I came for, I teleported out of his home and back to my own. Upon arrival, I unfolded the paper in my pocket and had a gander at what I could work with.

"Annie! You're back. *Great* . . ." I faked a smile as Annie joined me backstage for the morning show Jay was scheduled to appear on.

"Try not to let your enthusiasm overwhelm you," Annie said, straightening her fitted argyle jacket.

I checked my watch. It was quarter to nine. They'd be going live soon. Jay sat in a chair, a make-up artist doing final touch-ups to adjust the shine on his forehead.

"So you're feeling all better?" I asked Annie.

She nodded. "I haven't been that sick since I got river flu as a kid. Someone up there must have it out for me."

Someone up there, someone right here . . .

In truth, I still felt torn about the matter. Part of me felt bad about giving Annie so many sick days, and yet I also wondered if maybe I should've used more magic to make the illness last longer. I thought I'd made some progress with Jay, and with her reintroduction to the group I wasn't sure how our dynamic would be affected.

"And you didn't help matters." Annie glared. "Going rogue, letting your feelings get in the way of your job, not sticking to the schedule, forcing Jay off his path."

"I didn't force him off his path, Annie. I tried to help him stay true to it. You and I have very different opinions of what is best for him."

"That's where you're wrong." She pivoted to face me, somehow looking down on me though I was half a foot taller. "I don't have opinions about what is best for Jay. Not Jay the person, anyway. I was hired to do a job—get him elected. I'll do that job and operate in its interests first and foremost. If people need help with their morality or personal happiness, they go to a therapist. If people want to get into office, they come to me."

"Ten minutes!" one of the producers called into her headset. She glanced at her clipboard before coming over to me and Annie. "Would you ladies like to go to the viewing area with the seated guests? You can watch from the private box."

"No. We'll watch from here," Annie said. She glared at me one more time before striding toward Jay.

"Excuse us," I said politely to the producer, then followed Annie.

The make-up artist did a final brush dab and left Jay. He was reviewing notecards diligently as we approached.

"Do you need those?" I asked. "I've heard you speak; you're good on your feet, articulate, and smart. Just answer from your heart and you'll be fine."

"What are you, a greeting card?" Annie asked.

Jay's mouth opened to respond, but whatever sentence he was

about to form got replaced with a very curt curse word when he looked past me. I cringed; I wasn't fond of crude language. Annie and I wheeled around. Farah Jaffrey stood in the backstage area, speaking to the hostess of the show as a producer adjusted the microphone on her lapel.

Jay stomped over to them. Annie was on his heels. I was on hers.

"What is the meaning of this?" Annie demanded before Jay could say anything.

The hostess, a brunette in her early forties wearing the amount of makeup needed to pass for mid-thirties in LA, turned and smiled at us.

Hm, I wonder if she and Jay belong to the same prescription teeth whitening company?

"Good morning, Mr. Nichols, ladies. I'm Tiffany Thompson. You know Ms. Jaffrey." She gestured to Jay's rival.

"Happy Holidays, Jay," Farah said, dusting the sleeves of her royal blue suit jacket. "I'm excited to be here with you this morning."

"Our producer thought it would be good for ratings to invite Ms. Jaffrey to join us," said the hostess brightly. "As a bonus, your presence together is great promotion for your Christmas Eve debate."

"How does that affect the talking points you sent us last week?" Annie asked critically.

"Well, naturally we'll have to go off script." The hostess shrugged her bony shoulders, pronounced in her tight dress. "You can handle it though. It's not as if there is a script for running a state, and that's what you both hope to do next year."

"So true, Tiffany," Farah replied.

She and Jay sized each other up. She winked. I imagined steams of chimney smoke pouring out of Jay's ears.

"Three minutes," a producer came by, signaling with her fingers.

"See you out there," Farah said, following the producer to the stage left entrance.

"Annie," Jay said.

"Yes?"

"Fluorescents."

"On it." Annie took off down the hall.

I tilted my head at Jay.

"Softer light is more flattering," he explained. "When I go on TV with political rivals, Annie . . . convinces the lighting technicians to highlight my opponents with the least flattering lighting possible."

My eyes widened. "That's so . . . I don't even know the word for it."

"Genius?"

"Juvenile." I offered. I glanced at Farah, now on the other side of the set. "What exactly is your problem with Farah, apart from her being your political rival?"

"Farah represents everything I've always thought was wrong with government. She isn't running for governor because she wants to do something, it's because she wants to *be* something. She is only interested in politics because of what the right title could gain her if she plays her cards right—power, position, and money. We've been operating in proximity to each other for years and while her charisma and smiles can fool a lot of people, she can't fool me. She spends so much time in people's pockets I'm surprised she's not covered in lint."

"Welcome to TTFN!" The announcer's voice filled the space as the show broadcast to life. "Here's your host, Tiffany Thompson!"

Cheers flowed from the audience as the brunette strutted to

her cherry-colored, high-backed chair. Two smaller silver seats were positioned on either side of her throne.

"Thank you for joining us today," Tiffany said. "We have a special treat for you this morning. Our first guests are young and ambitious, and one of them will hold the fate of our state in their hands next year. Please give a round of applause for Farah Jaffrey and Jay Nichols!"

Jay took a deep breath and proceeded onto the carpeted stage. Farah entered from the opposite side. They waved at the audience, settling in their seats with wide smiles.

"Farah," Tiffany said. "Tell us, what does it mean to you to be in the running for the gubernatorial seat?"

"Well, it is humbling given how many great leaders have come before me, but encouraging because it shows how far we have come. If elected, I would be the first female governor of our state. That victory would be a symbol of diversity in government and women's empowerment that our country needs right now."

The crowd cheered.

"*I knew she'd get the word diversity in her first answer,*" Annie whispered cuttingly, appearing next to me.

"Why?" I whispered back.

"The diversity Jay brings to the table is part of what makes him a popular candidate. Farah is always trying to claim that position first so he sounds like a copycat if he replies similarly. His only move now is something unexpected."

"Jay," Tiffany pivoted. "Same question."

Jay raised his eyebrows at Farah. "You know, for a long time diversity has been a part of my headline—I check multiple boxes there and I am incredibly proud of my various cultural heritages. But if I get elected, I don't want that to be the first word people think of when they look back on my gubernatorial term. My actions, my character, and my experiences are what I want heading that resume. That's what everyone should want."

The audience applauded his response.

Tiffany and Farah exchanged a glance. When the clapping died down, the hostess readdressed Jay's rival with lots of energy. "Farah, I hear congratulations are in order. Your foundation for cancer research just went international."

"That is correct," Farah said. "My family has funded six children's hospitals across the country, but I wanted to make my own impact for this cause given my personal experience. As a thyroid cancer survivor, I count my blessings every day and work to help other people facing this battle."

Applause.

"Jay," Tiffany said. "I've recently been informed that your ex-wife Celia spent a year in rehab to recover from a drinking problem, during which time you filed for divorce."

Jay's face dropped.

"Do you ever feel bad for abandoning her during her time of need?"

Annie's eyes were wide as golf balls. "How did they find out about that?" she hissed.

Jay took a second to recuperate, then responded carefully. "My ex-wife's time in recovery is part of her personal journey. I don't discuss her business in public, except to say that I didn't abandon her. It didn't work out for us as a couple. We got a divorce. It's that simple."

No applause.

"Back to you, Farah." Tiffany turned in her chair. "What do you want the people to know about your leadership style?"

"I believe in giving the people what they want. It is a new day and it is time for a change. I would be honored to take the helm of ushering us into that."

"Jay," Tiffany said. Her demeanor shifted from bright and cheery to hostile and interrogative. "You've talked a lot in interviews about helping improve and sustain local businesses. Isn't it true that while you were working as a manager at a restaurant in college, the business—which had been operating for ten years—went bankrupt?"

"That diner was struggling for years," Jay responded more surly than normal, eyes narrowed. "I'd only been manager for three months when the owner decided to close."

"Farah," Tiffany said. "Any special plans for Christmas?"

"Well"—she touched her hand to her chest like she was a gushing Southern belle—"I am extremely excited that Jay and I will be appearing in our first debate on Christmas Eve. But on Christmas Day, I look forward to spending time with family, watching movies, and drinking hot cider. Assuming we have a Christmas Day that isn't over seventy-five degrees again."

The audience laughed.

"Do you have a favorite Christmas movie?" Tiffany followed up.

"Definitely *Home Alone*," Farah responded. "It warms my heart with feelings of family and forgiveness every time."

"Oh, absolutely," Tiffany responded. "I am a sucker for *Home Alone 2*. Every year when I watch it, I am reminded of our ability to do good, and the importance of love and family." Tiffany smiled warmly before switching her attention back to my boss.

"So, Jay, being governor means you will have an important seat on the national stage. Tell us what you think of our country's current employment situation in respect to the last decade, and how you would raise the economic success of our state in relation to those factors."

Annie and I exchanged a look. For once, we were both feeling and thinking the same thing.

The interview went on like that for another ten minutes. It didn't matter what kind of lighting the technicians used on Farah, Tiffany's softball questions put her in the best figurative light possible. Meanwhile, the hostess skewered Jay with queries that were extremely tough and invasively personal.

When the segment ended and the show went to commercial, Jay and Farah left the stage from opposite sides. Jay didn't say anything to me or Annie at first when he joined us. He watched Tiffany like a hawk, waiting for her to come backstage.

"What the heck was that?" he said to her angrily when she did.

"What do you mean?"

"You fed Farah easy questions to make her look good and had negative spins built into every question you directed at me."

"*Jay*," Tiffany said patronizingly. "Usually people who think their stories are being spun are seen as complainers—and more guilty—so I wouldn't get too hung up on this. Recover. Prepare better for next time. And if you're going to take on a rival, make sure you bring more ammo than they do." She shot a glance at Farah, who was exiting with her manager and assistant.

"You should have treated them both equally," I protested.

Tiffany turned her appraising eyes to me and scoffed. "Honey, I'm in the business of ratings. Ratings require human interest. And humans like to pick sides—hero versus villain, progressive versus old-school, cool and collected versus hot-tempered wild card. Farah gave me what I needed to assign those roles between her and your boss today." She pivoted to Jay. "My advice is that you take a page from your opponent's playbook and plan the way she does for these appearances, dirt and all. Otherwise, when the new year comes around, the roles I put you in today could become the roles the public puts you in permanently."

The backstage lights flashed.

Tiffany straightened her posture and smiled widely. "That's my cue. We're coming back from commercial. Thank you for being on my show. I hope we do this again. Merry Christmas."

She turned away from us. Annie and Jay glared daggers at her.

My emotions burst through the barrier I used to control them. Tiffany walked out on stage, waving at the audience as she approached her chair. I took a step back, quickly glanced around to make sure no one was watching me, then snapped my fingers. The banana charm on my bracelet dissolved into glitter. A second later, Tiffany experienced a Three Stooges–level fail. As soon as the LIVE sign lit up, she tripped on something invisible and launched forward spectacularly—falling face-first onto the stage. Her heavy make-up would surely leave a stain on the carpet from the way she plowed into it.

"*Merry Christmas, you filthy animal,*" I muttered under my breath.

Jay was notably less animated in the days that followed. Getting embarrassed on that morning show was rough, but it was Tiffany's "advice" that bothered him. I ghost eavesdropped on several private conversations he had with Annie, listening to them argue about what he should and shouldn't have said, and how they should and shouldn't proceed.

Narwhals, I wish Annie hadn't returned.

I felt like the time I'd spent alone with Jay had allowed me to nudge him toward better choices. Now he was more vulnerable. He was at a tipping point, and I could no longer go rogue in my Scrooge duties to influence the scale. For one, with Annie the guard dog back at her post it would be way more difficult, and if she caught me I would *definitely* be fired. Past that, I was pushing my luck. Though my soul compelled me to intervene with Jay, I was lucky—*and shocked*—that Specter One hadn't found out about my first firing mishap. My magical boss had an omnipresent way of knowing things. Whatever the reason I had escaped his vigilance this time, I doubted a second issue would go unnoticed.

And so, for the coming days I aimed to limit my ghostly efforts to what they were supposed to be: observe, take note, and prepare a CCD plan that treated Jay like he was already too lost to change on his own. Maybe he hadn't been when I started, but every day that went by I felt him taking steps in the wrong direction. The "different" kind of man and assignment I thought he'd been was disappearing. The morning show was a big push; Thursday night made his path to Scroogedom seem almost inevitable.

It was half past eight and my ghostly form stood outside of a restaurant on La Cienega Boulevard. Patrons in fine attire waited to be seated by the host. I skipped the line and phased through the smartly dressed clientele, several waiters, and a wall until I found Jay's party in a corner booth at the back—very old-timey mafia movie.

Jay's dinner with Friedman's Election Consulting was an intimate gathering consisting of my boss, two men in their sixties, and one in his fifties. The roomy booth had plenty of space to spare. I slid next to Jay on one side and leaned my spectral elbows on the table as I watched the exchange.

"I don't know how you expect me to respond to this," Jay said.

"In a word, wisely," said the guy in his fifties—trimmed salt-and-pepper beard, crisp wool sport coat.

"Farah may have handed me my face on a silver platter on TV, but I don't want to stoop to her level."

"So your whole plan is to beat her by taking the moral high ground?" one of the older gentlemen scoffed. He was overweight and, judging from the mountain of food in front of him, unashamed of it. "Good luck with that." He put a forkful of steak in his mouth.

"Look, Jay," said Salt-and-Pepper Beard. "Farah is bad for the people. You know it and we know it, but she's smart enough to make sure the people don't. The woman comes from a family of politicians and one percenters. She understands how to use her resources and cunning to pull the magician's gambit—distract people with something splashy while her real intentions are unfolding elsewhere. We paired you with Annie because she knows how to play the game to win. And you want to win. Not just for your own sake, but everyone else's."

"You've done well until recently," said the other older guy. His facial features were sharp and his glasses were round and small, similar to something Harry Potter might wear. "You have followed our advice and Annie's for how to talk to people—giving assurances without making commitments, endearing the public while looking out for your political interests. Now it's time to sink into the trenches. What that Tiffany woman told you is accurate—the media assigns roles in elections. If you don't want to be demolished next year, you have to fight fire with fire and get as much negative press about Farah out there as possible."

Jay shook his head, unconvinced. "It was one show."

"Exactly," said Salt-and-Pepper Beard. "In one fifteen-minute segment, Farah managed to label you as a man who abandoned his wife, a questionable leader, and someone who gets hot under pressure. If she can do that so easily this early in your campaign, you are doomed."

Jay gulped. "But I—"

"No more beating around the bush, Jay," interrupted Bespectacled Man. "Friedman's has invested a lot of time and money in you, and if you want that to continue, here are your marching orders. Stop questioning Annie at every turn. Let our people investigate Farah. Once we find skeletons in her closet, or at least dust that may seem sinister in the right light, we'll use that to paint *her* as the villain and you as the obvious choice next year. In the meantime, you need to make a public statement that officially distances you from your ex-wife and her former troubles."

"I already keep my distance," Jay said. "Her recovery is personal; she'll hate me for using it publicly for my own self-preservation."

"So?" countered Salt-and-Pepper Beard. "You hate her, don't

you? She took your kids from you. She replaced you in their eyes with that stuffy executive. Why do you care?"

Jay didn't reply.

The hefty guy stabbed his fork into his steak again and left it there like an axe in a tree stump. He signaled a passing waiter for the check and then turned to Jay. "Kid, we picked you because we thought you checked all the right boxes to get somewhere. You've worked hard and are a nice guy, but nice is not something anyone in the big leagues cares about. If you want to really do this, you need to stop behaving like the naïve college grad you used to be. The world is hard. You need to be hard. Or you could cut ties with us now and go back to losing for the rest of your life."

The waiter delivered the check and the hefty guy put it in front of Jay. "Let us know your decision tomorrow. Tonight is on you. Consider it backpay for how much we've built you up already. After all, where would you be if not for us? Making homemade pamphlets about your ideas and putting up posters with a staplegun?" He and the others laughed as they made their way out of the booth.

The three men left Jay without another word. I continued to sit beside him, silent and still, just like him. I think we were both wondering what came next.

"Hey . . ." I said timidly as I knocked on Jay's office door, poking my head in.

Friday had come and gone. I hadn't had the chance to talk with Jay one-on-one at all. Annie had assigned me a sizable project, which took me the whole day.

Multiple times I had considered finding an excuse to go see Jay, but the woman was ever-watchful and told me to leave him alone. I didn't even get to bring him his lunch like always; the delivery guy had more face time with my boss today than I did.

Maybe it was for the best. Having space from Jay for the day allowed me to think carefully about my next move. With Annie in the middle of a phone meeting in one of the other offices, now was my final chance to act on it.

"Frost, what do you need?" Jay didn't look up from his computer. His distraught expression had remained in place since last night. His voice was empty and tone dull, as if I were talking to an automated GPS.

"I brought you coffee." I crept in and placed a steaming cup on his desk. "I can put in a dinner order for you if you want; it's getting late and I'm not sure how long you plan on staying tonight. I also completed the research you requested on community programs that lost funding in the past five years." I slid the thick folder in front of him, noticing a white box on his desk tied with a candy cane striped ribbon.

"Thanks," he said, glancing up briefly before continuing to stare at his screen. "I don't need dinner. I'm not hungry. You can clock out early if you want."

I nodded and pointed at the wrapped package. "Someone give you a present?"

"What?" His eyes flicked to the box and he shook his head. "Kamie and Kingsley baked cookies with Celia and Eddie today. Kamie wanted me to have some, even though I couldn't make it. Eddie's assistant dropped them off half an hour ago."

"That was today," I realized with dismay. I'd been so preoccupied I had forgotten.

"Yup," he said.

"You were too busy to steal away a couple of hours?"

"What other reason would I have for not going?" he said sternly.

"You tell me."

He looked at the box again. "Can you take them actually? I'm not in a cookie mood."

"But your kids baked them."

"*Frost.*"

I picked the box up and cradled it under my arm. "So . . . I guess I'll head home then."

"Fine. See you Monday." He went back to his computer.

I turned for the door, but hesitated. "Jay . . ."

"Hm?" He didn't look up.

"There's really nothing else I can do to help you, is there?"

"I don't think so, Frost. You know your job. Stick to that."

My soul sank—not dramatically like a ship, but slowly like a deflating balloon.

"Yeah. I'll do that."

On Friday nights, I usually couldn't wait to jump in my inter-dimensional bathroom elevator and return to the CCD. Tonight, I stalled.

At quarter to eight, I paced around the loft uneasily. Marley sat in front of our magical exit door—watching me move from one side of the room to the other.

Eventually, I huffed. "I'll be back in a few minutes, Marley."

I closed my eyes, squeezed my fists, and suddenly I was some-where else. Honing in on Jay, my present powers had transported me to his office; evidently he still hadn't left. Everyone else had though, resulting in a darkened downstairs area and a sole bright stream of light coming from where my Scrooge dwelled.

My spectral blue body glided forward. Jay looked surreal through the glass walls of his office—seated at his desk in the glowing room surrounded by darkness.

I drifted closer and passed through the wall. He wasn't on the computer. He wasn't on the phone. He wasn't working at all. Jay lay back in his chair with his hands folded over his chest as he stared at the ceiling.

After a moment, he sat forward. He glanced at the Christmas tree bobble I'd put on his desk and flicked it once before picking up his landline phone and punching in a number.

"Jake Friedman, please. It's Jay Nichols."

Oh no.

The pit in my stomach that had been there since last night's dinner carved out more, like a spoon scooping out the contents of an avocado, leaving nothing but the shell.

"Jake. It's Jay. I thought about what you and the partners said, what you want from me." He paused a moment and closed his eyes. "You've got it."

I hung my head as my spirit accepted the state of things. Jay was right; I did know my job. My intervening had been an interesting side project, and for a moment I did think I was making a difference to him, but in the end it seemed that all roads led home. Jay *had* been unlike other assignments. As Bismaad noted, he wasn't technically a Scrooge yet because I had arrived before he made the choices that would cement his dark path. *He still had so much good in him.* I suppose I felt compelled to interfere because of that goodness. Try to save him before he became like the cynical, self-involved men and women I'd helped before. Sadly, none of my machinations appeared to have diverted Jay from his destiny as a Scrooge. He was going farther down that road every time I looked. I couldn't stop it any more than I could stop my previous Scrooges from reverting back to who they were before.

With another magic flash I returned to my apartment. Nothing to do now but prepare for the end game. I couldn't believe I had let myself get pulled off course—distracted, fascinated, and emotionally compromised because Jay was different. And yet . . . I understood why.

I had a deep desire to believe that people could really change, even if so many of my Scrooges had proven otherwise, and despite the doubt that had grown in my spirit over a century of watching how selfish and cruel people can be. *Given that*, I think the notion that maybe I could stop Jay from going bad had not only compelled me to try, but projected my need for spiritual renewal upon him. Perhaps if I could keep him from becoming a true Scrooge, I could prevent him from backtracking like the already damaged people I'd worked with did. He could change and *stay changed* with my help. I had seen him as an opportunity to renew my faith in Christmas, and in humanity.

Sigh.

Maybe I'd been around too long and seen too many of people's flaws for such faith to legitimately still be a possibility for me.

I sat on the edge of my couch—clawing my nails against my palm. Marley came over and sniffed me with concern. He licked my knee. I smiled softly and patted him in thanks.

In an effort to not get dragged under further by depression, I took out my phone and began scrolling through Tinsel. Allan had posted a picture of his Scrooge's grandkids with the status update: *"FEELING JOLLY"* #holidayvibes. Mezra's latest update read: *"It's Beginning to Look A Lot Like the Weekend!"* Jeremy had posted pics of the goods offered at his Scrooge's bakery with the caption: *"Life is what you bake it."*

I opened the post function on the app and my thumb hovered hesitantly over the keyboard. Then I updated my status the only way I knew how.

"FEELING HO HO HOPELESS"

With a sigh, I put my phone face down on the table and stood up.

"I'm going out, Marley," I said.

I grabbed my bag, then made my way to street level. I needed some fresh air, or LA's equivalent anyway. Hands in my pockets, I wandered the sidewalks. Occasionally I passed people wearing festive Christmas attire or carrying shopping bags. Restaurant windows glistened with twinkle lights, boughs of holly, and ostentatious bows. High up in apartment windows, the occasional Christmas tree or glowing string of lights twinkled. The city— once my city—for all its metals and cements looked warm, whereas I felt colder than I ever had.

After a while, I hailed a passing cab and caught a ride to the local movie theater.

"Which movie?" the teenager at the counter asked.

"Whichever one starts next," I replied.

"Is this really the answer?"

I'd been distracted, but now I locked eyes with the pale, pimply adolescent. His glasses were square, and crumbs dotted the corner of his mouth from the small tub of chocolate chip cookies beside him.

"Sorry?" I said.

"Spur of the moment ticket for one? Seems to me like you're running from something. Or you just don't want to be alone with your thoughts. Maybe hiding in a dark theater with the distraction of fiction isn't the answer?"

At first, I was surprised. Then my eyes narrowed. "Thanks for the advice, but I only have enough for the movie, not a therapy session." I shoved the money at him and took the ticket.

Can't a ghost wallow without strangers judging her for it?

With my stub, a soda, and a bag of popcorn, I proceeded into the darkened sanctum just as the previews were finishing. The movie began and the familiar, placating light of the big screen spilled over my face. I absentmindedly crunched on my snack.

"Frost."

I jumped in my seat with a yelp. People farther down my row shushed me.

"*Specter One*," I whispered. I glanced around then readdressed my true boss, who'd appeared in the seat beside me. "What are you doing here?"

He didn't answer the question. Instead, he grabbed a handful of popcorn from my bag and pointed at the screen. "Is this a good one?"

"I, uh . . ." My brain short-circuited as I watched my ghostly employer eat popcorn and stare at the picture ahead. I had been *extremely* surprised that he hadn't called me into his office or scolded me in any fashion for getting temporarily fired, but that had been a week ago, and I had gotten my job back almost immediately. To get a visit from him now was shocking, *especially* considering I'd never seen him on Earth before.

"Sir, should you be here? I mean, what if someone notices how . . . magical you look?" I alluded to the sparkles on his cheekbones, silvery swirls of his hair, and translucent irises.

"It's Los Angeles, Frost," he replied. "I'm sure people have seen stranger."

Fair point.

He reached over and took a sip of my soda. Evidently since we were both dead, he wasn't worried about germs.

"I considered calling you into my office after last week," Specter One said in a low voice, continuing to look at the screen. "But I thought talking to you on your turf would make you more receptive to the feedback I have."

He chewed and swallowed. "You have been going rogue with Jay Nichols."

I tensed. "I have."

"Did you get what you hoped for out of it?"

"No . . ." The answer deflated me and I leaned back in my chair. "I'm sorry, Specter One. I thought I could help him in a different way—fix him before he broke. I thought if I did, I wouldn't lose him long term like the others. I shouldn't have done it."

"That's correct," Specter One said. "You put your entire mission and your retirement at risk by wasting time trying to fix him preemptively instead of dedicating your full attention to creating his Christmas Carol experience. I only hope that lost time and focus doesn't cost us his soul. Or yours, for that matter. Mr. Nichols has to demonstrate a true change of heart by midnight on Christmas Eve to be successfully Scrooged and generate the magic that your existence—and in this case, your reincarnation—is dependent on."

"He'll get there," I assured. "I may have lost focus, but I'm past interfering and I can still get the job done."

"I'm worried that both those things may be untrue." Specter One finally angled to look at me. His eerie ice cube eyes reflected the colors on the movie screen. "I suspect your connection with Mr. Nichols may be deeper than you truly understand."

Apparently unafraid of being discovered, Specter One snapped his fingers and with a tiny burst of golden sparks, a notecard appeared in his hand. He gave it to me.

"No space of regret can make amends for one life's opportunity misused."

A quote from *A Christmas Carol.*

"Specter One, why would you—" I glanced up, but he was gone.

12

In the kitchen of my loft, I marked a tally on the whiteboard under the words: *"MOVIES SEEN THIS SEASON."* I was up to four. Not great, but maybe I could squeeze in another before Christmas. Hopefully in my next life I'd have more time to pursue this passion.

With Marley in one arm and Jay's box of cookies in the other, my realm-evator took off. We shot upward, the transport shaking as its walls glowed with jagged bolts of red and green.

5, 6, 7, 8, 9, 10, 11, and . . . 12.

DING!

The lift halted and the doors glided open. "Welcome back to the CCD, Miss Mason," the intercom said. I put Marley on the ground and we proceeded to my office. Once settled, I placed the box of cookies down, slung the briefcase off my shoulder, and emptied its files onto my desk. From there I made my way around the room and gathered all other files I had on Jay—strewn on my coffee table, bookshelf, even the fireplace mantle—then put those on the desk too. When everything was laid out like a secretarial avalanche I put my hands on my hips and sighed.

"Okay, let's get to work."

"We have one sample charm left," Specter Nine said. "Would anyone else like to share with the class?"

"I will!" Bismaad declared, sticking her hand in the air. Specter

Nine nodded and my friend stood, smoothing her thick-belted midi dress and adjusting her double braids.

Specter Nine handed her the most powerful charm we used. This was not included in our basic magic set, nor was it another miscellaneous, first-come-first-serve charm up for grabs when we reloaded in preparation for Christmas week. This was something terribly unique.

"Okay," Bismaad said when she arrived front and center. "So for my dramatic entrance tomorrow night, I was thinking a little shake and bake action. Observe."

Bismaad snapped her fingers and the charm dissolved into glitter. My friend took a deep breath and closed her eyes. When she reopened them, they were fruit punch blue and shone like meteors. Her braids floated away from her body as tinkling, high-pitched bells rang deafeningly through the class. The entire room started to shake. As the rumbling escalated, so did the volume of the unseen bells. Suddenly, the perimeter of the room erupted in sapphire blue flames. Parts of the ceiling fell. Cracks fractured the walls, then—*FLASH!*—it was all gone. The flames vanished, the ceiling and walls magically repaired themselves, and the shaking stopped.

Bismaad's eyes returned to normal, and she clasped her hands together and popped her heel out. "Ta-da!"

The class clapped.

"Excellent, Miss Hansra," said Specter Nine. "Your use of the elements is exemplary and your fear-to-discomfort ratio is greatly improved from last season."

Bismaad curtseyed as our ghostly colleagues applauded again.

"Your grand entrance charm allows for total magical manipulation of your environment for up to five minutes," Specter Nine reminded. "Unlike your other charms, which have one specific use, keep in mind that these can *be* and *do* anything;

they are only limited by your focus and your imagination, so I advise that you plan ahead like Miss Hansra clearly has. And remember, the most important thing to consider when planning a grand entrance"—Specter Nine pivoted and began writing on the board—"is to get your Scrooges to FREAK THE GEEK OUT." She underlined the four words she had written. "Most people do not believe in magic or spirits. And *these* people, your Scrooges, are used to calling the shots in their own lives. You have to get their attention, and get them to take you seriously."

My friend slipped back into her seat beside me.

"So, class," our teacher continued, "as we wrap up our last session of the season, I want to end with this advice. Be careful not to let anyone but your Scrooge witness you using magic. Keep your Scrooge at a distance; they're not meant to see behind the curtain of how or why we do things. Never let them feel like they can escape what is happening to them. And lastly, have fun with it!" She clapped twice. "Now go out there and scare the pants off some people then shove their hearts full of Christmas Spirit. Happy Holiday Haunting, everyone! Come see me at the front for your grand entrance charm."

We applauded a final time then journeyed toward the front of the room, falling in line with the other Ghosts of Christmas Present. "You know," Bismaad whispered to me. "I totally get why you weren't in a place to talk about it last week, but I would still love the details on your history with the Santas."

"It's not that big a deal," I replied in a hushed tone. "You know I've always liked kids. I met our current Claus's father Kris when he was a child. We got along well and bonded over the years. It was the same thing with the Santa you met, Nick, and Paul. I didn't actively go out trying to be friends with them; it just sort of happened."

"Santa implied you used to be closer than you are now," Bismaad prodded as we moved closer to the front.

"We were," I admitted. "But a time came when I realized with his situation it didn't make sense to stay that close. I pulled back. I didn't intend to become friends with Paul in the years that followed, but he was a weirdly persistent kid, and he had already known me for years before I tried to put distance between myself and his father. He liked me and kept coming to the CCD to find me—Christmas after Christmas. I couldn't shake him, so eventually I caved and we became friends, despite my best intentions."

"Your best intentions were to *not* make a lifelong friend?" Bismaad clarified, confused.

"Next." Specter Nine waved me forward.

"I'm done with this conversation, Bismaad," I replied—not harsh, but firm. I stepped up and held out my wrist. Specter Nine attached the grand entrance charm to my bracelet—a golden bauble in the shape of a fancy *YASS*, which stood for *You Are So Scrooged*.

I made my way to the lecture hall's exit. Bismaad caught up with me after receiving her charm. "I'll see you at the potluck tonight?"

"Oh, right. That. I should really concentrate on my mission, Bismaad. Goodness knows I strayed from the path enough these last few weeks."

Bismaad pouted. "Frost, you may not be keen on forming connections with people, but this may very well be the last week we ever see each other. I'd really like to make a few final memories with you. Please come and spend time with me." My friend's eyes looked like a dog's after you ate the last meatball without sharing a single bite.

I sighed. "Fine, I see your point. It *is* important we hang out while we still have the chance." I pulled out my phone and opened the group invite on Tinsel. Navigating to the food sign-up sheet, I wrote my name and added *"Cookies."*

Bismaad gave me a side hug and squealed with delight. "Yay! I'm so glad you're coming! We're going to talk and dance all night. Good luck with your team meeting. I'll see you later!"

We parted ways and I strode to my study room, mind on the mission. Today my team and I would put our final Scrooging plan together. Today we outlined the days that followed.

I was ready.

Jay's atypical Scrooge character had distracted me for a while, and stirred emotions I hadn't allowed myself to invest in this job for many years. I was over that now. I had to be over it. The more emotionally removed I was from my Scrooge, the better chance I had of engineering a concrete, secure plan of attack. If I just did the job and looked at Jay as what he was—a case I'd been appointed to—I could check all the boxes of our Christmas Carol formula, get to the finish line of this weird afterlife, and finally return to Earth for another chance at being human.

I grabbed the door handle of the Partridge Room.

Time to shine. Or at the very least, time to punch Jay in the face with a classic Christmas reawakening. This would be another methodical plan for another Scrooge who was nothing more to me than an assignment.

I gulped at the thought, like my subconscious had sent a wad of reconsideration up my throat.

He's just another Scrooge, I restated firmly in my mind. *You can't care about him. Just get the job done.*

I pushed the door open and addressed my team. "Let's nail this guy."

"How is it possible to be this tired?" Brandon said, his head in his hands. We'd been in the study room for hours—the efforts of our labor evident everywhere in the forms of notes, ideas, and timelines. Our table was buried in documents and we had plenty more taped to the wall. To an outsider, this level of elaborate scheming would suggest we were planning a break-in at the Smithsonian.

Midori reached out a bony hand and placed it on Brandon's arm. As always, she remained silent, but the compassion in her act was evident.

"I know it's a lot of work," I said to Brandon, joining Midori in her efforts to comfort him. "But this is the kind of detail that goes into a successful Scrooging. And we've come up with a smart plan. You should be proud. I know I am."

"Yeah," Brandon said, "but do we have enough time to make it work?"

I began taking our pages down from the wall. Brandon and Midori followed my lead as I continued. "The CCD did its due diligence when the agency came together. The Ghosts of Christmas Present begin the Scrooging exactly one week before Christmas Eve because it's the perfect amount of time to execute a Christmas Carol scenario—not too drawn out, but long enough for us to properly affect a Scrooge with our chosen visits to the past, present, and future."

With the last of the documents removed from the wall, I started gathering them and the papers on the desk into folders. "Trust me, Brandon, we'll be fine. We have our visits and their order set, and we've scheduled them perfectly around Jay's schedule to culminate on Christmas Eve. Like every other Scrooge before him, well before midnight on the 24th, he'll be putty in our hands and rejoicing in his new appreciation for love, mankind, blah, blah, blah."

I shoved the folders into my bag and glanced at my watch. It was already eight o' clock. "We were here a lot longer than I expected and that's my fault," I told the group. "I wasn't focused at our last meet up and that kept us from making more decisions earlier."

"It's fine, Frost," Brandon said, slinging on his backpack. "This is your final season. I'm sure you were just distracted by your magical retirement."

Yeah. Sure. That's what it was . . .

"Any chance as an apology you'll clue me and M in on the secret of what happens after you leave here?" He gave me a cheeky grin. Midori also looked at me with interest.

The kid's expression was compelling, but I'd broken enough rules this season—in regards to spilling the beans about retirement to Bismaad and Paul, and in a bunch of other ways.

"I'm not supposed to say, Brandon."

"*Please*," Brandon urged. "I asked Specter One about this last year *and* last week, and he told me not to worry about it."

I laughed slightly. "Yup, that sounds like him. Sorry, I'm not sharing either. I *can* tell you that it is a fantastic opportunity."

He huffed. "Something to look forward to after a hundred years, I guess."

I ruffled his ginger hair. "Exactly. Though if I were you, I would take it one Christmas at a time." I slung my bag over my shoulder then readdressed my teammates. "I'm getting up at dawn to line up at the equipment room. The better the charms I get, the more prepared I'll be. We can regroup at noon before I head back to Earth just in case we need to reconfigure the plan based on what charms I end up with, and to touch base in general."

"Go, team, go!" Brandon pumped his fist in the air.

"Love the enthusiasm," I said. "Now I have to go. I'm late for the Ghosts of Christmas Present Christmas Party. See you both tomorrow."

I scurried out of the room and to my office. My kooky Christmas sweater hung from a white wooden coat hook. The neck hole was tight, and as I struggled to get it on, I bumped my bookshelf roughly. Small thumps sounded behind me.

"Ow."

When I finally got my head and arms through the right holes, I noticed I'd hit the shelf so hard that some of the books had lurched forward and a couple of knickknacks had fallen on the floor. I straightened the former and picked up the latter. Then I stood before the mirror.

My sweater featured a giant unicorn throwing up candy. When I flipped a switch inside the sweater's sleeve, the candy flashed with bright lights.

Marley started to bark, startled by the special effects. "Calm down, boy. Here, I got you something too." I attached a set of glowing bells to his collar. "Don't you look fabulous."

I grabbed Jay's box of cookies, then Marley and I made our way to the Blitzen Ballroom, one of the CCD's larger venues. The room was packed with my colleagues. The ostentatious colors and prints of their holiday sweaters was enough to give a department store a stomach ache.

A bunch of glittery balloons floated above the dessert table, and I headed over to deposit Jay's cookies. When I opened the box, I discovered each treat was uniquely decorated. I plucked out a gingerbread woman—her hair and bow were made of frosting. Kamie's name was written on the cookie's torso in icing. The cookie underneath had Kingsley's name. The third cookie in the line up said *Daddy*.

My heart lurched. Sadness, regret, anger, and pity coursed through me as I looked at the cookies. Then I felt something worse—fear. More specifically, fear that I was feeling all these things. I was not supposed to care about Jay, not like this. That's what caused me to break away from my routine in the first place and interfere in Jay's life. I couldn't do that again so close to Christmas or I might blow the mission. That was not an option. And I'd literally just promised myself after talking to Specter One that I was over this, over deviating from the formula. The fact that something as silly as a sentimental cookie could draw me back in was—

"Frost, I'm surprised to see you here."

Allan leaned against the table. He wore a red argyle sweater embroidered with tiny gingerbread men under a tasteful tan blazer, a classy brown fedora atop his head. "I thought you would back out and go it alone like you always do."

"Excuse me for making work a priority," I replied.

He rolled his eyes. "Frost, come on. Work isn't a priority for you; it's a singularity. I still don't know how Bismaad or Paul Claus manage to ever get you out of your office now and then. Before I gave up on you, I must've asked you to hang out at least fifty times over the course of thirty years. But you always said no because you're stupidly determined to fly solo. Parties may as well be the plague to you."

"I didn't ask for your opinion of my afterlife choices, Allan. At least I followed instructions for *this* party. Unlike you. Is your wardrobe an interdimensional portal to the *Mad Men* costume department? This is a kooky sweater party. You don't need to look dapper all the time. We're dead. No one cares."

"Implying that you do, in fact, think I look dapper."

I ground my teeth. "I *think* you look like a ghost who takes my professional stance on relationships personally, and instead of accepting it, you throw shade."

He frowned. "Well, I guess you won't have to put up with that much longer."

"Here's hoping."

Allan snatched one of Jay's gingerbread cookies out of the box, bit its entire left arm off with a glare, then tromped away as Bismaad approached the table. Her sweater featured parasailing penguins. She did a double take at Allan's surly storm off.

"What happened there?" she asked.

"Just Allan being obnoxious. Nothing new."

"You never did tell me what went down between the two of you," Bismaad said, plucking a winterdoodle cookie from a platter and putting it on her plate. "I asked Allan once and he said you, quote, 'Prefer being the loneliest ghost of all time.' End quote." She took a bite of her cookie and shrugged. "Vague, but better than a lot of exposition I get from you. In the decades we've known each other you only mention details about your past sparingly, and I feel like years go by between the moments you do open up." She eyed me expectantly.

"I don't like to share, Bismaad."

"Don't I know it." She took another bite, still looking at me.

Her answer made me feel a little defensive. "I don't like to get too invested in people, okay? I never have. Plenty of ghosts have invited me to socialize over the last century—be in study groups, take part in winter activities, come to parties like this—and I always turned them down. Most ghosts take the hint after a few years, but Allan did not give up so easily. When he finally did realize I didn't want to be friends, he took offense. As if somehow me leaning into being alone was an affront to him."

"*Well* . . . in a way I can understand that," Bismaad said carefully. "I mean, you are not actually alone, so using that as an excuse to avoid those who are making an effort to connect with you could be seen as insulting."

I raised an eyebrow at her. "I *am* alone, Bismaad. If I wasn't, then my soul wouldn't be at the CCD, now would it? Relationships are a distraction from the truth." I stared at the floor, arms crossed. "And the pain of losing them is a great deterrent for avoiding close friends."

"Then why are you my friend?"

I glanced up.

Her inquisitive look bore into me. "It's true that you turn me down a lot when I try to include you in activities, but you do partake once in a while. And we have had plenty of good times together—we laugh, we talk, we listen to each other. It's been that way since I got here. Since the moment I shadowed you during my first season, you always made it a point to spend some personal time with me each year. It wasn't much at first, but over the years it's increased. I just never understood why. I didn't know if it was my place to ask, but I've wondered about it for a while. Why be open to being my friend, and Paul's, and no one else's?"

I raked my nails against my palm. "I already told you about Paul."

"Then what about me?"

I swallowed some guilt. "Let's just say you both are my exceptions."

"But—"

"Bismaad, can we please leave it at that?"

She chewed thoughtfully, eyeing me. Eventually she swallowed and put her plate down. "Fine. But only because I want to ask you about a matter weighing on me more dramatically. Since we're speaking of exceptions, I'm not usually the type to read too much into a social media post, but is there something you want to talk about?"

I frowned. "I'm not sure what you mean."

Bismaad whipped out her phone and held up the screen. It showed my latest Tinsel post.

"Wow that's a lot of comments and reactions," I replied.

"Well, of course, Frost. You're not alone here and people care about you succeeding. If you seem like you need help, we want to be there for you." She glanced at her phone. "I haven't been online since yesterday—too distracting given it's the last weekend before Scrooging begins. I turned it on tonight and saw this '*Ho Ho Hopeless*' post. What's up, girl?"

I shrugged. "It's nothing to worry about, I was venting. Jay had me hoping for a moment that maybe we could deviate from the normal Scrooge pattern. When I realized that hope was in vain, I felt pretty low. I'm over it now. I just needed to accept that while what we do here matters, things that matter don't always make a difference."

"I am sorry you feel that way, Frost," Bismaad replied steadily.

"Don't be," I answered. "I'll soon be reborn and I won't remember all the hopelessness about humanity I've come to learn over the last century."

Taking in my friend's face, I realized I'd bummed her out—a jerk move at a party. Specter One's note about my aloofness being a mask to cover the passion I'd buried came to mind. With each passing week my feelings had been bubbling over more and more, and I hadn't been able to contain them. Maybe after decades of keeping them sealed in jar, the building pressure of this job and my wrung-out soul were causing the jar to crack. Messy, unhelpful things were leaking out.

Bismaad forced a smile and recovered. She picked up her plate and put a hand on her hip. "No more sullen talk. Let's have fun, okay? I have to go judge the potluck's casserole contest, but I'll be back in ten minutes."

"You do you," I replied. "I'll find something to keep me busy."

She one-arm hugged me. I meekly returned the embrace with an awkward pat on her back. I was not a hugger. I hadn't had much practice, in life or the afterlife.

Bismaad scampered into the jolly crowds. I grabbed a bag of peppermint bark kettle corn and munched away as I wandered the room. Marley loyally remained two steps behind me. A few different ghosts tried to exchange pleasantries as I meandered, but I deflected them with amicable brief nods.

I had nothing against my colleagues; I just never saw a need to form connections with them. Our time at the CCD was supposed to be dedicated to our Christmas missions. And even though I had only recently learned the specifics of our retirement—like the orphanage—I always knew our time here was limited so what was the point of growing close?

There had been a period in the last century when I'd let that mentality fade somewhat where the Claus family was concerned. But after a difficult experience a couple decades ago, I'd been reminded of the repercussions of letting people close and had fully pushed Nick away after that. I wished I hadn't grown this close to Paul; it was unintentional. But thankfully my soul would soon be reborn and I wouldn't have to deal with the impacts of that mistake.

Things would be different when I started fresh with a family and the opportunity to love and be loved. For now, I was still Frost Mason. I was still the orphan girl who had not known what it was like to matter to anyone and who didn't want to relive the pain I experienced when I dared let people matter to me, even a little . . .

I gazed around at the gathering. Suddenly I felt overwhelmed and claustrophobic. Everyone around me was engaging in deep conversation, dancing, and cavorting. Things I was not used to doing and, frankly, things I didn't *want* to do.

I glanced down. "Marley, how would you feel about a movie in our room instead?" Marley wagged his tail and spun in a circle.

"Compelling argument." I took one more look at the party then nodded decisively. "This isn't for me. Maybe in the next life."

My dog and I escaped the gathering the way we came in and walked down the cold halls. Snow edged the windows like the thick icing on Jay's cookies. We strode through the isolated corridor with the warm glow of the party fading farther and farther into the background.

13

I gasped awake. It felt like I hadn't taken a deep breath in an eternity. Every part of me was tense and my eyes stung. My mind was a snowstorm—a whir of disorientation and bone-chattering shock. It took me a few moments to realize I was trapped.

With panic, I pressed my hands against the frosty blue wall six inches above my face. It was like a coffin made of ice!

"Help!" I banged my fists against the theoretical lid. "HELP!"

Terror pulsed through me, but after a minute of no one hearing my shouts, I forced myself to take a breath so the fright wouldn't consume me.

Inhale. Exhale. Inhale. Exhale.

Then I noticed something. Or lack of something. My hands were . . . flickering. One moment solid flesh, the next wisps of pulsing cobalt energy in the shape of hands.

Suddenly the ice wall above me began to lift. It *was* a lid, hinged on the side. Once it was out of the way I sat up rapidly. Swirling mist poured out of my enclosure as if I were some kind of below zero Dracula.

As the mist cleared, I saw something sparkly and golden coming toward me. A second later, I discovered that shine was the glitter on the cheekbones of a man dressed all in white. His plush hair swirled with silver shimmering locks and his eyes were as hauntingly transparent as the ice capsule I found myself in.

He stepped forward, hands behind his back. A gold Christmas tree brooch with **#1** on it was pinned to his lapel.

"Hello, Frost."

I blinked and stared at him. "Do I know you?" I glanced around. We were in some sort of igloo filled with medical equipment and small children in colorful tights and clothes.

Do those children have pointy ears?

"My name is Specter One," the mystical man said. "Welcome to the Christmas Carol Department. Your soul has been chosen to serve in a special agency dedicated to improving people, thus making the world a better place. Think of it as afterlife community service."

His words may as well have been in a foreign language. Was I dreaming? I climbed from my ice coffin, but when my feet hit the floor, I faltered and fell. I scrambled to my hands and knees after that, breathing fast as my palms flickered again.

Flesh. Light. Flesh. Light.

When they stayed solid, I grabbed the side of my coffin and carefully stood. Mine was one of four twinkling identical ice capsules, open and empty. I didn't see any other people. My head turned when I realized the beeping medical equipment in the background seemed to be mimicking a Christmas tune.

Slowly, one of the man's words sunk in.

"*Afterlife?*" I repeated.

He nodded. "At a quarter past two o'clock on January twelfth, your time on Earth came to an end. Now you are here in the North Pole for your December orientation."

My eyes darted around the room. "The North Pole? Like reindeer, elves, Santa Claus, partridge-in-a-pear-tree kind of North Pole?"

"Actually, partridges are jerks so they are no longer allowed within city limits, but yes to the other identifiers."

I focused on Specter One. "I don't understand. It's January, not December. January twelfth like you said. I went to work, I saw a movie, I saved a dog. Then I . . . died?"

"Correct," Specter One replied. "Except for the part about it being January. Being a ghost takes a lot of magical energy. And as the work of Christmas Ghosts is only performed during the month of December, you have been put on ice—pardon the poor turn of phrase—until now."

"I'm . . . I . . ." My mind was so full of ridiculous, surreal information that I couldn't think straight, let alone feel the depth of sadness one ordinarily would experience when informed they were dead and now a ghost.

Specter One put a hand on my shoulder. "Deep breaths, Frost. We'll take this slow. As it's your first season with us, this December you will complete orientation, training, and shadow a team in the CCD. Now come. It seems your form has solidified. We can continue this conversation in my office."

He headed for the arched exit of the igloo. I opened my mouth to respond, but someone tugged on my skirt. I glanced down at an elf with blushing cheeks and freckles like diamonds. She held up a tray of treats. "Cookie?"

Music began echoing around the igloo. Then the igloo began to vibrate. A moment later, my dream memory faded to white haze and disrupted—everything dissolving up like it was being slurped through a straw.

I awoke in my dorm room; I had fallen asleep watching a movie. Marley was upside down on my lap. He twitched in his sleep.

That same muffled music I'd heard at the end of my dream still continued. What was that? Something vibrated under me. I wiggled until I found my phone. I had passed out on top of it and the alarm had been going off for ten minutes!

"Fudge in a jar!" I shouted, leaping up.

Marley whined, disgruntled by the disturbance. I didn't have time to comfort him. It was D-Day and the equipment room was opening in half an hour.

Ghosts didn't need to shower or brush our teeth, so I speedily straightened my hair bun, dusted popcorn off my dress, then left Marley in the room and ran across the CCD. The equipment room was in the lowest level of the main building. An elevator took you most of the way, but the sole means to descend the final floor was a grand, red carpeted staircase straight out of *Hello Dolly!* with balustrades intricately woven with garland and lights.

Elves wearing no-nonsense sunglasses like *The Terminator*, sparkly combat boots, and olive t-shirts with "*D-Day*" printed on them were stationed along the stairs as I made my way down. They whooped and cheered as I descended, tossing sparkly snow at me with glee.

At the bottom, I discovered a formidable crowd had already gathered around the Yeti-sized double oak doors. Using stealth and elbows, I tried to wriggle through. Unlike the powers of Past and Future Ghosts, the powers of Present Ghosts didn't work in this realm. I couldn't exactly cut the line by phasing through.

A ten-foot-tall tower stood on each side of the doors, elves hung out atop them. A bridge above door height connected the towers.

"Welcome, Ghosts of Christmas Present, to D-Day."

We all turned. Across the hall, a 60-inch TV monitor was mounted to the wall. Specter One had just appeared on the screen. He sat at his desk with his hands folded.

"I want to wish you all good luck. Remember, the Senior Specters and I will be monitoring the progress of your targets through the Merry Meter app so *make sure you don't lose focus.* The sooner your target gets successfully Scrooged, the better."

I could've sworn he looked at me during that last part.

"We know you can do your jobs, but if Merry Meter detects any major red flags in your Scrooge's Christmas Spirit progress, we'll call you back to base for a one-on-one. This is not a threat, nor a punishment. We want you to succeed and will do anything we can to facilitate that.

"For those ghosts experiencing their first Decembers with us, remember that your magic is only meant to last the Christmas season, which ends at midnight on Christmas Eve. As noted by your watches, magic runs out the more you use it. However, time eats away at how much you have left too. Your powers naturally fade the closer you get to the Scrooging deadline. They are tied to that ticking clock *and* to your assignment. Meaning the more Christmas Spirit your Scrooge starts to show, the more your powers will be sustained until Christmas. The less spirited your Scrooge, the faster your tank will empty. So be careful and work as effectively and efficiently as possible. When your Scrooge's soul is fully 'saved,' he or she will reach 'Maximum Christmas Spirit' on Merry Meter. Then your powers will recharge and you'll be done for the season. So with that . . . Happy Holiday Haunting, everyone!"

Specter One vanished from the monitor. The screen was taken up by the words *"D-Day"* for a moment, then a special effect like a wintery wind blew the letters away, replacing them with: *"DICKENS DAY!"*

The elves in the watchtowers lifted up massive, *Say Anything* style boomboxes. With the press of a button rave remixes of holiday music blasted out as the doors to the equipment room snapped open. My colleagues and I rushed the entrance. An elf handed me a shopping bag as I entered and I was on my way.

The room was modeled like a fancy jewelry store that displayed charms in its cases and on racks. There was vast inventory—

everything from refills on our basic charms to classic favorites to the newest magic innovations we'd learned about in our seminar this month. As we only were allowed to take twelve charms, I had to bob and weave quickly. It was a loud, noisy endeavor. Speakers near the ceiling blasted the same music as the boomboxes outside.

"Excuse me! Excuse me!" I pushed my way to the frying pan charms. I grabbed two and put them in my basket. As I reached out for a third, Allan elbowed me out of the way.

"Excuse you!"

I harrumphed but let it go. I had to keep moving. It was like Earth's version of Black Friday in here. With determination, I dashed and darted and swirled and twirled around the room, gathering the charms I deemed would be most effective in my team's plan for Jay.

Finally, I made it out.

SPLASH!

The moment I exited, giggling elves on the bridge over the doors gleefully dumped a barrel of cold apple cider over me like I had just won the Super Bowl. They cheered and high-fived, and I got out of the way as the pair picked up another container for the next ghost departing the equipment room.

I noticed Bismaad at the end of the hall speaking to a ghost named Susan. Both were dripping, as I was, but unperturbed. I wasn't particularly bothered either, now that the shock had worn off. The elves always good-naturedly pranked us on D-Day. Last year they dropped a pile of snow on top of us. The year before was a twenty-one-marshmallow salute.

"Hey!" I said, migrating over to Bismaad as Susan strode up the stairs. "How'd you do in there?" I gestured to her shopping bag.

"Fine." She barely looked at me before beginning to climb

the steps. Her wet, marigold chiffon saree clung to her arms and body.

A red flag rose in my mind.

"Is something wrong?" I asked, pursuing her.

"Nope." She checked her phone, as if trying to ignore me.

"Really? Because you seem different this morning."

She stopped and turned to face me, nostrils flared. "I *am* different, Frost. I have been in the afterlife for a few decades now and have gotten a lot of perspective on who I was on Earth and who I want to be with whatever kind of existence I have now. You know who *isn't* different? You."

My brow furrowed. "I don't understand."

Bismaad sighed, pinching the bridge of her nose like a tension-relieving tactic. "Frost, you told me that when we retire from the CCD, we get to be reborn into any situation on Earth we like."

"*Shhh . . .*" I glanced around to make sure no ghosts or elves were near enough to hear. "I told you that in confidence. Only retiring ghosts are supposed to know what comes next."

"Relax. I'm not going to tell anyone. I'm just sad for you. Because this grand opportunity is going to be wasted."

My eyes narrowed. "That's a mean thing to say."

"It's not mean. It's the truth. For decades, I've listened to you talk about how alone you were on Earth, how you distanced yourself from anyone that could've mattered because you were afraid of getting hurt. I get that. *I lived that.* So did most of the ghosts here in one way or another. Like you said last night, that's why we ended up at the CCD. But being dead is not an excuse to stop growing. Once a year, we're tasked with helping people on Earth change, but it's an annual opportunity for us to learn from *them* too. I definitely have, but you haven't. I am no longer the same girl I was on Earth. My soul is fuller, more hopeful, and more open. I've made good friends here and at the North Pole. So I know that I can change, and when my time comes, when I'm reborn, I will have a genuine chance at a happy life. But you . . ."

She sighed. "I don't think any kind of do-over is going to make a difference to you. You could be surrounded by countless opportunities for connections, but you'd still be you. Which means you'd still push people away. You're incapable of doing anything else."

Her words bit deep. In fact, they stung drastically. "That's not true, Bismaad. I . . . I can change. And I don't *always* push people away. I have friends here too. You and Paul obviously."

"Congratulations, Frost. After one hundred years, you have exactly two friends who are at your bedside when you're sick, console you when you're sad, and invite you to go out. It only took a century, and even after all these years you still hesitate to be vulnerable with us and shy away from closeness. You ditched me at the Christmas party last night. Just like you've ditched me plenty of times in our afterlife. And frankly, when you are present, sometimes it's like you're not *actually present*, like you're just checking 'socializing' off some to-do list in your brain."

Bismaad shook her head disappointedly. "You didn't need to be reincarnated to make connections with others, Frost. *We are right here.* We've been here the whole time, and I'll bet we were there on Earth too, but you didn't give us a chance. So why should your second life be any different?"

We stared at each other for a long moment until a pair of elves came over to us. They offered up embroidered towels to wipe away the cider dripping from our faces.

"Thanks," I replied.

Bismaad and I each took a towel. Then we ascended the stairs together—side by side, but in silence.

"The good news is that I managed to get a decent number of charms for countering technology," I told Brandon and Midori as we conversed in the lunch line of the CCD cafeteria. "The bad news is that I only got two TV charms and two lightning bolt charms. Overall though, I am happy with the range we have to work with."

"With the basic charms you have left, it sounds like we're in good shape," Brandon said as an elf with a hairnet gave him a modest scoop of Jack Frost's famous Winter EnCHILLadas. Brandon made an impatient waving gesture to indicate the elf needed to keep it coming.

I nodded, glancing at my wrist where my original snowflake, heart, and cage charms twinkled next to my new charms.

Brandon eyeballed my bracelet then signaled the elf to stop after her fourth scoop. We slid our trays farther down the line. "Can you write down a list of all the charms you have?" Brandon said to me. "I don't have the magic charm handbook completely memorized. There may have been a team snowball fight at the North Pole when I was supposed to be studying last weekend . . ."

"Sure thing," I said. "I was going to do that anyway so we'd all be on the same page."

I held my tray up for the twin elves offering salsa and guacamole. I only motioned for salsa. When Brandon's turn came next, he gestured for both.

"Guac is extra," the elf on the right said.

"*Seriously?*" Brandon replied. "Even in the afterlife?"

"Take it up with the universe." The elf shrugged.

"It's fine. Lunch is on me today, Brandon," I replied, ruffling his hair. "It's my treat for both you and Midori. Ghosts of Christmas Present spend so much time on Earth that we never come close to using our full meal allowance."

We arrived at the register and I handed over my CCD ID. Once we were all rung up, the three of us wandered to an empty table. The cafeteria was packed today; it seemed like all the Christmas Carol teams were regrouping over lunch before my kind departed for Earth. I saw Bismaad at the back with her own team. She noticed me too, but redirected her gaze immediately. My soul churned. I'd have to deal with that in the next few days. I didn't like her being mad at me. I *really* didn't like the things she'd said to me.

"The first charm I'll use, of course, is the grand entrance charm," I continued as Midori sat on my left at the round table, Brandon on my right.

"Wish I could see that," Brandon mused as he forked his enchiladas. "So cool that with one charm, you Ghosts of Christmas Present can warp your environment however you want."

I nodded. "It is cool. Most of our charms have strategic value instead of pizzazz, but I love getting to open with a grand splash. It's important and it's fun."

I swallowed a forkful of enchilada. "If anything with our timeline changes I'll check in with you two. Right now, I don't foresee any problems. Jay isn't my first Scrooge with father issues, and he's certainly not my first Scrooge with an estranged family. *He isn't as unique as I first thought.*" I said that last part adamantly, as if trying to convince myself.

I cleared my throat and pulled apart my bread roll to get at the fluffy white center.

"So we're all good to go then?" Brandon said with his mouth full.

"Not quite. I know it's your first year, Brandon, but remember our powers are quite different. You can visit the past; that is set in stone. I can visit anywhere in the present; since it's happening now, that is beyond meddling too. However Midori's powers allow us to visit the future, and the future—no matter how strong a plan or person—is always in flux. Sometimes even the smallest choice or variable can have monumental effects. I've had plenty of Scroogings where we've had to revise the plan at the last second for one, or even all three visits to the future. For now, we're preparing to end with the funeral scene—it's a classic that works every time. But if Midori sees a change in Jay's future sometime this week and a different visit may have a stronger impact on him, we'll alter course."

Brandon stabbed his fork into his food so it stood straight up, folded his hands under his chin, and looked over at Midori. "What do you think, M? Are you gonna knock us out of the park with a curveball or play it straightlaced?"

Midori's eyes locked with his. She tilted her head slightly, then removed Brandon's upright fork and placed it beside his plate.

Brandon looked at me. I shrugged and raised my glass of ice water.

"What she said."

14

The waxing moon hung in the December sky. Despite the natural haze of smog and the distraction of LA's skyscrapers, which tried their best to outshine it, the lunar beacon beamed like a blessing . . . or a warning.

I knew Jay's habits well by now and, as suspected, discovered him burning the midnight oil in his office. He sat at his desk working by the glow of his computer, its blueish illumination making him seem ghostly too.

In my invisible, intangible form I looked around, making sure we were truly alone. Times were different. Every year, CCD operatives had to deal with a higher risk of exposure. Which didn't pair well with the fact that every year we also had to make a bigger splash to get people's attention. CGI and special effects in movies had desensitized people. Once upon a time, a girl could just unleash a little mist and flicker some lights and a Scrooge would be putty in her hands. Nowadays people were harder to surprise and scare. Once you got used to seeing spaceships explode, dinosaurs on rampage, and berserk aliens, classic spooky just didn't cut it.

Oh, Earth. You got so weird in my absence.

I didn't want to terrorize Jay. It wasn't how I liked to work, and all-out terror was a cheap tactic. Great scary movies were elegant. You needed to ease into them, set the stage.

In the cast of the daring moonlight, I strode across the second level of the office to the window wall facing the city. For grand introductions, I always chose to wear attire from the early 1900s. It was what I felt most comfortable in, and it enhanced my specter vibe. Antique style simply went well with a quintessential haunting experience. Nobody ever expected to be haunted by a ghost in loungewear or a pantsuit.

From my position I could still see Jay through the glass walls of his office. I shook out my shoulders and readied myself. It was time. With one snap of my fingers, for the next few minutes I could manipulate this environment however I chose. The only limits: my imagination and focus.

I raised my wrist.

Snap.

My *YASS* grand entrance charm disintegrated into glittering gold particles that, unlike with my other charms, trickled up my arm and over my body. I tingled with power and twinkled like a Christmas tree.

Magic activated, I touched my finger to the window and drew downward. The glass cracked in my digit's wake—a long break like something a raptor's claw would leave behind.

The cracking sound made Jay glance up from his computer, but after a moment he shook his head and stared at the screen again, thinking he was hearing things. I placed my palm on the center of the fracture, causing it to suddenly multiply twentyfold and splinter out like a web or cruel snowflake across the entire glass wall. *That* got Jay's attention. He stood and exited his office, then stepped back in surprise when he noticed the damaged glass.

Still invisible, I took a deep breath and released a drawn-out exhale like a yoga instructor in Jay's direction. The moment it left my body, that breath transformed into a frosty, powerful wind that gusted against Jay like a slap in the face. He stumbled several feet before he found his balance. The wind had caused icicles to develop on the edges of his suit and tie. It also frosted over every window and converted the floor into an ice rink, tendrils of curling blue across the entire thing.

Jay whirled in the direction the wind had come from, slipping on the ice but managing not to fall. I made a single light flicker on the lower level of the office.

"Is someone there?" Jay shouted. "Who's doing this?"

I stomped one foot into the ground. Loud bootstomps echoed all around us. The room shook in rhythm with the stomps, as if some giant from atop a beanstalk were on his way.

The ice on the floor began to stretch up the walls—climbing toward the ceiling like jagged vines up a trellis. The glass of the conference rooms and individual offices started to fracture. Every computer screen on the lower level seized with green and red light as an unsettlingly slow version of "Jingle Bells" played from all the monitors at once.

Jay's face now looked like the glass walls of his office—*cracked*. Oh yes, I definitely had his attention now. I made the stomping footfalls louder and louder. I clapped my hands and the light at the top of the elevator flashed on to signal the arrival of a car.

DING!

I silenced everything, shut down all computers, stopped the shaking. Jay spun around as the elevator doors opened. There was nothing inside but darkness.

"Good evening, Jay."

Jay turned to find me ten feet behind him, sitting on a throne made of ice. The fractured and frigid glass wall behind me cast my form in shadow. There were so many emotions fluctuating on his face, I thought he might pull a muscle.

"Frost, what are you? How are you?"

"Quiet now." Suddenly, he and I switched places. I stood where he had been and he sat in the ice throne, but bound and gagged from head to toe with glittery garland. His eyes were wide with confusion, fear, and anger, and he struggled against the bonds.

"Jay Nichols," I said in my most deadpan tone. "The universe has singled you out as someone in need of special attention. Within the next week, you will be visited by three Christmas Ghosts who will show you your past, present, and future. You have already met one. *I* am your Ghost of Christmas Present, and I have been assigned as your guide through this transformative experience. By midnight on Christmas Eve, you must learn to embrace the potential for good that you have in your heart, commit to changing your ways, and truly embrace the Christmas Spirit, or deal with the consequences."

Jay glared at me, still struggling to free himself. I strode forward. "There is no escape from this. I will remain in your life over the next week to take you on this journey. Any attempts to make your situation known to others will lead to . . ." I glanced at his restraints. "Magical interference."

I bent over so we were at eye level, our noses inches from each other. "I think it goes without saying that you can't fire me from *this* job."

I turned and walked away. "I'll see you tomorrow, Jay," I called back. "Get some sleep. You're going to need it."

I stepped into the open elevator. Once inside, we exchanged another glance before I snapped my fingers. The ice on the walls began to dissolve, the cracks mended themselves, and Jay's garland bindings and throne vanished into thin air. He dropped to the floor. The elevator doors started closing as he scrambled to his feet.

"Frost!"

He raced forward, but it was too late. The doors shut then I teleported back to my loft.

Marley trotted over giddily when he saw me. I lifted him into my arms and tapped his nose affectionately. "I've still got it, boy."

Half an hour later, Marley and I were lounging on the sofa in front of the TV—fully engaged in movie night mode. I wore a red pajama set covered with a pattern of snowflakes and had a bowl of popcorn beside me.

"See, Marley, this is what I'm talking about," I said, gesturing at the screen. "This film gets a thumbs down from me. Big hype drama might distract some people from lack of story, but not me."

I tossed another popped kernel into my mouth. Suddenly, a knock came at the door. Not in the movie, in my actual apartment.

What the . . .

I got up gingerly.

"Hello?" I called out.

There was no answer. Then the rapping of knuckles against the door sounded again, only more aggressively.

I scurried over, not making a sound thanks to my fuzzy penguin socks. I couldn't see anybody through the door's peephole. I glanced back at Marley. He had not been designed as a guard dog, so he just lay on the couch watching me curiously.

"Lazy," I said to him.

Whatever. I didn't need a guard dog. I was over a century old and armed with magical powers. I glanced at my charm bracelet.

I snapped my fingers and one of the newer charms—shaped like a baseball bat—turned to glitter. A major league baseball bat appeared in my hands. There was an engraving on the side:

Holiday Creep Stick
For when you spring from the bed to see what is the matter.

I threw the door open as I raised my weapon, ready to swing. Jay and I both shouted in surprise. I was so dumbfounded I did nothing to stop him as he barged into my apartment.

"What the heck, Frost?!" he demanded.

I lowered my bat, still shocked. "Jay, what—what are you doing here?"

He turned and looked at me. "Seriously? You're a magical ghost who just punked me at my office and scared the sh—"

"Hey!" I interrupted, lowering the bat and kicking the door closed behind me. "I don't care for bad language. And as I'm the, quote, 'magical ghost' here, I'll ask you to respect that and answer my questions when I ask them. How did you find me? The address I provided to your HR team isn't real. You've probably been sending my checks to a PO box or an abandoned building."

"Yeah, I noticed that," Jay said with a glower. "I just took a car to a locked warehouse in San Pedro Harbor with a pile of mail at the foot of the door. So thanks for that wild goose chase. How did you—" he abruptly shivered and rubbed his hands against his arms. "*How cold is it in here?*" He stomped over to the thermostat and tried to change it with no success. I let him fiddle with it in frustration for a moment as my mind raced. I still couldn't believe he was *in my apartment.*

"You weren't supposed to try and find me, Jay. I mean, who does that? You get a spooky holiday ultimatum from a ghost and your first instinct is to call an Uber and go after her?"

"You posed as my personal assistant for a month. Then you tied me to an ice chair and told me I'm living in some sort of parallel Dickens universe. Who does *that?*" he countered.

"Actually, the Christmas Carol Department where I come from existed for quite some time before Dickens wrote about it. Santa thought it would be good for humanity to read the story, so he allowed the author to go forward with the printing and—wait." Bat still in hand, I made a T for timeout. "Why am I explaining this? You still haven't told me how you found me."

"Rocco dropped you off at this building after I fired you. There are only four floors. I knocked on doors until you opened up."

"Son of a snowman," I cursed.

Jay huffed, a tiny bit of amusement slipping through despite his irate state. "I thought you didn't like bad language."

"Shut up. It's fine if it's holiday-themed and appropriate for an eight-year-old."

I paced, patting the bat against my open palm in anxiety. We were *never* supposed to let our Scrooges find out where we were staying. I'd been so upset and flabbergasted after I got fired that I'd slipped up.

I whirled around and pointed the bat at Jay. "Okay, here's what's going to happen. You're going home. You're not going to come here again. Tomorrow I'll show up for work and when it's time for one of your ghostly ventures I'll let you know and we'll proceed as normal."

"Normal?"

"Normal for a Scrooge. That's you in this scenario, in case you haven't figured it out."

Jay opened his mouth, then looked down. Marley was chewing on his pant leg. "You have a dog," he said. "Can ghosts have dogs?"

"Would you prefer it if I had a snake made of mist or a flock of crows?"

He ignored the comment and bent down to scratch Marley's ear. My dog ceased his chewing and thumped his leg excitedly.

"Traitor," I said to my pet.

Jay straightened and readdressed me with more seriousness. His anger seemed to be subsiding. "Why me? I'm not a bad person, Frost. You said so yourself."

I sighed. My grip loosened and I put the bat down. "Not right now, but it's inevitable that you become one. We've seen your future, Jay. Choices make us who we are. You've been choosing poorly."

"Is that an *Indiana Jones* reference?"

"Yes, but don't let that detract from the importance of my point. We're all one bad decision away from sealing our fates. Don't think of this Christmas Carol experience as a punishment. Think of it as an intervention. You're in danger, Jay, of having your life mean nothing but missed opportunity and emotional casualties. I get why you're mad. And for once—though it's probably unwise for me to admit it—I kind of feel bad about it. But this is happening one way or another, so I advise you to get on board."

Jay took three long strides toward me so we were barely a foot apart. "And if I don't?"

For dramatic effect I engulfed my body with my magical blue aura like I was about to teleport. His eyes widened, but he held firm. "Are you familiar with the song 'Governor Got Run Over by a Reindeer'?"

"It's '*Grandma* Got Run Over by a Reindeer'."

"Not the way I heard it."

We glared at each other.

After a beat, Jay conceded the staring match and marched toward the door. He flung it open, but paused on my penguin welcome mat and pivoted to address me from the hall. "You know, just because you're haunting me doesn't mean you can be bad at your day job. Be on time tomorrow, follow Annie's orders, and leave the bat at home."

"Whatever you say, Mr. Nichols," I snarked as I followed him to the door. "Can I get you anything else? Cookie? Comfy pillow?

A thank you card you can write me, acknowledging my efforts for making sure you don't die miserable and alone?"

"No. I *will* take an assistant who doesn't dress like an overgrown eight-year-old though." He gestured at my pajamas. "You look ridiculous."

I glanced down at my festive nightwear, soured with embarrassment, then slammed the door in Jay's face.

"I can't believe I'm going back to Earth," I said to my CCD mentor Marsha, my dream memory dropping me into the first December of my afterlife.

The teenage Ghost of Christmas Present smiled reassuringly. "My first time back was a bit jarring too. It shouldn't seem that unfamiliar though. You only died eleven months ago."

"Attention, new recruits!" Specter One announced from the front of the room.

My fellow first-time spirits and I had been training and studying hard during these past few weeks. We'd also undergone *a lot* of grief counseling. I still couldn't believe the North Pole had such a great mental health care plan. How many elves had nervous breakdowns over the course of the holiday season to require this?

The other new ghosts in attendance were Ty Watanabe and Bill James. They'd both been selected as Ghosts of Christmas Past whereas I'd inherited the role of Ghost of Christmas Present. Alongside our mentors for the season, we'd gathered for casual cocoa, cookies, and a motivational speech in one of the North Pole's conference rooms. I'd swiped a finger across the wall earlier and discovered it was made of gingerbread bricks with icing in lieu of mortar.

"I realize that it is going to be strange returning to the mortal world," Specter One said. "To tame any desire to visit places and people you knew in life, we have assigned you to teams stationed far from where you lived on Earth. Stick with your mentors, don't interfere, and—"

"Enjoy yourselves!" Santa Claus burst through the doors of the gingerbread room. He snapped the straps of the mulberry overalls over his Christmas tree patterned turtleneck. A small child, maybe five years old, scuttled in behind him, playing with a toy airplane.

"Season's greetings, ghosts!" Santa declared. "I understand it may seem sad to not be alive, but take solace in knowing you are all part of something miraculous now. You get to spend your afterlife producing joy, helping people become the best version of themselves, and increasing the world's goodwill. From here forward, every moment you are awake will be Christmastime and your whole existence will revolve around spreading the magic that makes it, quite literally, the most wonderful time of year."

The child zigzagged between the tables, making plane sound effects.

Santa smiled and gestured at the kid. "My son Kris, everyone. I tell you, the invention of the airplane didn't just make Earth noisier; the youngster loves them. Anyway, I—"

"Whoa!" Kris abruptly tripped and fell. The plane flew from his hands and skidded across the floor to land at my feet. One wing had broken off the body. When Kris clambered up and retrieved the toy, he realized it was damaged and started to cry. I bent down.

"Hey now, it's okay. It's not broken; it just shape-shifted. May I?" I gestured for the toy.

He looked at me hesitantly, then passed it over. "Trust me,

okay?" I snapped off the remaining wing and then played with the hull, making wave motions with my arm and *glub glub* sounds. "See? Now it's a submarine," I said. "All it takes is a little positive perspective."

Kris sniffled then smiled at me. I offered him back his repurposed toy. He took it and I patted his head. "I'm Frost."

"Kris," Santa called. "What do you say to Frost?"

"Thank you, Frost." He scampered out of the room making *glub glub* noises. I watched the kid go. A touch of warmth that I didn't know cold ghosts like me could feel flickered deep inside.

I stood only to find Santa in front of me.

"That was quick thinking, Frost. I'll have to keep my eye on you. There's wonder in your heart. You think outside the box." Santa pivoted to the group. "Now then, everyone. Have a good time this week. Merry Christmas. And thank you for your service."

Santa waved and exited the room. Specter One finished his own send-off and after some awkward mingling, we departed for Earth.

Christmas week went by in a flash; my dream memory played through multiple scenes from that time in a montage. I observed as Marsha and her Past and Future colleagues worked their magic on their assigned Scrooge—a wealthy factory owner in New York City. There was lightning, snow, tears, yelling, spooky glowing, and finally the ultimate breakthrough on Christmas Eve when the target finally let the truth, and the miracle and meaning of the holiday, overcome him—Christmas Spirit filling up his heart in every possible way.

It was beautiful, humbling, and heartwarming. Maybe Santa, Specter One, and my elf therapist were right. Maybe there was meaning in my death. I *could* enjoy this. What wasn't there to enjoy about helping humans get a second chance? We were saving people and pumping positive energy into the world.

Huzzah, right?

Following the successful Scrooging, we returned to the CCD at half past seven in the evening. Marsha patted me on the back. "We finished a little later than normal, but we got there in the end."

I dusted off the snowflakes from the blizzard in Central Park.

"Isn't the deadline midnight?" I asked as we walked down the hall from the CCD's realm-evator lobby.

"Yes," Marsha said. "Midnight in whatever time zone you started in. Regardless, teams typically finish way before their deadline. Our three-ghost Scrooging technique is consistent and effective. The latest anyone ever gets done is around nine o'clock, which is good because in addition to running out of magic simply by using it, our powers diminish on their own the closer it gets to midnight. They weaken even faster if our Scrooges are not progressing enough. Hence the motivation to wrap things up as swiftly as possible."

"So now what?"

"Now we have the holiday party." She glanced at her watch. "Keep pace with me, Frost."

We hurried through the CCD, its grand windows blanketing the skybridge with the greens and purples of the aurora borealis twirling outside as it did every night. I paused to stare out at the vacant terrain, nothing but endless snow visible up to the horizon. Unlike the North Pole, there were no animals and no additional buildings past our CCD compound—no signs of life anywhere beyond our agency in fact.

"Marsha, what's out there? Past the snowbanks I mean."

She paused and turned around, coming over to me. "It's nothing."

"You can tell me," I said.

"No, really," Marsha insisted. "It is actually nothing. Our realm isn't round like the Earth. If you go too far off into that snowscape, this world just *ends*, and if you reach that point, you vanish too. The same goes for the edge of the North Pole."

"Have you ever gone and seen it for yourself?"

"And risk ceasing to exist? Definitely not. Our souls are fragile and only survive on this plane of reality through a lot of magic we're not meant to fully understand. If we push that luck, we could be lost. Now come on, Frost. Your questions are too morose for such a festive evening." Marsha continued down the hall and I reluctantly followed, but my eyes lingered on the snowy horizon.

It was the last thing held in my mind's eye before my dream memory ended and I woke in my LA bed. My alarm went off barely a second later and I shut it off and lay there for another minute. Last night with Jay had been weird and entirely unexpected. I was angry and frustrated. *Of course* my last Scrooge had to be extra difficult. And just when I was set on treating him like all my other assignments, once again he had to go and be unpredictable.

With a huff, I threw the covers off and began preparations for the day. Five minutes later as I stirred the cocoa in my mug with a candy cane, a loud *BANG* sounded from my "bathroom." Cup in hand, I hurried around the kitchen counter just in time to see Brandon stumbling out of my interdimensional lavatory. Marley barked.

"I think it'll be a few Christmases before I get used to that," Brandon said, eyes wide and a bit off balance. He was dressed normal enough for a kid these days. He had only died a year and a half ago, so this world was pretty similar to the one he'd left behind.

"To be honest, I never got used to it," I admitted, taking a sip of my cocoa.

"That's encouraging." He rolled his eyes. "So how'd it go last night?"

"Well, great at first. Then less so. Jay is proving to be a real pain in the pine tree."

"Sorry to hear that."

I sighed. "It's fine. I'll figure it out. I need to leave for work in a few minutes. I'll come back later to get you for your first run at the past. In the meantime, you can make yourself at home. I have TV, food, and a dog. That should be enough to keep you occupied."

"You had me at TV. The CCD does not get any streaming services, and just because I died doesn't mean I don't want to finish the shows I was watching."

I cracked a smile. "I completely understand. Here. Let me show you something." I strode to my bed, set down my cocoa, and pulled my precious wooden box from under the frame.

"This is my memory box," I explained. "Ghosts don't amass many possessions, but this is where I keep the things that are most important to me." I opened the box and Brandon came over to look at the contents.

There were a couple of outliers—a set of gold, shiny bells connected by a red ring and a century-old toy airplane without wings. Other than that, the treasure of the box was my collection of ticket stubs.

"Movies are my thing. Whenever I'm on Earth, I see as many as I can in theaters and rent a bunch more. When the season is over, I store the box in my dorm at the CCD for the next year. I think that souls—even in death—will always be drawn to what made them feel alive. Getting wrapped up in other people's stories was always my escape, and I still love getting lost in them."

He nodded in appreciation as I shut the box and put it away. Then I handed Brandon the remote for the television. "Have fun."

Forty minutes later, I was at the office. I stepped out of the elevator and it was like nothing had changed. All traces of my magical grand entrance had vanished, the office staff none the wiser. My coworkers typed away at their computers. Phones rang. The watercooler *glub glubbed*. Colleagues conversed. I would say it felt busier than normal though.

Annie was in the middle of giving orders to a few staffers when she spotted me and waved me over. "Did you sleep in, Frost?"

I checked my watch. "Annie, I'm five minutes early."

"Didn't you get my email last night? We're starting an hour early every day this week. I hope you don't have Christmas plans with your family, because this job comes first for the next seven days."

"I didn't get your email, but I am in complete agreement with you; the job *does* come first this week."

"Um, excellent," Annie replied, a bit surprised. "Now then, Jay and I are sitting in on a City Council meeting first thing this morning."

"When do we leave?"

"He and I leave in fifteen minutes. You're staying here for the day to work with Bobby and AJ on getting out press releases."

My brow furrowed. "Wait, shouldn't I be going with you?"

"Jay insisted you stay here all day and work on this instead." Her phone buzzed. She answered and began walking away without so much as an excuse me. While she was distracted, I mounted the stairs and barged into Jay's office.

He glanced up. "Do you always have to dress so Christmassy?" he asked with contempt, eyeballing my crimson plaid top tucked into a cream skirt.

"You said no pajamas."

"I guess this beats the pre–Depression Era housewife look you wore last night."

I put my hand on my hip. "I'll have you know that dress was really in style when I was alive."

"Just like I'm sure loin cloths were all the rage in caveman times. But if a half-naked ghost shows up at the office next, don't expect me to be cool with it."

I shook my head, aggravated, then noticed the Christmas tree bauble I'd given Jay in the trash. I frowned but chose not to address it.

"What's the big idea making me stay here all day?" I asked. "You don't actually think you can ditch me and get out of this, do you?"

"I *think* that you're not going to channel your hocus pocus with witnesses present. So unless you're planning on going all M. Night Shyamalan with an audience, you'll have to work around my schedule and won't be able to interfere with the week I have planned. At least during working hours."

"You can't—"

"I can, Frost." He stood and faced off with me. "You have a job to do. Fine. Hit me with your best shot. But I have a job too. My whole life and career are on the line this week. I've been distracted enough by you, my family, and my doubts. Now I have to focus and there's no turning back. You and your wintery witchcraft can deal with it and plan around me."

I glowered at him. "You're being absurdly difficult, Jay. I am trying to help you. You could be a dash more grateful and a little less snippy about it."

"Take it up with HR," he replied, waving me off as he sat down and took a sip of coffee.

In a moment of irritation, I snapped my fingers and the charm on my bracelet that looked like a splotch disintegrated into glitter. Jay suddenly spilled a large swill of hot coffee over his lap. He scowled and leapt up, shocked.

"Take *that* up with HR," I said. I left his office in a huff, then scurried down the stairs to the restroom. Alone inside, I stared at myself in the mirror. My fieriness subsided and was soon replaced by confusion and concern.

What is the matter with you?

Taking a shot at Jay had felt good, but it was unprofessional. As his ghostly guide, I wasn't supposed to let his denial and anger with the Scrooging situation get to me. Scrooges were never happy when they found out what was happening to them. They lashed out and were rude because lack of control in their lives terrified them. It was nothing new. What *was* new was me getting emotional about it. How many times did I have to remind myself not to do that with Jay? How could he so easily counteract my commitment to restrain my impulses? I must've been broken. That had to be it. After a century of ghosting, my spirit was malfunctioning.

"Get a grip," I told myself, clutching the edges of the sink.

As if he could sense the disturbance, my phone sounded and I saw a text from Specter One. *"Hope things are going well. Remember to focus. No more deviations. Your future is on the line."* Thumbs-up emoji. Ghost emoji. Smiley face emoji.

I sighed and texted back. *"Things are fine. Moving right on schedule."*

I added an octopus emoji to throw him off before I pocketed my phone. Then I met my frosty eyes in the mirror.

"Remember what you're working for. Remember what's at stake. *Just do your job.*"

After taking a couple minutes to compose myself, I exited the restroom, plastered a smile on my face, and went to touch base with Bobby and AJ. The guys had a salesman can-I-interest-you-in-a-timeshare vibe, but were nice enough.

"What's this about a press release?" I asked.

Bobby handed me a memo. "Jay wrote this up over the weekend for damage control. We're supposed to make sure it's blasted everywhere in response to the debacle that was last week's morning show."

I started reading sections of the document.

"For the sake of our children, I did everything I could to help Celia make better choices and support her while we were married . . . When her self-destructive decisions put our children at risk, I realized for their best interest, and hers, that she needed to seek professional help . . . I did everything in my power to help her fight her demons. We mutually agreed to file for divorce. Then I single-handedly cared for our children while she chose to work on herself. When she was no longer a danger to herself or others, our children were reintroduced into her life. Since then, I have been keeping a close eye on them, just in case she relapses."

I could not think of a holiday-themed curse word grandiose enough to react to this.

My eyes darted to Bobby and AJ. "Please tell me this hasn't gone out yet."

"An hour ago," AJ responded. "I'm in charge of print media.

Bobby is handling the bloggers. It'd be great if you could pull out small snippets and publish them on social media."

Jay came out of the men's restroom—changed into fresh clothes after I'd ruined the previous suit with coffee. He moved to meet Annie at the elevators just as the lift doors opened. They stepped in; I took off after them and slid inside before the doors closed.

"Frost, I told you to stay here," Annie said.

I ignored Annie and held up the document. "Jay, this is a mistake."

"It's already done, Frost." Jay didn't meet my gaze, but there was the smallest grain of remorse in the corner of his eye.

I just stared at him until the elevator doors opened again and he and Annie exited. I watched them cross the building lobby before the doors shut in my face and I rode back up.

I gulped and plopped down at my desk, powering on my computer. It took *way* too long to start up and I fidgeted with angst. With a grunt of frustration I pulled out my phone and absentmindedly scrolled through Tinsel. I tapped my finger against the screen as my mind tremored with anxiety.

I couldn't text Bismaad right now; she was mad at me. In an attempt to vent, I opened my post function and took an elfie (what elves say you should call selfies around the holidays). To complement the image of my frowning face, I added the caption: "*How it feels when your Scrooge digs himself into a deeper hole and won't let you take away the shovel.*"

I stared at the press release. For a second, I considered going rogue again. Then Specter One's message flashed through my mind.

"*No more deviations. Your future is on the line.*"

I groaned and got to work.

I spent most of the day at my desk. Annie kept me busy with plenty of assignments—via text and email when she was out of the office, and barking orders at me once she and Jay returned.

At five o'clock, the burnt orange glare of the SoCal December evening streamed in through the windows. At last, with a chunk of staffers having gone home, I had a moment to call my team on SpaceTime from a quiet corner. Midori answered first. She was wearing old-timey airplane pilot goggles for some reason.

"Um. Hi, Midori."

She nodded. Brandon picked up the call a second later and he split the screen with her. A lollipop stick popped from the corner of his mouth. "How goes it, Frost?"

"I'm sorry you had to wait all day, Brandon, but things got intense here."

"What happened?" the kid asked.

The elevator dinged open and Celia stomped out. My jaw dropped.

"Where's Jay?" she snapped loudly. The whole office fell silent. Papers halted shuffling. Fingers stopped typing.

"Hold on. I'll call you back," I whispered. I hung up the phone as Annie went to meet Celia at the front. The former touched Jay's ex-wife on the arm.

"Celia, listen. You don't want to cause a scene. Why don't we—"

"Why don't *you* back out of my personal space, Annie?" Celia plucked Annie's hand off her arm. "Did you and your media spinning monkeys really think you could say all those awful things about me and not get this visit? I am going to talk to my ex-husband."

"He's busy, Celia. You can't just barge in here."

"Call security," she retorted over her shoulder as her heels clicked up the stairs. I darted into the bathroom—*coast clear*—and phased into ghost form. I teleported into Jay's office just as Celia stormed in. Jay was on the phone. His eyes stretched beyond the recommended size when he saw her.

"Uh, Patrick, let me call you back." He hung up the phone and laced his hands together. I sat on the edge of his desk and readied myself for what was about to go down.

Celia, who'd been all rage by the elevator, spoke with calmness now, her voice steady though wounded. "How could you do this?"

She held up her phone and began quoting snippets from the release. "*Self-destructive, put our children at risk, chose to work on herself, in case she relapses . . .*"

"That isn't untrue, Celia," Jay said carefully.

"It's cruel, Jay. I had my problems, yes, but you made me sound like a monster. More importantly, you completely disrespected and insulted me. You may not understand my condition, and you may not want to, but it's mine and you had no right to talk about it publicly. Furthermore, you and the kids were never in 'danger.' I just got lost in depression after my parents were killed in their car crash and I didn't know how to deal with it in a healthy way. That's not an excuse, but it is a reason."

"I don't think having a reason means you get a pass to let down all the people in your life," Jay responded.

Celia's brow twitched with anger and frustration. "You're right. Goodness knows you have plenty of reasons for disappointing your family, and that certainly doesn't ease the blow." She strode forward and planted her hands on the desk. "Jay, *I'm sorry* that I'm a human being and my flaws are too much for the perfect, politically groomed image you are trying to cultivate. But while it is important that I make amends to the people I affected, in my recovery, moving forward is not about letting those people make a villainous caricature of my past."

Jay's temperament remained even. "I'm sorry you think it's a caricature, Celia. But when I wrote that, I wrote from the heart. You have no idea how much it hurt to watch you lose yourself after I went down that road with my mom and watched her drive away my dad. You put Kingsley and Kamie in danger of dealing with the same broken hearts I dealt with as a kid."

"Don't speak to me like I don't know you, Jay," Celia responded flatly. "This isn't your heart. This is a tactic. Eddie and I watched that show you did with Farah. You're doing to me what she did to you—throwing a disparaging light on the easiest target so that you look better."

"Isn't that what you do to me every day?" Jay's voice rose a little. "Painting me to look like the absentee father who doesn't care about his kids when it's you and Eddie who are making it impossible for me to spend time with them?"

"You only want to spend time with them if it fits into your schedule, and if Eddie and I aren't anywhere near them, as if we can't exist in the same setting without the sky falling apart."

"You took Christmas from me."

"You're taking Christmas from yourself!"

Celia stopped. She took a deep breath to calm down then backed away, hands raised. "But you know what? I forgive you, Jay. For this. And for treating me like a scar on your life. I forgive you because it's impossible to feel anger toward someone you feel sorry for. If you want to be the kind of man who brings down others to look better, go for it. The only people you have to answer to are yourself, and an optimistic kid named Jay Nichols I met in college who thought being good was the most important prerequisite any public servant should have."

A lull hung in the air.

Eventually Celia shook her head with a sigh and looked at Jay without ire—only vulnerability and sadness. "Don't you feel guilty about it *at all*, Jay? You're disrespecting what we *did* have. Saying all these things . . . it makes it seem like you don't have any happy memories of our relationship or our family left."

Jay paused then delivered the final blow. "I honestly have no memory of us being happy, Celia. The hardship you brought on our life together is all that remains for me now."

And I thought I was cold.

Celia stood still and studied him. "Then that hurts me more than this ever could." She alluded to her phone. "Because I genuinely don't know if you mean that, or if you're just adamant to convince yourself, so selling me out and burying your past is easier."

Celia left the office. Jay stared at his desk as if it were an endless sea.

"Geez, I feel like I needed popcorn while watching that horror show."

Jay jumped in his chair. With no one around to see into his clear view office, I'd turned visible.

"Frost!" All his forehead lines crinkled.

"You're lucky," I said wistfully. "I thought for sure she was going to punch you at one point. You definitely deserved it."

He glowered at me. "That was a private conversation."

"Nothing about your life is private where I'm concerned," I said, dismounting from my seat on his desk. "But seriously, this is what I tried to warn you about this morning."

"I know," he said getting up and starting to pace. "But it had to be done."

"*Why* did it have to be done?"

"My career is on the line."

"Your *soul* is on the line."

He turned to me. "You're being melodramatic. I'm not doing anything with the intention of being cruel. Farah is an evil person. *She* does malicious things purely for self-interest. I do things so she doesn't bury me in the dust. The ends will justify the means. I deserve to be governor, not her. I'm not going to spend the rest of my life losing to people who don't actually care about making the world better."

He resumed pacing. I crossed my arms. "Whether you deserve something or not doesn't matter, Jay. Good people and bad people don't get what they deserve all the time. I'm warning you not to let your fear of rejection turn you into someone who, as Celia noted, the younger you never wanted to be."

He paused and looked at me with a glimmer of genuine vulnerability. "Does anyone ever turn into the person they wanted to be?"

The sadness in his voice surprised me. I held his gaze before responding. "We try. My bosses keep attempting to convince me that's what matters."

He tilted his head. "You don't agree?"

"Sometimes it's hard to when I continuously meet people like you. It's not easy to keep Christmas Spirit alive in your heart when the people you want to help foolishly waste life's most precious gift every day."

"What's that?"

"The fact that you don't know only proves how much work I have left to do." I paused as I settled on an idea. "Talk to you later."

I went invisible again before marching out of Jay's office. It would be suspicious if I exited after Celia and, even if it was a short distance, my powers weren't meant to transport me anywhere aside from my loft and close to Jay.

I headed to the women's restroom where I could take my normal form again. Once done, I checked for feet in any of the stalls. Having verified I was alone, I got Brandon and Midori back on the line.

"Sorry about that," I said to the pair. "Brandon, I may not be home for a while, depending on when everyone clears out of here. In others news, I think we should switch the order of our three visits to the past. Jay's press release has unleashed all kinds of damage with Celia. Let's swap the first and last visits."

"Are you sure?"

"Absolutely."

Someone entered the restroom. I smiled awkwardly.

"Bye, guys," I said to my teammates before snapping the phone closed and exiting. When I came out, Jay was leaving his office. Our eyes met for a moment, then Annie captured his attention and AJ took mine.

By half past six, everyone had gone home. Technically that included me. Annie liked being the last person at the office, apart from Jay. I waited across the street in the shadows of a restaurant awning until she vacated the premises.

Time to get this show on the road. I just needed my co-star. Once I saw Annie get in a car, I flashed home.

"What the?" My floor was covered with muddy shoe prints. The sheets, pillows, Christmas tree, and chairs had been converted into a fort. The TV was running a nature show. Some kind of batter was slopped over the kitchen cabinets and floor.

"Brandon!" I called.

He poked his head out from the fort, wearing a construction paper crown. Marley stuck his head out beside the boy.

"Hey, Frost!"

"What happened here?"

His eyes shone. "You said I could do the things I missed on Earth. I missed playing in the park, forts, *Planet Earth* documentaries, and pancakes. I had to watch a few online videos to experiment with the last item on that list, but it didn't go well. I don't know where I went wrong."

I shook my head. "I'll show you how to make them some other time. For now, it's time to go. Jay is finally alone, which means we can take him on his first journey to Christmas Past."

Brandon rose slowly and took off his paper crown, fiddling with it. "About that . . . I'm not sure if I can do this, Frost."

I raised an eyebrow. "Why do you say that? You've done all the training. You contributed in our team meetings. I have total confidence in you."

He lowered his crown and kicked at the floor. "That makes one of us." He sighed. "Having magic is cool. I like the elf soccer team I joined. The food in the cafeteria is great. And a penguin in the North Pole owes me a lot of money. But I'm just a kid, you know. It's kind of overwhelming. I didn't ask to be a ghost, and I don't know if I want to be one. This random person's soul is partially in my hands. What if I didn't do enough research? What if I show him the wrong thing and scar him? Or what if I waste one of my visits on something that's not important and he doesn't find his Christmas Spirit because of me?"

He plopped on the floor, deflated.

I took a knee and put my hand on his shoulder. "I didn't ask to be a ghost either, Brandon. Just like I didn't ask to be an orphan." I tilted his chin up. "Same as you."

He met my gaze. "How long have you known?"

"The whole time. When new recruits are assigned to our teams, Specter One gives Ghosts of Christmas Present some background to understand them better; it helps us accommodate your CCD transition. I didn't want to say anything to you about it though. Just because you're a Ghost of Christmas Past doesn't mean you're obligated to talk about yours."

He nodded. "Thanks . . . Maybe someday."

I sighed and sat beside him on the floor. "Look, neither of us asked for the lot we were given in life or the afterlife, but no matter what plane of the universe you exist in, all you can do is work with what you've got and try your best. I've seen how hard you've been preparing. You're ready for this. You're going to make an awesome ghost, we're going to save Jay's soul, and I'll be there the whole time to back you up just in case."

Brandon looked at me. Then he threw his arms around me. If I'd had a beating heart, it would have warmed. I patted the kid on the back. Then I stood. "Come on. Let's get this guy."

I offered Brandon my hand. The kid's sticky fingers gripped mine and he got to his feet. I willed my radiant blue ghost energy to cover us both and a second later we arrived at my desk in the downtown office. I let go of Brandon's hand, returning us to normal.

"Count to fifteen then follow me," I whispered.

I ascended the stairs and opened Jay's door. He seemed startled at first, then played it off. "No dramatic entrance?" he asked, returning his attention to the computer.

"I don't like to be repetitive."

"Glad to hear it. Now beat it, Casper. I'm busy."

"Yeah, that's not going to fly with him."

"With who?"

"You're getting Scrooged, son!" Brandon burst in and marched up to Jay's desk. Before Jay could stop him, the kid outstretched his arm and swept all papers, pens, and even Jay's phone to the floor—everything except a glass soda bottle. Brandon grabbed it, smashed it on the end of the desk, then waved the broken bottle at Jay like he was challenging our target to a bar fight.

"Whoa! Dial it back, Brandon," I said. He glanced at me. "Love the enthusiasm though." I gave him a thumbs up.

"Sorry," Brandon said. "One of the elves taught me that."

"Um, Frost?" Jay said, uneasily leaning back in his chair. "What's with the violent ginger kid?"

"This is Brandon," I explained. "He is your Ghost of Christmas Past. My advice is that you cooperate. He's a new hire, and whereas I have patience from years of practice, he's nine, recently dead, and hopped up on questionable pancake batter. He may not be as tolerant of your attitude as I am."

Jay scoffed with disdain and stood. "Fine. You both have my attention. I've seen the movies. Where are we going? Back to my childhood so I can see how happy I used to be when my family was together?"

"Not exactly," Brandon said. "I'm gonna need your hand, bro." He put down the bottle and offered Jay one hand, extending the other to me. We both accepted.

"What happens now?" Jay asked.

"Hocus pocus," I replied.

Brandon's eyes whirred with energy while ethereal wind swept the office. Our trio became fully coated in a blue aura as papers swirled around the room, trapped in the cyclone of magic. Then *BAM!* We dropped roughly onto a carpeted hallway.

"Ow." I winced, going to a knee.

"My bad!" Brandon apologized as we clambered up. "I got a little too excited and didn't focus on the landing."

Jay stared down at himself in awe; he was now blue and translucent like Brandon and me.

"We can see, hear, and touch each other," I explained.

"But you're invisible to everyone else. And mostly intangible too."

He took in our surroundings. Although the carpet, walls, and doors were monotone shades of beige, many of the doors had festive touches—wreaths, paper snowflakes, twinkle lights, even a tinsel Star of David.

"I recognize this place," Jay said in a daze. "This is my first apartment after college. Once we graduated and got married, Celia and I lived here for years." He wandered over to the door covered with cutout snowflakes. Rainbow lights hung around the frame. Jay reached out tentatively. When he discovered his fingers could pass through the door, he stepped forward so the rest of him could phase inside. Brandon and I followed.

We entered an endearingly merry scene. A five-foot Christmas tree embellished with glistening baubles sat in one corner. A sleek white record player played holiday tunes that drowned out the TV. Battery operated candles gave the room extra warmth. An old schnauzer slept in a plaid basket by the window. On top of the coffee table, a slender vase held a bouquet of fuchsia-veined white flowers with pinkish rims.

Across from the TV on the couch a younger Jay and a much smaller Kingsley sat cross-legged, deeply involved in some pretend play with action figures.

"Okay, boys. Make room for Mom!" Celia entered through the open archway with a plate of cookies in one hand and baby Kamiė in a frilly Christmas dress cradled in the other arm.

Jay lowered his legs and scooched over so that Celia could settle in beside him. She passed him the baby and he held the fragile creature tenderly.

Celia gave Jay and Kingsley a cookie each before taking one herself. "Let's see how these peppermint reindeer pies came out.

On three, everyone." They each held up their treat as she counted off. "One, two, three!"

The trio took synchronized bites of their cookies, munching loudly.

"So what's the verdict?" Jay asked after everyone had swallowed.

"Can I have a couple more before I tell you my answer?" Kingsley asked.

Jay grinned and affectionately noogied his son's head. Then he looked at Celia. "I think these are better than the sugar doodles we made last year."

"But not as good as the peanut butter ripples we made two years ago," Celia responded thoughtfully, finishing off her cookie. "I say we go down a peanut butter road again next year. Peppermint isn't my true calling."

"Then you won't mind if I take that then?" Jay reached for the plate of cookies in Celia's lap. She playfully slapped his hand away.

"Peppermint may not be my calling, but cookies in general are. That aside, I know you, Mr. Nichols. If I give you this plate, you'll have finished them before we're halfway through the movie. And we have to save some of these for Santa."

"Mom's right, Dad," Kingsley said. "Santa needs nine cookies—one for each reindeer and a big one for himself. We have to think of them before us."

"Good point, buddy," Jay said. "Your mom raised you right."

Jay and Celia exchanged a quick but loving kiss then Celia touched Kamie's cheek before picking up a remote.

"Jay, can I turn off Mr. Joel?"

"Whatever you like, my Uptown Girl."

Celia smiled at him and used the remote to power off the

record player. Then she pivoted to her husband. "Okay, Mr. Nichols, it's your year to pick the Christmas movie. What'll it be?"

Jay looked at Kingsley then Kamie then Celia. "You know, I think I'll pass my turn. Whatever makes you happy is fine with me. I couldn't ask for anything more than I have right here."

Without a word, our Jay—invisible, blue Jay—moved past Brandon and me and phased through the front door. We exchanged a look before joining him in the hall.

"Cheap shot, Frost," he said, staring at the floor with his hands in his pockets.

I raised my brows. "Really? That's your reaction?"

"You're trying to make me feel guilty about what I did to Celia today."

"Brandon and I are trying to show you what it was like when you and Celia were happy. I was moved by what she said to you this afternoon, Jay. Like her, I genuinely don't know if you can't remember being happy because so much anger and pain have buried those memories, or if you are just blocking them out as a means to put distance between you two. Either way, you needed to be reminded of this—the joy and love and family you once shared. You may find it simpler to think of Celia as a villain. It lets you justify how you push her away and made throwing her under the bus today easier. However she is not a bad guy in your life story. You loved her. She made mistakes. You're both different people now, but there's no reason you can't still connect with her. You clearly got along before."

"You're assuming the woman in that apartment is still a part of Celia in present day." Jay waved at the door. "Too much has happened for that to be true. You said so yourself—we're different now. Those people in there are as dead as you two are."

I put my hands on my hips. "People change, Jay. I don't know present-day Celia well enough to say how similar or dissimilar she is to her younger self, but neither do you because you've never tried to get to know her. You may find you really like new Celia if you gave her a chance."

Jay gazed back at the door to his past life for a second, then snapped his attention to us. "Are we done here?"

"We will have two more visits to your Christmas Pasts," Brandon responded. "But we only do one visit on the first day. Time travel can be pretty overwhelming. You may be experiencing an unsafe number of feelings."

"I'll stop at the grocery store on the way home and buy extra tissues," Jay said dryly. "Now let's get back to reality."

I frowned at him as we took Brandon's hands. With a flash our trio returned to the office, fully tangible again. Jay checked out his surroundings—papers and personal items blown chaotically everywhere. "I don't suppose there's any chance of you two picking up this mess?"

"That's not in our job description," I replied.

"Of course," Jay answered. "If you're not annoying me, then you're not on the clock. Got it."

"See you tomorrow, Jay," I said flatly. "Come on, Brandon." I offered the kid my hand and we teleported back to my loft.

"How do you think that went?" Brandon asked.

"About how it typically goes," I replied. "No matter what part of the past we open with, most Scrooges are resistant at first."

"Are most Scrooges that sarcastic?"

"No. He's a special case where that's concerned . . ." I considered something. "Truthfully it doesn't bother me much. I'm kind of enjoying leaning into it by not pulling any punches with my responses. It's my last year doing this, and I'm tired of playing nice while dealing with egotistical, stubborn mistletools. Throwing decorum out the window feels oddly refreshing."

"I get that," Brandon replied. "Sometimes it feels good to tell people where to shove it."

I laughed. "Yes, that is one way to put it. Well, we're all done for the night. You can head back to the CCD."

Brandon traced his foot bashfully on the wooden floor. "Well, I could . . ."

I watched as his eyes wandered to the blanket fort he'd built and his fingers fidgeted. The part of me that had a weak spot for kids wavered. Brandon was sweet, weird, and full of moxie. I felt bad for him—a kid who died so young. I felt connected to him with our similar pasts. And, I don't know, I guess I felt protective of him too. A soul with this immense purpose thrust upon him, trying to get used to the enormity of our ghostly purpose.

"Or . . ." I mused, breaking my rules about forming non-professional relationships for the first time in decades, "since you have to come back tomorrow anyway, you could camp out here tonight."

His whole face brightened. "You wouldn't mind?"

"Are you kidding? I was just telling Marley the other day that this apartment desperately needs a blanket fort. And I'm not even tired after that Scrooging visit. Why don't we whip up a batch of pancakes and watch a movie? Your choice."

"That'd be great!"

His excitement was endearing. Brandon dashed to the kitchen as I took a deep breath.

This was so unlike me. I'd worked with new spirits before but always sent them on their way when we weren't on the clock. Why was I opening even a small sliver of personal connection now? It felt foreign—a rusty trick I hadn't performed in a long time.

As uncomfortable as it was for me in terms of routine though, it also felt like the right decision. Just like with Paul all those years ago, this kid had gotten under my skin. More than that, I had empathy for Brandon. It took me years to get good at being alone. He'd just had a big day and I felt bad sending him back to the isolation of a frigid dorm in our ghostly dimension. I may not have needed anyone, but I couldn't turn away a teammate who did. Especially one with such a similar background to mine. Brandon had a century of afterlife to adjust and cope with loneliness. I would be gone next year, hopefully, and wouldn't be able to help him through it. So if I could detract from his emptiness this season—give him a smile and some guidance before I left—I wanted to.

"Frost, come on!" Brandon called from the kitchen.

I walked over and ruffled his hair. "All right, kid. You get the flour. I'll get the mixer."

16

"I love this place," I said, startling Jay as I popped out from behind a display of poinsettias. The flowers were such pure red they'd make a color wheel cry.

I'd phased here and been waiting for him to be alone. It wasn't hard; I blended in well. My beret matched the poinsettias' shade, my turtleneck was black like the tiered display stands, and my ankle-length, flowy green skirt went flawlessly with all foliage.

"Frost, what are you doing here?" Jay asked.

I came around the display and leaned against a wall of the bustling shop. "Well, not that helping the fundraising team call supporters and ask for donations isn't *riveting*, but I am kind of on a deadline with you so being left at the office all day isn't ideal."

"I don't have time for your ghostly shenanigans right now. I only have an hour for this photo opportunity, then I have four interviews, some holiday jamboree thing, and—"

I held up my hand. "I know your schedule, Jay. Calm down. You think you're the first big shot I've worked with? I—"

A woman holding so much baby's breath you couldn't see her face wormed her way between us and knocked me back.

"Your third interview isn't real," I continued once she'd gone. "I put that in your calendar last week to block out time for me. Honestly, did you really think there was a blog called *HoliDaily News*? Annie will be getting a call from Brandon in a little while, pretending to cancel at the last minute."

"Brandon is a kid."

"He'll disguise his voice."

"You have it all figured out, don't you?" he said, rolling his eyes. We moved aside as three Hispanic women charged through the flower shop with armfuls of pinecones and pine branches. Then Annie came charging over herself.

"Okay, Jay, we have three news stations present, a photographer from *LA Magazine*, and—" Annie finally looked up from her phone. "*Frost?* Why are you here?"

"Jay texted me," I replied. "He left his fact cards about the flower district on his desk and wanted me to bring them." I reached into my pocket and handed Jay a few index cards.

Jay exhaled in frustration but played along. "*Thank you, Frost.* Annie, is the rep from the American Florists Exchange ready?"

Annie gave me a suspicious look. "Yes, he's here, along with a senior member of Southern California Flower Growers, Inc. Let's go. It's time for on-camera introductions."

"I'll be there in one minute," Jay replied. "Get them to film me coming out of this shop. Gives it a more casual, Huell Howser approach." He waved for Annie to exit.

When she left, Jay turned to me and held up the notecards. "You need to work on your lies. Campaigning for governor may have taken me all over California, but LA is my city, and history has always been my favorite subject. I may review notes before TV interviews, but I don't need cheat sheets for something like this. After I showed you the Palace theatre and The Last Bookstore, I presumed one thing you knew about me was that I value preserving the entrepreneurship that makes this city and state special. I thought you understood that, and I thought you appreciated those places I took you to. I guess you were just playing along, doing your job."

Jay handed back the stack of cards. Disappointment instead of anger marred his expression and that caused me to soften.

"I'm sorry," I replied. "I didn't mean to insult you. You're in political mode so often that it can be hard for me to tell what's genuine, but you're right. I do know that you really care about these places."

He nodded.

I pocketed the notecards as he moved toward the door for the waiting cameras.

"Jay?" I called. He turned. "For the record, I *have* appreciated the places you've taken me to. LA was once my city. It's nice to meet someone who cares about it so much. My interest and enjoyment during those trips was not a part of any job."

Jay studied me a moment. Then he shook his head and sighed. "Come on, Frost."

I caught up with him and we left the shop together. On the sidewalk, Jay activated his charm like a superhero powering up and introduced himself to the various media and flower district reps that had shown up. Annie gave me a subtle wave, indicating I should step out of the shot. I obliged and fell back, following from a distance as Jay received a private, on-camera tour of the flower district.

I didn't mind tagging along from farther away. Taking in the sights for myself was lovely. This was the most Christmassy setting I'd been in since returning to LA. While my CCD employee morale was typically low, I did love Christmas itself. And seeing, smelling, and hearing the wonder of the season was a good distraction whatever your problems.

The Los Angeles Flower District was an explosion of color in a concrete jungle. With all the different shops, and the enormous span of downtown real estate it took up, there must've been two thousand vendors. Every kind of flower and arrangement you could imagine lined the streets; it was an event planner's playground, a florist's mecca, a botanist's daydream. And at Christmastime, there wasn't a single shade of red or green missing from the party. Hundreds of holly vendors, thousands of thistles, millions of mistletoe, garlands galore—the options (and my ability to alliterate them) could go on.

I strolled in a contented daze, keeping an eye on my target and his posse but also enjoying the scenic holiday atmosphere. In this place, a girl could forget that snow wasn't meant to fall here.

Jay stopped periodically to meet vendors, ask questions, and pose for pictures. Soon enough the venture was over and conclusion handshakes were exchanged.

"Miss Jung?" said one of the reporters. "Can we ask you a few questions regarding Jay's upcoming events?"

"Yes, of course," she replied, glancing at her watch and turning to Rocco. "Ask Lucas to pull the car around."

Rocco nodded.

"Have fun?" I asked, sidling up next to Jay. Having bid goodbye to the press, he stood on the sidewalk lost in thought. "From far away it's hard to tell if your smiles are genuine."

"*Yes*, Frost. I enjoyed myself. Like I was saying, this place is a perfect example of how small businesses can thrive when cities respect them enough to give them the space and a chance. This market is over a hundred years strong and still thriving."

I nodded. "It's inspiring to see. When the LA Flower Market got started in the early 1900s over on Spring Street, it was just an idea—a vision of local Japanese-American growers. Then that led to the establishment of the city's first major Flower Market in 1912. And now here we are. Like The Orpheum turning into the Palace theatre, or The Last Book Store, this place has changed and grown, evolved with the times, but continues to be beautiful."

"Someone was paying attention during the tour," he commented with a small smile.

"Actually, I wasn't," I replied. "Like *I* was saying, LA was also once my city. The original version of this flower district was only getting started when I was still alive. I didn't know what it would become and neither did anyone else. But that's the thing about people with vision—they don't need the ego-boosts of others to know they're creating something special."

Jay's expression shifted and he crooked his brow. "Frost, how old are you?"

The SUV pulled up.

"Jay, don't you know it's rude to ask a lady her age? Dead or not, that's still what I am."

We buckled up and zoomed away, headed for our next event. Jay gazed out the window—innumerable flower shops whizzing by. His face was that of someone lost in a sad memory. I was familiar enough with the expression to know. Annie was absorbed in her phone, so I kicked Jay's shoe lightly.

"Hey, what are you thinking about?"

"I used to come here every year around this time," he said, speaking in a daze. "Celia and I had our first date Christmas week. I brought her a bouquet of Christmas Roses. It's a more unique holiday flower a few vendors here carry; I think their proper name is the Helleborus niger? Anyway, bringing her the flowers for Christmas became a tradition after that. I've driven through this market since our divorce, but I think this is the first time I've stopped."

Annie glanced up. "Christmas Roses. Those are the white things with pink hues, right?"

He nodded. "They're supposed to represent purity and hope since they bloom during the darkest months of the year when everything is frozen. Funnily though, they're also poisonous."

"That's the same with Christmas's infamous love plant, mistletoe," Annie commented. "And holly, too, now that I think about it. Strange how some things so wonderful in certain respects can be so dangerous in others."

"It's not that strange." I shrugged. "Aren't human beings the same? So much good and beauty marred by the potential to do great harm."

Annie and Jay stared at me.

"Quite the cynic, aren't you?" Annie said, raising her eyebrows.

I shifted in my seat, unsettled by the accusation and who it was coming from. I was fully aware that I'd become jaded in a lot of ways over the years, and I had cynical thoughts on occasion where the CCD's work and our Scrooges were concerned, but no one had ever outright called me a cynic before.

Is that what it'd come to? Is that who I was?

I hadn't meant for it to happen; I'd never identified myself that way. Maybe the thing about disappointment and bitterness was that they were like poisons too—the true effects could sneak up on you. That was . . . something to think about.

"I've just known a lot of Scrooges in my time." I gave Jay a quick glance. "Trying to do good can sting after a while if the people you'd like to help keep pushing back self-destructively or ignoring the negative consequences of what they're doing."

"Only if you care," Annie replied with a shrug. "Let Scrooges scrooge themselves. If people choose to crash and burn, that's their problem. There is no 'we' in humanity, but there is an 'I.' And *I've* found people do best in the world when they look out for themselves. We're not exactly a species with great long-term odds anyway. Why sour the time we have worrying about how other people fare?"

"Now who's the cynic?" I countered.

Annie shot me an annoyed look then pivoted to Jay. "It's a long ride to Costa Mesa for your first interview. Let's go over your updated schedule for after the holidays. You'll be on the road for a few months straight following the new year, and there are still a lot of decisions to be made."

"Yeah. Sure, Annie," Jay said unenthusiastically.

As the two of them began looking over documents in Annie's briefcase, I sent a text to Brandon. *"Everything is running smoothly. See you in three hours."*

At half past noon, Jay had finished up his interviews in Costa Mesa.

"I love it when we're ahead of schedule," Annie almost sang as we walked through the parking lot. "Now on to—" Her phone rang. "Hello." Her brow furrowed. "Fine. Please text me if anything changes." She hung up and huffed with irritation. "That was our next interview. It seems the reporter we were going to meet at *HoliDaily News* was called away for an emergency. They cancelled. Can you believe that?"

Lucas pulled the car up and Annie hustled us inside. "Your final interview of the day is in Irvine, Jay, so we'll just get there early." Our vehicle started to drive out of the parking structure as Annie continued. "When we get there, I have a few people who have been wanting to meet you; we can stop at their offices beforehand."

"Hey, look at that!" I pointed excitedly.

Not the most original diversion, but it worked.

In the moment Annie and Jay glanced out the window, I snapped my fingers and the tire charm on my bracelet turned to glitter.

Annie looked back at me. "What—"

KERJUNK!

The car bounced abruptly and screeched to a halt on one of the parking structure's descending ramps. Annie unbuckled immediately and stepped outside. The woman would've made a great Girl Scout troop leader; she was always ready for action.

Jay darted his eyes to me suspiciously. "Is this you?"

I checked on Annie—speaking into her phone at such aggressive volume that we could hear her through the closed car door. "Hello? I have a flat tire. I need service immediately. No, no, I don't care about the wait time. Let me talk to your supervisor . . ."

"Yes," I replied to Jay. "And in the interest of full disclosure, *this* is also me." I snapped my fingers and the satellite dish charm turned to glitter. I alluded out the window to Annie.

"My name is Annie Jung and I'm—*Awg*." Annie yanked the phone away from her ear, looked at it, then put it back. "Hello? *Hello?*" she barked. She knocked on Rocco's window and he got out. "No signal. Give me your phone."

There was no luck with his either. I'd used enough magic with that charm to cause all our cells to short-circuit, which Annie realized within the next minute of testing them.

Following a huff, she addressed us.

"I am going back inside the building to use a landline. You two wait here. Jay, review your speech for the jamboree. Rocco, come with me." She shut the door again and marched off. I laughed. Jay raised an eyebrow.

"What?"

"Is she your campaign manager or your babysitter? That woman has boundary issues."

"You're one to talk—assistant by day, Gengar by night."

"Really? A Pokémon reference? How old are *you?*" I lowered

the divider of the car. "Lucas, Jay and I need to have a private conversation. Can you not disturb us for ten minutes please?"

"Yes, ma'am."

I raised the divider, made sure all the tinted windows were rolled up, then turned back to Jay. "And being a ghost isn't a night gig. It's a full-time job. Wait here. I'll be right back."

I flashed away, leaving Jay dumbfounded in the SUV. A few seconds later, Brandon and I reappeared. The kid rubbed his hand on the leather seat of the interior.

"Sweet ride." He clambered across the car. "Is this thing like a limo? Are there free sodas in here like in the movies?"

"Brandon," I said. "We'll get snacks later. We're working with a limited timeframe."

"Right, right." Brandon nodded. "Hands please."

I took hold. My colleague and I stared at Jay expectantly.

"*Fine*," he groaned.

In a flash, we were standing in front of a house adorned with twinkling lights. Our ghostly blue bodies were iridescent in the darkness of evening. Jay let go of Brandon's hand and took a few steps toward to his childhood home. In the doorway Jay's mom, stepfather, and twin sisters watched as the kid and his dad trotted down the driveway toward Marlon's truck.

"I remember this Christmas," Jay said. "This is the first year my sisters chose our mom and Raymond over our dad."

"That's one way to put it," Brandon responded. "Serious question though, bro—do you remember what that Christmas was like for you?"

Jay blinked. "Yeah, my dad picked me up with a special apple like always. We had dinner out and then went back to his place. We made a blanket fort in the living room and stayed up late watching movies."

Brandon and I exchanged a look.

"Hey, Frost, do you know if there's a Sunglass Hut nearby?" Brandon asked. "Because I think our pal Jay needs to get his rose-colored glasses cleaned."

The kid pivoted and looked up at Jay. "In all seriousness, man, you weren't much older than me in this memory, and at our age, we tend to see what we want to see. Memories aren't always accurate because of that. You're in your thirties now. Time and resentment have a way of warping the truth."

Brandon took our hands and we moved from that scene to a burger restaurant—a drive-thru with a few tables on the sidewalk. Jay and his dad sat at a table eating. One of the fluorescent light bulbs flickered slightly and a car alarm went off in the distance. They ate in silence. Ten-year-old Jay happily munched on his burger, not noticing how frequently his dad checked his watch.

Still holding onto us, Brandon changed the scene to later in the evening. We landed in a small apartment without Christmas decorations, rusting fire escape visible through the dusty window. What Jay called a blanket fort looked like an inflatable mattress, a few pillows, and some sheets draped over a couple of chairs. Jay lay on his stomach watching TV. Marlon sat in an old armchair, tuning his guitar. The clock read nine o'clock. Brandon suddenly turned the clock forward in time to half past eleven. Jay was now asleep on the mattress. His dad whispered on his landline phone, hung up, glanced at Jay, then slipped out of the apartment. Finally Brandon flashed us to the man's destination. At a little past midnight, Marlon was at a bar playing cards with some guys.

Brandon returned us to Jay's mom's house where we had started and let go of our hands.

Jay glared at us. "So my dad had meager means to work with. That doesn't make him a bad father, and it definitely doesn't make me look down on our time spent together. Felicia and Monica may have had a problem with it, but I don't."

Brandon slapped a hand to his head. "Man, it's not about that. The point is that *he* didn't really value his time with you. Seeing those moments from this Christmas was supposed to make you question how you've romanticized the past." Brandon flicked his eyes to me. "I used that word correctly, right?"

"Nailed it," I replied. I tagged in and stepped forward, addressing Jay with hands on my hips. "Now go look at what you and your dad missed out on." I pointed to the house.

Jay frowned, but turned and walked toward it, curious despite himself. Brandon and I followed at a distance.

The inside of the dwelling glowed with warmth as Jay's mom, stepdad, siblings, and various members of their extended family gathered at the table with hands joined and eyes closed. Two chairs remained empty beside the twins.

"Bless this family, bless this meal, and bless those who could not be here with us," Raymond said. "We are thankful for the gifts of the past year, the promise of the future, and most of all, for right now."

The family began digging into the feast. Brandon grabbed us both and his eyes glowed with meteor brilliance as he moved the scene forward. The evening sped around us. We watched the family have dinner, relatives make elaborate gestures with wide grins as they told stories, cookies come out of the oven, presents get opened beneath the tree. It was a whirlwind of laughter, frolicking, and fun. Jay observed his family with a blank expression and a glimmer of hurt in his eyes the whole time. When Brandon finally ceased control over time as the clock struck midnight, our Scrooge continued to stand frozen.

I nodded to Brandon then the kid enveloped us in light. A second later, we were back in the SUV in the parking lot.

Jay seemed wounded and glowered at us. "You think I don't know that I missed out on the fun of traditional Christmases during those years that I went with my dad? After he died, I spent every Christmas with my family until I left for college. I know my mom did the holiday right. Why do you think I resent her? She drove my dad away and then made me choose between the holiday and being with him."

"*But she didn't make you choose*," I argued. "She didn't make him choose either. Brandon and I have poked through your past thoroughly, Jay. Every year, your mom extended the offer for your dad to join them for Christmas. *Every single year*. He could've spent the holiday with you and your sisters, but his pride and bitterness kept him away, just like yours has kept you away when Celia and Eddie ask you to join them."

A pause hung in the air.

"Incoming busybody," Brandon commented, pointing through the window at Annie, who was stomping across the parking lot toward the SUV.

I rapidly reached for Brandon's hand, dropped him off at my loft, then reappeared in my seat barely a moment before Annie opened the door.

"Help is on the way. We should be out of here in fifteen minutes," she said, climbing into the back seat. Then she saw the frowns on both our faces. "Did I miss something?"

"No." I stared at Jay. "Jay, how about you? Did *you* miss something?"

His return glare held strong before he went for the door handle. "I need some air."

Fashion Island.

When I learned of this place during a ghostly return to Southern California years ago, I excitedly wondered if some fashionistas had taken boats to Catalina Island and seized control of the land for their own shopping purposes—turning it into a mecca for clothes and accessories. Regrettably, Fashion Island was just a fancy outdoor shopping plaza located in the heart of Newport Beach.

Though there were plenty of designer shops in the area, the plaza's main attraction was free. Fashion Island's epic Christmas tree was forty feet high, dotted with no fewer than five hundred ornaments, and surrounded by giant, glittering packages adorned with bows. The tree's lights shined, but mildly. Night hadn't fallen yet; the sun was only beginning to set somewhere far off and it looked like someone had spilled guava juice over the sky.

Jay stood on a stage next to the tree, his charm turned up to maximum.

"Once again, I want to thank you for having me. Now let's give it up a final time for the Corona Del Mar High School band and your talented local youth choir!" He clapped along with the many spectators. The band began to play "Gloria" to the fluid harmony of the choir.

Jay dismounted the stage. At the end of the performance, everyone applauded again before reporters and cameramen made a beeline for him. Annie abruptly shoved some cash at me. "Bloomingdale's has a restaurant. I'd like a latte, one sugar, iced." Without waiting for my response, she trotted after Jay. I crumpled the money in my hand but did as I was told.

When I returned, the crowd had dispersed and I had to wander a bit before I found Jay by Santa's Village, taking pictures with families while Annie hovered nearby.

I handed her the coffee and change. She accepted without a thank you and waved me away. With a deep breath intended to provide prolonged patience, I moved to stand next to Santa's house, out of the way.

The Santa impersonator came over to me, drinking from a

to-go cup and eyeballing the crowd around Jay. "Tough season," he quipped. "I can't believe I have to compete with a politician for attention."

I smirked. "Politicians come and go. You'll never go out of style." I gave the Santa a quick glance. Then I did a double take. *"Paul?!"*

He pulled down the fake beard a moment. "Keep it down, Frost. You'll blow my cover."

"What are you doing here?"

"My dad makes me and my sister periodically work these kinds of events every December. I never mentioned it because I thought you'd make fun of me." He slapped the stuffing of his fake belly, jiggling it like gelatin. "My elf trainer dies a little inside whenever he sees me cover my abs with this, but Dad says the experience is good for us. Can't run a business if you don't know the customers, right?"

"Hi, Frost." Margo Claus popped up next to me on the left, dressed as an elf. Her wavy, orange-bronze hair spilled down to her waist, and her green eyes sparkled like her cutesy dress.

"Margo has to be an elf," Paul explained. "The beard doesn't work with her."

His sister raised an eyebrow. "Facial hair doesn't exactly compliment you either. Next year, I'm having the costume department make me red overalls and you can wear all these jingly bells."

"That's a hard sell, sis."

She shrugged. "The CCD Scrooged an executive at Coco Cola recently. I'm sure with a little persuasion they'd put my face on a series of cans for their winter ads campaign then BOOM! Lady Santas could totally be a thing."

I cleared my throat to get their attention otherwise their sibling back-and-forth could go on for a while.

"Right," Paul said, regrouping. "Anyway, Frost, I couldn't believe it when I spotted you in the audience at the Christmas tree jamboree and thought I'd surprise you. How's it going with your Scrooging?"

I crossed my arms. "I *think* it's going okay. Targets always fight back during the Past Phase, usually getting angry and defensive. It can be discouraging, but Jay should be turning around soon."

"He's cute," Margo commented, eyeballing my Scrooge in the distance.

I glanced at Jay as he shook hands, finishing up with the crowd and cameras. "Glad you think so," I replied.

"Hey, Frost," Paul said then. "Did you do something to Bismaad? We hung out last night and when I mentioned you, she seemed ticked off."

I scratched at my palm anxiously. "I ditched her at a party and she got mad."

"Well, that's weird."

I nodded. "She's totally overreacting."

"No, I mean it's strange that she's letting it bother her now considering how many times you've ditched her over the course of your friendship."

My attention sharpened—defensiveness settling in—and my eyes diverted from watching Jay to fully looking at Paul. "I'm not that bad, am I? I don't like socializing as much as other ghosts or people do, but that doesn't make me a bad friend."

"Isn't socializing *part* of being a friend?" Margo asked. "I mean, other than my family I only hang out with elves, so maybe it's different with humans, but Twinkie and Bibbly Bap are my best friends. Even during the busy season we still make an effort to have brunch every week."

"I'm not a brunch kind of girl or ghost," I replied. It was frustrating that people never understood where I was coming from. "I'm good at being alone and don't need to be around other people constantly to feel happy. Isn't that a strength—being independent and self-reliant?"

Paul shrugged. "Sure. But you realize there's a difference between being independent and isolated? I accept you as you are, Frost; I always have. But I think that if I didn't go out of my way to hang out with you every December, we probably would go years without speaking, like you and my dad. You don't naturally invest the time or vulnerability that friendship requires unless provoked. And even then, you pull back."

I glanced at Margo, as if for a second opinion. She shrugged. "Girl, you and I aren't close, but if my brother were wrong, wouldn't you have more friends after a century?"

I frowned. That's more or less what Bismaad had told me.

"Frost . . ." Paul said, putting a hand on my arm. "Needing people may not be a requirement to feel happy, but it is a requirement to feel human. If Bismaad got mad at you, it could be because she's worried that if both living *and* dead you didn't figure that out, your next life may be just as empty. And then you'd end up back at the CCD."

My eyes widened with horror. I *genuinely* had not thought about that.

Could that happen?

"Frost?" Jay strode over, having finished his schmoozing. "We're going soon." He paused and raised an eyebrow when he noticed Paul's hand on me. "Hi, Santa."

"Paul Claus," Paul said, extending his hand.

Jay shook it. "Nice to meet you. Word to the wise though, you probably shouldn't half commit to the role; there are kids around. I recommend always introducing yourself as *Santa* Claus when you're on duty. Paul doesn't exactly scream 'North Pole' as far as names go."

Paul chuckled. "Solid tip. Thanks."

Jay took me by the elbow and led me a few steps away. "Annie and I are going to use one of the department store dressing rooms to change for my next event. Can you do your pretend job and contact the office? We need the latest guest list from Councilman Walden's secretary. Annie wants to go over it in the car, make sure I know the right things to say to the right people."

"And here I thought buttering up people for personal gain came naturally to you."

"Just do it, Frost."

"Aye, aye, pretend boss." I mock saluted.

Jay rolled his eyes and walked off to join Annie. I waved to Paul and Margo. "Bye, guys. I'll see you later."

"I hope so, Frost . . ." Paul said.

Something about the way he said it made me pause. Then I shook my head and stayed the course.

17

Once I had finished my assistant task, I headed into the department store where Jay and Annie were changing. I found them outside the dressing rooms. Jay was straightening his tie and looking in a mirror when I arrived. Annie sat on the edge of an armchair, now wearing a pair of black trousers and a silvery collared shirt.

"We're eight minutes ahead of schedule. Let's move." Annie gave me a sideways glance, eyeing the pine needles and various smudges I'd gotten on my skirt at the flower district. "Should I assume you are going like that?"

"I can change my look if it's important to you."

"There's no time for shopping."

"I don't need to go shopping." I pulled down my ankle-length skirt, revealing the slim-fit black pants underneath that matched my turtleneck. The pants were tucked into my knee-high wine-colored boots. I stepped out of the skirt, took off my red beret, removed my scrunchie, and shook out my brown hair. All done, I picked the skirt off the floor and put it on an armchair. "Bam. Ready. Not super fancy, I know, but it's a clean and chic beatnik look."

Jay and Annie blinked at me. It took a lot of chutzpah to make these two speechless. The latter opened her mouth to say something, but then just sighed and waved us forward.

We wormed our way across the busy department store. Jay

stiffened when we moved through the perfume department. His brow pinched tautly.

"It's because of Celia, isn't it?" I whispered, sidling up to him.

"What?"

"You dislike flowery perfume because that's what Celia wears. I first noticed her scent when she crashed the school visit, and have smelled the same potent perfume on her the other times she's been close by."

Jay's eyes—facing forward until now—finally looked down at me as we walked. "I hope they pay you good money at your ghost job. You're creepily observant."

"We're more of a room-and-board situation. But thanks."

"It wasn't a compliment, Frost."

"Depends on your perspective."

We exited the store. Dark had fallen, the guava sky of dusk replaced by deep twilight. Night settled in completely by the time we pulled up to the posh home of the councilman. Sparkling lanterns and hedges stuffed with white twinkle lights framed the long driveway before we reached the main entrance. Several massive lit-up snowmen decorated the main lawn.

After being dropped off, we made our way up the brick steps to the three-story home. A handful of guests were waiting in line to enter ahead of us. I felt a little more casually dressed than the others, but being a magical Christmas Ghost gave you a different outlook on self-esteem. I had an enchanted closet, but I'd been in enough situations over the last century to know it didn't matter what you wore in the end, or who you looked like—executive, assistant, zookeeper, maid—if you met someone in the eye with confidence, you'd command their attention.

"Can you do me a favor?" Jay whispered to me, catching me off guard. "Give me a bit of space in there. This house is full of important potential donors and I'm not going to be able to concentrate if I keep having to worry about you and Oliver Twist crashing the party."

I was inclined to shut down the request—after all, I was on a schedule—but there was something about the look in his eyes. Jay wasn't giving me an order. He was genuinely asking.

"That's the wrong Dickens story," I replied. "But fine. I promise to give you two uninterrupted hours. After that, Brandon and I are taking you away for another trip. Your Christmas Past visits need to be completed tonight. Deal?"

"Deal."

We were greeted enthusiastically at the door and another merry mingling montage commenced. Though I kept an eye on Jay, most of my evening was spent scrolling through Tinsel or checking out the Christmas decorations. My only interactions were with the occasional waiter carrying hors d'oeuvres. Oh, and this one random guy who stopped to talk to me.

"Decent party."

A handsome man with wavy blond hair like a young Thor stood beside me. He sipped a glass of milk from a wine glass. Unusual beverage choice for a grown man at a party, but Jay liked a glass of milk during his private time. Maybe adult men had become more complicated in the twenty-first century.

"It is," I agreed.

"You're here with Jay Nichols, the candidate for governor, right?" the guy said.

"I'm his assistant."

"I once heard a saying that those who can't do, teach. Are assistants those who'd rather concentrate on helping others versus themselves?"

I pivoted; now this guy had my full attention. "Not that it's any of your business, but I like helping people. And *I* don't need help."

His eyes seemed to dance with laughter. "Are you sure about that? Sometimes people latch onto those with similar problems as a way of healing themselves. But that just keeps you from realizing the truth that could let you move forward."

The comment felt like a jab to my sternum, though the wave of offense allowed me to not analyze why. Who did this guy think he was? Maybe twenty-first century men had also gotten a bit too comfortable voicing their unwarranted—*and incorrect*—opinions.

I checked my watch. Two hours had passed and it was time to get going. "I have work to do. Excuse me." I pushed past the obnoxious partygoer.

After fetching my ghostly colleague and leaving the kid in a safe place, I waited for Annie to leave Jay's side. When she'd gone, I came up behind him.

"You and I have business," I said.

He groaned, turning to face me. "Annie will only be gone a minute. She went to find the owner of some pistachio empire I'm supposed to schmooze."

"What, was the almond king unavailable?"

He released a laugh, despite himself.

"Don't worry. I have distraction contingencies for Annie." I spotted the woman heading toward us from the foyer, accompanied by a tall guy with slicked back hair. I stepped behind Jay for cover and snapped my fingers. The heart charm on my bracelet fizzled into glitter. I stepped around my Scrooge to observe the result. As Annie and the pistachio man passed beneath the archway connecting the rooms, a sparkling sprig of mistletoe sprouted above them. The gentleman stopped suddenly, looking mystified.

Annie paused to see why he'd faltered. Stars in his eyes, he glanced up at the mistletoe. Then he planted the biggest kiss on Annie I'd seen since *The Princess Bride*. She actually looked into it for a second; it certainly got the attention of the crowd around her. Then she pushed the guy away and slapped him. High-pitched indignation ensued. Her rage drew the attention of the crowds, providing ample distraction.

I took Jay's hand in mine. "We have a few minutes before that gets sorted." I led him down an adjoining hallway and to the kitchen.

Brandon waited for us inside, sitting on a countertop as he chewed a leg of turkey like a Viking. Three Christmas cookies were stuffed in his left pocket. Staff members buzzed around—cooks prepping more food, servers waiting for fresh trays of appetizers.

"Watch your feet," I said to Jay. I hopped on the countertop beside Brandon. Then, with my hand low to conceal the magical effect, I snapped my fingers to activate another charm. Two seconds passed and then—

"RAT!" yelled one of the cooks.

The kitchen staff started freaking out. People either fled in fear or joined the team chasing the rat down the hall. The room was empty in ten seconds. I dismounted the counter and shut the sliding double doors, locking them from the inside.

"Now then, Jay." I approached him steadily. "In all seriousness, I need you to have an open mind and calm disposition for what we're going to show you. Sometimes when Scrooges get disillusioned about their pasts, they don't take it well."

Brandon offered us his hands. Jay accepted hesitantly. The kid activated his powers and, following a swipe of spectral magic, we stood in an apartment living room.

Six-year-old Jay sat by the artificial silver tree playing with a plastic truck while his baby sisters waddled in the adjacent pen. Ghostly Jay let go of Brandon and put his hands in his pockets as he took a brief look around. Then he shrugged.

"So my parents' first apartment is messy and modest. Way to oversell the trip, Frost."

"Wait for it," I said.

Arguing voices grew in the background, soon becoming yelling. Jay furrowed his brow and headed toward the kitchen; Brandon and I trailed behind.

Jay's mom pointed a wooden spoon at his dad. "I can't believe you lost that money. That was for the kids' presents, Marlon. You were supposed to go straight to the store after work to pick them up, not out with your scum friends."

"I'm sorry, Sandra," he said, though he didn't seem very apologetic. "I thought I could double it. You know my band has been struggling. If I'd won, I could've used the money to help us, maybe buy you something nice too, like a necklace or a new dress."

She slammed the spoon down. "I don't need a new dress, Marlon. I need a husband who has a real job. A husband who doesn't blow our kids' Christmas present money on a gamble."

Marlon rubbed the back of his head. "Actually, it wasn't just that money . . . See, I was ahead for a bit, and you know you can't interrupt a hot streak. Besides, with the rent money—" He stopped himself and grimaced.

Sandra had gone perfectly still. Then ire filled her eyes. "Marlon are you telling me—"

"Mommy?" Little Jay trotted in with his truck under one arm. "Why are you guys yelling?"

"We're just arguing about which reindeer is the fastest," Marlon said quickly, squatting next to his son before Sandra could respond.

Jay wiped his nose with the back of his hand. "That's easy. Dasher. It's in the name."

Marlon forced a smile. "You're probably right. Come on, why

don't you play in the living room for a bit longer while your mom and I finish cooking."

Marlon escorted his son back to the play area. We watched as the man turned on the record player and cranked up the volume. Loud Billy Joel music filled the small apartment before Marlon returned to the kitchen.

"There. That ought to keep the kid from hearing us." Marlon paused. Sandra was adding a large, empty glass bottle to the trash in the kitchen. It was one of several already collected in the bin. She shut the lid of the trash forcefully then went to the counter and collected a glass with her lipstick on it. She promptly moved to the sink to wash it, her hands shaking slightly. Marlon hovered over her.

"You should try to change in the new year. For our family's sake," he said.

She laughed once. Darkly. Then turned off the faucet with a rough smack of her hand. "What great advice, Marlon. Now if you're not going to make yourself useful in here, either go to the store and buy me another bottle or go play with the kids. Pick one and then get out of my way."

Marlon stepped back, then leaned against the counter watching his wife as she continued to work, her eyes mistier than before. He didn't intervene. He just stood there.

Ghost Jay left the kitchen abruptly. "I've seen enough," he said. "Take me back."

We didn't argue. After linking hands, Brandon returned us to the kitchen of the councilman's home. A muffled commotion sounded outside, but in the kitchen everything felt still.

"I know that couldn't have been easy to see," I said to Jay, letting go of Brandon's hand.

"My mom had a drinking problem," Jay said, looking at the floor. "I already knew that. As it got worse, it became more difficult for my dad to deal with. That's why it's especially hard for me to forgive Celia. She knew how I felt about the issue. I don't drink because of that. I never have. When Celia lost herself to the same problem, it was a betrayal."

I shook my head, aggravated. "It's not a betrayal, Jay. Don't be so self-centered. Celia's drinking has nothing to do with you. That is a real struggle that she has to deal with every day. Same with your mother. But they both were strong enough to recognize the problem and get help. From what Brandon and I have seen of the past and present, it's clear they have stayed committed to their recovery one day at a time. And their futures look good too. That aside . . . we didn't show you that scene to bring up painful memories regarding Celia or your mom. This was about your dad."

Jay's eyes narrowed. "You guys can't expect me to rewrite my entire opinion of my dad based on a snapshot of one bad holiday. People make mistakes. That doesn't make them bad."

"We're not saying he's a bad guy, bro," Brandon responded. "We're just trying to—"

"Tarnish the memory of someone who is already gone," Jay cut him off harshly. "Both of you should reevaluate how you do your jobs. If I'm in danger of being a Scrooge for the rest of my life, maybe you should focus your little time field trips on the people who are still in it." He turned and unlocked the kitchen doors. "And you two *especially* should know better than to speak ill of the dead."

He stormed off. Brandon and I stood in silence for a moment before the kid picked up his turkey leg and huffed. "That went well."

It was half past nine when Jay and I left the party. Annie was staying for what she called "late night networking." Like a strict parent though, she insisted Jay go at a reasonable hour so he could get rest for tomorrow; she'd summon a car to take her home later.

My Scrooge and I rode quietly on the freeway for a long while. Our bodies were soaked in shadow except for when Jay pulled out his phone and his face became illuminated by its digital glow. When we entered downtown LA where the glistening skyscrapers and apartment towers concealed the sky, I finally turned to face my Scrooge.

"I think we should talk about your father."

Jay didn't look up from his phone. "Hard pass."

"Come on, Jay. This Scrooging is supposed to help you open up, not crunch you into a tighter ball."

"Okay, how about this." He looked at me expectantly. "I'll tell you about my dad if you tell me what it was like when you went through puberty."

"*WHAT?*"

"Exactly." He stuffed his phone in his pocket. "Prying into people's personal business is easy but no one wants to share details about their own sensitive issues. So get off your high horse and leave me alone."

The glassy spark in his eyes provoked me. I crossed my arms and leaned back with confidence. "The year was 1905. It was a warm springtime in Los Angeles, and little did I know I was the next flower about to bloom—"

"Whoa, whoa, whoa. What are you doing?" Jay cut me off, eyes wide.

"If the price of you sharing is me sharing, I'll pay it. I'm a ghost, Jay. Subtlety and shame were left behind in my previous life. You're underestimating how important it is to me to see this job—i.e., you—through to the end successfully."

Jay wiped his hand down his face and groaned in frustration.

"Frost, is it so wrong that I only want to remember good things about my dad? That I want to forgive him for any mistakes he made and just cherish the memories I have? Isn't that healthier than being angry at someone who is gone?"

I leaned forward, my hands clasped as if in prayer. "There is absolutely nothing wrong with focusing on the good in people. And you're right; carrying resentment for someone who is no longer part of this world is unhealthy. What Brandon and I are concerned with isn't that you're focusing on the good, it's that you're denying that bad even happened. You have this vision of a perfect father in your head, and the man was far from perfect. He wasn't there for you, your siblings, or your mother the ways he could have been. In fact, I'd venture he may have driven your mother deeper into her drinking issue."

Jay glared. "You don't get to speculate on that."

"I do when your emotional well-being is my business. You blame your mom's problems for driving your dad away, when the truth is that he was a catalyst for breaking your family apart."

A chilling, uncomfortable quiet ensued. I tried to find something else to say, but before I could, the car stopped. We'd arrived at my building.

"Think about it and get some rest," I told Jay as I unbuckled. "You'll see things differently soon enough."

Jay crossed his arms, looking away from me. "I doubt that."

"This week is a marathon, not a sprint, Jay. If people like you were easy to rush to realizations, ghosts like me wouldn't need so much time to work with you."

Lucas opened the door for me and I stepped out. Jay didn't acknowledge my departure. I stayed on the curb until the car pulled out of sight, taillights disappearing down the avenue.

"Why aren't you dancing, Frost?" Marsha asked, migrating over to me with a glass of cider in hand. She stirred it with a cinnamon stick before taking a sip.

The CCD Christmas Party was in full swing as the realm neared midnight. The noise and crowds and bonding were not my scene. Given that it was my first season back from the dead, it all felt a little disorienting.

"This is a lot to process," I replied. "When I was alive, I never went dancing. As a ghost, I doubt my rhythm would be much improved. Past that, this is not my idea of relaxation. After this week, I am simply looking forward to getting some sleep."

Something about Marsha's face changed; a nervousness set in and she twirled the end of her blonde ponytail as she took another sip of cider. It was like she felt guilty or something.

The clock struck midnight and silver confetti fell from the ceiling. The ghosts cheered as Specter One took the stage and the music lowered.

"Everyone, thank you so much for your work this holiday season. If Santa wasn't somewhere over the Atlantic, I know he'd want to personally express his most sincere thanks as well. For all our returning ghosts, we'll proceed with the normal slumbering order—Past Ghosts at 1:00 a.m., Future Ghosts at 2:00 a.m., and Present Ghosts at 3:00 a.m. To our ghosts serving as mentors this season, please escort your trainees to their designated rooms immediately. DJ Dizzle and DJ Dazzle, let's keep this party going as long as possible. Hit it!"

A pair of elves wearing glossy helmets twisted knobs and pulled levers on their command center, causing music to flood the ballroom again. Marsha put a hand on my shoulder.

"Come on, kid. It's time to go."

Marsha had become serious and tense, and that worried me.

"I have two questions," I said. "One, should you really be

calling me kid if you died as a teenager and I'm in my twenties? And two, where are we going?"

Marsha directed me out of the party. The other ghosts who'd been in my recruit class, Ty and Bill, exited with their respective mentors too, but while they headed up the hall to the right, Marsha and I went left.

"I may have died in my teen years, Frost, but I have been at the CCD for three decades. In terms of maturity, that makes me way older than you," Marsha replied as we walked. "And to answer your second question, we're going to prep you for next Christmas."

The tinsel hanging from the ceiling cast snakelike shadows in the glow of the Northern Lights, worming above us as we migrated over the skybridge.

"I can't believe you've been in the afterlife for a full thirty years," I commented. Marsha escorted me to a regular elevator— the kind meant to take us to different floors of the CCD, not other realms. She scanned her ID. All of a sudden a glowing button that I'd never seen on the panel shimmered into existence. It read *BF*. Marsha pressed the button.

"Basement Floor?" I guessed as our lift descended.

"Yes and no," Marsha replied uneasily. "And I haven't been a ghost for thirty full years, just thirty Christmases."

The elevator was built on the side of the CCD, allowing us to view the wintery realm beyond our home through the glass walls of the lift. After descending all the aboveground floors, I watched our elevator drop past the snow line, sinking to a windowless sublevel. Iron walls surrounded us now. Five seconds later, the doors opened and we stepped into a huge warehouse.

Rows and rows of large ice capsules, like the one I'd woken up in, were present—some laid out and resting horizontally like coffins, dozens more racked in rows behind them. I assumed it was as cold in here as it was outside because huge parts of the metal walls and floor were frozen over. The ceiling, laden with massive icicle stalactites, seemed constructed of the same glittery material as the igloo infirmary I'd started the month in.

I watched in awe as elves in coveralls drove cranes and moved capsules to ground level from the racks they were stored in. Other elves held clipboards, running equipment checks with the assistance of polar bears in bright orange vests.

Specter One was waiting for us, standing ten feet away in front of an ice capsule that had been brought down from the nearest row. I didn't know how he'd beaten us to this place, but I did know this place was not where I wanted to be.

"Hello, Frost," he said.

I looked at Marsha. "Just thirty Christmases, not thirty years," I thought aloud. "That's what you said."

Marsha sighed. "Frost, existing in this form of afterlife takes a lot of energy, magic, and cold. One soul saved provides just enough magic and energy to rejuvenate the team of three ghosts assigned to a Scrooge. But only for another month. Once Christmas is over, we go back into these enchanted ice chambers; they preserve us until next season when we're needed again. This is the storage facility for Ghosts of Christmas Present—the Body Freezing room."

An elf cranked a lever and the lid of the ice capsule behind Specter One snapped open, hanging off its hinges on the left side. Mist from the capsule poured around our boss.

I took an uneasy step back. "You're telling me that we need to go back into those things every Christmas Day? *That's* our reward for spending a whole month trying to save some-one?"

"It's not that bad," Marsha commented. "It's not as restful as being asleep, but it's better than being dead. And although ghosts can't dream, as you have noticed this month, we can relive past memories."

I took two more steps back. "No way. I am not being entombed. I didn't sign up for this. I didn't ask for this. I have no interest in being a ghost if it means spending eleven months of the year frozen in an ice coffin reliving my memories on loop. That's enough to drive any person insane."

Specter One came toward me. "A person maybe, but you're a ghost, Frost. Trust me, you'll get used to it. Everyone here does. Eventually you'll look at this eleven-month stint as a restful vacation and your job in December as an adventure."

"He's right," Marsha chimed in. "I resisted at first. We all do. But after a couple of seasons, you get into a rhythm and realize how wonderful it is to be a part of this. I am sorry we had to spring the truth on you this way, but"—she glanced at Specter One—"Santa and the Senior Specters have found it's best to reveal truths about the CCD to us in phases so we can adjust and not become overwhelmed or overburdened."

"What if a spirit wants out?" I asked, pausing for a moment. "Could you set me free? Can I just go wherever other souls who weren't chosen head after they die?"

"I'm afraid not," Specter One said. "We didn't choose you specifically, Frost. Ages ago, Santa Claus Twelve sought a way to recruit others to help him spread Christmas Spirit on Earth. He embedded magical contingencies into the universe to redirect the right souls here. Your soul was caught in our 'mystical net,' so to speak, because you met the qualifications that this ancient Santa set forth. The only way your soul can move on from here is if you save one hundred Scrooges. The magic generated from a century of successful seasons will allow us to help you do that. More on this later though. For now, it's time to go to sleep."

"No, I can't. I won't—" I turned and bumped into a large polar bear standing on his hind legs. He scooped me up in a big bear hug and carried me over to the open ice capsule. I struggled desperately.

"Frost, it'll be okay," Marsha said reassuringly, though she looked sad.

The polar bear put me in the capsule and before I could escape, the lid closed. I banged on the ice, seeing Marsha and Specter One's faces looking down on me. Mist started to pump into the chamber, and my hands began to flicker with blue energy.

"No! Let me go! Let me—"

"Frost?"

I bolted up in bed with a fearful cry. Brandon and Marley reflexively scampered into the blanket fort. After a moment they poked their heads out with concern.

"That must've been some memory," Brandon commented, emerging in plaid pajamas with a matching old-timey nightcap.

I blinked and took a moment to adjust, then rubbed my face. "It was."

"Was it a memory from your original life or afterlife?"

My fingers clutched the edges of the bedsheets. "Afterlife. The end of my first season with the CCD, my training year."

Brandon's face shifted. "The refreezing?" he asked knowingly.

"Yeah," I replied, staring vacantly at the Christmas tree in the corner.

An acidic chill crept through my body. Pain accompanied it. I wondered if this is what it felt like to be holly or mistletoe or a Christmas Rose. I was supposed to embody Christmas Spirit, but venom pumped through me.

Suddenly I glanced down in surprise. Brandon's small hand squeezed mine.

"We can't take Jay on any more trips to his past, Brandon," I said, thinking he meant to activate his powers. "What do you want to show me?"

"Nothing," he said. "Except that I care. And that I get it."

I tilted my head at him.

"I didn't have any family on Earth," Brandon said. "I like you, Frost. I appreciate how you've looked out for me. You're the best sister, aunt, maternal figure, ghost mentor I ever had. Sorry." He rubbed the back of his head. "I'm not good at guessing ages. How old were you when you died? Twenty-five? Thirty-five? Fifty?"

I laughed, loudly and heartily.

"What's so funny?"

"I've never been so insulted and complimented at the same time." I put my hand over his for a second. "I like you too, Brandon. And for the record, I'm in my twenties. Now come on." I got out of bed and squished into my slippers. "Let's make you a solid breakfast before you head back to the CCD."

"Chocolate chip pancakes? Or blueberry?" he asked.

"You just finished your first solo round as a Ghost of Christmas Past, kid. I think that earns you both."

"So how long is this power outage supposed to last?" Jay asked.

We watched from the side of the auditorium as maintenance workers with flashlights escorted guests out.

"I didn't use much magic, so half an hour at the most," I replied. "I should warn you that I have the means to do this trick a second time." I held up my hand and jingled my bracelet. One lightning bolt charm remained.

"This was an important lecture for me, Frost," Jay said crossly. "I went to this college. These political science students came back to campus between semesters just for me. I was looking forward to telling them about what a real life in politics is like."

"Just tell them to see a Liam Neeson movie; it's the same thing. The stakes are high, but there's a lot of disappointment. Anyway, you're hardly the best example for them. College is when you first compromised your political character. I doubt you were going to lead with that inspiring story."

Jay had made a lot of faces at me—most of them shades of irritation or fatigue—but I think this was the first time he appeared genuinely hurt. He opened his mouth but only air came out; the right words eluded him.

I sighed. "I know about the fixed fraternity election, Jay."

"I didn't cheat," he responded in a hushed tone. "I could've won. I should've won."

"Could've and should've are the favorite words of a guilty conscience."

The last of the students filed out. Annie stomped across the stage with several maintenance men in her wake. That woman was never at a loss when it came to giving orders.

"I did a great job as vice president," Jay told me firmly. "I could have done a great job in any of the other dozens of positions I tried to achieve in my life. But no one will ever know because no one ever gave me a chance. That position in college became my chance. It could've been my only chance for all I knew. So I took it. The only consequences were a year of excellence in my fraternity and a star on my resume that led to the job in the councilman's office that I got the following year."

"I'm glad it worked out," I replied nonchalantly. "But sometimes a morally questionable choice that doesn't have bad consequences is worse than one that does. It gives you a taste for something, and it creates a precedent for the future when you have to make other tough decisions." I glanced over at the stage.

"Annie!" She looked my way. "Jay and I are going to get a coffee. We'll be back in fifteen."

Without waiting for her to answer, I took Jay by the arm and escorted him up the aisle of the auditorium. All the students were milling about outside, killing time on their phones. I directed Jay to a dark corner of the auditorium's foyer by the bathrooms then used a frying pan charm to cause the security camera across from us to spark and die.

"Let's put a pin in all that," I said. "Although your political motivations are important, I don't want to let up on where we left off last night. It's time to confront your family issues, Jay. This time in the here and now." I offered him my hand.

"Where's the little rascal?"

"Brandon's time is done. I am your Ghost of Christmas Present; your next three journeys are with me alone."

He didn't reach out, so I took his hand myself. Blue energy surrounded us, then we were inside a beautiful two-story home. Natural light from plenty of windows made the space pleasant and inviting. Red ribbon encircled simple white columns holding up the living room's archway, resembling giant candy canes. Crocheted Christmas throws covered three couches. A six-foot noble fir sat in the corner, wrapped in homemade rainbow paper chains and surrounded by presents. Over a dozen stockings with embroidered names hung from the wooden staircase.

Jay glanced around. "Where are we?"

"The fact that you don't know says way more about you than I think you're going to like," I replied.

An older woman came out of the corridor behind us. She wore a vibrant marigold dress with a matching sweater and a bold red necklace. Her face was sweet, wrinkled, and focused as she set down a bowl of delicious-looking pasta salad on a dining table, centered within an alcove off-shoot of the living room. Utensils, plates, and napkins were already there, along with serving dishes loaded with corn muffins, greens, and chips.

"Mom," Jay said, shocked.

Sandra passed right through him to go back the way she'd come. Jay turned to me, unable to form words.

"She can't see or hear you," I reminded. "In this form, you're as much of a ghost as I am."

Jay moved around the room, taking in the space anew.

"This is your mother and Raymond's house," I explained. "They moved here seven years ago. Not that you would know. You haven't visited once."

Sounds of talking and laughter echoed from upstairs. Suddenly a swarm of kids surged down the steps playing laser tag. Half the group had blue shooters and chest packs strapped on; the rest sported green accessories. Among the kids were Kamie, Kingsley, two additional young girls, and a boy around Brandon's age.

"For glory!" Kingsley shouted as he jumped and rolled over a couch, firing at Kamie on the opposing team.

"Take cover!" a girl near Kamie's age exclaimed.

The *pew-pews* of shooters continued until the sound of loud clapping overpowered them.

"Okay, kids, take it outside." A tall woman about thirty with thick arms and perfect eyebrows shooed them away from the couches.

The kids scampered off laughing. Kingsley opened a glass sliding door and led the pack into the backyard.

A second woman with a similar face and body came into the living room holding a pitcher of lemonade. "I am regretting getting Chadwick that laser tag set for his birthday," she said. "One of these days, someone is going to break something."

I glanced at Jay condescendingly. "In case you can't tell your twin sisters apart after avoiding them for so long, Felicia is the one with the lemonade; Monica is the other woman."

He scowled. "You're the worst, you know that?"

The sliding door opened again and three men entered. Two carried platters of flank steak and the third older man held a tray of freshly grilled corn.

"Food's ready!" called the guy in front. I had never seen a more pronounced, well-groomed mustache.

"Thank you, love," Monica said, giving him a kiss on the cheek. She took the other plate of meat from the skinny guy, who was in his mid-twenties. "Ray, tell the kids they have five more minutes to settle their war or I'll come out there and end it for them."

"Easy, sis," Ray said. "No war is ready for your kind of fire-power."

Monica smacked him affectionately on the arm. Ray trotted outside.

"Ladies!" Felicia pivoted and called out. "Lunch is—"

"They can hear you in Timbuktu, honey," Sandra said, entering arm in arm with Celia.

Jay's face fell so flat that I wondered if he was beyond recovery. His mouth hung open as he watched his family. The older man exchanged a quick kiss with Sandra before holding the chair out for her and serving her a plate.

"Thank you, Raymond dear."

"Eddie was sorry he couldn't get off work for lunch today," Celia said as she sat down. "He has a presentation."

"Please, girl," Monica said. "If my man made the money yours does, I wouldn't mind if I only saw him once a week. No offense, love." She pivoted in her chair and cupped her husband's chin in her hand then gave him a sassy kiss.

"None taken," he said with a smile.

"Oh no, I'm hit! Medic! Medic!" Ray yelled. The adults turned to see him flopping dramatically on the grass as several of the kids ran around him firing wildly.

"Ray!" Monica yelled.

"Oh, leave him be, Mon," Felicia said. "Maybe getting drilled by those kids will inspire him to mature and join us on this side of the adult fence."

Ray made whooping sounds as he got up and pursued the children.

"From your mouth to God's ears," Sandra commented. "Now then, Dion." She gestured to Monica's husband. "Please pass the corn muffins."

The family started eating, still talking and laughing. Eventually Jay turned to me, hands in his pockets and face now masked with his normal, cocky mistletool attitude.

"So, what? Your plan was to get me to reevaluate my whole life because my family is having a barbeque I wasn't invited to? I'll try not to cry myself to sleep at night."

"You *were* invited, Jay." I unfolded a document from my pocket; the page was ghostly blue since I had teleported with it. "This is the schedule Celia gave you that lists the activities your family would be participating in during Christmas week. She was trying to involve you, but apparently if Annie doesn't approve your itinerary, or if a meeting doesn't include cameras, you can't be bothered."

I handed him the document. He glanced over it for barely a second before he shoved it back at me.

"Hollow offers," he said. "It's like extending a party invite to someone who you know is busy. They're fully aware I have a lot going on, so I probably couldn't make it even if I wanted to. Which is fine because they honestly wouldn't want me here.

Look how close they all are. I've barely spoken to any of them in the last decade. I'm about as welcome here as coal in a stocking."

"Oh, for the love of—" I lost my cool, grabbed Jay by the tie, and yanked him across the living room to the staircase. I pointed up dramatically. Each stocking was embroidered with a name. The kids' names were closer to the bottom; adults branched toward the top. Above our heads, between Felicia and Sandra, was a snowman-pattern stocking printed with the name *Jay*.

My Scrooge blinked. I released my hold on his tie. "Still think you're unwelcome? Still think they've tried to replace you?"

Jay drifted over to the glass door and stared out at the kids playing. After a moment he moved past the adults at the table and glided through the wall. I went after him, but when I phased through he was farther ahead of me than expected—already down the hall. I kept chase until I caught up with him in the kitchen. He stood frozen in front of the counter, staring at a bowl of fruit. A bowl of red apples.

"I wanted to show you, but you beat me to it," I said steadily. "Brandon can see your past Christmases from your perspective, but also the perspective of people who are part of your past. We've been thorough. In doing so, we've been enlightened. We know about those people out there—who they are and how much you missed out on because you've been too stubborn to face them."

I migrated to the counter then concentrated my magic so I could grab an apple—make it ghostly too.

"They've continued their own version of your dad's tradition for years," I said, turning the fruit over in my hand. "Every Christmas week for over a decade, they've kept red apples in the house, eating one a day in tribute to your dad's memory and his culture's Christmas tradition."

Jay's attitude, confidence, defiance—it all melted. All that remained was confusion.

"But why? You and Brandon saw my dad's faults. You think he was the reason why our family broke apart and the cause of my mom's issues. My mom left him. My sisters moved on from him. They no doubt know he had flaws too. Why keep this up?"

"The same reason adults with babies too young to grasp the concept still put out milk and cookies for Santa. Belief, Jay. Belief isn't about shrouding flaws and pretending things are perfect; it's about accepting that they aren't and choosing to focus your heart on the good that exists around them. Your family may be fully aware of the negative aspects of who your dad was, but that doesn't mean they have to believe he was a bad guy. They can choose to concentrate on the positives and believe he was fundamentally a good guy who just made mistakes."

I put the apple down. Jay phased through the wall again. I followed him, ending up outside. Beams of sunshine passed through our translucent forms in dizzying, dazzling streaks.

Jay's back was to me.

"I didn't throw out that list," he said after a moment.

"I know." I came to stand beside him. "But you hid it away. Like your spirit. Not gone. Buried. But not impossible to find if you're open to it."

He didn't say anything.

After a moment, Jay extended his hand to me. I accepted and transported us back to the university auditorium. Coast clear—I made us visible.

"Any more trips today?" he asked emotionlessly, straightening his tie.

"No," I said. "I thought I'd give you a break. Wednesday is called hump day, after all. I think with one more push, tomorrow you'll get over this one."

Wordlessly, he headed across the auditorium foyer to the main doors.

"Jay . . ." I called. He paused. "Whatever you may think of me, I'm not here to haunt you. I'm here to help you break free of the ghosts that've been haunting you for years. But at some point, you have to be open to letting them go."

He remained there another second. Then he left me standing alone.

18

My dream memory brought me to Christmas Eve. It took me a moment to figure out which one.

I watched from across the street as my Scrooge ran into the church, only a minute after Christmas Eve mass had started. I smiled proudly. Franklin, a plump Ghost of Christmas Past, and Moira, a bespectacled Ghost of Christmas Future, stood with me.

"I love a dramatic finale," Moira gushed, wringing her braid like a dishtowel. "Elliot really put up a fight at the beginning. He's come so far."

"A proper pain in the keister he was," Franklin agreed in his Alabama accent. "Fella was this close to blowing it."

"And yet, we're all wrapped up at five o'clock," I said, checking my watch. "And with half a dozen charms on my bracelet to spare. I know this is only my fifth season running a Scrooging mission, but are they always supposed to be this easy?"

"Aw, kid," Franklin said. "The hard part isn't the job. It's dealing with the aftermath."

"How do you mean?"

He sighed and shook his head. "You'll find out."

I eyed him. A red flag rose in my mind.

"Shall we phase inside and listen in on his big moment before heading back to the CCD?" Moira suggested. "I adore an impassioned speech."

"You two go ahead. I don't feel up to it."

"Are you sure, Frost?" Moira asked. "I know how much you like films. A changed Scrooge's grand, dramatic revelations are very cinematic."

"Agreed. But since this is my first assignment in Los Angeles since I died, and I don't know when I'll be back, I think I'd rather just walk the streets of my city before heading back to the CCD."

"Okay, dear." Moira pushed her glasses up on her nose. "Two pieces of advice though. First, I wouldn't recommend thinking of this place as your city. Trust me, that can make it hurt more when you return."

I stared at her. "Why?"

"Well, because there will come a time when you come back 'home' and realize it's not your home. Five years is nothing. In a few decades, you'll see the toll time takes and it can be difficult to accept that while you remember the city, the city has forgotten you . . ."

I hadn't thought about that. I gulped and looked at Moira with a touch of unease swaying my stomach like a rough sea. "The second piece of advice?"

"Be careful and stay out of trouble. Your powers are fully recharged now that Elliot's soul has been saved, but that magic needs to be conserved for our hibernation period."

I nodded innocently, then Moira and Franklin strolled across the street. Once they were in the church, I stretched my hands, released an anxious breath, and did the opposite of what my colleague had been advising; I activated my powers. Now that I *was* fully recharged, blue energy wafted off me like fire. Magic sizzled beneath my skin.

The teleportation abilities that came with my Ghost of Christmas Present mantle had several designated purposes. However, I'd wondered for a while if these were simply suggested uses. After all, if I was a magical being that the laws of physics didn't apply to, and my charms could create tiny or huge effects depending on how much magic I output, who was to say with enough of magic I couldn't stretch my teleportation powers outside of their typical uses.

Now that I was at maximum power, I decided to try something beyond normal teleportation to my Scrooge or Earth homebase. It was something I'd been aching to do all month but couldn't risk attempting until after I'd finished my mission, given that my magic had to be dedicated to my assignment first.

I closed my eyes, clenched my fists, and concentrated on one name.

It felt like I was vibrating, as if the mystical atoms that comprised my ghostly body were being shaken by a bartender with a vendetta. I also felt like I was burning up a bit. A rush of wind abruptly filled my soul and caused my mouth to burst open with a gasp.

My eyelids fluttered and my form flickered unsteadily. I stood in a hallway now. Sconces lined the walls, red bows tied to each of them. Laughter and the creaking of floorboards came from a room on the left. I wandered in. As I took in the scene, my soul welled up with a slew of emotions no therapist nor scientist could fully break down.

There he was. Wyatt Glass—the boy who'd once looked at me with affection and asked nothing more of me than my attendance to a dance.

I hadn't seen him in over a decade. He'd clearly been busy in that time. Across the room two children played with handcrafted toy swords by a modest Tannenbaum while a third, younger child sat on the ground tying on new ballet shoes. Once she had tightened the ribbons, Wyatt offered the little girl his hand and twirled her.

He looked good. He was in his thirties now and had grown a

beard. Abigail Wakeman also looked good. Her smile was bright and as kind as the day I'd met her downtown. The woman's hair was longer than I remembered, and her perfect bronze curls bounced on her shoulders as she moved beside Wyatt and twirled the little girl too.

I guess he'd married her.

I guess I was glad for him.

My invisible stomach sloshed again. I closed my eyes. This time my powers were harder to channel. In fact, my normally cold body felt like it was being lathered with flaming lotion. It was a clear warning that using my magic this way wasn't a casual, no big deal experiment like I'd tried to convince myself.

My teleportation powers weren't meant to find miscellaneous people. I'd read the ghost guidebook during training five years ago; I knew the rules. My conscience may have tried to forget that in favor of doing whatever I wanted, but my body was punishing me for it.

And yet . . . I continued to ignore the warnings and pushed through anyway.

When would I be in LA again? I couldn't attempt this misuse of power from another city, let alone another country. My magic definitely wouldn't be strong enough to handle that if I could barely do this.

I concentrated. *David Varot.*

Pain rushed through me. It was surprising. I honestly didn't know ghosts could feel pain. The physical kind anyway.

My ghostly body churned like I'd swallowed an earthquake for dinner and a cyclone for dessert. Then, in a surge of magic I landed in a fancy music room. Though the setting was more lavish, the situation was reminiscent of Wyatt's home.

It seemed David—the man who'd presented me with an opportunity of marriage all those years ago—had found himself a different wife. The lovely blonde creature sat at the bench of a grand piano, her fingers dancing across the keys. On the bench beside her, a teenage daughter sang in accompaniment to the Christmas carol being played. David resided on an adjacent floral sofa with four younger children, his arm around the smallest one. They seemed content, calm, perfect.

I drifted closer and sat down in an empty chair between the piano and the sofa. I studied David's matured face with some sadness until my CCD watch started flashing red. It had never done that before.

The song ended and David and his kids applauded. I tried ignoring the watch, but I couldn't. I phased into the connecting hall and tapped the accessory, trying to understand what was wrong. Not able to figure it out, I teleported back to the church, honing in on my Scrooge like a homing beacon. Used as intended, my powers were painless.

My watch continued to flash as Moira and Franklin, both smiling, exited the church. They met me under a glowing lamppost. Franklin raised an eyebrow when he saw my watch.

"What did you do?"

"How do you mean?" I placed my arm with the watch behind my body.

"Have you heard that saying about the bearded Big Guy?" Franklin asked. "He sees y'all when you're sleeping and knows when y'all are awake, yada yada?"

I blinked.

"None of us know the exact extent of Specter One's powers," Moira explained. "However, he got his magic from Santa, so he has a mystical way of keeping track of us. Our CCD watches only flash like that for two reasons. The first is if we are dangerously low on magic. That only happens if time is running out on Christmas Eve and our Scrooge's Christmas Spirit has not progressed enough. The second is if we misuse our magic." She stared me down.

"Oh." My soul tensed. I guess I would have to deal with the consequences. Without another word, I held out my hand to Moira and Franklin, transporting us back to my LA apartment. When we took the realm-evator to the CCD, the journey was absolutely silent. The situation did not improve upon arrival. An elf met us in the CCD lobby and handed me a note closed with a wax seal—shaped like a **#1** within a crescent moon:

"My office immediately – Specter One"

I raked the nails of one hand against my opposite palm as I rode the lift to my boss's frigid domain. The sleek ice construction would've made Hans Christian Andersen's *Snow Queen* proud, possibly envious.

"Miss Mason," Specter One said, gesturing to the ice bench in front of his desk. "Have a seat."

I made my way over the steel floor, feeling as if at any moment that giant ice chandelier was going to come down and skewer me like a ghost popsicle.

"The Senior Specters and I can track your magic status through those watches too." My boss pointed a finger at my wrist. "When you're alerted, we're alerted. Tell me, do you know why your watch is flashing now?"

I nodded. "Moira told me. It's because I used my magic inappropriately."

"Correct." Specter One came over and took my wrist in his hand. He twisted the tiny knob on the side of my watch three times forward, one time back. I always thought that was just for adjusting the time, but it made the flashing stop.

"Misusing magic causes extreme stress on your ghostly form," he said, releasing my wrist. "Your powers are gifted to you for intended purposes. Violate those purposes and we have a problem. Tonight you were lucky. If you had done it a third time, we would have a much more serious issue on our hands and Santa may have had to get involved to help."

"I didn't realize . . ." I bit my lip, totally abashed. "It's not in the manual."

I really *had* read the guidebook when I'd started this job—cover to cover, multiple times. It was how I knew that Moira and Franklin wouldn't be affected if I went rogue tonight. We each had our own magic supply that we spaced throughout the month. The number of times Franklin visited the past for research, for example, didn't affect my magical tank. He kept track of his remaining power the same way I kept track of mine. The only way that we were linked was that saving a Scrooge recharged all three members of our CCD team. And as the Christmas Eve deadline approached, our assignment's spirit or lack thereof affected us equally too, i.e. our magic drained faster or sustained longer depending on our Scrooge's state of mind and soul.

Specter One wandered around the desk and took a seat in his chair, hands folded. "I don't expect our ghosts to follow an exact formula, but your powers are meant to help your Scrooges reignite their Christmas Spirit—not be used as a tool to stalk old boyfriends."

I cringed with embarrassment. "I was not stalking them, sir. I was just . . . curious."

"About what could have been?"

"Aren't all dead people interested in aspects of their lives they left behind?"

"Perhaps. But Wyatt Glass and David Varot were not part of your life. You left them behind long before you died. You went to visit them because you were curious about what may have happened if you'd made different choices while you were alive, not if you hadn't passed on." He nodded solemnly. "'No space of regret can make amends for one life's opportunity misused.'"

The phrase sounded familiar. "*A Christmas Carol* quote?"

"One that I have found clings to certain spirits who've passed through here the way shadows adhere to the living." My boss sighed and leaned against his chair. "You're not going to be punished this time, Frost. I've been doing this long enough to know that most ghosts in the CCD eventually come to terms with their own reinvention as they help Scrooges find theirs. Just don't do it again."

I nodded, glancing down at my watch. My gaze lingered on the ticking second hand.

Tick. Tick. Tick.

It got louder.

Tick. Tick. Tick.

I opened my eyes and discovered a pigeon on the ledge outside my loft window, pecking at the glass. Pale pink and fading gray light caressed the whole apartment.

Marley rested in his basket—not asleep, trying to reposition himself. I whistled lightly to get his attention. He lifted his head and trotted over, hopping on my bed and snuggling up to me.

"How would you feel about getting out of this apartment today, boy?"

He wagged his tail.

"Yeah, that's what I thought."

"Good morning!" I said cheerily when Jay opened the door to his condo.

"Nope." He slammed the door in my face.

I phased inside with Marley in my arms as Jay was walking

back toward the kitchen, rubbing his eyes. I could just teleport directly next to my Scrooge, but today I chose to add a cushion of space out of consideration. Mistake.

"I was trying to be polite," I said, setting Marley down as we returned to normal, tangible form. "Evidently you didn't feel like returning the favor."

"Frost, it's seven in the morning. Can't you keep your ghostly business to human working hours?"

"Not today, I'm afraid. The clock is ticking. You need to get dressed." I stared at his dark gray sweat pants, gray t-shirt, and bare feet, which seemed to make him self-conscious.

"What?"

"You gave me a hard time about *my* pajamas. You look like a lump of charcoal. I guess I know what I'm getting you for Christmas."

"Would it make you feel better if I told you I have on candy cane boxers?"

I raised my eyebrows. "Do you?"

"You'll never know. You're a ghost, not a TSA agent." He turned on his coffee machine. "So where are we going that's so time sensitive?"

"It's a surprise. Now hurry up and change before we're late. I'll make the coffee. I've been doing it for a month anyway." I shooed him out of the kitchen.

He spotted Marley lying on the couch contentedly. "He's not going to pee on that couch, is he? It's expensive."

I scoffed. "Marley doesn't do that."

Marley yapped in agreement. Jay sighed and patted the dog on the head.

Fourteen minutes later, my Scrooge emerged in one of his many suits. I handed him a steaming mug of coffee and let him take one long sip before I took it back and set it on the counter.

"Marley." I snapped my fingers and my dog bounded over. I scooped him under an arm and offered Jay my free hand.

A moment later, we appeared in a park. It was a crisp morning; the preamble of dawn was departing the sky. Tents and tables were scattered across the grassy area. Volunteers in lime green t-shirts and elf hats carried boxes of supplies, passed out snacks, and held up signs. From the parking area, families and kids in athletic gear migrated into the park in herds. Farther off a DJ played peppy music near a finish line marked with colorful banners and a balloon arch.

"What is this, a race for kids?" Jay asked as we passed a face painting station with an eager line of boys and girls.

"Kamie is a part of an organization called Girls on the Run." I set down ghost Marley. "It involves running, but the overall focus is helping girls believe in themselves and working to achieve their goals. This morning is their annual winter 5k. Eddie, Celia, Kingsley, and Kamie are all participating. You were invited too . . ." I drew the same itinerary from yesterday out of my pocket and held it up. "But you'd rather talk about poll numbers and campaign donations."

I folded the document and put it away before pointing ahead. "There's your family now. Eddie and Celia took the day off from their jobs. People do that sometimes, you know."

Jay turned to see the foursome striding across the grass. While Celia adjusted the superhero cape that Kamie wore over her t-shirt, Eddie walked with an arm around Kingsley. Jay's fists clenched.

Marley suddenly bounded away from us, chasing a squirrel that couldn't see him.

"Give me a moment," I said to Jay. "Marley!" I chased after the dog. When I grabbed him and turned back, ghostly Jay was sitting on one of the benches, watching his family warm up for the race. The golden streams of sunlight through the trees highlighted his ghost form, poking holes in him like he was a sad slice of ghostly Swiss cheese.

It was a fortunate thing no one else could see him. It wasn't right that a person could look so depressed on such a beautiful December day. I moseyed over to the bench, placed my dog on the ground, and sat next to Jay. His expression was resentful as he watched Celia interact lovingly with their kids.

"They were too young to remember how reckless their mother was, how much damage she did," he said darkly. "They don't remember that I was there to get her the help she needed, then pick up the pieces when she was gone and look after them on my own. All they know is who she is now—the polished version of her, and the big house and suburban life she and Eddie have built together. And all they know of me is the guy on TV and posters who comes and goes as quickly as the mailman."

We sat in silence together, taking in the vibrant signs of life around us—not interacting, just observing.

"Jay," I said eventually, "Brandon is only allowed to take you to three Christmas Pasts, but as I alluded yesterday, we've poked around every Christmas you've ever had. You didn't influence Celia's drinking like your dad influenced your mother's, but in the aftermath you've treated Celia and your kids the way your dad treated your mother, you, and your siblings after they split up. Resentment and pride made your dad deny opportunities for all of you to be together, and over time that created distance. The distance embittered him more and rather than push through it, he pushed you guys further away. The same thing is happening with you, Kamie, and Kingsley now. You hold so much resentment toward Celia and dislike for Eddie's presence in your kids' lives that you can't even be around them."

I shifted on the bench to try and make eye contact with Jay, but he refused to meet my gaze. So I got off the bench and sat down on my knees on the grass in front of him—addressing him head on.

"Jay, just like your dad forced your sisters to choose, your refusal to adjust and accept how your life has changed is forcing Kamie and Kingsley to pick between you alone and the rest of your family—both Celia and Eddie, and your mother and siblings who you're also blocking out because you still don't accept Raymond or forgive your family for loving him."

I sighed and shook my head. "I've seen how depressing and isolated your last few Christmases with the kids have been—they're like guests in your life. Now that they've voiced they want to be with their whole family for the holidays, you're looking at it as a betrayal against you. Just like you saw Felicia and Monica's decision to stay with your mother and the rest of the family as a betrayal against your dad. But it wasn't, Jay. Your dad could have had it all. He didn't have to choose distance and neither do you."

My phone gave a short jingle.

"That's my alarm," I explained. "Your workday starts soon. I have to get you back."

Over the loudspeakers, the DJ cut into her music. "Racers, it's time to meet with your teams! Our first wave of runners will be taking off in five minutes!"

Celia and Eddie began to walk away with the kids toward the starting line. As they headed off, Celia signaled Eddie and gestured to a coffee cart nearby. He nodded and jogged over. Jay lifted up his head, watching his kids intently. My gut twisted. I had an idea. An idea that wasn't in the CCD guidebook as an appropriate use of my ghostly magic, and wasn't a part of my team's plan, but it resonated within me. And it wouldn't cost me hardly any power, so what was the harm . . .

"You could stay if you wanted," I said. "Traditionally I'm not supposed to let you interact with the places I take you to, but if you'd like . . . I mean, we can do it if you want. I could make you visible."

Jay looked at me. He checked his watch. He bit his lip. Then he stood.

"Okay."

I leapt to my feet. "*Okay?*"

Marley trotted over, curious about my enthusiasm. I scooped him up.

"Just for a few minutes. To say hi to the kids," Jay said. "Then take me back. No other journeys for the rest of the day. Deal?"

"Deal."

He met my eyes. "You have to turn visible too though. It'll feel less awkward being around Celia and Eddie if you're there."

"I guess I could do that."

"Actually, I was talking to the dog. He's got a likable vibe; you I'm still on the fence about." He smirked and scratched Marley behind the ear.

"Oh, hush," I replied.

I waved Jay behind a tree, took his hand, and made us visible and solid. I felt a low-grade burning in my gut and terrible ache in my system, but ignored it. My watch started flashing red.

"Another alarm?" Jay asked.

"Something like that." I cleared my throat, putting Marley down. "Go on, before they start the race. Catch up with them."

Jay hustled ahead of me. I stayed back a moment and twisted the small knob on the side of my watch three times forward and one time back to make the flashing stop. Specter One had no doubt already been alerted, so I'd have to deal with that later.

I checked my power supply. I was down to a 55% full magical tank now. Not bad, but not great.

"Kamie! Kingsley!" Jay called as he caught up with his family. They turned around and looked absolutely shocked.

"Dad?"

"Jay?"

"Daddy!"

Kamie cantered over and gave Jay a huge hug. Kingsley hugged him too.

"Jay, I can't believe you came," Celia said.

My Scrooge straightened himself. "Is that code for hoping I wouldn't?"

"*Of course not.*"

An awkward lull passed.

Jay glanced over his shoulder and saw Eddie paying at the coffee cart.

"I can't stay," he said. "But I did want to say hi to you both." He patted his kids on their heads. "You know that I love you, right? Even if I'm not with you a lot, I hope you know that."

"We know, Dad," Kingsley said. "But it'd be nice to see you for more than a few minutes at a time. Are you going to come to Christmas Eve at Grandma's house?"

"Honestly, buddy . . ." He glanced at the hopeful faces before him. "I'm busy that night with my campaign—there's this big gala and then the debate with my opponent, Farah." He swallowed, holding in volumes of unspoken emotion. "I think it's for the best that you and your sister will be with the rest of your family for Christmas this year. I'm not as much fun and I have a lot of important work things going on right now. But hopefully things will be better next year."

Kingsley hung his head a bit. "Yeah, okay, Dad."

Jay patted his son again, this time with less heart.

"Jay." Eddie joined the group, to-go cup in each hand.

"Eddie," my Scrooge replied flatly.

Eddie gave Jay a stern look. "You know, one of these days you and I are going to have words about what you said about Celia in the press."

"It's fine, Eddie," Celia replied curtly, putting a hand on his arm. "I'm over it. Just because Jay isn't big on forgiveness doesn't mean I have to hold similar grudges."

The couple stared at my Scrooge.

"*Frost*," Jay called anxiously.

I rushed over from where I'd been watching the exchange, Marley at my heels. "Yes?"

"You all remember my assistant, Frost," Jay said.

"Hello." Eddie nodded to me.

"Hi," Celia said.

"We should head out." Jay glanced at me.

"Actually, you can stay a bit longer if you want," I replied. "I can get us back pretty quickly. Traffic is *not* an issue."

"Better safe than sorry," Jay stated finitely. "Bye, kids. Have fun today. Hopefully I'll see you soon."

"When?" Kamie piped in. "Christmas?"

"No, sweetie. Like I told you, I have to be on TV on Christmas for my debate."

"That's stupid," Kamie said, crossing her arms. "Christmas is no time for political stuff or arguing with mean people who don't get it. Come be with us, Daddy. We're more fun."

Jay gulped. He looked at Celia and Eddie—not answering right away—then turned stone-faced. "I'm sorry, Kamie. I can't. Maybe another time."

"Racers, this is your two-minute warning!" the DJ announced over the loudspeakers.

"Come on, kids," Celia said. "Daddy has to go, and so do we. Thank you for coming, Jay. Whether you believe it or not, I hope I see you soon too."

Eddie nodded at Jay as the foursome continued across the grass. Jay released a deep, frustrated exhale.

"That's not how I expected this would go," I said, failing to keep the disappointment from my voice.

"What were you hoping for exactly?"

"I thought you heard me, Jay. I thought that maybe—"

"Maybe seeing my kids' faces would cause me to completely forget years of resentment, forgive years of bad blood, and throw my career responsibilities out the window?"

I took a deep breath and clenched my teeth.

"No," I said coldly, scooping up Marley. "Because that would be silly, wouldn't it? It would be *absolutely mad* to expect that any person, when faced with a chance at redemption, would pick the simplest path to betterment. *How foolish of me* to think for a second that if presented with reason and opportunity, someone could just open their eyes and see what matters in the long run, rather than quell the desires and fan the grudges of the here and now."

"You said it, not me," Jay retorted.

He stuck out his hand. I grabbed it, squeezed it, and flashed us away.

"I went off script, but it wasn't for personal reasons like that time with Wyatt and David, I promise," I told Specter One over our SpaceTime call. The women's restroom at the office had surprisingly good interdimensional reception.

"*Both* of those times," Specter One corrected.

"Right . . ."

"Was it even worth it, Frost?" Specter One asked. "That move cost you a chunk of power. Meanwhile, Jay's Merry Meter doesn't look much better than it did at the start of the week. You're on

Day Four, and we usually see an uptick in Scrooge Christmas Spirit by now."

I sighed. "Jay is stubborn. I think the reason I went off book and let him talk to his family was because my gut sensed he was on the verge of a breakthrough."

"He clearly wasn't."

"Well, hindsight is always 20/20, isn't it?" I shook my head dejectedly. "Maybe I pushed too hard. I've been hitting the family angle nonstop with all my team's Christmas visits. It's probably for the best that the next one we have planned addresses his career. His family issues can marinate for a while as I switch gears. Speaking of which, I should get going. I'll be back at the CCD tonight if you want to admonish my behavior in person."

"That won't be necessary for the *immediate* time being, Frost. Just focus. I don't want any more misplaced emotions disguised as gut instincts causing you to get lost in this assignment. I have been afraid for you these last couple of weeks—that you're letting Jay's progress, and your own, become entangled. That's why I paid you that visit at the theater."

I paused. That encounter had been on my mind for days.

"Specter One, why did you give me that quote at the movies last week? I had a dream memory recently, and realized it's the same Dickens quote you said to me all those years ago when I misused magic for the first time to check on Wyatt and David."

"I gave it to you back then because most ghosts at the CCD are distracted to some degree at first, but in time they come to terms with their regrets and move forward, focusing on their jobs and who they want to be now. You are different. Change has not come naturally to you. I reprised the quote this month because I am worried the regret you never properly faced is having a resurgence due to your similarities with Jay. And that is causing you to become dangerously invested in the situation."

Suddenly a woman walked into the restroom. I paused in panic, but she barely acknowledged me and entered a stall, locking the door. I waited a moment, then whispered at my phone screen. "What similarities to Jay? I'm not—"

My boss and I both froze as we heard the woman . . . relieve herself.

Specter One sighed. "Go back to work, Frost. You'll figure it out. For your sake, and your team's, I hope you do anyway. I'll leave you with this final advice. It's not wrong to care, but you should try to understand why you do."

He hung up and I pocketed my phone. When I reentered the office, I could not find Annie or Jay anywhere. They weren't on the main floor, in his office, or in any of the conference rooms.

I stopped at the nearest desk. "Ken, where is Jay? I have it on my schedule that he has focus group testing in five minutes, but he's not in any of the offices."

"Oh, they do those in the conference rooms two floors up. It's hard to get honest opinions from folks when you put them in a glass room like we have here."

"Fair enough. Thanks." I took the elevator upstairs and poked around until I found Jay pacing inside a small room, glancing every so often at a two-way mirror that observed a much larger room with a conference table.

Over a dozen people sat there. Annie walked around the table with a clipboard. "Thank you for participating today, everyone," she said. "Our goal is to get your overall impressions of this candidate." She clicked a remote and a projector displayed Jay's face on a slide. My Scrooge stopped pacing and approached the two-way mirror.

"Hey," I whispered, shutting the door carefully as I came in. "This must be refreshing for you. Usually you only have me telling you what I think. Now a dozen strangers can do it."

"Yup," Jay said, not meeting my eyes. "Nothing says pleasant afternoon like a bunch of people picking you apart like a bread roll."

"Sorry?" I moved to stand near him.

"I don't like crusts. I only eat the centers of breads. I don't know; the analogy made more sense before I said it." He shook his head. "Never mind. The point is that focus groups are awful. They help us understand what voters like and don't like about me, but they also make me want to smash my head through the mirror. Like, I once heard a guy comment that he couldn't vote for me because my eyebrows were untrustworthy. *People can be so aggravating.* I'm trying to do good here and they don't seem to care. They'd rather be angry with me or distrust me for stupid reasons I don't even think they fully understand."

"I know the feeling," I said, crossing my arms.

Jay's face—formerly locked in self-pity and angst—changed. His expression grew serious. Then he surprised me.

"I owe you an apology, don't I?"

I raised my eyebrows. "Are you asking or offering?"

"Both. The latter." He huffed. "If I'm being honest, I'm not used to apologizing. But I think I was a little cruel to you this morning. You were trying to help me, and you went out on a limb to do it. I may not be a fan of you being here, and I don't like the literal and figurative ghosts you're making me confront, but I can appreciate that you're just trying to make a difference. Like me. The very least I could do is not reject you without giving you a chance. I know how demoralizing that is."

I was astounded. For a moment, I would even say I felt . . . alive.

"Thank you, Jay. That means a lot. Saving your soul is my mission, but if *I'm* being honest . . . though I'm not completely sure I understand why, I've come to care about you too."

He glanced at me and smirked. "You're not falling for me, are you, Frost? You wouldn't be the first assistant who has."

"HA!" I loudly scoff-laughed. "Sorry, Jay. I'm the spiritual awakening kind of ghost, not the kind you make romantic pottery with."

"Good," he said. "Because I'm about as lousy at ceramics as I am at relationships."

"You don't have to tell me. Had Nora Ephron poked around your past like I have, she would've hit you upside the head."

Jay smiled, amused. One of the focus group attendees spoke up in the background. "Has anyone else noticed how aggressive his gestures are when he's giving a speech? It's like he's trying to mash an invisible potato."

The smile left Jay's face. He groaned, putting his hand to his forehead.

I patted him on the back. "There, there."

"So what do you think?" asked an eager woman in a tight blazer.

We'd returned to our offices for an afternoon presentation from Jay's advertising team. My Scrooge sat at the head of the table with Annie and I on either side of him.

As the ad faded from the large screen set up opposite him, Jay fidgeted. "They're a bit negative, aren't they? I am far from being in Farah's fan club, and your ad nailed it—she is a career politician who hasn't done anything—but isn't it better to come out the gate talking about why I'm the right choice, not why she's the wrong one?"

"Actually, sir," said a clean-shaven young man, "our polling shows that people are more united by having a common enemy than a hero. You can do awesome stuff for the state, but it's not going to get the same PR as dirt on an opponent."

"Farah is already running ads that highlight your inexperience and naïvety," said the woman in the tight blazer. We gave her a questioning look. Her eyes widened and she quickly corrected herself. "Farah's words, not mine."

"I actually heard from Friedman's Consulting Group shortly before this meeting," Annie said. "They have dug up dirt on Farah's ex-husband that we can compromise her with. He's currently under investigation with the SEC for insider trading."

Jay leaned back, surprised. "Was Farah involved?"

"The charges weren't brought up until after their divorce, but that hardly matters." Annie shrugged. "I like the ads," she said, turning to the team. "Let's start running numbers one and four in the new year, and try to develop another that questions Farah's financial integrity."

"Hold on," I interrupted. "Jay has done good things for a lot of communities. He wants to do even more. It's not really in the spirit of leadership if he's throwing mud at people who get in his way."

Annie stared at me. "I'm sorry, did I accidentally hire you for moral consultation? Oh no, wait, I remember. I hired you to get coffees and send emails. Why don't you go do that? This room is a little too crowded."

"Annie," Jay interceded. "I don't think Frost is wrong."

Annie sighed. "Jay, I respect your commitment to decency, but I need you to respect that I am following through on my commitment to help you. And I know how to do it better than Frost does." She tapped her pen aggressively on the table. "I'll tell you what. Let's run the ads in the new year like I suggested. We'll just test them for one month, and then based on the results, we can decide what to do afterward. Okay?"

Jay paused but agreed. "Fine."

The meeting wrapped up. As I was exiting the conference

room, my phone jingled in my pocket—a text message from Paul.

"Have you made amends with Bismaad yet? Also . . . CLICK THE LINK BELOW to watch the BEST video of a baby flying reindeer sneezing."

I clicked the link and watched the short, hilarious video. When the baby reindeer sneezed, he flipped through the air backward and took out two elves. Despite my Annie-soured mood, the clip made me laugh.

Oh technology, you giveth and you taketh away.

"What's so funny?" Jay asked.

I glanced back to make sure Annie was busy giving her final commands to the advertising team. Then I held up my phone and showed Jay the video. He laughed.

"Special effects are great. That reindeer and the elves look so real."

"They are real, Jay," I found myself saying as I stowed the phone in my pocket. "Baby reindeer sneeze all the time, but when the flying ones do it's amazing."

He blinked twice. "Your ghost department has elves and reindeer?"

"No. They're from the North Pole, I'm from—" I stopped. My eyebrows shot up in panic. I wasn't supposed to be telling him any of this. What the heck was I doing?!

"Jay," Annie interrupted. "We have that meeting with those key donors in forty. The car is picking us up in five."

Jay saluted her with a bit of sass. She marched toward the elevator. He started pursuing her, but then paused and glanced over his shoulder. "Are you coming?"

"You're not going to try and ditch me again?"

"What's the point? Anyway, the nine-year-old kid in me has about eighty-five questions for you regarding the North—"

"*Shh.*" I thudded him on the chest. Annie, who happened to be looking in our direction, glared. I took a step back, correcting my overly familiar behavior.

"Jay," I whispered, "Christmas Carol ghosts are not supposed to reveal the ins and outs of our magical dealings. Just forget I said anything."

"Are you serious? You have to give me something," he prodded as we walked.

I rolled my eyes—irritated, but angrier with myself. "One question. *Choose wisely.*"

"Callback to the *Indiana Jones* reference?" he asked.

"More than you know. I may admittedly like you, Jay, but if you reveal anything about your magical Scrooge journey, well . . . let's just say face-melting in movies is nothing compared to when a ghost does it in real life."

Annie gave us a pointed look when we joined her as the elevator doors opened. We stepped inside. "What are you two whispering about?" she asked suspiciously.

"Magical Christmas secrets," Jay responded.

I stared at him wide-eyed. *What the heck, man?*

"Hilarious," Annie replied, shaking her head.

Jay returned my shocked expression with a smirk as if to say: *See. She doesn't believe me anyway.*

We rode through the city in heavy traffic. The clouds congesting above were thick and gray. A storm was coming. The California equivalent of one, at least.

About fifteen minutes into the drive, I drew out my phone. I tapped my finger on it anxiously as I thought of what to say. Reaching out to people for personal connection was not my forte. I was like mayonnaise; for me to go on I had to stay cool and sealed tight. It was how I made it on Earth. It was how I managed in the afterlife. Nevertheless, I hadn't meant to hurt Bismaad.

I decided to go with a casual approach and communicate with Bismaad through her favorite medium. Scrolling through the pics on my phone, I posted a shot to Tinsel of me and Bismaad from three Christmases ago. I smiled fondly at the memory. We'd competed in a North Pole sledding contest with penguin partners. I came in second and Bismaad came in first. I tagged her in the photo and wrote a simple, truthful caption.

"In a world where sometimes it feels like you're Fa-La-La-La Failing, it's nice to remember the good times and good people you care for." #snowbuds #afterlifeoftheparty

SEND.

Well, they were out there now—my feelings. It wasn't a grand gesture, I know, but it was an olive branch. Like Jay, I wasn't used to apologizing.

I took out my phone several more times to stare at it throughout the ride, trying to telepathically will a response from Bismaad. She'd never been angry with me before, although according to Paul I'd given her plenty of reasons.

Maybe I *wasn't* what a friend should be . . .

When we arrived at our destination, droplets of rain started to come down. The frigid air frosted the car windows and the speckles of water sticking to the vehicle's taillights sparkled.

Rocco opened the car door, holding up an umbrella to shield us as we stepped onto the slick curb. I was a fan of the Christmas tree patterned tie and matching green pocket square he was wearing.

"Be careful, Frost," he said as I got out.

"Thank you, Rocco."

"No really," he said with genuine concern. "Be careful. You're on slippery ground."

"Uh, yes, thank you," I replied, looking at him in confusion.

A loud, basketball-fan-esque whistle called my attention.

Annie.

"Frost. You're making us late. Let's go."

I scurried after her and Jay. We rode up in the elevator and when the doors opened we were greeted by a bony receptionist with a dazzling smile. "Welcome, Mr. Nichols, Miss Jung, and Miss Mason. Please follow me."

We made our way into an intimidating conference room. Instead of a traditional table, a desk wrapped around the room—forming a huge, hollow circle with two dozen black leather chairs spaced around it. Above, a grand light fixture the same size and shape as the desk glowed powerfully a la Tolkien's "One Ring to rule them all." Three of the walls were chrome while the fourth was a single pane of glass overlooking the wettening city.

Were we here to plan the end of the world or discuss campaign donations? I shuddered, hardly comforted by two poinsettia plants in the corner.

The receptionist gestured for us to take our seats then poured water from a pitcher into crystal glasses at our settings.

I fidgeted in my chair then leaned over and whispered to Jay, "This place looks like the *Dr. Strangelove* war room. Or FIFA headquarters. I keep expecting General Buck Turgidson or Gianni Infantino to walk in."

He laughed.

Annie glared at us and Jay leaned away from me. The doors opened.

"Jay!" The man at the head of the group extended his hand as he walked in. He was thick and wide-chested like a retired football player.

"Mr. Randall." Jay stood and went to greet the man. Annie and I followed his lead.

"Please, call me Mike," the large man replied. "You remember Zamir and John from the fundraiser last month?" He gestured at the two men on his right. Jay shook their hands. "And this is Dora Claremont and Lamar Franklin." Mike alluded to the pair on his left. Jay made the rounds with them and then introduced Annie and me. The group nodded at us—apparently we weren't important enough to receive handshakes—then moved to take their seats. The receptionist poured water for them and then departed the room with a dramatically loud thud when the door sealed shut.

And then the Volturi attacked!

No, just kidding. But that's how on edge I felt. I was mentally referencing a *Twilight* movie, for goodness' sake. The whole vibe of this place was making me anxious. A deep protective instinct was buzzing inside me, and I felt like my Scrooge shouldn't be here. I raked my nails against my palm as I waited to find out why.

"Thank you for coming to our offices," Mr. Randall said, addressing Jay. "My daughter has a ballet recital this evening, so I want to make this short and sweet, but for these kinds of matters, I prefer the in-person approach. These days you can't be too careful with electronic communication. Don't know who's watching, am I right? Speaking of which . . ." he pointed at me and Annie. "Do you trust these two?"

"I do," Jay said. "Annie has been my campaign manager for a while. There's no one better. Frost may be new to our team, but I know for a fact she only has my best interest at heart." He glanced at me a moment. "Anything discussed here is secure."

"Good," Mr. Randall replied. "No formalities or beating around the bush then. Jay, we represent significant influence and financial backing that would completely change your campaign. With our support, your momentum and reach would be able to compete with Farah who, as I'm sure you know, is backed by some very powerful people."

"Powerful people who are excellent at staying in power and shaping the landscape and minds of the public," said Dora. Her painted arched eyebrows were severe but could not compete with the sharpness in her hazel eyes.

"I am aware of that," Jay said. "Your support would be invaluable."

"And yet, the thing about writing checks is that value is the most important component," said Zamir. He had the mustache of an old-timey train conductor and a chic gray-suit-pink-tie combo. It looked liked something Allan would wear back at the CCD.

"If we are going to invest in *you*, Jay," Zamir continued. "We need to be sure that you are going to be able to offer a return on that investment. All of us have some mutual interests that need safeguarding. Are you willing to work with us to protect those?"

"Of course, assuming they don't contradict what I stand for. What did you have in mind?" Jay asked.

"Let's start with your small business crusade," said Mr. Randall. "You'd like to institute a reduction in taxes for small business owners while adding a surcharge on all non-local business-related developments. My colleagues and I have vested interests in various foreign enterprises as well as national brands that would like to expand into communities that are on the rise across the state. We would need your commitment to not interfere."

"I can understand that bigger entities and companies can help communities in their own ways," Jay replied. "But it depends on the details. I'm open to ideas different than my own for how to benefit people, but I can't just up and announce I've changed positions on the subject and suddenly be all about big business versus small business across the board. People would think I'm a flake on my promises."

Zamir nodded. "Of course. And we wouldn't ask you to do that. You can continue stating your passions to the public, and I'm sure there will be some measures you can take to support small business." He said it as if the words tasted bad. "But you know how it is once a person gets in office—the paperwork, the bureaucracy, the daily minutia. Plenty of politicians never get around to enacting the changes they set out to. Things slip through the cracks. Priorities shift. All we're asking is that when matters of importance come into play—*matters we advise you are important*—you relax a bit on what you're willing to consider. And in the name of an open mind, when it comes to how you benefit the people, you behave . . . flexibly. Both in regards to large business interests against small business interests, and other areas of policy we may need your support on later."

Jay stayed silent for a moment. Then he looked at me. I gave the slightest shake of my head—*No*.

Annie observed our interaction and annoyance creased her brow.

"Jay," she interceded. "They're not asking you to give their interests special treatment. They are asking that you not directly harm their livelihood and consider their counsel on issues in the future. That's a fair ask if they're going to be on our team."

Jay responded. "How many issues are we talking about?"

Mr. Randall smiled. "We're not a demanding bunch, Jay. We can work it out as we go. The value of our support will mirror the value you bring to the table."

A long pause hung in the air.

"I don't know what you heard about me," Jay said finally. "But I'm not for sale. I'm not that kind of candidate."

Dora's gaze held Jay's mercilessly, as if seeing if he would crack under the pressure. Then she shrugged. "Respectable. And bold, considering your laughable election history."

"*What?*" Jay said, eyes narrowing.

"I don't mean it to be an insult, but it's fact, isn't it?" Dora said. Her colleagues watched Jay with hard expressions. "You may be on a hot streak lately, but you've been losing elections your entire life."

"I lost a lot when I was a kid," Jay admitted hesitantly. "That doesn't mean I'll keep losing in the future. People will see the good I can bring; they'll appreciate my experience, passion, and potential."

"Perhaps," Zamir said. He folded his hands on the desk and stared straight into my Scrooge's soul. "But let me paint you an equally, if not more likely picture. Jay . . . There are way more diamonds in the rough than the people who run the world would like you to believe. The fact is, this world is full of people with intelligence, integrity, and the ability to shine and be remembered. But most of them *stay* in the rough. Most of them will never get the chance to be who they are truly meant to. Not because anyone purposefully tried to take them down, not because they weren't good enough, and not because they made the wrong choices. Simply *just because*. Life isn't fair. We can blame it on background, race, gender, or a dozen other hot-button topics, but most of the time, the reason things don't work out is pure chance. Your whole life, you've been beaten down by chance and people's refusal to *give you a chance*. Statistically speaking, you don't break free of that without help. Powerful help."

I felt the urge to say something, to do something. I watched Jay's body's slump—I could almost feel his soul shrinking like a child running from monsters. Thunder ricocheted across the stormy sky outside.

Mr. Randall sighed, feigning empathy. "Jay, in an ideal world, you would win the election and get to enact the kind of change you always dreamed of. Sadly, the odds are against you. Those odds crumble further when you're in direct competition with people who don't play by the same rules. That's why you need us. We're not a band of super villains looking to take over the world; we want the best for this state, just like you do. Our chance at success is yours, so let us be on your team. Let us help you get where you've always wanted to go. It's a long road to November and you can't run on fundraising phone banks forever. Sometimes, to get what you want, you have to compromise a little. It's for the greater good in the end. You can't change the world if no one knows or cares who you are. What's the use of all that talent— all that drive, intellect, and passion—if no one ever hears you? Wouldn't you rather get someplace fantastic and do a third of what you set out to than cling to your ideals and die without having accomplished anything?"

I gulped. This was like watching a scary movie that I couldn't walk out on. I so badly wanted to yell at the main character to run.

Compromise was a deceitful, clever word. On the one hand, making compromises in life was not a wholly bad thing. Sometimes they were necessary to make relationships, partnerships, and plans work. But compromising an agenda or attitude was very different than comprising a moral principle or part of your character. I knew enough about human nature, politics, and prose to understand that while these people were dressing up Jay's need to compromise as the former interpretation, they were prodding him toward the slippery slope that eventually led so many to the latter—to a downfall of who they used to be for the sake of money and power.

Jay looked at the desk, his eyes dark.

I'd lost him.

I knew Jay's past as well as anyone. I knew his triggers, his desires, his deepest fears. These people were targeting all three, and he wasn't strong enough to fight them—who would be? Not alone anyway . . .

"Jay," I tried.

"Frost." Annie skewered me with a fierce glower. "Don't interfere."

"*Jay*," I insisted.

He refused to meet my gaze. Instead, he addressed the donors.

"I won't agree to anything that directly goes against the platforms I'm running on. I'll bend, but won't break. I would like your support, and I can be amendable and compromise in the name of the greater good, but I'm not going to change who I am."

Mr. Randall's smile returned. "We would never ask you to."

As if on cue, the thunder crashed again.

Midori, Brandon, and I stood on the streets of LA. Then reality fizzled away. Bit by bit, like a decomposing hologram, the setting disintegrated until we were left in an empty room with walls and floors made from laptop-sized, white shimmery bricks. Fluorescent backlighting lined the rim of the room.

Just as Present Ghosts had use of more detailed files, reels for the screening rooms, and books from the Naughty & Nice Department, Past and Future ghosts had their own unique tools for researching our targets.

"I love these future drill rooms," Brandon marveled. "It's like being in a videogame."

Ghosts of Christmas Future had Choice Chambers. While Brandon poked around Jay's past and I infiltrated his present, Midori spent every day in one of these rooms using her magic to make trips forward in time—inspecting the Decembers that awaited our Scrooge.

Visiting the future was much more difficult than visiting the past or present because the future was always in flux. Any little change in a Scrooge's life could alter his or her destiny. Midori had to be thorough and creative. Half her trips in here were visits to the future paired with specific conditions input into the chamber settings, allowing her to run theoretical scenarios—like when I asked her to see how Jay's future looked with "avoidance of rejection" as the driving factor behind his choices. The rest were straight-up visits to whatever future existed out there for him as things stood now—no extra influences applied.

While I was down on Earth executing our plan, it was vital that Midori kept up her work here. It helped us track our progress with Jay and ensure that we'd selected the most important parts of his future to show him for driving home our mission. After all, it was always visits to Christmases yet to come that got through to Scrooges the most. No matter how much they fought back during the Past and Present phases, this always worked. It was the kill shot, the game-winning basket at the buzzer, the final countdown.

"Thank you, Midori," I said. "As much as I want to have faith in Jay's good intentions, after that meeting today, I realized this future is inevitable. I just had to be sure. I mean, he's surprised me before. Even as recently as today . . ."

"If he could change on his own, he wouldn't be in our hands," Brandon said, patting me on the arm. "Don't second-guess yourself. It may be dramatic, but I like your drop-and-ditch plan for tomorrow. It works well paired with Midori's opening move of showing Jay the future of LA." He offered Midori his raised palm and to my surprise she gave him a high-five.

My team parted ways and I returned to my office on the other side of the CCD. I opened the door and found Bismaad sitting on the couch, petting Marley.

"Hi!" I closed the door behind me. "After I didn't get a response from you, I thought you were ignoring me." I sat on the edge of my coffee table, facing her anxiously.

"I *was* ignoring you," Bismaad replied. "A tagged post isn't exactly the Everest of apologies, Frost. You're over a hundred years old; frankly that felt juvenile and non-committal as far as amends go."

My stomach clenched. I raised my hands in defense, but in a teasing sort of way. "Hey, you're the one always pushing social media. I was just trying to speak your language."

"I think you were trying to talk to me in the most non-vulnerable way possible. But ..." she sighed. "I'm going to choose to appreciate that even lowering your walls a little and reaching out is a big deal for you. That in itself is kind of sad." She shook her head. "Still, the fact remains that you're retiring this season and you've been a friend to me since serving as my mentor during my first season. You may not want to hang out often, or try as hard as friends should to spend time with each other, but I know you care about me and I care about you. So let's just put this behind us so we part on good terms when the time comes, okay?"

Relief filled me. "I'd like that. Thank you."

Bismaad stood. "You want to get dinner? There are Feliz Navidachos in the cafeteria tonight."

I frowned, looking at my watch. "I was planning on reviewing my Jay schedule for tomorrow."

Bismaad shot me an *Are you serious?* look.

"But I can do that later," I said quickly, setting down my book bag. "Let's go."

She smiled and I did too. I was so glad she'd forgiven me. Our friendship may have started off unusually, but I valued it. Even if I didn't show it enough. Even if I thought relationships were a liability and I always kept her at a bit of a distance because of that.

My soul enlivened with gladness as we headed out together, and it wasn't just because of the impending nachos.

19

"Righteous!" Rick said.

Rick Marvin, Ellie Pastor, and I watched our Scrooge make out with his long-time love in the center of a cheering crowd gathered at Griffith Observatory. The iconic triple-domed building glowed with tender light amidst the blushing holiday sky.

"A successful Scrooging fills my heart with more jollies than a polar bear at a pizza parlor." Rick clapped and whistled, even though the crowd couldn't see or hear us. He was one of the more enthusiastic Ghosts of Christmas Past I'd worked with.

"Not how I would phrase it, but I quite enjoy the feeling as well," Ellie commented. "And kudos to your leadership, Frost. I've never wrapped up a Scrooging so early on Christmas Eve." The Ghost of Christmas Future shook out her luscious curls, a reflex like the way I scratched my palms, only more ladylike.

"All right, team. Let's get out of here," Ellie said. "I am so over Los Angeles. This smog is not doing my hair any favors. And *freeways*—yikes."

"I don't know," I mused. "I'm proud of my city. Freeways and all."

The occasional opportunity to live in LA was one part of my job I still looked forward to. After the news I'd received this morning, I needed to cling to something I could count on.

"*The* city," Ellie corrected, giving me a sideways look. "I can't believe after all this time you still have a sense of connection with this place."

"It feels familiar," I replied with a shrug. "Like I could step into my old life as simply as putting on a sweater. Yes, a lot has changed since I was here thirty-seven years ago, but the vibe is the same and I think some of the changes are pretty groovy."

"For instance?" Ellie asked.

"This observatory," I replied, "the Pantages Theater, we have a basketball team now, oh, and that Disneyland park everyone keeps talking about. I didn't get to check it out this month, but I'd love to if it's still here the next time I get assigned to this part of California."

Ellie snorted. "A theme park centered around a giant castle and a mouse wearing gloves? I give that place two more years, tops."

"Hey, you ladies want to get drinks at The Nutcracker before the CCD party?" Rick asked. "My treat."

"Love it! I'm in," Ellie squealed.

"I'm going to pass," I replied.

"Oh, come on, Frost," Rick said with a groan. "You never want to come out. Let loose and have a couple cocoas with your team. It's not like it's gonna *kill* you."

"Hilarious," I said. "But no. Thank you." I sighed, deciding I owed them some explanation. "Truthfully, I'm feeling a bit down. This morning I found out another one of my former Scrooges reverted back to who he used to be. His Christmas Spirit is gone. That's the fifth Scrooge I've lost in the last decade. It's getting ... tiring."

"Shake it off, kid," Rick said, squeezing my shoulder. "Take it from a ghost going into his eighth decade. You can't let human beings bring you down. Well-intentioned souls like us try our best to help and do right by the world, but long-term change is nearly impossible for most people. We just have to be grateful for the time they do try to put their best foot forward. Your bad news is all the more reason to come out with us tonight. Three cocoas and a mountain of whipped cream, and you'll be right as rain."

"I think I just need to be alone, Rick. Thank you though. Hands please." Once we were linked up, I used my renewed magic to phase us back to my small house across LA.

"You go first." I gestured at my interdimensional bathroom door. "Don't wait for me once you're back at the CCD. I have to clean up here."

Within minutes, Ellie and Rick had departed. I went to the main door of the house. The red bow waited for me there, above the frame. I took one final glance at my LA dwelling—the furniture, appliances, and decorations. I sighed. Another season come and gone so fast.

I pulled one of the tails of the ribbon, undoing the entire thing in a swift yank. When I did, not only did the entire bow vanish, everything else in the cottage did too. Every piece of furniture and hardware suddenly disappeared in a puff of white smoke. The décor, artwork, and rugs dissipated in waves of golden sparkles. A glistening silver flash passed over the entire house—a final elimination beam to wipe this place clean of any magic or trace of me. At that, a ticking clock appeared on the bathroom door, counting down from twelve minutes. The words "*FINAL BOARDING CALL*" flashed above it.

"Goodbye, house." I drifted to the window at the back of the living room. "Goodbye, LA. Until we meet again."

I decided to take one last look at my city, one more breath of Earthly air before I was forced to go to sleep again. I activated my ghostly form and made my way out to the sidewalk. Clouds were setting in above; Kris would have bad visibility landing on rooftops tonight.

Suddenly sirens blared. An ambulance came whizzing down the street on my left. I took a cautious step back. Even after all these years, fast-moving vehicles still put me on edge. To my surprise, the ambulance stopped at a house up the block. I couldn't say what drew me to it, but in my ghostly form I glided up the sidewalk.

By the time I arrived paramedics were transporting an old man out on a stretcher, an oxygen mask over his face. He looked about seventy and had silvery hair. His eyes were closed, but at the exact moment when the stretcher passed in front of me, they fluttered open.

Holy—

"Mrs. Glass, you can ride in back of the ambulance with your husband," one of the paramedics said. He assisted an elderly Abigail into the vehicle. The woman who'd fallen in love with Wyatt more than half a century ago was wrinkled and worried.

Several younger adults had come out of the house with her, along with some kids. One of the adults accompanied Abigail into the transport while the others got into their cars to follow.

The ambulance took off into the night. The lights on the vehicle pulsed, getting farther and farther away with every second. I looked back at my house. When my eyes returned to the ambulance, I discovered it turning the corner and leaving my sight.

My spirit throbbed. I bit my lip. Then I clenched my fists and focused.

Wyatt Glass.

With a surge of magic, I caught up with the ambulance. Actually, I teleported inside of it. My stomach did a burning flip and my ghostly body tremored. I ignored both. Wyatt struggled to breathe and keep his eyes open. The younger adult had his hand comfortingly on Abigail's back.

"Wyatt," Abigail said, holding her husband's hand and kissing it. "I want you to know that meeting you on Christmas Eve so many years ago was a gift, but you've made all my days feel like Christmas since then just by being here to live them with me. I am grateful for all those days and hours and moments we had to build a life together, even this moment now."

I stood invisible at the foot of Wyatt's stretcher. Ghosts didn't have working hearts; they were as frozen as the North Pole. And yet, I felt pain where mine should be.

I never loved Wyatt. We didn't have a romantic relationship. But we did have *a* relationship. We were friends. I didn't know if that could've evolved into something like Abigail had with him, or if we could have simply strengthened our friendship as the years went by and we mattered more to each other. The answer to this would've only been found had I not kept him at a distance, had I actually invested the time and vulnerability to find out.

That chance was gone now. Lost to time like I was.

With every labored breath Wyatt took, my own soul found it harder to stay upright. Then the ambulance hit a bump and I tumbled back—phasing right out of the vehicle's rear door and onto the street.

When I hit the road, my body flickered like a TV channel with a bad connection. I stared at my quivering, spectral blue hands.

Honking caused me to whip my head up. Headlights sped at me. I gasped and covered my eyes, but the car passed straight through me. It'd been honking at a vehicle ahead. For a moment I'd forgotten I was invisible and intangible. I stood up uneasily and moved to the side of the street, dodging the oncoming cars like a reflex.

On the sidewalk, I glanced at my watch to see how much

time I had before the realm-evator left without me. The watch face pulsed red.

I'd broken a rule. I hadn't done that in almost forty years. Specter One no doubt already knew. I shouldn't make the situation worse. Plus, I only had three minutes left to return to my house for my lift back to the CCD. And yet . . .

Standing there on the darkening sidewalk, Christmas lights powering to life, I found I couldn't do it. As the lights went on, so did my instinct.

"David Varot," I thought aloud, focusing my magic.

FLASH.

White hot fire seemed to replace where human blood flow would be—searing heat pumped through my body while my stomach felt like an orange being squeezed to its core for every last drop of juice.

I opened my eyes just as several people passed through me. My disorientation slowed my recognition of where I was at first. Finally I handled the sensations and realized.

A cemetery.

Many gravestones were decorated with tinsel, ornaments, ribbons, and even some tiny, fully adorned Christmas trees. The lights of the cemetery illuminated the property and caused impressive shadows to extend from the visitors who were there to offer tribute to lost loved ones.

A chill different to the cold of the North Pole sunk into me. I turned around hesitantly. Several people were laying flowers down for the gravestone behind me. The inscription read:

David Varot
1892 – 1963
Beloved Husband, Father, & Grandfather

I stumbled backward. It was too much. I was as dismayed as I was shocked.

I thought I'd been careful during my life not to get too close to people so it wouldn't hurt to lose them. I'd pulled back from David and Wyatt to avoid the risk of love. I'd put up walls between me and the nuns and orphans—knowing my time with them would expire when I aged out of the orphanage. I'd opted out of any chances to be adopted even after learning the truth about my mother because I couldn't take another parent betraying and leaving me. Despite all that, it seemed my soul was still involved, even if it was just a little, and even if it was a long time ago.

Suddenly, Los Angeles didn't feel like my city anymore. My home. The only people I had mattered to at any point in my life were gone or about to be gone, and they probably had forgotten my name long before. David and Wyatt likely stopped remembering me decades ago. Why wouldn't they? They'd filled their lives with people who actually made an effort to be in them, people who didn't run out of fear of being rejected or hurt again.

Sad acceptance settled into me.

This city may have had a similar beating heart to the one it'd possessed decades ago, but I didn't. I *couldn't* just slip back into normalcy. The world moved on without me and I had no place here anymore.

My watch pulsed brighter. I felt like I wanted to cry, but no tears escaped. My eye sockets were barren like this desert I used to call home. No more.

With my jaw clenched, I teleported back to my little house and took the elevator to my realm of origin. When the doors slid apart, I found Specter One waiting for me.

"I'm disappointed in you, Frost."

Caught red-handed. Or red-wrist-watched, I suppose.

"I'm sorry," I said, stepping around Specter One into the

realm-evator lobby. "I only did two inappropriate teleports. I remembered from last time you said any more than that would've caused a serious problem."

"So that makes it *okay?*" Specter One asked pointedly.

"No." I huffed. "Again, I apologize. I didn't intend to do it. You have to believe me. I crossed paths with Wyatt by accident and then I had to check on David too. I just needed . . ." I shook my head. "I honestly don't know what I needed. Wyatt and David weren't mine to love so they shouldn't be mine to mourn."

Specter One sighed. "Frost. You and I will have a conversation about professionalism and best ways to handle your uncertain feelings later. For now, you are wanted by *my* boss. I told Santa about what you did. He is in the middle of his trek over Central America right now, but he requested that you see him anyway."

Specter One removed a set of gold bells from his pocket, joined together by a red ring. He handed them to me. They gleamed like enchanted treasure.

"Beaming Bells," he explained. "Elves use them to teleport to Santa's sleigh in case of emergencies."

I tried to imagine what emergency a flying sleigh would have. Repairs mid-journey? Injured reindeer? Run out of cocoa?

"Shake them three times and whistle loudly."

Though still surprised by the turn of events, I did as told. In response, a miniature tornado of snowflakes shot up from my feet and whisked me from the realm-evator lobby. The next thing I knew, I was on a soft bench surrounded by stars. A bearded, tubby man sat on my left and a brunette, adolescent boy with glasses sat on my right.

"Uh . . . hi, Kris," I said to the man, trying to play it cool. "Or maybe I should call you Santa since you're on the job?" I pivoted to the kid. "Hi, Nick. How goes it?"

"Dad let me go down the last chimney by myself!" the kid

said, pushing the glasses back up his nose. "It was awesome. And the cookies were great!"

"Frost." Kris kept his eyes on the eight reindeer pulling us through the sky. "I hear you've been naughty."

My gaze fell to the floor of the sleigh. "It caught me off guard," I said, shoving the Beaming Bells in my pocket.

"Seeing former friends?"

"No. Seeing death." I looked up and did something I never did—allowed myself to be vulnerable. "I know decades have passed since *I* passed. I understand that life has continued on Earth without me—the world turning and turning, causing the people I used to know to age until they expire. But until tonight I'd never come face-to-face with that so personally. When your father died, Kris, I was sad, but he was already old when I met him. It's different because I knew David and Wyatt when they were young."

I sighed and leaned back, staring up at the sparkling night as wind whistled around us. "Seeing them reach their ends was surreal. Staying the same age in the afterlife while everyone else changes has depressed me for a while now—I first started to feel it when *you* passed me in age—but tonight was like a punch in the face and I feel conflicted about it."

"How so?" Kris asked.

"Well, part of me regrets caring about David and Wyatt at all because if I hadn't, maybe I wouldn't feel this way now. The other part wonders what would've happened if I'd allowed myself to care about them more, like I do for you. You're probably the closest thing I've had to a good friend, and that terrifies me."

"Dad, Dad," Nick urged. "Give her the present."

I straightened and looked from the kid to his father.

"Frost, you're not the first ghost to have trouble adjusting, and you probably won't be the last," Kris said. "Specter One and the

Senior Specters share the responsibility of keeping all you spirits calm, focused, and from going off the edge. Every soul is different, but I think with you, a gentler approach is necessary. Plus, as someone who considers *you* a good friend, I have taken an extra special interest in your case." He gestured to Nick. "Now, son."

Nick twisted around and dug inside the massive sack in the back seat.

"The CCD isn't in the habit of gift exchanges," Kris explained. "They don't make sense when you spirits are only active for one month a year and are immaterial in nature. But I remember that you gave me a gift the day we met when I was only five years old. I played with that toy submarine for months and it endeared me to you."

"It was just a broken plane, Kris. Imagination did the work."

"I believe you called it positive perspective," he replied. "Something I hope you hang onto, even as time tempts you to cynicism. Anyway, I would like to give you a gift now. The first one, I reckon, you've received since you died."

A high-pitched yap caught my attention. I turned. Nick held a fully-grown Westie terrier in his arms. The creature wiggled and waggled. A sparkling red bow was wrapped around his neck. Nick handed the dog to me. He immediately began licking my face and I couldn't help but smile.

"A dog?" I said.

"Not just a dog," Nick piped in. "This thing doesn't need to be fed, cleaned up after, and it won't age."

I blinked in astonishment.

"I know a lot about you, Frost," Kris said. "Both from decades of Christmases spending time together, and the personal files that Specter One shared with me when I took over as Santa. I *know* you're not good at making friends. You favor isolation too much, even for a ghost. I figure maybe you need a surrogate to help you open up some." He alluded to the dog. "That's why Nick and I have been working on this present for you. Since he doesn't age like a regular dog, you'll at least have one being in your life you don't have to worry about growing old on you. The pair of you will always be exactly as you are now."

I was astounded and grateful beyond words. Despite my cold ghostly nature and the frosty winds, a warmth grew inside me that I hadn't felt in a long time. The dog yapped excitedly.

I looked at my friends on either side of me. "Thank you, Kris. Thank you, Nick."

"You're welcome," Kris said. "Just please promise me that one of these holidays you'll try letting *people* in. Being dead is no excuse to stop learning, Frost. And while I don't want to get into it now, it's *essential* that you find the ability to change. Otherwise, there's no point in the long run."

I opened my mouth to voice a question, but Nick tugged on my sleeve.

"So what are you gonna name it?"

The dog's tongue licked my cheek. Then my vision faded to blackness and I awoke from my dream memory to find present day Marley standing on top of me. His small but persistent tongue lapped my face.

I glanced around, realizing I'd fallen asleep on the couch in my CCD office. "Come on, boy, we should go to our room. Taking naps here isn't the most comfortable . . ." I saw the speckled light on the floor. Abruptly I sat up and twisted around to look at the window. That wasn't moonlight; it was daylight! It was morning!

I checked my watch. I was supposed to be at Jay's office in fifteen minutes!

"Gingersnaps! I'm late!" I hurriedly swiped the contents strewn all over my coffee table back into my bag and threw open the door. "Marley, let's move!"

My dog dashed into the hallway. I slammed the door shut behind me with way too much might. *BAM!* I winced as crashes sounded from inside—reverberation force no doubt shaking objects from my bookshelf to the floor. No time to worry about that; I'd clean up later.

"Where's the fire, Frost?" Allan mocked, passing me in the hall.

"Shove it up a chimney, Allan."

I didn't break stride and thirty seconds later, Marley and I were jettisoning down in our interdimensional lift. After a quick change in the Fa-La-La-La Fashion Pod, I tried to teleport to Jay's office directly to save time, but once there I couldn't find a place to reappear clandestinely. Jay was in a meeting with several staffers, the conference rooms were busy, and the bathroom and elevators were teeming with people. And then—because the universe wasn't cutting me any slack this morning—I discovered that maintenance was painting the stairwell.

Cookie crumbs!

I gave up and teleported back to the loft.

I guess I'm going on foot.

With another wave to Marley, I bolted downstairs to exit the apartment complex. The crisp, sunny LA morning collided with me. I was tense, but at least it was a gorgeous day. The city was damp, clean, and smelled fresh. After being hammered by rain last night, the soil and soot had washed away. If only rain worked that way on sins.

I hustled up the block as my mind swirled with conflict. Jay's concession to the donors last night was a whopping domino pushing him toward the dark futures Midori had been showing me and Brandon for weeks. Since the beginning of the month I'd struggled believing they were his destiny because I just didn't see him as bad, but my doubts kept springing up like daisies—

or weeds depending on your perspective. I went back and forth because of the time I spent with him. His soul drifted away and then came back. His hardness and stubbornness took over then his softness shined through. He gave me a glimpse of the kind, good man he was and then just as swiftly the anger he held, resentment he bore, and fears that haunted him would draw him back on track to doom.

I hated that I kept fighting the very idea that he was supposed to be a Scrooge. And it bothered me even more that I cared for him in a non-professional way. I wanted to save the souls of all my assignments, but I'd never wasted so much energy and emotion trying to stop them from needing saving.

Now it was too late for that anyway. With every passing day, Jay needed saving more desperately, and I was the ghost to get the task done. I had to. I couldn't let him end up like—

"Hey, watch it!" an angry driver yelled.

I leapt back frightfully as a sedan sped around the corner. Once my nerves calmed, I checked my watch. I was never going to make it.

"One more try for good measure," I thought aloud.

I darted into an alley and looked around for cameras. Once I felt safe, I turned ghostly and used my powers to latch on to Jay. When I beamed to the office I found he was still in a meeting so I made for the stairwell. Since the painters would've seen me turn tangible, I hustled all the way to ground level, phased through the door to the lobby, and got in an elevator. I had to ride with a bunch of different people for several minutes, listening to casual jazz elevator music all the while. Thankfully, eventually a time came when the car cleared. *Finally* alone, I returned to human form then pressed the button for Jay's floor.

Just then my phone dinged—a Merry Meter notification. I

opened the app to the familiar "Bah humbug!" and discovered the UnScrooged update.

"Oh, come on, Karen, really?!" The elevator doors slid open precisely as I exclaimed in frustration. The office staff stared at me.

I laughed nervously and pocketed my phone. Without meeting anybody's gaze, I proceeded toward Jay's office. My face forged a perfect scowl as I mounted the stairs. Frustration and ire pumped through me like blood through the veins of the living.

My team and I had saved Karen Thatcher's soul only six years ago. I couldn't believe she'd backtracked so quickly. What was happening to the world? Was it really so hard for someone to stay committed to being better in this day and age?

I approached Jay's office just as two of my colleagues were exiting. I entered, then stopped. To my surprise, I spotted the Christmas tree bauble I'd given Jay. It was back on his desk.

"So I was looking at my schedule this morning," Jay said as he glanced up from his computer. "My remaining focus groups have been pushed to tomorrow and today I have something labeled 'Holiday Obligations' in my calendar. The whole morning is blocked out for it. I take it that's you?"

"Correct. I moved your focus groups because we have our final Ghost of Christmas Present visit today. I want one of your drivers to take us somewhere first, though. It'll look weird if you suddenly disappear from this office without having used a car."

"Fine. I'll text Rocco," he said, picking up his cell.

I blinked. "That's it? You're not going to go off on me again for interfering with your schedule? After your last meltdown, I at least expected some yelling."

"I'm not thrilled about it. Annie won't be either. But if you were going to get me out of anything, I'm glad it was this. I would much rather go on a field trip with a dead woman than listen to a focus group."

"How flattering."

The click-clack of stilettos announced Annie's arrival. She entered the office and nodded at me before addressing our boss. "I just looked at my calendar. Jay, I thought we had focus group testing this morning. Did you move it?"

He nodded. "Sorry, Annie."

"You do realize cancelling on people at the last minute does not send a good message regarding your leadership style," Annie remarked, eyes narrowing. "What are these *holiday obligations* anyway?" she spoke the words like they were foreign in her mouth.

"Uh..."

"He's doing some Christmas activities with his family," I interceded.

A hint of annoyance creased Jay's face. "Uh, yeah. I'll be back in two—"

"Three," I interrupted.

Jay glared at me. "*Three* hours."

"And we're going to be late if we don't leave now," I added. Jay exhaled tiredly and got up from his desk.

"Frost is going with you?" Annie asked, markedly perturbed.

"To assist," I responded. "That is my job, isn't it?" I held open the door for Jay, but Annie stopped him, standing in his way.

"Jay, may I speak candidly?" He nodded slowly and she continued. "I am worried about you and I think Frost is a bad influence. You made the right decision to work with the donors last night. But it scares me that you would look to her for approval and listen to her opinions over mine, even for a second. Frost has been here a month. I have been by your side for a year. After your Friedman's dinner, they assured me you were going to stop mucking around and make the hard choices, listen, and focus. I haven't been seeing that from you enough, and I think that's partly because Miss December here is making you second-guess. That needs to end. You're a smart man, Jay, and you have a strong command of the issues, but I'm not interested in backing a horse that won't run on the track. There is no alternate route. To win a race, you have to concentrate on the prize ahead and keep your blinders on to all distractions."

Jay looked between me and Annie. Then he put a hand on Annie's shoulder. "Annie. I *am* invested. I *am* focused. This week has just been crazy. I promise after the holiday I'll buckle down. Whatever you say. You can even hire a different assistant. Frost is leaving us after Christmas." He turned his head to me. "Aren't you?"

I nodded, but didn't speak.

Annie crossed her arms. "Okay, Jay. Fine. For my own peace of mind though, just look me in the eyes and promise me that you meant it when you gave your assurances to the donors last night and to our backers at Friedman's. You're committed to winning, right? That's what matters the most here."

"I promise, Annie," he said, face serious. "Nothing matters to me more."

His words haunted me as we rode the elevator downstairs.

"Rocco texted. The car is being pulled around," Jay said as the floor numbers whizzed by.

I didn't respond.

We exited the building and stood on the busy curb. Jay looked at me after a moment, vexed. "You know, you shouldn't be mad at me for the new assistant comment. If anything, I should be angry with you for scheduling time with my family without my permission. Seeing them yesterday at the 5k was painful enough. I'm not in the mood for another awkward run-in."

"I'm not upset about the assistant comment," I said, eyes forward. "And we're not spending time with your family. That was a lie for Annie's sake."

Our vehicle approached. "The Los Angeles Women's Center please, Rocco," I told the driver before raising the divider between the back and front.

We merged into Friday-before-Christmas traffic. The streets were stressed from too much obligation; the mood between me and my Scrooge remained just as tense.

"Are you mad about last night?" Jay asked after a few minutes. "Because while I'm not thrilled to have to compromise on some parts of my platform, everyone has to compromise at some point in life. Compromise can actually benefit a lot more people than being a stickler can. That's how the world works—they give me something; I give them something. It's not like doing that means I'm going to the dark side of the force."

I didn't respond. Which spoke volumes considering I appreciated the *Star Wars* reference. I merely stared out the window.

Time passed.

"Hey, I thought of my question," Jay eventually said.

I frowned and looked at him. "What question?"

"You said I can ask one question about . . ." He lowered his voice even though the divider was up. "The North Pole."

I sighed. "All right, let's hear it."

"Is Santa immortal?"

My whole body stiffened. A pause hung in the air before I responded.

"No."

Jay blinked then leaned forward like an impatient child. "I'm going to need more than that. How does it work then? What happens to him when he dies? Who takes over?"

Crossness built in my body and tone. "I said you could ask one question."

"But you gave half an answer. Come on, Frost. You can go back to uselessly nagging me about my life choices for the rest of the weekend. You owe me this."

Now I was mad.

"Jay, I don't owe you anything. In fact, you owe me for dedicating an entire month to trying to save you. All you Scrooges have no idea how lucky you are to be given a second chance. Then when you backtrack, it feels like a smack in the face to me for believing in you and thinking maybe this time would be different, maybe not all human beings are so . . ."

I stopped. Jay was staring at me.

I took a deep breath. The news about Karen was filling me with too much distress. I hadn't expected so much fury or frustration to come out. Like Sergeant Roger Murtaugh from *Lethal Weapon*, I was getting too old for this.

"Forget it," I said. "Santa is magical, but he's mortal. He gets married and has kids like most people. Not an experience I can personally relate to, but there you go. His oldest child takes over for him when he retires or dies. I don't know what happens to him after that. Souls end up in different places in the afterlife."

Jay had never looked at me with concern before. It made me uncomfortable. I was supposed to be the one helping him through his issues, not the other way around.

"Frost . . . why are you like this? How did you end up a Christmas Carol ghost?"

I gazed out the window at the busy streets—alive with people going through the rhythms of life. A slew of good reasons came to mind to not tell him. It was none of his business. It was against the rules. I'd already told him way more than I should. I didn't like to open up to people.

"It's a consequence of my time on Earth," I found myself saying. "If a person has a great capacity to love while alive but dies without meaningful connection to anyone, you end up a ghost tasked with saving souls for one hundred years. We do that by resurrecting people's Christmas Spirit—you know, that goodwill toward humankind, warm, and hopeful feeling you fill up with whenever you watch a holiday movie. Christmas Spirit dwindles every year as the world becomes more complicated and it just gets harder to be a person. Ghosts like me imbue the world with an extra infusion of that miraculous energy every time we save a Scrooge."

"That sounds very . . . noble," Jay said slowly.

I huffed. "That's a nice way to describe it. Sad would also be an apt term. It's not easy to see time pass, the world change, and people die. It's even harder when the Scrooges you've invested in let you down."

"So . . . you died without anyone you cared about?" Jay asked, voice soft.

"In order to become a Christmas Carol ghost, there can't be anyone—alive or dead—who truly matters to you *and* who you truly matter to."

"That's . . ." Jay paused. "Well, I guess sad is the right word."

"Yes, I know."

A lull passed.

"It's strange," Jay commented. "When I first met you, I thought you were the human embodiment of the holidays. Your festive clothes, your cheery attitude—you even smell like sugar cookies. But the more I've gotten to know you . . . I guess I go back and forth. Sometimes you seem like this optimistic Christmas Spirit spirit—so alive and full of passion and warmth that I see you as a person. Other times you're morose, cynical, and distant, and I am reminded that you're a ghost."

My chest clenched. I wasn't sure if I felt offended or hurt or what. But I felt *something*.

And I didn't like it.

"Let me clear things up for you, Jay. I am as much a ghost as you are a Scrooge. Our roles are clear and fair. I can't hold it against you for making destructive choices any more than you can hold it against me for being cynical. Annie was right, that *is* what I am. Or at least that's what I've become even though I never wanted to fully admit it. But we are what we are."

"For now," Jay said. "I mean, your whole point of being here is to try and change me, right? Can't you change too? Don't you want to? I get that dying without mattering to anyone or anyone mattering to you is a bleak way to go, but shouldn't saving people and working to make the world a brighter place help you move on?"

"Ten minutes out," Rocco said over the intercom.

I stared at my Scrooge. "Jay, I *have* moved on. I've accepted the way the world works anyway." We turned a corner and drove past a theater. My eyes held onto it, the marquee glimmering in the LA sun. "I think that's the main reason I like movies so much . . ." I thought aloud in a daze. "Why even in death, even in my state of dwindling hope and optimism, I still make time for them every season. Movies are a chance for happy endings."

"You don't think life has happy endings?"

"It can. People just tend to get in the way. You know that as well as anyone." I took a deep breath and faced him directly. "Though I didn't like how you acquiesced to those benefactors last night, I don't completely hold it against you because not everything they said was nonsense. Who knows the good you could've done over the years if people had given you a chance? You could be so much happier right now if people had simply cooperated."

"I think about that all the time," Jay said distantly, a little resentfully.

He sighed. "I guess maybe that happy ending thing is another reason I like movies too. We have that in common."

He and I shared a moment until the alert that had been sounding on low volume inside me went off much louder. I sat back and cleared my throat. I couldn't believe how open with Jay I'd just been. I guess one of the unanticipated consequences of keeping to yourself is that after enough time, given the right stress—the right trigger—you may open up when you weren't planning on it.

Now it was too late to take it back and frankly, I wasn't sure I wanted to. Despite the rules, and myself, I didn't regret the conversation. Something inside of me felt . . . lighter having shared my feelings with Jay. Still, it was time to refocus.

"This isn't about me though; it's about you. Before we get where we're going, I need to talk to you about my magic."

His eyes went wide. "I'm all ears."

"I'm sure you are." I straightened up. "Look, it's against the rules to share info about my ghost deal with my Scrooges. The venting I just did . . . let's call it a weaker moment. That being said, my team and I did agree to bend this rule regarding a partial explanation of my powers. It's necessary so you understand what's about to happen."

I took a deep breath.

"My powers allow me to teleport myself anywhere you are and take you three places for our special visits, which I've selected in advance. That's my main function. Plus, as you've experienced, I can make myself and whoever I'm traveling with invisible and intangible."

I felt the car slowing down. "Perfect timing."

Jay and I exited the vehicle before Rocco could get out and I came around to the driver's window. "Rocco, can you pick us up here in exactly two hours?"

Rocco looked to Jay for confirmation and my Scrooge nodded.

Our ride departed and we strode toward the women's center that Jay had debuted at the start of the month. When we were close, I pulled Jay into an alleyway and used another frying pan charm to disable a street camera. With that done, I took his hand and we transformed into ghost states before entering the center.

I couldn't help but smile at the life buzzing around us. As we wandered the rooms, Jay following my lead, we saw kids and adults with Christmas decorations, baskets of clothes, and wrapped gifts. The kitchen and dining room bustled with activity and delicious smells. Women worked on computers, made calls, and conducted meetings in offices. In the main room, a bunch of kids watched holiday cartoons on a big TV.

"So why this place?" Jay asked as we came to a pause. "All our field trips to my past and present have focused on my family so far."

"How you treat your family is only half the recipe for how you turn out," I replied. "I've given it a lot of attention because your denial, touchiness, and resentment make the situation more complicated. Today we're going to address the other half of your recipe."

At that moment a familiar young woman escorted two men and a plump lady in a teal pantsuit into the room. The men began taking pictures of the space.

I couldn't believe the good luck and gestured for Jay to come closer to the group.

"The lighting is better over there," the young woman instructed. "Get some shots of the different ornaments on the tree. The kids made those."

The plump lady crossed her arms. "Please make sure you have

enough photos for the rest of the week, dear. You've done an excellent job, but the clock is ticking. The holidays are our best time to get donations, and the stronger the social media reach, the better."

"Yes, ma'am," the young woman responded. "Mr. Nichols gave us a great head start with his promised three years of funding, but I'm not taking that for granted and will do him and you proud."

"Mommy!" A four-year-old boy trotted over from the TV circle and hugged the young woman's leg.

"Hi, sweetie. I'm so happy to see you." The young woman patted his head then addressed the photographers again. "Make sure to blur out the screen in any shots you get with the TV. We don't want it to be clear what they're watching."

The photographer she was talking to winked. "For sure. Nothing says Christmas bummer like copyright law."

"That's Nia," I explained to Jay, pointing to the young woman as she continued conversing with the teal pantsuit lady while holding her son's hand. "The day you opened this center she asked me to tell you how this place has given her a job, a home, and a chance at a better future with her son. She wanted me to tell you that she says thanks."

Jay nodded. "That was the idea. Sometimes people hit a bad break in life and need help to move forward. I'm glad this place can give women in our community an opportunity to do that."

I laughed.

He raised an eyebrow. "What?"

"That is verbatim what you told a reporter last time you were here. No one with a camera can see or hear you right now, Jay. You can relax with the pretense. Especially considering I know only a third of what you promised these people is going to reach the center. *The Jay Nichols Community Relief Fund*," I said to him pointedly.

Jay's face soured. "The money in that fund is meant to help communities. I can't help anyone if I lose. My team and I are keeping this place afloat for the next year, then once I'm elected I can continue to help. For now, the remainder of the funds has to get me to that position. Otherwise my efforts and goals for improving communities will mean nothing. You can't help anyone if you *aren't anyone*."

"That sounds like Annie, not you Jay," I replied. "And believe me, I've come to know you well enough to hear the difference. You try to pretend like you can turn down the volume on your heart for the job's sake, but it's strong. You should listen to it more."

I offered Jay my hand and used my final present trip to transport us to a busy street in the middle of downtown. Mom-and-pop shops, restaurants, and other local gems were carved into the booming city around us. I strolled along the sidewalk with Jay following me suspiciously—sun, smog, and people phasing right through us.

"Is this it?" he asked after a few minutes. "Your best attempt is a guilt trip at a place I'm trying to help followed by a casual afternoon downtown?"

"Sort of," I replied with a shrug. "I want you to look at this city—really appreciate it for all the wonderful pockets of business and life that it has. You've told me how important it is for you to preserve this. *You care about this*."

I stopped in front of him.

"I do," Jay said warily. He knew I was up to something but couldn't figure out what. "I want people to be able to grow and thrive and have their best chance. It's my whole reason for running for office."

"It's the only reason anyone should run for office," I corrected. "That's neither here nor there, though. As I said in the car, this is about you. And the best way for me to help you understand the consequences of your current choices is by immersing you in how things are now before showing you what they become."

I gestured at the lively city surrounding us then met Jay's gaze. "You remember how my powers work? Well, this is why I explained them to you. I'm leaving you here, Jay, for some personal self-reflection time. No phones. No schedules. No distractions. Just you and the city you came from. I wouldn't bother fighting it; no one can see or hear you. But don't worry. I'll find you later, wherever you are."

"Wait, what? Frost, you can't—"

I vanished and reappeared in my loft, Jay's shocked and panicked expression lifting my mood a bit. I did truly enjoy the tough love portion of a Scrooging experience.

I whistled for Marley as I flopped down on the couch. My loyal pet trotted over and hopped next to me as I put my feet up.

"Hey, boy. I've got a couple of free hours. What movie shall we watch?"

20

"Boo!"

I found Jay in the Historic Arts District downtown. He whirled around when I spoke, his expression furious.

"FROST!"

"You're mad. I can see you're mad."

"Mad? You turned me into a ghost and then left. I've been wandering the city for hours."

"Hence why I cleared your schedule," I replied, unfazed. "I made sure you didn't miss any important appointments. I'm a responsible ghost." I winked at him.

His expression remained unchanged.

"Look," I said more seriously. "I wouldn't have done this to you if it didn't matter. I already received a phone call from my boss questioning my tactics, and I had to take his stern lecture on behalf of my team. So if I'm willing to put myself in hot water with my magical ghost supervisor, you could at least be a bit more patient with the process."

His body language and clenched jaw remained tight, but he backed down. "Fine. Just get me back to the office."

"That's the plan." We clutched hands and I beamed us to the women's center. We ducked into the adjoining alley to resume our human forms and when we emerged spotted Rocco's car.

"Couldn't you have just beamed us back to the office?" Jay asked as we walked over.

I shook my head. "Each ghostly visit is a round-trip ticket.

Past, present, future—we have to teleport back to the same place we came from."

Buckled up, we rode for twenty minutes before Jay cut the silence. "Frost." He looked at me. "Do you still have that list of my kids' activities for the week?"

"Yes . . ."

"Can I see it?"

In a state of shock and cautious excitement, I dug around in my bag. No schedule.

Tannenbummer.

I must've left it on the table in my CCD office.

"I can bring it to you later. Why do you want it?" I asked, trying to downplay my hope.

"I'm not saying I agree with what you and Brandon have pointed out to me, but being alone for the past couple of hours gave me time to think about my kids. I'm not going to be able to spend Christmas Eve with them, but maybe I can squeeze something in tomorrow. You did schedule 'Holiday Obligations' for me today. Maybe I should complete some of those for real."

My spirit rose. "That's a great idea, Jay. I'm proud of you."

"Yeah, yeah." He got out his phone and began to text, then paused and flicked his eyes to me. "No more surprises for the rest of the day though. Okay, Frost?"

I saluted him then smiled with some satisfaction as my Scrooge became absorbed in his phone. With some time to kill in traffic, I took out mine as well and texted Bismaad.

"Hey, I hope things are going OK in the UK." Smiley face emoji. *"Since you're eight hours ahead, when you get back to the CCD, can you please look for a folded itinerary in my office? Should be by the table, maybe the floor. Then text me a pic. Thank you!"*

Things were finally starting to turn around, and right on

schedule. I guess this old ghost did still have some tricks up her sleeve.

"What are we watching?"

"Jesus!" Jay gasped as I appeared next to him on the couch in his condo.

"Nope—a lot of people celebrate his birthday in a couple of days though." I reached over and grabbed a few pieces of popcorn from the bowl on Jay's lap.

The lights were dimmed, so the glow of the TV illuminated us quite spectrally if I did say so myself. Jay stared at me. "It's my favorite Christmas movie," he said warily as I chewed. "*Die Hard*."

"Of course it is," I replied reaching for the bowl again. "That's such a boy answer."

"It's an awesome answer," he corrected. My hand went for the popcorn a third time and Jay smacked it away.

"Hey!" I protested.

"Hey yourself. I thought we agreed no more surprises for the day."

"Yes, but now the day is over. Night is fair game."

He shook his head. "Did you at least bring me that list of my kids' activities?"

I winced. "Annie had me stay late at the office. I haven't had a chance to retrieve it. And the friend I asked to send me a pic of the schedule hasn't responded. I'll bring it to you first thing tomorrow. By the way, if you were wondering if you were Scrooge material before? Having your staff work on December 23rd and Christmas Eve, which also happen to fall on a Saturday and a Sunday? Come on, Jay."

"You know perfectly well how important the next two days

are for my campaign. I'm not chaining anyone to a desk. The staff took these jobs knowing how demanding they'd be. Maybe you should be haunting them and having them reexamine *their* life choices."

He paused the TV. "So then, ghost friend, let's get this over with. Where are we going?"

I raised my eyebrows. "So we're friends now, are we?"

He huffed. "It was a figure of speech."

"Uh huh." I looked at him curiously. "Well, before we get to the where, I have a who that needs explaining. There's someone I'd like you to meet." I tilted up my chin, signaling that he should look behind him.

"Geez, Frost!" Jay jumped when he found Midori sitting on the armrest of his couch, her dark eyes staring into his soul.

Classic Midori.

Jay got up quickly and took three steps backward.

"This is Midori." I gestured at the petite Japanese woman, who remained perfectly still. "She will be your Ghost of Christmas Future, showing you exactly what is in store if you don't learn the error of your ways, repent, and forge a new path."

"Hi," Jay said to her uneasily.

Midori continued staring at him.

I should talk to Specter Nine about recruiting her to teach a seminar on intimidation tactics.

The navy robes Midori wore glimmered with silver embroidery that shone like her gray hair. My colleague's charcoal shawl rested on her narrow, stooped shoulders. Her raven black eyes were darker than any night sky LA had ever seen.

"She's not much for small talk," I said. Then I pointed at Jay's outfit. "I see you have sneakers on. That's good. Is that sweatshirt, sweatpants combo warm enough for outside?"

"Uh, yeah."

I nodded to Midori. "It's time."

My colleague stretched out her thin, wrinkly hands. I took hold. Jay hesitated but I didn't blame him. Holding hands with Midori felt similar to holding hands with an undertaker. I'd grown fond of her these past few weeks in a creepy-old-neighbor-who-occasionally-waves-at-you sort of way, but I was dead and therefore inherently harder to spook.

When Jay extended his hand, he flinched as Midori's fingers slowly curled around his. Then she squeezed—roughly. An ominous breeze tore at the skirt of my dress and the long sleeves of Midori's robe. The wind was laced with blue energy that circled us with a deep moan. The lights of the condo flickered. Midori's eyes opened wider until her lids were no longer visible, the white of her eyes soaked in magic.

The blue winds consumed us. Then with a *WHOOSH* we re-appeared in the darkened streets of downtown LA. Jay could not let go of Midori's hand fast enough. He glanced around. "This is where you found me today. The Historic Arts District."

I nodded. "Any starting point downtown would do for tonight, but this seemed appropriate given your adventure today. Notice anything different about the area?"

Jay walked away from us, head swiveling as he studied the streets.

While sparse streetlamps, some Christmas lights in apartment windows, and the distant luminescence of the city's bigger towers provided light, at ground level it was notably a few degrees too dark. It was the result of all the shadowy vacancies. Shopfronts and businesses were shut down—boarded windows, chained doors, faded and peeled store signs.

"There was an Italian restaurant there this morning." Jay

pointed across the street. "And a mom-and-pop grocery store over there. And I think an antiques shop here? What's going on? Midori is a future ghost; when are we exactly?"

"This is fifteen years from now," I told him solemnly. "Congratulations would be long overdue by then. In this timeline, you won the election, Jay. You won a couple more after that too, but as you made compromises to get to those wins, the things you started out fighting for kept moving to the bottom of the pile."

Jay's face lit up. "Seriously? I win?"

Midori and I exchanged an exasperated look. I smacked my hand to my head.

"Jay, not the point. Your compromises on individual matters snowball into compromises in character and purpose, like they do for a lot of people. On your current path, eventually protecting small businesses and the livelihood of the average person become just that to you—small, average problems you don't concern yourself with."

Jay put his hands in his pockets and frowned at me, voice defensive. "You can't blame me for a few places closing down, Frost. Eighty percent of privately owned restaurants go out of business within five years. With the advent of online shopping, brick-and-mortar shops have to fight for their lives. This isn't my fault. Anyway, no matter what position I hold, no city is ever going to live and die with me. I'm just one person."

"All it takes is one person," I replied. "A single soul, even a single decision, can improve the world drastically or ruin it dramatically. Maybe you didn't *cause* this to happen, Jay, but a soul as strong as yours certainly could've helped prevent it. You still can. You're at your beginning now. The road you're going down with Annie and those donors from last night and Friedman's has a slippery slope. Don't be complicit in doing nothing where your passions are concerned like they want. You're better than that."

Jay turned and gazed down the street. The occasional car whizzed past us, oblivious to the three glowing ghosts on the sidewalk.

"You remember when I ditched you this morning so you'd properly appreciate the city for what it is in the present?" I said.

Jay pivoted slowly. "Yes?"

"Sorry, I'm going to have to do it again."

His eyebrows went up. "Frost, don't you—"

Before he could finish, Midori grabbed my hand on cue and rushed us back to the present with another *WHOOSH*. We solidified in Jay's condo.

I glanced at my spooky but not unpleasant coworker. "I figure we can pick him up in two hours. That's how much time I gave him to wander this afternoon."

Midori blinked at me then nodded. I looked around awkwardly. My eyes fell on the TV. "I don't suppose you like action movies? I could catch you up on what's going on."

My colleague blinked again, then sat down and stared at the paused TV screen—her back perfectly erect and eyes focused on the frozen image of Bruce Willis talking into a radio.

I guess that's a yes.

I sat down beside her and picked up the bowl Jay had left on the couch, offering it to her. "Popcorn?"

She looked at me, looked at the bowl, then took a single piece of popcorn and put it in her mouth before staring back at the TV.

I shrugged and pressed play. I'd had weirder movie nights.

Two hours later, Midori and I found ghost Jay slumped on a park bench. When he saw us, he didn't react with intense emotion like he had this afternoon when I'd picked him up. He simply stood and sighed.

"How was it?" I asked.

"Discouraging," he said. "There were too many vacant places where small businesses should be. Way more big chain stores than I remembered. The homeless population is out of hand. The women's center is gone." He shook his head. "A guy can cover a lot of ground in a two-hour walk with limited street traffic and the ability to phase through things."

I put a ghostly hand on his shoulder. Midori tilted her head and gave me a sideways glance, causing me to withdraw. I was getting better at reading her looks—this one said, *Kind of a personal gesture, girl. Keep it professional.*

"This is just one city," I told Jay, "but Midori and I have explored your future thoroughly. The places you wanted to protect all across the state have deteriorated. It doesn't have to be this way though. You can make different choices. You may not be able to help everyone and do everything you set out to accomplish, but as long as you fight your hardest with the mindset that you can, then you have the best chance of living your best life."

I nodded to Midori. She offered us her hands and transported us back to Jay's living room in the present. He glanced around in a daze for a moment before addressing us. "You've given me a lot to think about. Now can you both leave me alone? Please? I have to . . . I'll see you tomorrow, Frost."

Jay disappeared down the hall that led to his bedroom. Midori grabbed my hand, and this time I used my magic to return us to my loft.

"How about that, huh?" I said, feeling pleased. "We set up that visit to the future perfectly. He's shaken and totally reevaluating things." I extended my palm for a high-five. It hung midair for a moment, then thankfully Midori reciprocated the gesture.

I whistled for Marley and gathered him in my arms. "Ready to go?" I asked Midori, jutting my chin toward the realm-evator door. "We can call Brandon on SpaceTime when we're back. Give him an update."

She nodded and we boarded. Upon stepping into the icy CCD lobby I set Marley down then phoned Brandon and did a walk and talk. "Things went great with Jay tonight. I think we bridged a major hurdle. Tomorrow I'll connect him with his family in the present like he requested and then hammer home the consequences of his political ambitions. I—Marley!"

I snapped my fingers at my dog, who'd wandered off and seemed to be considering licking one of the beautiful ornaments on the lobby's "*Future*" Christmas tree.

"That's awesome," Brandon said. "I'm sure Midori was raving about it."

I adjusted the phone to Midori as we continued down the hall. She gave Brandon the thumbs up. I smiled and readdressed the kid. "Let's meet for breakfast at seven tomorrow. Talk more details."

"Awck. That's aggressively early, Frost. I don't know if I have that kind of energy."

"In two days you're going to sleep for almost a year. Dig deep," I said.

We hung up as I reached my office. I waved goodbye to Midori and strode in, almost tripping on a book. Several volumes and a few knickknacks were scattered on the ground from my door slam this morning. I began putting them back as Marley settled in his favorite spot.

I picked up a golden reindeer figurine, a Nancy Drew book I'd had since the seventies, a pack of candy cane flavored gum, a fantasy book called *Crisanta Knight* I'd bought in Alabama five years ago, a framed picture of Marley in an elf costume, and . . . *Whoa.*

I carefully touched the last book that'd fallen—it was open on the carpet, its pages spread out like the wings of a dead butterfly. I retrieved it from the floor and closed the text, wiping dashes of dust from the leather cover. My fingers traced the words: "*A Christmas Carol by Charles Dickens.*" It'd been such a long time since I opened this book—this story that once meant so much to me. I sighed and put it back on the shelf.

When I migrated to my coffee table I discovered a few documents that I had, in fact, left behind. One of them was Jay's itinerary. I stashed it in my bag before checking my phone. My message to Bismaad had the *SEEN* notation next to it since this afternoon, so why hadn't she responded?

I sent another message.

"Hey, is something wrong? You're probably asleep now, but DM me when you wake up. I'm kind of worried."

Strange. Bismaad was one of those instant responders— sometimes it felt like I barely hit send on a message and she was already responding. Hopefully I'd talk to her in the morning.

"Bedtime, Marley. Let's roll. Tomorrow we turn things around."

I clapped my hands and my dog yapped excitedly, following me out the door.

I wondered if reliving trips to a doctor's office through dream memories counted as actual visits. Ghosts like me would've needed a very inclusive health insurance plan if that were true, as we never knew when our dreams would deposit us in such places.

"Doctor Pebbles, I hardly think this is necessary," I said sitting down on the gingerbread-brown velvet couch in the elf's office. Marley sprang up on the cushion next to me.

"Frost, Specter One wouldn't have referred you to me if it *wasn't* necessary."

Dream me huffed indignantly. In the six decades since I'd been here as a trainee, this office hadn't changed much. Vases of blooming snowdrops were positioned around on abstract shelves. The carpet was fluffy and white like a polar bear's backside. Behind the doctor's desk were framed oil paintings of igloos. The gold sign on the wall next to me gleamed with her credentials.

THISTLE THERAPIES
Doctor Roberta Pebbles
North Outer Pole Institute of Technology
MD, Ph.D., LCSW, MFCC, LMNOP

Dr. Pebbles pushed her glittery glasses up her nose with her pen. "According to Specter One, you have been progressively distant during the last few Christmas seasons. Also, in their end-of-year reviews, your team members have noted that you are"— she held up her clipboard and quoted from her notes—"effectual, but cold. Focused and a good leader; however, subtly pessimistic enough to be a bummer. Present, yet somewhere else—like her head is in the game, but her heart isn't."

My therapist looked at me.

"Technically ghosts don't have working hearts," I corrected. "If we did, at least half of us would've died again by now from a coronary due to all the cocoa and cookies we consume."

Dr. Pebbles blinked at me. She was not amused. She flipped a page in her clipboard. "I've seen this before, you know. Most ghosts take success and failure with their Scrooges in stride, accepting that most humans can't sustain change on their own long-term. But some, like you, become disenchanted with the CCD's effectiveness and thus humanity as well. Disenchantment is dangerous. It makes you less productive and eliminates your ability to contribute to society. That is the case in every dimension. On Earth, thankfully, with most people the stakes aren't so high. In your line of work, however, disenchantment can cost souls."

I crossed my arms. "My outlook on what we do and its impact may have soured a bit over the years, but I'm still checking all the boxes. You heard those reviews; I am focused, effectual, and a good leader. Why is it anyone's business how I feel inside if I conceal it from my Scrooges and get the job done? It's not as if you can fire me. So why are we wasting our time here? Everything about the CCD is stagnant; we're on a holiday loop. I've made peace with that."

"You've made peace with giving up on humanity? How oxymoronic. And disappointing considering that your favorite book on Earth was *A Christmas Carol*."

"It's an inspirational, beautiful work of fiction," I replied, my nails raking my palm. "The ghosts and magic in it may be real, but the idea that any person can permanently change, breakaway from a lifetime of patterns after a week of ghostly intervention—that's not realistic. Yes, there are some outliers who do alter after the experience and live up to the potential for change that Dickens preached is possible, but most don't. *Most people* are only human. As you're an elf, I don't see how you can help me cope with that. You don't understand the affliction."

I stood and Marley hopped off the couch in solidarity. Then I stopped.

"And for the record, I haven't given up on humanity. I still believe that people can change; it's just disappointing how few people follow through. Regardless, I approach every Christmas with the attitude that maybe this Scrooge will be a winner. Maybe this time will be different. I hope for the best, but I prepare for the worst. That's not being a cynic; that's bracing myself so being let down doesn't hurt so much."

"Frost," Dr. Pebbles said. "Sit."

I sighed, but obliged.

"I am going to take your word because other than those two incidents of magic misuse on your record, you have been a model ghost," Dr. Pebbles said. "However, Specter One has expressed increased concern for how you haven't changed. You've been with the CCD for over half a century. And other than your intermittent friendships with members of the Claus family, you haven't formed a single close bond with anyone since your afterlife began."

I glanced at Marley and opened my mouth to respond, but Dr. Pebbles broke in. "That's a dog, Frost. And an abnormal one at that. It doesn't count." She sighed and removed her glasses before leaning toward me. "Specter One fears that if you remain on your current closed off path one day your suppressed emotions will bubble over and keep you from successfully Scrooging an assignment. He can't have that happen, for the Scrooge's sake and yours. Failure is not an option at the CCD. As such, Specter One has instructed me to assign you a friend."

"I'm sorry?"

She sat up straight and replaced her glasses on her nose. "We have a new recruit beginning training this season. Bismaad Hansra. She has been chosen as a Ghost of Christmas Present. She will be shadowing you this season, but your relationship will continue past that. Every December from now until your retirement, you must get together with Bismaad for at least three in-person social visits outside of work requirements."

"That's nuts."

"That's intervention. And your prescription." Dr. Pebbles

handed me an actual slip of prescription paper. "Merry Christmas, Frost. We are forcing you to make a friend. Maybe in time, you won't need our interference and will choose to change on your own. Or should I hope for the best, but prepare for the worst where that is concerned too?"

I glared at the piece of paper with the doctor's practically illegible cursive handwriting. Marley and I left the doctor's den and returned to our own. I huffed in aggravation and stared at the prescription, pacing my office. The nerve of Dr. Pebbles and Specter One. I didn't need friends on Earth, so why should I need them here? We were all just biding time anyway—one hundred years of service until our souls went somewhere else without our consent.

I cut to my bookshelf. Every office in the CCD came with a copy of *A Christmas Carol*. It was a welcome gift when we arrived. I pulled mine off the shelf. It'd been a while since I'd held it. I ran a hand over the leather cover and sighed.

"What happened to you?" I voiced to myself.

I opened to a random page of the text and thrust the doctor's prescription inside. Then I shoved the book on top of my bookshelf. Out of sight and out of mind . . .

JINGLE! JINGLE! JINGLE!

My morning alarm went off, but my brain was already throbbing on extra alert.

The prescription!

I tossed aside my sheets, disturbing Marley, and bolted out of my dorm room in my snowflake pajamas with phone in hand and my loyal dog chasing me with concern.

It'd been such a long time since I thought about Dr. Pebbles. My copy of *A Christmas Carol* had been forgotten at the top of my bookshelf for decades and I hadn't dream-remembered it in years either.

I burst into my office and went for the book, flipping through the pages. The prescription was gone.

Bismaad. What if she'd come into my office at my bequest and found it! What if she thought . . .

I checked my phone. Last night's message had been seen too, but there was still no response. Bismaad would already be back in England now, working her second-to-last day on the job like I needed to do soon. There was no time for me to pursue her in person. I sent a quick message for her to call me and nervously bit a fingernail.

Hopefully I was just overreacting.

Brandon and I gazed around at the futuristic cityscape that Midori had transported us to.

"It looks the same as it did yesterday," I said. "Should we try another street?"

Midori glowed fervently and the landscape around us morphed once, twice, then a third time. The places that Midori took us to remained as rundown as they had been when we'd explored LA's future landscape the day before.

"Still the same," I murmured.

"I don't get it," Brandon said. "If you got through to Jay, shouldn't this future be different now—less . . . *bleak*?"

After the fifth street, Midori brought us back to the present and the bright white walls of the Choice Chamber replaced the mirage of the city.

"That's not necessarily a red flag . . ." I thought aloud, trying to convince myself as much as the others. "Last night was only Jay's first visit to the future, and Scrooges never have their grand revelations before Christmas Eve, so we're fine."

"You sure?" Brandon asked.

Midori's eyes asked the same question.

"Yes," I replied. "He and I are in a good place. He's coming around. I'll talk to him when I get to the office and I'll see *you* later." I pointed at Midori. "Come down to my apartment whenever you want. Marley is already used to you, so he won't be alarmed."

"Whoo! December Eve eve!" Brandon pumped a fist in the air. "Now someone get me some pancakes. I'm beat."

"Sorry, kid. I have to go." I ruffled his hair, nodded at Midori, then picked up my dog. We rode down to the loft. The Fa-La-La-La Fashion Pod dressed me in a stylish red turtleneck, olive skirt, and knee-high boots then off to work I went.

I expected a lot of things to happen today, but my place of work melting down was not one of them. When I got off the elevator, I was taken aback by the frantic state of the office—phones ringing like mad, people scampering to different desks and conference rooms, staffers aggressively brainstorming in groups. I was instantly on edge. I didn't like surprises. I hadn't seen dying coming. I hadn't seen a century of ghost-life coming either.

While Christmas Carol work was tiring, annoying, and often disheartening, one aspect of my repetitive CCD servitude I found calming was the rhythm to my job. Scroogings weren't meant to go off the rails, especially this late in the game. And as a team leader, I was supposed to have everything under control.

"AJ, what's going on?" I asked, grabbing my coworker by the elbow as he passed by.

"Frost?" He cringed away from me. "You may want to get out of here."

"Why?"

"FROST MASON."

The whole office froze and AJ took a step sideways to allow

me a clear view of Annie atop the stairs. Her hand was on her hip, a newspaper was folded under one arm, and her eyes seemed to will me to burst into flames. She pointed a finger at me and curled it toward herself, beckoning me to come forward.

"Everyone else, back to work!" she barked.

I guardedly went up the steps, then followed Annie into Jay's office. When I pushed the door open, Jay was sitting at his desk and couldn't meet me in the eyes.

"What's wrong?" I asked.

Annie slapped the newspaper on the desk. Across the front page were an assortment of cropped shots of me and Jay—sneaking around corners, whispering to each other, even holding hands as I led him to the kitchen during that party at Councilman Walden's house. The headline read *"Nichols Disregards Campaign Commitments for New Assistant Fling."*

Well, I just died for the second time.

"Annie . . ." For once I regarded her with total humility. "This is an outright lie. All those photos have been taken out of context. Jay is *literally* just a job to me."

"Whether I believe that or not isn't the issue," Annie retorted. "This isn't just in one newspaper; it's online now and gaining traction." She turned to Jay. "I told you we should've committed way more to getting dirt on Farah. She certainly didn't hold back. I just confirmed that the photographers who took those shots work for her. Farah is going to kill you in the press now. This little scandal will dominate the news cycle for a week, maybe two. Not only will it distract from all the great things you've done this month, it'll be ammo against you at the debate tomorrow and completely overshadow anything else we do for the rest of the year."

A knock came at the door. One of the PR guys popped his head in. "Annie. I have Channel Five on the line for you. They're looking for a statement. And the mayor's office just called. They cancelled lunch today."

"Oh for the love of—" Annie waved the guy away and her eyes burned straight into me. "Frost, you're fired. Get out of this office right now."

"Annie, you can't fire her," Jay finally spoke. "Trust me."

"Jay, you can't be serious?" Annie whirled around. "The best thing we can do for damage control right now is keep anyone from seeing you two together. She has to go."

He rubbed his forehead. "She can't. It's complicated in ways unrelated to this garbage story, but she has to stick around for the next couple of days. Maybe we can come to a conciliation though . . ." He glanced at me, exasperated.

I nodded twice, still in shock. "I'll . . . I'll leave the office for the day. Give you both some space." I headed for the door, only pausing to blurt, "I'm sorry. I didn't mean to—"

"Get out!" Annie yelled.

I hurried from the room and left the office to curious stares. In the elevator, I found myself shaking. Rather than face the streets again, I teleported myself home. I walked past Marley in a daze, dropped my bag on the floor, and flopped on the couch— clutching my head in my hands.

What did I do?

I paced around my kitchen. It was half past two. Nothing had been able to distract me from the morning's events and I was going crazy.

I made a third attempt to call Jay, but once again he didn't answer.

In my state of shock this morning I'd agreed to give Jay space and not return to the office, but practically speaking I had just wasted the majority of a workday on Christmas Eve eve. When we were this close to the Scrooging deadline I needed to be with my assignment constantly; this was the most pivotal, vulnerable time for them. These were my final and most crucial hours! Any progress Jay had made could slip away if I wasn't at least in communication with him, a persistent voice in his conscience. That's assuming his progress hadn't already been blown to smithereens when that "news" story broke.

In frustration, I teleported my ghost self to his office to check on him. The staff continued going bananas in the main part of the office doing damage control. Conversely, Jay remained in his den, creepily calm. He wasn't on the phone. He wasn't even doing anything of value on his computer. He absentmindedly scrolled through an avalanche of unanswered emails as he drank a cup of coffee.

I pulled out my phone—invisible like me—and dialed his number. Jay's cell buzzed on the desk. He glanced at it, then hit the ignore button.

Oh, that is it.

Since I didn't want to show myself at the office in person, I returned to my loft and snapped my fingers. One of the TV-shaped charms on my bracelet dissolved into glitter. I closed my eyes and concentrated.

"You're ignoring my calls? Really?"

Jay spilled his coffee and almost fell out of his chair when I appeared on his computer screen.

"*Frost,*" he said in a harsh whisper. "*I thought you were going to give me the day.*"

"I said I'd leave the office, not stay away from you entirely. You know I can't do that. That's why you didn't let Annie fire me—you understand the ticking clock I'm dealing with. I have to complete my work with you on Christmas Eve. Midnight at the latest. It's not just tradition. My future is as much at stake as yours."

"How do you mean?"

"Never mind," I waved my hand dismissively. "That's not your concern. The point is that I am not going to fail or back away. Neither of us can afford it."

"What would you have me do?" Jay asked genuinely, desperately. "The whole office has been royally Scrooged since this morning. Annie was right; the media is obsessing about this."

"Can't you just . . . I don't know, ignore it? None of it's true. Go about your plans and keep being you. There are much bigger things happening than petty personal attacks. You saw the city fifteen years in the future. You understand what could happen if you let the game consume you."

"What you showed me was depressing, Frost, I stand by that," he replied. "But let me ask you a serious question—that future you showed me, is it set in stone?"

"No," I responded. "The future is always changing. Midori checks every day because even small choices can cause huge ripples."

"So that future can be avoided in a lot of different ways then."

"I mean, theoretically—"

"Not theoretically. Actually," he said firmly. "I didn't realize I could let things slip through the cracks so badly if I became successful. Now I know they can, so I'll keep an extra close eye on these issues no matter how high I rise in my career. Basically since I'm aware of the dark Christmas future that one potential timeline holds, I can be hyper vigilant to prevent it. I'll alter small choices in the present, like you said, to cause ripples that change the future. Easy."

"No. Not easy. We both love good movies, Jay, but this isn't the time for any Christopher Nolan time-travel shenanigans.

Theorizing about messing with random choices for a hypothetical outcome is a luxury neither of us have time for. You can't finagle your way out of fate solely on the idea that you will do better in the future. You need to commit to doing better right now. Get out of the trap you're falling into; don't willingly step into the trap thinking you are armed with the proper tools to handle it."

Jay glanced up. "Someone's coming. If you have another box to check, find me after working hours."

He got up from his desk, straightening his tie.

I abandoned his computer screen. My soul returned to the loft. I checked my watch. It was late evening in Bismaad's time zone. By now she'd be back at the CCD for the last meeting with her team before going into the final twenty-four hours of their Scrooging. This might be my last chance to talk to her before then.

"Marley, I'll be back."

I quickly sent a text to Bismaad:

"Can you come to my office after meeting with your team? I took a break from Earth."

I rode the realm-evator north. As I made my way to my office, I checked to see if Bismaad had responded. Nope. She'd seen the message, but there was no reply. I was still being ghosted. Quite literally.

I pushed my office door open then, for my second surprise of the day, discovered Bismaad sitting on my couch with her ankles crossed on the coffee table.

"Bismaad, I'm so—"

"'*You are fettered,*' said Scrooge, trembling. '*Tell me why?*'"

"Bismaad?"

I drew closer and noticed the book in her hand. She was reading from my copy of *A Christmas Carol*.

"'*I wear the chain I forged in life,*' replied the Ghost. '*I made it link by link, and yard by yard; I girded it on of my own free will, and of my own free will I wore it.* "Bismaad stopped and looked at me. "Funny. This was the page the book was open to when I found it on the floor yesterday. It's fitting, don't you think?"

"Okay, you found the prescription . . ." I held my hands up cautiously like one would to calm a hysterical dog. I went over to Bismaad and sat down across from her on the coffee table. "Let me explain. Decades ago, when you were assigned to shadow me as a new recruit, Specter One had become extra worried about my growing pessimism with Scrooges and my lack of socialization with other ghosts. He did mandate that I hang out with you, but I haven't thought about it that way for years. You're not an obligation anymore, Bismaad. You are a great friend to me."

"I am, Frost," she said, shutting the book with a snap, taking her feet off the table so she could sit forward. "But you're not one to me. I was thinking back trying to remember how many times each season we hang out together, excluding work, and most of the time it does fall around three. As prescribed."

I shook my head. "That's a coincidence. I haven't kept track in like a decade."

"You really expect me to believe that?" Bismaad's laugh was dark. "I now understand why you were always so distant—the most un-present Present Ghost of all time."

"Bismaad—"

"But for the sake of argument, let's say I did believe you—that you're not spending time with me out of obligation anymore. Well then, that means the only reason you still put up walls and treat me like an optional accessory in your life is because *you want it that way.* And that's just so . . ." She threw her hands up as she searched for the word. "*Sad,* Frost. The ghosts who end up in the CCD were alone on Earth, but while sometimes people end up alone on accident, staying alone is a choice. You built that situation for yourself in life, just as you did in the afterlife. And that emptiness inside you is why you're so much more miserable than the rest of us."

She sighed and shook her head in a pitying way. "It's a hundred times easier for cynicism to bleed in and spirit to fade when there's no one around to fill the craters in your soul with love and support. Which you could have if you just got out of your own way and tried to change. Not because someone—or even a team of ghosts—is making you, or scaring you, or pressuring you, but because that's what you want. That's the flaw, don't you see? That's where our efforts go wrong and why some Scrooges backtrack. It's not because we didn't do our jobs well, it's because *they* didn't want it enough. They didn't want to change enough to sacrifice who they were and take a scarier, less certain path. *Just like you.*"

She stood and studied the book in her hands then pointed at me with it. "You forged that chain of cynicism and isolation and regret for yourself, Frost, link by link, with each choice you made, and now you wear it and strangle yourself with it every day. You'll form a new chain in your next life, I'm sure. And then I'll see you back here for another round of afterlife for souls who wasted their time on Earth."

Bismaad tossed the book at me. I caught it and stared at the cover as she stormed out. After a moment, I reached into my bag's outer pocket and removed the quote card that Specter One had given me in the theater. I flipped through the text and held the quote next to the passage on the page Bismaad had read. Two quotes from two people warning me of the same thing.

I was my own worst enemy. And the person most responsible for my dwindling Christmas Spirit was me.

21

To my disbelief, when I returned to Earth and used my powers to track down Jay, I was teleported to a mall.

The shopping center was thriving with activity, not surprising considering that tomorrow was Christmas Eve. I found Jay a dozen feet away wandering around the handbags department. I hustled to a nearby dressing room to turn visible again then approached him slowly, not sure what state he'd be in.

"Hey."

Jay looked up and did a double take. My Fa-La-La-La Fashion Pod had made an atypical adjustment when I'd changed for my next trip to the future with Jay. I guess it knew I needed to blend in given the media scandal, so my outfit consisted of a pine green hoodie, dark wash jeans, and fake glasses like Bismaad wore.

"How was the rest of your day?" I asked, pretending to peruse purses while keeping my hood up.

"I can't say," Jay responded, picking up a small backpack with kittens on it. "You don't like curse words. How was yours?"

"I can't say for the same reason."

He glanced at me again. I cleared my throat, continuing my fake shopping. "What are you doing here exactly? I would think you would be laying low."

"That's what Annie wants me to do," he replied. "But I had to come. For obvious reasons, my plan to see my kids today went out the window. I may not be able to visit them tomorrow, but I can at least have someone messenger over a couple of gifts."

"You haven't bought your kids Christmas presents yet?"

"You've seen how busy I am. Anyway, I'm here now, aren't I?" He held up the cat backpack. "What do you think? Is this something a six-year-old girl would like?"

"I haven't been six for over a century, Jay. And I'm a dog person."

He sighed and put the backpack down.

"You know . . ." I tried. "I finally found your kids' activities list. There's still time for you to be with them. Yesterday your instincts told you to go to Kamie and Kingsley, and you shouldn't suppress that feeling. I know your kids would prefer seeing you over random messengered gifts, and it would be a healthier choice for your long-term relationship with them."

I pulled the kids' schedule from my pocket. "Tomorrow they're baking cookies in the afternoon again and then performing in a youth choir recital at their church's midnight mass. Maybe after your debate you could—"

"Where do you get off?" Jay said a bit too loudly, causing a few people to look our way. He ducked around the purse display and met me in the corner, hidden from view. "Frost, do you really think I have the luxury for your lectures? You were supposed to help me, yet your presence in my life has done nothing but cost me."

"I'm genuinely sorry about what happened today, Jay," I said. "But you have to let me finish doing my job. We're so close now. Please don't go backward. You have no idea how lucky you are to be getting this gift from the universe."

He scoffed. "You know what, I'm not interested. I've humored your little haunting, but I've been thinking about it all day and

I'm done. I didn't ask for this gift, but I *am* returning it. Go back to the North Pole, or the underworld, or wherever it is you came from."

He took off into the crowd. I hustled after him.

"Jay," I called, bobbing and weaving around the throng of shoppers. He cut into the cosmetics department. I bumped into several people and started to lose him as he bee-lined through fragrances.

Wait, fragrances!

Keeping my hand low so people wouldn't see the magical effect, I snapped my fingers and the cage charm on my bracelet turned to glitter. A flock of saleswomen wielding spray bottles assembled faster than a team of Transformers. They came around their counters and surrounded Jay with a thick perimeter—spraying products on sample cards or their wrists then aggressively holding them out to him.

"Try our new floral fragrance."

"Jasmine and plumeria?"

"Our Violet Vapor is to die for."

"Care for a sample?"

Jay stumbled back, revolted. He got turned around as the perimeter of perfume-wielding women tightened, cutting him off no matter which way he tried to escape. It allowed me to close in on him. He actually was so distracted that he full on rammed into me.

"Is this you?" he asked, eyes wide and panicked.

I lowered my hood.

"It's always me, Jay. Now you're coming to the future."

"This was a nice trick, Frost, but you can't go ghost mode and magically transport us out of here without anyone noticing."

"Are you sure?"

I clicked my fingers and the hourglass charm melted—magical sparkles trickling off my wrist. Just like that the world stopped.

Jay stepped back in awe. The entire department store—every shopper, every escalator, every salesperson, even the clouds of perfume that had been sprayed in the air—had frozen in time. No one and nothing moved except me and Jay.

"The effect will wear off once we leave," I explained, holding out my hand to him. "Midori is waiting in my apartment. Let's go."

Jay poked a guy in the face who'd been about to bite a soft pretzel.

"Jay?"

His fascination converted to annoyance as he turned to face me. "*Fine, Frost.* You got me. I give. But if you ditch me again—"

"I won't," I said. "It's in neither of our best interests if you keep getting angry with me. I need you to trust me."

"I think that ship has sailed. Or, to put it in more festive terms, I think that sleigh took flight a long time ago."

He gave me his hand and we emerged back in my loft. Marley bounded over and greeted Jay like they were old pals. He bent down and scratched my dog's ear.

"Where's the tiny crypt keeper?" he asked.

I pointed to his six o'clock.

Jay jumped out of his skin when he found Midori two inches behind him, staring expectantly. He straightened his tie out of nervous habit.

"So what dark and deserted place are you going to try and haunt my dreams with tonight? An empty dock? A murdery alley? Maybe a junkyard?"

"Actually, the opposite," I said, taking off my fake glasses and tossing them on the couch. I took Midori's hand and Jay did too.

We became wrapped in her trippy wind-energy and were swept forward in time.

When we landed, I think Jay came about as close to having his mind blown as any human possibly could.

We stood in the Oval Office. The full-on President of the Unites States, commander in chief Oval Office that only important leaders and security-cleared tours were allowed to access. Jay looked at it the same way I had looked at Santa's Workshop the first time I saw it—like I had stepped into a dream that my imagination and heart hoped I'd someday see, but logic taunted otherwise.

At the moment, the office was empty. Jay walked slowly across the patriotically blue carpet, passing between twin beige couches to the grand seal on the floor in front of the Resolute Desk. He glided his ghostly hand just over the polished surface of the desk. Nothing but night came through the three windows behind it, framed by contrastingly bright marigold curtains. Eventually Jay came out of his stupor.

"Why did you bring me here? You don't mean—"

The door opened and a security detail escorted a distinguished man into the room. About fifty, he wore a pristine suit, his hair and beard were peppered with gray, and his eyes were more than familiar.

President Jay strode across the Oval Office. Ghost Jay stood adjacent the American flag with eyes wide like a goldfish. A staffer followed and brought in a silver tray with milk in a brandy glass; he set it down on a coaster upon the desk then scurried out. After a few quick words, President Jay dismissed his secret service detail as well.

"Merry Christmas, sir," said the men and women before departing.

"Merry Christmas," President Jay replied. When his team

had gone, he sat at the Resolute Desk. He drummed his fingers on the fine wood, glancing at the clock. It was half past eight. Following a huff of frustration, he pressed an intercom button on his desk phone.

"Sydney, any calls or messages from them?"

"I'm afraid not, President Nichols. Would you like me to try and connect you to their residences?"

"They won't be home. My son is in New York with his wife's family for Christmas and my daughter is in Los Angeles with her mother and extended family."

"Yes, sir. I can pull up the contact info for either if you'd like to try and reach them there."

"No. They have my direct number. They'll call if they aren't busy." He paused. "Sydney, are you sure you sent them the White House Christmas card and some gifts?"

"Yes, sir. I don't know exactly what was sent off the top of my head, but I can get our personal shopper on the line right—"

"No need," he interrupted. "As long as it's taken care of."

"Yes, sir."

There was a long silence.

"Would you like me to have the kitchen send something up for a late-night snack, sir? Or I could have the staff prepare the screening room. I have a list of the Christmas movies you watched last year, so I could—"

"Sydney." A pause. "I'm fine. Truly. You can head home and be with your family now."

"Yes, Mr. President. Thank you, sir. Merry Christmas."

"Merry Christmas."

President Jay ended the call and picked up his brandy glass. He swiveled to face the windows. A small table in front of them held a collection of framed photos. Most featured Jay shaking hands with important-looking people. However, there were a few sentimental pictures.

He reached out and held up a frame in his free hand. It was a picture of Kamie and Kingsley as young children—as I knew them now. There was also a graduation picture of Kamie in a cap and gown with Celia, Eddie, and Kingsley smiling proudly beside her. A wedding photo where Kingsley stood with his bride and wedding party. A Christmas card featuring a family photo taken on the staircase in Sandra and Raymond's house.

The sparse pictures of Jay's family all had one thing in common. Jay was not in any of them. Ghost Jay realized it too. I could tell. When his future self turned around again and began flipping through a briefing folder on his desk, ghost Jay leaned down and stared at the photos with great consideration.

"This is a lot to take in," he commented eventually, stepping back. He marveled at the office in a slow pivot, trying to absorb every detail. Midori positioned herself on the armrest of one of the couches while I followed our Scrooge as he traced the room.

"Sticking with your current path, you become very successful in your career," I said. "You win the governor election and are reelected a few years later. After that, you serve as vice president before outshining your number one and being elected to the presidency the following term. This Christmas—right now— marks the completion of your third year in office."

"I can't believe I did it . . ." he said, thinking aloud as he passed in front of a bookshelf.

He turned to face me. "I mean, when you're a little kid, you dream these giant dreams and want to believe that maybe some- day all your hard work will pay off, but you don't *know*, you know? This is incredible."

"In some respects, yes," I replied. "It's also not a shocking revelation that if you align yourself with wealthy, powerful people who lack a moral code, you can go far. The choices you made in your first gubernatorial election—the donors you placated, the officials you accepted as backers, the consulting groups you let guide you—they did what they promised and got the job done. They got you elected. Once you were in office though, they didn't go away. You had to pay the piper. As you proceeded in your career, and got hungrier to keep winning, you fought back less and less against their 'compromises.' Then you ended up here. As that guy." I gestured to the president.

"What's so wrong with that guy?" Jay asked, offended.

"Two things," I said, raising a pair of fingers. "You've already realized the first. You have no family, Jay. All those things Brandon and I tried to warn you about came to pass. You never got over your resentment toward your ex-wife and mother, which put increasing distance between you and the kids. With every election you became busier, and that distance widened to a chasm. At this point in time, you haven't seen your kids in person for two years. You haven't seen them at a non-political function in four. You didn't even make it to Kingsley's wedding, let alone Kamie's graduation. Work and responsibility became the perfect excuse to let them go. And for what reason? Simply because you couldn't forgive and move forward."

Jay's eyes shone with pain—remorse he wouldn't voice. He glanced at the photo table before readdressing me. "What's the second thing?"

"You wasted everyone's time."

There was a beat where he stared at me, nonplussed.

"I don't understand."

With a sigh I crossed my arms and paced away from him a few steps, the room itself inspiring me. "I had a Scrooge who worked here once." I said. "It was a long time ago, but I remember this place well."

I turned back around. "There's a quote from John Adams engraved in the mantel of the State Dining Room. 'May none but Honest and Wise Men ever rule under This Roof.' Unfortunately, that statement has not always held true because people often trade slices of their soul for success, but I think this statement always has *a chance* to be true. On any given day on any given year in any given decade, there is the possibility for a person to walk into this room with nothing but good intentions and a soul that's not for sale. After all, the young boys and girls out there who dream about reaching this place don't know the words moral compromise. They all start good and want to do good. Like you. Life just warps them along the way."

I walked in front of my Scrooge and met him on the seal of the carpet.

"Jay, you once told me the thing you dislike most about Farah is how she appears to be in other people's pockets. By this point in the future, you've been in positions of power going on two decades. Even with bureaucracy holding you back, in that time you could've done so much for the people you pledged an oath to serve. But your hands were so tied by obligations to folks who made sure you got in those big, fancy chairs that you were never able to truly follow through on things you once cared about. You moved within the limits of *their* wills and desires. As a result, you accomplished nothing of lasting value to help the world because you got corrupted by the game from the start. Sixteen years as a glorified seat filler. The world slipping a little every year into something less bold and beautiful."

Jay stared at his older self for a long moment, taking it all in. After a sizable pause, he met my gaze. And he expressed the opposite sentiment I'd been expecting.

"I don't believe you."

Now it was my turn to make goldfish eyes. "*I'm sorry?*"

"You and your ghoul posse have only taken me to Christmas seasons in my timeline. That's one month a year, but there are eleven others. You're looking at me and my choices and my life through a specific lens. I know myself and I don't believe I would waste any kind of opportunity, let alone the opportunity to make a difference."

I put my hands on my hips. "*Are you seriously suggesting—*"

Midori cleared her throat.

I looked at her, then back at Jay. "We can finish this argument in the present."

Jay and I glared at each other as we took Midori's hands. When we got back to my loft, I turned to my colleague. "Go back to the CCD. I'll meet with you and Brandon tomorrow."

Midori glanced at the bathroom door and her eyes seemed reluctant, but I had neither the mindset nor patience to try and decipher what she was trying to tell me. "Midori, please just go."

She nodded. Then she patted Jay on the arm unexpectedly, entered the interdimensional transport, and shut the door behind her. This got Jay's attention.

"Where is she going?"

Alarms went off in my head. That's what Midori must've been trying to communicate!

"Oh, sugar cookies, you're not supposed to see that!" I tried to cover Jay's eyes like a mother shielding her child from a scary movie commercial, but he pulled my hand away in time to see my bathroom door shaking and bleeding red and green light.

"Frost, what is—"

"You know I'm not from this world, Jay. Let's leave it at that. Back to more important matters, I still am having trouble processing that you don't believe me when I *literally* showed you proof of what you become."

"Snippets of proof," Jay countered. He tore his eyes from the bathroom door. "No one can be summarized by a few moments in life. We're a mash of everything mixed together. That little future field trip isn't going to convince me that one day I'll wake up and the man I am now will just be gone. It's not possible, and you judge me too harshly. Maybe I don't accomplish a lot of the things I want to. Such is life. But as people we can try our best, and I certainly have always given my best. I've struggled and fought my whole life. It's engraved into my character. To assume that part of me will be wiped away completely at some point is insulting, and the fact that you think you know me well enough after a month to make that call is arrogant."

Marley trotted over and whined. I'm not sure he'd ever been around arguing, and today he was getting a healthy dose.

I got in Jay's face. "Do you know what is insulting and arrogant? You thinking that your soul is immune to corruption. You've taken steps in that direction a handful of times this month alone, as recently as Thursday."

He got in *my* face. "It's compromise, Frost, not corruption. I am trying to think of the greater good. If I am elected and can get even a small portion of what I want accomplished, then it will be worth it. It will be more than the zero I'll be able to do if I lose and stay a nobody forever. Those donors, and Friedman's, and Annie aren't wicked masterminds twirling their mustaches and laughing maniacally off-camera like you seem to think. They just have priorities in terms of maintaining their own well-beings. That's not monstrous and I can play ball with it. They're not going to wreak havoc and I'm not going to be corrupted. This isn't some movie where evil is waiting to swallow me if I make a wrong move."

"Jay—" Marley started to whine again, but I ignored him. "Evil has to be eased into. You really think Hitler started out with, 'Follow me and we'll mass murder a chunk of the population, create a creepy cult salute, and bomb a bunch of countries'? *Of course not.* If he'd done that no German would've responded with 'Sign me up, bro.' He made promises that he'd make things better, they believed him, and the darkness crept in. Everyone always starts out hoping for the best. Everyone believes they'll make the right decisions because they trust their own character. At the end of the day though, we're all vulnerable. You especially, given the future at stake, your frustration with your past, and the anger in your heart in the present."

Jay fumed. I did too, as much as my naturally icy body temperature would allow anyway.

"I'm going home. The old-fashioned way," Jay said, storming for the exit.

My phone started sounding off loudly, an alarm I'd never heard. I bit my lip and whipped out the cell. A flashing Merry Meter notification had appeared on screen.

"*Danger: Scrooge Spirit Levels Low – Intervention Necessary*"

My Scrooge slammed the door behind him.

"Jay, wait!" I shoved my phone in my pocket and dashed after him. Marley joined me as I ran into the hall and down the stairs. Jay moved fast; for once I was grateful to be wearing modern jeans instead of an early 1900s dress.

"Jay!"

He'd already crossed the busy street. He was getting away. I looked both ways. Cars were coming, but I had an opening and went for it. I made it to the opposite sidewalk, ten feet from my target. "Jay, you can't—"

YAP! YAP!

I spun around, only then fully grasping that my dog had

followed me out. Marley was in the middle of the street, licking a sewer grate. Cars were seconds from reaching him.

"MARLEY!"

Without thinking, I ran into the street to save my dog. I was feet from him when the bright lights of an oncoming vehicle blinded me. My head turned at the sound of a car's horn. Then—

YANK.

I toppled onto Jay, who'd pulled me out of the way. The loose rocks of the road by the sidewalk crunched into the palms of my hands as screeching brakes screamed in my ears. I whipped my head toward the street where Marley had been. The scene seemed frozen for a moment as my brain processed it all—the cars stopped unnaturally in the middle of the road, the honking of horns, the white and fluffy body lying off to the side, unmoving.

"Marley!" I scrambled to my feet and raced toward him as several people got out of their cars. I slid to my knees beside the dog. Jay was right behind me. He took a knee, and whereas I was all horror, his panic turned to confusion.

"Are those *wires?*" he asked.

Marley's side was split open—not exposing any kind of biological gore, but metal parts and splaying wires. Electric sparks flashed in my dog's eyes. Marley whined and moved his front legs in a jagged motion.

"Oh no, is the dog okay?"

"Did he get hit?"

"Call an ambulance!"

The spectators were getting too close. I hastily bundled Marley in my arms. "He's fine. All fine. I'm a vet." Without regarding the humans any further, I sped back inside my building and up the stairs.

"Frost!" Now it was Jay's turn to chase me.

The door to my loft was still open. I rushed in and carefully lay

Marley down on my bed. He yapped and kept moving his legs, but cringed as wires within him sparked. His metal exoskeleton was cracked in several places and some kind of mist was escaping from him like steam from a locomotive stack.

I grabbed my phone and called Santa. No answer. I called Paul. No answer.

Jay approached the bed and stared at Marley in shock.

"He's not a real dog."

"*He is a real dog*," I snapped. "He just also happens to be a toy. A previous Santa and his son made him for me decades ago, but the latter isn't answering." I checked my watch, my breath panicked and hands starting to tremble. "They must already be on their gift delivery route."

"But it's December 23rd."

"Why do humans always assume the world revolves around them?" I huffed irately. "*Countries move on different time zones, Jay.* Australia, for example, is seventeen hours ahead of California. It's already Christmas Eve in plenty of places across the world right now. Santa's gift delivery cycle is a full thirty-six hour adventure with a few breaks in between."

"So how do we fix the dog then?" Jay asked, gesturing at Marley who'd stopped yapping and was starting to seizure a bit.

I felt like I was having a heart attack, or a stroke, or at least a dozen other mortal reactions it was impossible for me to have.

I bit my nail. "I don't know. Santa could be anywhere right now, and the only way to reach him in emergencies is—" I started waving my arms dramatically at the realization. "The bells!" I dashed for my bed and clawed at the floor space beneath it, looking for my box.

"Jay, wrap Marley in a blanket," I ordered. "I think he's already lost a few parts. I don't want any more falling out."

Jay did as he was told while I found what I was searching for. I thrust open the special wooden box.

"Beaming Bells," I declared, clambering to my feet. "These will take us to Santa." I snatched the bells and slung my bag over my shoulder.

Marley was cradled tightly in Jay's arms, wrapped in one of the throw blankets from my couch. My pet continued to short-circuit. I grabbed Jay's arm and shook the bells while whistling loudly like I had all those years ago. A mystical mini tornado of snowflakes wrapped around our threesome. In the blink of an eye, our surroundings changed to thick clouds and muffled moonlight. Eight reindeer galloped ahead of us. Jay, Marley, and I found ourselves squished between a very surprised Santa and Paul.

"Frost!" Santa shouted.

"Jay?" Paul exclaimed.

"The Claus from the mall?" Jay said, looking closely at the man beside him.

"Santa!" I interceded. "I'm sorry to drop in. I know I'm probably breaking dozens of rules, but you have to help. It's Marley." Jay lowered the folds of the blanket so Santa and Paul could get a better look. "He was hit by a car, and he's broken and dying. You and your father built him. With your father gone, you're the only person who may be able to fix this."

"Frost . . ." Santa cringed. "I'm so sorry, but I am kind of on a deadline here. We're halfway to Singapore right now. I can't just—"

"*Please, Nick,*" I begged, my eyes pleading with him even more than my words.

Santa stared at me a long moment. Then—

"All right. Everybody hang on. We're making an unscheduled

landing." Santa pulled on the reins and we all swayed dramatically to the left as he changed course. Within minutes we were landing on the darkened beach of some tropical landmass. The sleigh skidded into the sand. Once the reindeer stopped, Santa gestured for us to get out.

"Let me have a look." He indicated for Jay to pass him the bundle. Jay did so with a dazed nod. Santa placed Marley gently on the seat and popped the glove compartment of the sleigh, pulling out tools.

Jay, Paul, and I awkwardly and anxiously waited by the reindeer.

"So . . . you're a professional Santa in more ways than one?" Jay said to Paul, taking in my friend's red overalls and white, long sleeve muscle shirt.

"Yup." Paul looked to me. "Frost, I'm sorry about Marley, but you do get that bringing this guy here—exposing North Pole secrets—is a huge violation of the CCD?"

I rubbed a hand over my eyes. He was so absolutely right and I hadn't even considered it.

"I'm sorry. I wasn't thinking, Paul. I got scared. Marley is the most important thing to me. He's the strongest relationship I've ever had. And he's the *only* being I've ever had in my life that didn't die and that I didn't push away. Without him . . ." I gulped. "I'm sorry. I panicked."

"I understand," Paul said. "I'm not the one to apologize to though. You will need to answer to Specter One."

My body tensed. "I know."

"Frost," Santa called. I darted over. He sighed deeply, scratching his head. "I can't fix him here. I don't even know if I can fix him at all. I was like twelve when my dad built Marley for you; I mainly just watched and passed him tools. Your dog is the most advanced toy I've ever seen. If I have any shot at saving him before his system completely shuts down, I need to get back to my workshop." Santa pivoted to Paul. "Son, I know you've never done a solo run before, but can you manage on your own for the next couple of hours?"

"Yeah, Dad. I got this."

Santa wrapped Marley up again and stood between me and Jay as Paul hopped into the sleigh and punched some buttons on the console. A device like a soda gun popped loose. Paul aimed it at us and glimmering particles sprayed out, sticking to our skin and clothes. Our bodies became hazy, then we melted into mist.

When we solidified again, we were standing in Santa's private workshop. Elaborate model train tracks covered the ceiling— no problem for the gravity-defying trains that puffed out cute smokestacks as they chugged along. A bronze hot cocoa machine the size of an armoire stood in the corner. Santa's desk was as beautifully crafted as the Resolute Desk in the Oval Office. Falling snow could be seen through massive windows at the back.

Santa took Marley over to a worktable. With the flip of a single switch, he powered on a plethora of different lamps hanging over the table. Santa then kicked a horse-sized tool chest and about twenty different drawers spewed open, giving him access to the fullest range of hardware in existence.

"You two should wait in there," Santa said, pointing with a wrench toward a set of doors. "Best that no one knows we're here."

I nodded. Jay and I entered the side room—set up with a cot, couch, and fancy cookie dispenser. I shut the doors.

"Santa sometimes likes to pull all-nighters," I explained halfheartedly in response to Jay's mesmerized expression. "This is his nap room."

A small window at my chest height overlooked the Stuffed Animal District four stories below. On a normal night, the streets would be full of traffic—elves pushing wheelbarrows of buttons and driving tiny vehicles with stuffing in their truck beds. Tonight, with Santa already gone on his Christmas Eve route, the elves were off at their party. The North Pole streets stood as barren as I felt. In a state of frigid stillness, I watched the snow fall. Jay came beside me and took in the sight with the wonder of a child and the mystification of an adult.

"I can't believe this," he muttered.

"That's the second time tonight," I replied without emotion.

A deep, pensive quiet hung between us—a true silent night even though all was not calm or bright.

"I don't want to fight with you anymore tonight," Jay said after a while.

"I don't either." I sighed and rested my forearms on the windowsill. "Though I have a feeling tomorrow isn't going to be easy. For either of us."

"No. I doubt it will be." He studied the magical landscape with his hands in his pockets. "So you knew the previous Santa too?"

"I did. I've known Paul and this Santa since they were born and I met the previous Santa as a kid. It's been hard to have them in my life, my afterlife I mean."

Jay crooked his brow. "Why's that?"

"Being a ghost isn't easy, Jay. When you know someone as a child and then see them pass you in age and then pass *on* . . . that changes you. It darkens you. I guess that's why the only friend I've never pushed away is an immortal toy dog."

I shook my head and began to pace. "This is torture. It's only been minutes and it feels like hours."

Jay sat down on the couch and motioned for me to sit too. Reluctantly, I did.

"Frost, we have a lot in common. Like me, movies—stories—help distract you. They calm you. Tell me a story about yourself. You know a ton about me. Tell me who you were when you were alive, and who you've been since you died. It'll keep you from freaking out."

I stared at him, then shook my head. "I may have slipped up a few times with you this week, Jay, but traditionally I'm not a sharer. Past that, this is hardly the time for a get-to-know-your-ghost story hour. I am majorly losing my mind with worry right now."

"I'm not a sharer either, Frost, yet you drag personal things out of me all the time. In part, I resent that—you've gotten on my nerves like no other this month. But I'd be lying if I said I haven't found it *occasionally* nice to talk to someone about what's going on with me. It's been a while. Past *that*, I know you're losing your mind worrying about Marley, and I'm telling you the best way to deal with that is to distract yourself."

I hung my head. "Do I have to distract myself with something so . . . personal?"

"The best distractions always are personal."

I leaned back against the couch and studied him a moment. "You know, I haven't opened up to anyone in a long time either. At least not willingly. Then you came along . . ." I sighed. "Are you sure you want to know? Mine is not the happiest story."

He looked at me with the sincerest compassion. "I'm not going anywhere."

The words stirred me and my reservations at last lost the battle.

I took a deep breath. "Okay . . ."

With hesitance and faith churning within me, I adjusted on the couch and folded my hands over my lap. Staring at the ceiling, I began to submerge in recollections I'd spent a century drowning so deep only my dreams could access them.

"I guess my story starts on the streets of LA about a century and a quarter ago." I paused a moment and swallowed the pain. "I was four years old, walking hand in hand with a woman whose face I can hardly remember..."

22

"And that's how I ended up with Marley." A knock interrupted my story. I whirled around as Santa entered, then leapt to my feet—my soul pounding and shaking at the same time.

"Well?"

Santa opened the door wider and the familiar sound of feet scurrying against the ground preceded Marley scuttling in, tail wagging. He yapped when he saw me and bounded over.

"Marley!" I dove to the floor and scooped up the creature in my arms, hugging him tighter than I ever had. "I thought I lost you, boy."

I got to my feet after a moment and with Marley still clutched in one arm, I threw the other around my bearded, old, *old* friend. "Thank you, Nick."

"You're welcome, Frost."

I smiled at him, regarding the spritely eyes behind his glasses. They were encircled by wrinkles and framed by the white hairs of his brows, but if you studied them closely, they were as kind and lively as they had been when he was a kid. I saw that kid in him now; for a second it felt like no time had passed.

The connection broke when the Billy Joel song "We Didn't Start the Fire" started playing from Jay's pocket. He hastily took out his phone.

"Sorry. I didn't realize the North Pole got service." He sent the call to voicemail and pocketed the phone sheepishly.

"You two had better get where you're supposed to be," Nick

said. "And I had better get back to Paul. Frost, I will need your Beaming Bells please."

I grabbed them from my bag and handed them over.

"Take the private exit from my office," Nick instructed. "Then get Jay to one of the realm-evators before Specter One finds you. I'm sure he'll call you into his office eventually, but my advice is to lay low for the rest of the night."

"I will. Thank you again. I *am* sorry for interrupting your flight. It was selfish of me, I know. And irresponsible to bring him too." I threw a thumb in Jay's direction. "You didn't have to do this, Nick."

"That's what friends are for, Frost. It's not selfish to reach out for help when you need it; a true friend comes through whether it's convenient or not." He patted my head and strode back to his main office.

"Santa!" Jay suddenly called.

Our red suited host paused and turned around. "Yes?"

"Which reindeer is the fastest?"

Nick chuckled. "Dasher of course. It's literally in the name. Now be good, Jay. I'd rather not see your name on the Naughty List again." He shook the Beaming Bells with a whistle and was whisked away.

I led Jay to a sparkly platform behind Nick's desk, roughly the size of a two-person trampoline. "Can't you just use your magic to take us home?" he asked.

"My magic has limits," I said. "It doesn't work in the North Pole or my other ghostly realm I told you about. Even if it did, I need to be conserving it. Ghosts start to run out of steam the closer we get to midnight on Christmas Eve, particularly if our Scrooges aren't progressing the way that they should." I crooked an eyebrow at Jay before moving him onto the platform and standing next to him.

"This is the quickest way in and out of the workshop." I held Marley close.

"Is it like a *Star Trek* beam-me-up-Scottie kind of thing?"

"Not at all. In fact, we're going down." I yanked the lever on the wall shaped like a foot-long candy cane and the circular platform beneath us vanished. Jay, Marley, and I plummeted in freefall for two seconds before our butts bumped the plastic of a slide and we went on a twisting journey. Colorful strobe lights decorated the inside of the slide, making it feel like we were falling through a kaleidoscope.

"WHOAA!!!" Jay and I shouted, smushing together as we slid.

Seconds later we were shot out of the tubular adventure and landed on an SUV-sized stuffed teddy bear. Marley yapped excitedly. I slid off the bear's belly and stood. Jay followed my lead but didn't stick the landing as well. I grabbed him by the suit collar to keep him from toppling over.

"We Didn't Start the Fire" began playing from his pocket again. He checked his phone. "It's Annie," he said, stashing it back in his pocket. "She's the one who called while we were in Santa's office too."

"You don't want to get that?"

"This is more important. *And interesting.*" He gestured with wide eyes at the room we'd landed in—the Gumdrop Room. The walls were made of thousands of gumdrops while innumerable shelves held glass jars filled with the same candy. The North Pole's entire gumdrop supply was stored here. Muffled music thumped from just outside the room.

"Stay close to me," I said. "I'd rather get you home without anyone asking any more questions. Thankfully, pretty much all the elves will be in the workshop right now monitoring the sleigh's progress while breaking out the celebratory cider. You haven't seen an office party until you've been to the North Pole when the elves have finished up the season. Just look."

I walked over to the striped blinds covering the window on the purple door and pushed them up a bit, beckoning for Jay to spy beside me. We peered through. Directly ahead you could see important parts of the Claus operation. On the main floor of the factory, a floating globe the size of a parade float turned slowly. Golden sparkle clusters displayed denser versus lighter populations of "Nice" souls. On the back wall, three enormous screens showed where the sleigh was from different map views. A control panel of elves monitored these from a high platform.

The rest of the room, however, celebrated like it was 1999.

Having been here in 1999, I could make that reference with confidence.

There were hundreds of elves. Soaring streamers. Confetti poppers going off every seven seconds. A pair of elf DJs spinning records from a hot air balloon hovered around the room—hence the music we'd been hearing. Breakdancing penguins impressed whooping crowds. Spotlights whirred. Flying reindeer jetted all over. Yetis with bowties served hot appetizers. There was an ice luge, a raw bar, and a fondue fountain that put the Trevi to shame.

Jay's eyes couldn't have been wider. "Holy—"

I raised an eyebrow.

"Town of Bethlehem?" Jay finished. "This is the craziest party I've ever seen."

"And it'll continue through the 25th. I'm told most of the elves pass out for days afterward. And plum pudding sales go up significantly in the cafeteria."

Jay gave me a look.

"It helps with sugar hangovers," I explained. "Now come on. We need to get back where we belong." I escorted Jay out a side door and we found ourselves in a snow-covered alley. In order to avoid detection, I led him around the backs of the buildings. He shivered more with every minute whereas I didn't even flinch.

"Aren't you freezing?" he eventually asked, powder still steadily falling over us.

"Ghosts run cold," I explained as we delved into a patch of frosty pine trees. Marley leapt through the snow—sinking a bit each time he landed but seeming to enjoy it.

"It actually helps us survive," I continued. "I have to say, while the fact that I have a frozen heart is a mood-killer, I do love the cold. I was born in LA like you, but snow always fascinated me. Not only does it match my namesake way better than sunny skies, but it really makes it feel like Christmas."

"I've always wanted a white Christmas," Jay mused. "Like in the movies."

I looked over my shoulder and smiled at him. "Like in the movies."

I pushed a branch aside and the realm-evator depot came into view. Once inside, Jay's phone rang a third time as I summoned a lift. He silenced it again. The doors slid open and I gestured for him to enter. I held my badge over the reader, then pressed the Earth button. The doors started to close, but I held them open with my arm a tad longer.

"I'll see you tomorrow," I said. Then I paused. "Assuming you don't think that's going to make the media focus on fake scandal instead of your big debate?"

"You know what, the media is going to do whatever they want," he said sadly. "The damage is done. I have to focus on the things I can control. Plus, I can't ask you to stay away from me any more. It would be selfish. You have a job to do and you're already going to be in a ton of trouble with your boss for tonight."

I grimaced. "Yeah . . ." Then I glanced down at Marley, grinning at me. "But it was worth it." My expression relaxed as I turned my attention back to Jay. "Thank you for being here with me by the way. It means a lot. I haven't been so scared in a while."

Jay had a small smile on his face. "What a world where a politician can share a ride with Santa and a ghost feels scared."

"What a world indeed." I shook my head in astonished amusement. "Hold tight, Jay. This elevator will take you back to my loft. Oh . . . and in case it didn't come across how paramount it is that you not tell *anyone* about *anything* you've seen or I've told you—"

"Frost. You can trust me. You may think I'm meant to become some soulless politician, but today—here and now—I think you know that my word does mean something. After all, I have zero chance of ever getting off the Naughty List if I spurn a Christmas Ghost and spill Santa's secrets."

He gave me one of his more teasing grins. I released a light laugh.

"Good night, Jay."

"Good night, Frost."

I let the door go and my Scrooge vanished from sight. Marley and I proceeded to take another realm-evator to the CCD. On arrival, with dread I checked my phone but was surprised to see no new messages from Specter One. I also realized that the alert I'd received before Marley's accident had disappeared. I wasn't sure when, or why, but I considered it a win.

I was not so naïve to think I'd get away with all the lines I'd crossed this evening. However, I was definitely not in the mood to poke the polar bear tonight by pursuing answers about the Merry Meter alert, or having a confrontation with my boss.

That was a ton of feelings for a few hours. My Scrooge had made me angrier and more frustrated than any assignment, or any person, had made me in my entire life and afterlife. I was scared about my job performance and whether I could get this mission done successfully. I'd almost lost a pet that meant the world to me. I'd felt renewed warmth and affection for Nick, a man I'd pushed away for decades. And I'd been vulnerable with him and ten times more so with Jay, a man I'd only known a few weeks.

I was a ghost and girl who had gotten used to going by a playbook, suppressing passion and emotion in favor of systematically getting a job done without meaningful interaction. That ghost and girl had disappeared tonight like one of the magic charms on my bracelet and been replaced with someone else. I didn't know if I could sustain her—this more vulnerable, open version of me—come tomorrow. Given the weight and exhaustion on my soul, I didn't know if I wanted to.

The only thing I knew for certain was that I had to be brave, suck it up, and play it by ear. After all, tomorrow was not about my soul; it was about Jay's. And he desperately needed my help. For although he'd been sweet, helpful, and deeply honorable tonight, just before that he'd been cold, stubborn, and so full of anger that he couldn't see reason. His darkness may not have consumed him entirely yet, but it was there and I needed, *I wanted*, to save him from it.

My dog and I returned to my dorm room. I kicked off my shoes and collapsed on the bed, Marley nestled beside me. I started going through my bag, mind still running through everything that had happened while my hands kept busy organizing. I wasn't looking for anything as I did this, but I found something anyway. At the bottom of the bag—buried under a pencil holder, a sunglasses case, and a silk handkerchief—I located a piece of plastic. I pulled it out.

It was the Billy Joel CD that Jay had gifted me weeks ago.

I'd never listened to it.

I got up from my bed and opened a lower drawer of my

armoire. Decades ago, I'd written "*OLD TECH*" on a piece of duct tape to label it. Inside the drawer was a technology graveyard—a VHS player, a small record player, a ten-pound video camera, a cellular phone bigger than a banana. I grabbed the handle of a portable boombox and plugged it in the corner. With the sleeve of my hoodie I wiped away some of the dust then took my CD out of its case and loaded it in.

I hit play and lay down on my bed as the machine hummed and clicked to life. With Marley resting on top of my stomach, I stroked my pet as the opening verses of "We Didn't Start the Fire" resonated through the room.

I found myself walking across the skybridge in the CCD. Everything around me was hazy at first, like a frosted windowpane, but with each step further into my dream memory the setting solidified, as did the people around me.

"Maybe the reason you don't like parties is because you haven't been to a proper one," Bismaad said as we walked to our Saturday Seminar on Beanie Babies.

Marley followed at our heels.

"You died before the twenties in America even got properly roarin'," Bismaad continued. "I died when music and glamour were at their greatest heights across an excess of countries. I've been here over a decade and you come out with me hardly every twelve times I ask. One of these Christmases, I'm going to throw a party that's so splendid you won't be able to turn it down."

"Bismaad . . ." I sighed then stopped walking to face her. "It's more than my lack of party appreciation that causes me to withdraw. I've been kind of down these last few Christmases. I realize it seems silly that an actual spirit could lose her spirit, but I feel like that's what is happening. I've been fighting it for a while now, but this is getting harder every year."

"What's getting harder?" Bismaad asked.

I gazed out at the wintery terrain beyond the windows a moment, lost in another memory within this one. For the first time since being forced to befriend her, I found myself offering Bismaad some unprovoked openness.

"When I was just starting out at the CCD, a Ghost of Christmas Past warned me that completing a Scrooging wasn't the hard part; it was dealing with the aftermath. Now I understand what he meant. It's easy to feel on top of the world when we finish an assignment. We get to see people at their best, their freshest, when they're most in touch with the people who—deep down—they always wanted to be. It can feel like humanity has limitless potential and what we are doing here is important. But in the years and decades that follow . . . we have to deal with the fallout. Half of the Scrooges I've saved have eventually returned to the selfish, self-destructive people they were before."

Bismaad's multicolored chunks of bangles jangled as she wrung her hands together—searching for a silver lining. "Well, I mean, they all give it a go . . . And some of our Scrooges do make it the distance. But change is difficult, Frost. It's a lot to ask of a person to keep it up every day forever without magical forces like us to remind them to stick with it."

"Miss Frost! Miss Frost!"

We spun around as an elf in sequined overalls cantered down the corridor. The second she reached us, she took me by the hand and started pulling me in the other direction.

"I'm Trixie. Santa Senior is asking for you. Please come."

"Is something wrong?"

The elf pulled harder. "Not at liberty to say."

I glanced at Bismaad. "Take notes for me. This must be important. Come on, Marley."

I hustled with Trixie across the CCD and took the realmevator to the North Pole. Once we arrived in the lobby of the winter wonderland and stepped outside, I was astonished.

"Whoa." The sky churned with dark clouds. Snow fell thickly. All the magical creatures that usually cavorted on the snowbanks were gone. I picked up Marley and held him in my arms to shield him from the elements. "I've never seen the North Pole like this. Do you guys even get storms?"

"Only in our darkest times," Trixie responded. She led me over a couple of ice bridges and we rode a reindeer-pulled trolley to the Claus family home—a three-story building modeled like a ski chalet. The outer wooden walls were carved with depictions of elf history. Enormous peppermint sticks served as beams to hold up the second floor balcony. Most impressive of all, the world's most exceptional chimney attached to the structure's left side. It was decorated with a mosaic of rainbow tiles interspersed with glittery gumdrops and large blocks of shimmery ice.

Inside, Trixie guided me through the warmly lit hallways. I hadn't been in Santa's home for maybe a decade. As my outlook on my ghost job and the CCD's purpose had faded, so had my already-limited efforts to connect with others.

More than that, the older Kris grew, the less comfortable I became around him. I knew his clock was running out. Spending time with him and Nick, who'd passed me in age long ago, felt more like a solemn reminder of how fleeting friendship could be, and how emotionally dangerous the endeavor was as a result. It made me want to pull away—withdraw from the only bonds I'd allowed myself to make in the afterlife because I remembered perfectly well what it felt like the last time I lost people.

I set Marley down and he stayed close as we continued. I

marveled at the bronze, antique sconces, the plates of cookies on every end table, the thick boughs of garland hanging from chandeliers. Every nook and cranny looked like the backdrop for a Christmas portrait. There were certainly hundreds of those dotting the walls—all the Santas and their families that had existed since the beginning.

Eventually we stopped at a set of double oak doors, which Trixie pushed open. Inside on my right, a fireplace roared beneath a large framed photo of Kris and his family. To my left, all the members of his family were gathered around Kris as he lay in bed. His breathing looked shallow and his eyes were closed.

Had my heart still held the ability to beat, it would've stopped. Kris—the five-year-old kid I'd met close to eighty years ago—*was dying.*

His entire form was literally fading. Little by little, he was becoming intangible as if he were turning into a ghost too.

I drifted over to the bedside and Kris's family parted. His wife Irena was there. She didn't appear broken with despair; she simply looked at her husband with pure love and held onto his vanishing hand—one moment clutching skin, the next energy. It seemed she was at peace with what was happening. Actually, all the Clauses—though sad—seemed calm.

I stopped to stand next to Nick. He was forty-six now and had taken over as Santa three years ago. His white beard was a lot trimmer and sleeker than his dad's.

Nick put a hand on my shoulder.

"What's happening to him?" I asked.

"He's moving on to whatever comes next," Nick said.

I tilted my head.

"Claus spirits are unique," explained Nick's wife Beth from the foot of the bed (the current Mrs. Claus). Her two children were beside her—young Paul and younger Margo.

She soothingly stroked Margo's hair as the child quietly gazed on at her disappearing grandfather. "Whether by blood or marriage, the Christmas Spirit is a central part of who we are. *Our spirits*, therefore, don't die in the traditional sense. They change forms."

Nick looked at me. "We know about as much about our after-life as humans on Earth do. The difference is, we have faith that so much warmth and heart doesn't simply end. My dad is not dying. He is leaving to spread his magic in some other way. Kind of like you and the ghosts at the CCD. Strong spirits and good hearts are too precious for the universe to lose."

"Hmm. Peppermint Schnoodle," Kris mumbled from his bed.

"Is he hallucinating?" I asked.

"No, he wants a cookie," Irena said.

Paul—who was a scrawny but scrappy seven-year-old at this point—fetched a plate of cookies from the end table and moved beside his grandfather. "Here you go, Grandpa."

My elderly friend opened his eyes and smiled. "Thank you, Paul." He took the cookie and munched on it slowly. Fascinatingly, when he swallowed, it turned to glitter that absorbed into his ever-fading body. Paul tugged on my dress as his granddad continued eating. "You want one, Frost?" He held up the plate.

"No. Thank you, Paul." I patted his head and noticed the large scrape on his cheek. "What happened to you this time?"

"I got in a fight with the puffins at the ice rink."

"Frost?" My old friend had finished his cookie and beckoned me closer. I took a couple hesitant steps toward him.

"Since I am about to retire from this life, I wanted to give you something. A parting gift." He gestured for me to open the drawer of the end table. My eyes widened when I did.

"The broken airplane . . ."

"The submarine," he corrected. "Or have your sense of wonder and positive perspective gone completely since last I saw you? Specter One told me you seem to be going through the motions these last few Christmases. It explains why you don't visit much. Nick and Paul say they've only seen you twice this season."

"A lot of my former Scrooges have thrown away the gift we gave them. It's been getting harder to shake it off. And with you three, I just . . ." I gulped, feeling my throat close. "That doesn't matter right now, Kris. You . . . you're . . ."

"Moving on," he said, a small smile on his lips. "I don't know what comes next, but I know that wherever I go, I'll never entirely leave the people I love. Spirits tie themselves to one another, you see. Even when they part in one realm, that connection can never be severed."

His form faded faster. My eyes widened as more of the pillows and sheets underneath him became visible. "Good luck, Frost. Thank you for being my friend." He reached for my hand, but in a reflex of fear and sorrow, I pulled away and took a step back.

Kris seemed saddened by this, but he shifted his attention to his family and said some final words to each of them. I moved backward as he did, closer and closer to the door.

Suddenly Kris's ghostly form shone with vivid angelic light. He inhaled deeply, closed his eyes, and on the exhale all of him became golden glimmering energy that twinkled and then dissolved.

I heard myself gasp.

My soul seized up, however my body fled. I left the room and hastened down the hallway. I didn't know when I started to run, but before I knew it I felt my feet pounding on the snow outside. A couple dozen yards from the house, I halted in my tracks, looking up when I realized the storm had stopped.

Literally.

It had frozen as if someone had pressed pause. Snow hung

suspended in midair. The wind had vanished. Above, the clouds no longer swirled with dark power. Only one thing fluxed in the atmosphere—bright beams of sun shooting through the clouds. Their brilliant grace continued to puncture the gray like a hole puncher through paper, illuminating the snow in a vibrant, almost blinding manner. I didn't know what to make of it, but I did know that the effect did not bring light to the dark, heaviness inside of me.

I wandered to the closest ice bridge and sat down on the edge, letting my boots dangle over the sloshing river.

I hadn't even noticed Marley had followed me. But then he always did. He licked my hand, but the sweet gesture had no impact. It only drew my attention to the broken plane I clutched in my grip.

I felt dizzy, nauseous, drowned in despair. Then . . . I cried my first tear in over eighty years. I didn't even know I could still produce them.

A single drop went down my cheek—cold like ice and so strangely sharp that it hurt when I squeezed it out.

"Your pain must be excruciating."

Surprised by the high-pitched voice, I glanced down and discovered a puffin wearing an aviator helmet riding a small fuchsia narwhal. Marley barked at them.

"What?" I wiped away the frozen tear.

"Ghosts aren't meant to be able to cry," the puffin said. "Afterlife is supposed to numb those pesky negative emotions that make humans suffer. You know, so you can focus on happy things. *You* have problems." The puffin patted the narwhal's horn with his flipper. "Onward, Mr. Kerfuffles!"

The narwhal reared up a bit and whinnied like a horse, then hurriedly continued downstream, splashing me with his tail in the process.

Now I was dumbfounded, depressed, and wet.

Thanks, Mr. Kerfuffles.

"MERRY CHRISTMAS EVE, MISS MASON! TIME TO WAKE UP!"

The dream memory violently shattered as I sat up in my CCD dorm bed—startled by the loud, high voice and insistent pounding on my door. I checked my watch. It was barely five in the morning. Someone had beaten my alarm to its job. I went to my door and opened it. An elf I recognized with red pigtails and rubies on her cheeks skipped in.

"Uh, good morning, Wobbles," I said. "I kind of have a busy day. Can I help you?"

Wobbles stopped in front of my bed and bent to be at eye level with an interest-piqued Marley. They stared at one another.

"Wobbles?" I repeated.

Marley blinked.

"Hah! Gotchu!" The elf spun around. "Specter One requests your presence in his office immediately. Btw, that request is actually a demand. Have a great day!" She skipped out, oblivious that her news meant my chances of having a great day had substantially decreased.

I readied myself in all senses of the word, left Marley in my room, and headed for our boss's office. I was stunned to find Midori and Brandon already sitting on the ice bench in front of Specter One's desk when I arrived.

"Have a seat, Frost," Specter One said, not getting up.

The expressions of my teammates were unreadable.

"I've just finished telling Brandon and Midori about your escapades last night."

I took a deep inhale-exhale and held my head high—ready to take my comeuppance.

"I know what I did was wrong from a professional standpoint, but I regret nothing. I did what I had to do. I accept full responsibility. Please don't blame Brandon and Midori. Bringing Jay to the North Pole was my choice alone."

"I am glad you regret nothing, Frost," Specter One said, folding his hands on his desk. "As it happens, I don't either where the latter half of your evening is concerned because it seems to have saved you."

I frowned. "In what way?"

"Brandon and Midori are here because of your failure earlier that night. I believe you received a very dangerous, very rare alert through Merry Meter."

I gulped. "It said my Scrooge's spirit level was dangerously low and intervention was necessary."

"We got the same notification on our phones," Brandon said, taking his CCD issued cell from his pocket and holding it up. "I freaked out at first and tried calling you, but you didn't answer. The alert went away after a while on its own so I tried not to panic more and planned on asking you about it today. Then Specter One called us in here . . ."

The three of us directed our gaze to him.

"Our Scrooge success rate is 99.5%," Specter One said. "That alert hardly ever happens. When it does, I intervene. *However*, it would seem I may not have to anymore."

Specter One waved his hand across his icy desk. A blue hologram of a keyboard appeared and he punched in some numbers. A screen displaying Merry Meter analytics for Jay Nichols shimmered into existence beside us.

"For the past few days, Jay's readings have concerned me." Specter One gestured at a line graph. "During the first half of Christmas week, Scrooges tend to fight back so their spirits almost always remain low. However in the latter half of the week we gradually see upticks. We rarely see lower levels than those that we started with. Unfortunately, that's what we've experienced with Jay." He looked at each of us before returning to the graphs. "On Friday his spirit seemed to be lifting, but fell again yesterday—getting worse throughout the day. After your second future visit with Midori, it plunged below the danger threshold, which set off the alert. But after your adventure last night . . ."

Specter One pointed to the upward turn of the red line on the graph. "His spirit shifted and rose out of the danger zone. It is still much lower than what we should be seeing on the morn of Christmas Eve, but it is not hopeless."

Brandon looked at me. "I guess a trip to the North Pole was just what the guy needed. Nothing boosts spirits like elves, flying reindeer, and Santa."

I sat quietly for a moment. "I'm not sure that's what it was. I think . . . we bonded. In my distress over Marley, I was vulnerable—which I know I shouldn't have been—and we connected. Our second trip to the future didn't impact Jay the way I thought, and we got angry and frustrated with each other, but all that negative energy dissipated when we thought Marley was dying and he was there for me."

Specter One nodded. "Nothing is better for the spirit than helping others. By allowing Jay to help you in a time of crisis, his own attitude shifted. That is your only saving grace here, Frost. The saving grace for your whole team really. I *am* still concerned though."

He made the screen disappear with a flick of his wrist. "The consequences of failing a Scrooging mission are far worse than the barn cleaning and charm room organizing you've been assigned as punishment in the past, Frost."

Brandon side eyed me as Specter One continued.

"If Jay were still in the danger zone, the three of us would be having a very different conversation. Since that is not the case, magical agreements forged with the ancient Santas forbid me from divulging additional acute particulars, and I am to let you proceed without intervention."

Brandon raised his hand. "I barely just mastered the word romanticized. For those of us who didn't get a chance to major in literature in college, care to rephrase that, boss man?"

"As long as Jay stays above the spirit danger zone, I am magically forbidden from telling you what happens if you fail a Scrooging mission, as that would interfere with normal procedure." Specter One clarified. "I will warn you though; *the three of you need to buckle down.* Jay may just be one man to you, but no soul is an acceptable loss in the universe, and Jay's in particular has the potential to make an incredibly high impact. His life, the future of those he can affect, Brandon's and Midori's futures at the CCD, and, Frost, your retirement are all at stake. Do I make myself clear?"

The three of us nodded in unison.

"Good," he said. He leaned back in his chair—not in his usual confident and casual way, more tense than I had ever seen him. That concerned me. Specter One was our magical, everything-is-under-control leader. Why was he so worried? What wasn't he telling us?

"Have you picked out the best possible Christmas future to show Jay for your finale?" Specter One asked, glancing at Midori and then at me. "Or should I say the worst."

"Since Jay dies in a December month, we're going with the traditional funeral scene," Brandon said. "It's a classic, and after Midori showed us Jay's, even I was crying. It'll work."

Specter One gave me a pointed look.

"*It will work,*" I assured him. "Midori has spent all month combing through Jay's Christmas futures, and this will have the greatest impact. We have watched it in the Choice Chamber nearly every night and nothing has changed. How he dies and how he is remembered will finally shake and break him."

"Very well," Specter One said. He waved us away. "Now off you go. Frost, you should return to Earth immediately. And, Midori, keep going through Jay's possible futures every hour for the rest of the day. Take Brandon with you and inform Frost of any changes as she works with Jay. We can't afford to leave anything to chance here."

"Yes, sir," Brandon and I said. Midori nodded sharply.

We got up and crammed into the elevator together. When the doors slid open on the lower level, I stepped out first and turned to face my teammates.

"For the record, while I am not sorry about what I did to save Marley, I am sorry for not considering how it would affect our team. I'm supposed to be your leader and that means putting the good of the group before the good of the individual."

"It's fine, Frost," Brandon said, patting my arm. "You heard the boss. You may have gone off the rails, but in this case, it saved us. You got Jay back on track and that's what matters. Besides, Midori and I are as much at fault here. It's our jobs to pick the glimpses of the past and future that will affect Jay the most. If his spirit isn't budging, we're accountable too."

Midori nodded in agreement.

"That being said ..." Brandon bit his lip. "Specter One had a major doom-and-gloom vibe in there. Frost, you've been here the longest. Do you have any idea what happens to ghosts who don't complete their Scrooging mission?"

"I don't," I said warily. "Specter One mentioned that the CCD has a 99.5% success rate, which would indicate that someone at some point has failed. But as far as I remember, for as long as I've been here, it's never happened ..."

"Okay team." I addressed the assembled members of Jay's staff from the foyer of the grand auditorium where tonight's debate was being hosted. It was the morning of Christmas Eve and I was pumped up on a weird combination of enthusiasm, fear, hope, anxiety, and hot chocolate that I'd *mixed into* a latte for some extra buzz.

"I realize the last twenty-four hours have been difficult, but I want to clarify a couple of things. First off, the rumors about me and Jay are completely false. Second, we are not going to let those rumors destroy him. Latest polls show Farah at 45% and Jay at 36%, with 19% undecided. This Christmas Eve debate—although ill-timed in my opinion—is our best chance to close that gap and go into the election year strong. AJ, Abigail, and Jake, you three will be talking to reporters, providing facts, and serving as our general media spin team. Josh, Cara, and Langford, you'll be doing the same with regards to online presence. Tom and Lonna, you two are our runners and aides in case Jay needs anything. Questions?"

"Where's Annie?"

"Shouldn't she be giving us our assignments?"

"What time will the debate be over?"

I took a deep breath. Jay and I had been calling and texting Annie all morning with no response. We decided it was best to keep that between us so as not to throw everyone else off.

"Annie will be here when she can. I have her notes, so for now you'll be following my lead." I straightened and tried my best to look commanding. "As to the debate question, it's scheduled to start at nine and end at ten. We expect you all to show up at eight sharp. I know it's hard to leave home on Christmas Eve, but at least you'll have plenty of time to have dinner with your families beforehand."

I spotted Jay approaching. "Okay, everyone. Go familiarize yourselves with the environment a bit then head back to the office." The team broke apart. Jay joined me, clearly stressed. He kept glancing at his phone. "No word from her?" I asked.

He shook his head. "It's not like Annie to flake. I'm starting to get worried. And I feel bad. Maybe I shouldn't have ignored her calls last night."

"It was late. And you were in the North Pole. You were busy. Contrary to what Annie may want, you can't be on the job all the time."

"Speaking of jobs, if you ever decide to stop being an undead Christmas crusader, you may have a career in politics. That speech to the troops was solid."

"Glad you think so. I'll keep that in mind for my next life. Now come on." I glanced at my agenda. "According to Annie's notes, right now we should check out your green room, the control room, and the media viewing gallery."

Jay and I made our way through the busy building. All sorts of tech and event planning folk were getting things squared away. We took a shortcut through the auditorium, walking down the slanted aisleway between two large sections of seats. This place could hold in the neighborhood of five hundred people.

We visited the control room and introduced ourselves to the workers assigned there. The area had twelve monitors displaying the main stage at different angles, backstage, and assorted audience views. Jay's green room was next; it was furnished with a TV, Jay's favorite snacks, and plenty of water. Last was the media viewing gallery. Roughly the size of a hotel banquet room, it featured a massive screen taking up the front wall. Employees were busy setting up chairs to face it.

"And check," I said as I crossed off the item on my to-do list.

I turned to Jay. "That's it for this morning. Next we should head to—Annie!"

Jay spun around as his campaign manager strode toward us. She wore a fitted black dress with a sparkly snowflake brooch pinned to the lapel of her blazer. It wasn't the most Christmas-forward outfit I'd ever seen, but I appreciated the effort.

"Where have you been?" Jay asked, relief and annoyance tinting his tone. "You were supposed to be here an hour ago."

"Jay . . ." Annie stopped in front of us and took a deep breath. A bad feeling crept up my specter spine. "Do you remember what I told you when you hired me?"

He blinked, taken aback. "You told me that you don't compete; you win."

"Exactly. I've won every campaign I've committed myself to. That's because I am focused, I understand how to play the game, I make tough choices, and I partner with people who are the same way. I've ignored the warning signs with you because, to be honest, I like you, Jay. You actually could do some good for this world. But I don't think you have what it takes to get elected. Putting family time before campaign commitments, fighting and questioning me at every turn, associating with people who are"—she looked me up and down—"a distraction. I've wavered on what to do and wanted to talk with you about it last night. I think subconsciously I hoped you would change my mind. But when you ignored all my calls it gave me the final push I needed."

She held her head high. "I quit, Jay."

Jay's face fell. My face fell.

"You can't," he protested ardently. "I need you."

"What you need is to ask yourself what you truly want," Annie replied, firm but somewhat caring. "Politics is no place for the weak or soft-hearted. It's a gladiator arena: kill or be killed. And if you come out a victor, there will only be countless more opponents that come to take you down. I don't know if you can take them. But I do know that you'll have to do it without me because as is . . . I wouldn't bet on you."

"Annie—" Jay tried.

"Goodbye, Jay. Good luck tonight." She pivoted and walked out.

Jay stared at her retreating form—his expression filled with vulnerability and panic.

"What am I going to do . . ." he said.

Crumb cake!

23

As Jay finished his talk show appearance, I checked my phone for the tenth time that morning. Merry Meter showed a solid decrease in Jay's spirit since Annie's departure. Thankfully, last night's escapades had gotten us high enough that we weren't in the danger zone—yet.

"Now, Jay, tell us," said one of the hosts. "These rumors about you and your assistant—who I believe is backstage right now—is there any truth there? How will this affect you in the debate tonight?"

I glanced up and gulped.

Jay's jaw tightened, but he retained his composure. "Those photos were taken entirely out of context. My assistant Frost Mason is doing her best to handle a difficult job. It won't affect me in the debate tonight because it is irrelevant to my character and my campaign."

"Strong words from a passionate candidate," the host replied. She pivoted to face the cameras. "How passionate? Find out tonight at nine o'clock as Jay Nichols and Farah Jaffrey discuss the issues and the upcoming election year. We'll see you back here after the break."

The showrunner escorted Jay from the stage and handed him off to me.

"We have to get going right away," I said. "Your press conference is in an hour and a half, and it's a long drive. Come on."

"Should I be apprehensive that you're super concentrated on

this job at the moment and not your actual one?" he asked as we moved through the building.

"My actual job only gets done if your spirit stays intact. In order to do that, I need you to not dwell on Annie and all the awful things she said."

"All the accurate things she said," he countered bitterly.

I scooted Jay into the SUV waiting outside the studio doors. The car took off for five seconds before it became locked in bumper-to-bumper traffic.

"Why can't people just go to work or go home? What's with all this traffic? It's ridiculous," Jay huffed, staring in aggravation at the gridlock.

"You're right," I said sarcastically, trying to be playful. "People out and about on Christmas Eve? It's criminal. You should make reforming that a part of your running platform."

Jay gave me a look. "Can you check the sass, Frost? I'm not in the mood."

"Fair enough . . ." I tried to change the subject to something lighter. "Hey, I listened to that Billy Joel CD you gave me. 'We Didn't Start the Fire' gave me a bit of a headache, but overall it was good."

Jay's eyes remained distant, but he cracked a small smile. "If you'd said otherwise, I would've told Rocco to pull over and let you out right here."

A moment passed.

"Jay—"

"Frost," he said, still looking out the window. "Can we not talk for a while? I'm not . . . I need some time to think."

I nodded. "I understand."

And I did. Jay was in crisis right now; space was a fair thing to ask for. Unfortunately, I couldn't back away. This was the time that I needed to intervene the most. His soul was being con-sumed. I wasn't about to watch him sink from the sidelines.

Saving Jay was my mission, but it was no longer a job. It was a deep desire. Because, as shocking as it was to me, after all these years I'd accidentally made a new friend. After last night I couldn't deny it anymore. He was a person I cared about. I'd lost those before—some left me, others were stolen by time—and I wasn't going to lose another one.

Our car merged onto the freeway. As Jay gazed out the window, I looked through one of my folders until I found Celia's contact details.

"Fifteen minutes until places," I told Jay as we walked across the hotel lobby and darted around the bustling crowds. It was just past one o' clock and the excitement of Christmas Eve felt palpable in the air.

I grabbed Jay's elbow and directed him outside. "So you have time for this. In fact, after what you went through this morning, I'd say you *need* to make time for this."

My Scrooge and I descended some stairs to the hotel's rear courtyard. An epically tall Christmas tree with ocean-themed décor and a giant starfish on top towered to the left. The bright sun cast the tree's magnificent shadow across the grass. At seventy-two degrees with bright blue skies, Southern California had apparently not gotten the memo that Christmas was a winter holiday.

We approached an outdoor table with several people seated around it.

"Celia!" I called.

Jay halted in his tracks as Celia turned in her chair. She

set down her glass of water and stood up. Kamie and Kingsley waved with ice cream cones in their hands while Eddie stood and nodded to Jay.

Jay gripped my arm tightly. "What are they doing here?"

"I invited them," I said simply. "They only live half an hour away so I went out on a limb and asked if they could come."

"Merry Christmas Eve, Daddy," Kamie said, traipsing over to us. Unlike the previous times I'd seen her greet Jay, there was some hesitance in her gate. No running or bounding hugs. Kingsley trotted over too, but kept a few feet away.

Celia and Eddie followed the kids and joined us.

"Frost said that Annie quit, and that you could use some extra support," Celia said to Jay, looking at him with sympathy but guardedness.

"I'm fine," Jay said. "I'll get by okay on my own."

"Your answer for everything," she said with a modest sigh.

"Dad . . ." Kingsley said. "We came to watch your press conference. We want to be with you. Do you want to be with us?"

The direct question took all the adults aback, myself included.

Jay knelt so he was at eye level with his son. "Kingsley, of course I want to be with you. There's just a time and a place for all things. I have to be a certain person to do this job."

Kamie took a lick of her ice cream cone, then cocked her head. "Isn't it bad if your job makes you be a different person?"

Jay sighed and shook his head, standing. "I know it's hard for you to understand, Kamie, but I *am* trying my best here. Your mom and Eddie only want me to spend time with you on their terms, so it's hard."

Celia's eyes twitched. I think lightning just about shot out of them. "Eddie, can you take the kids to see the tree for a second?"

"Mommy, we can see the tree from here," Kamie protested.

"Come on, kids," Eddie said, herding Kamie and Kingsley away.

Once they were out of earshot, Celia glowered at Jay. "How dare you imply to the kids that other than your job, I'm the reason you don't spend time with them."

"You are, Celia."

"No, *you are*, Jay." She drove her pointed finger into his chest. "I offer amends; you reject them. I invite you to be a part of our lives; you run away. I extend a chance to reconnect with your family and you opt to go it alone rather than let go of all that anger inside you. And for what? Jealousy? Resentment? A grudge?"

"Maybe I just don't want to go through it again," Jay snapped.

I looked at him.

Celia raised an eyebrow. "Go through what again?"

Jay paused a moment. I saw the veins in his neck strain, like he was trying to hold back, then passion overrode his normal walls and he spoke low and fast. "I had a family as a kid. It had problems, but it was whole and it was mine. That was destroyed. Then I built a new one with you and that came crumbling down too. In both cases, everyone else moved on and filled the holes with someone new. The men who left were replaced as easily as"—he gestured vaguely—"as a flat tire on a car! My dad wasn't interested in being a broken part for an already complete set and neither am I. The fact, plain and simple, is that I don't have a lot of time to give because of the career I've chosen. The time I do have I don't want to spend in a situation where I feel like I'm an optional add-on—a piece of an old life, a relic being replaced by a better model. That's how my mom and Raymond made my dad feel, and it's how you and Eddie *make me feel*."

He shook his head, eyes on the ground. "My world is only getting busier and more complicated. Since you two have dominant custody and time with Kamie and Kingsley anyway, the wiser choice for me is to just lean into the distance. I'm used to being alone now, and I'm good at it. And I need to be one hundred percent focused on this election anyway." His voice grew softer. "I can't do what has to be done if someone else breaks me any more than you, and my mother, and so many people already have."

My eyes widened.

O HOLY NIGHT!

I understood now. The piece I'd been missing. What Specter One had been trying to tell me. Why this case was different.

Celia regarded Jay critically. Her expression alternated between frustration and compassion as she strummed the fingers of one hand against her crossed arms and thought for a long moment.

"Okay, Jay, I'll tell you what . . ." she ultimately said. "I'm going to roll the dice here because I want what's best for Kamie and Kingsley. And because, believe it or not, I still care about you too." She turned to face me. "Frost, what's his schedule for the rest of the day?"

"After the conference he's free until four. Then he has to get ready for the gala."

"Fine." Celia nodded. "Jay, I am going to leave Kamie and Kingsley with you until four. Eddie and I will go so you can have your precious alone time with them. Deal?"

Jay was dumbstruck. "Celia, I don't know if—"

"I'm giving you a chance here, Jay. Don't make me regret it. Otherwise, I'll be the one trying to distance the kids from you. I can't have you crumbling their worlds either."

"They'll be in good hands, Celia," I jumped in. "They can watch the press conference with me and then we can have a nice afternoon."

Jay seemed nervous but confirmed the plan with a single nod.

"I'll hold you to that," Celia replied. The she glanced over her shoulder. "Kids! I have some exciting news." She walked across the grass to join her family.

Jay pivoted toward me. "What am I supposed to do with them? I don't have anything planned. And honestly, I've been in a pretty lousy mood since the Annie thing."

"You'll figure it out," I said. "I'll help. This is important, Jay. I get it now."

"Get what?"

"Dad!" Kingsley said, trotting over. "Are we really going to spend the afternoon together?"

"That's right, buddy," he said. "I have to get ready for the press conference now, but Frost will find you a good spot to watch it. I'll see you afterwards."

Jay nodded to Celia and Eddie before going back up the stairs and inside the hotel. The couple looked at me.

"It'll be fine, right?" Celia asked warily.

"Yes. Absolutely," I said, trying to sound as confident as possible.

I never liked disaster movies. I'd seen several over the years, but I hated the dread that filled your stomach knowing doom was coming to the unsuspecting main characters. Though in retrospect, maybe that trepidation was a gift, because at least you could brace yourself for the shock.

Real life was not that kind.

"We have time for one more question," said the moderator of the press conference.

Jay had been doing well. He firmly but politely answered questions regarding yesterday's scandal. He reminded the public of who he was as a candidate—his values, experience, and true passions. And he drummed up awareness for tonight's debate.

I watched the conference on a monitor in a side room with the kids, keeping a low profile from the press. The moderator called on a young reporter in the third row.

"Mr. Nichols, what are your feelings now that your former campaign manager, Annie Jung, has joined Farah Jaffrey's campaign team?"

Jay froze. I stiffened.

"What are you talking about?" he asked.

"My contact at the Jaffrey campaign says that Annie Jung accepted a position with Farah an hour ago," the reporter said, looking at her phone. "An announcement welcoming Annie to the team just went up on the Jaffrey campaign website and social media. Care to comment?"

"I . . . uh." Jay's hands clutched the podium. His brow crinkled while his eyes sparked with panic and ire.

My phone suddenly started to blare. Kamie and Kingsley looked at me. I pulled out the device. To my dismay, the screen was blinking with the same scary red notification from last night. *"Danger: Scrooge Spirit Levels Low – Intervention Necessary."*

"Oh no . . ." I thought aloud.

"What's wrong?" Kingsley asked.

"No comment," Jay said on the monitor. He pushed back from the podium then brusquely left the stage with Rocco and Lucas on either side of him. Reporters barked follow-up questions and cameras flashed, but he exited, ignoring them all.

"I don't get it," Kamie said. "Does that Annie lady work for someone else now?"

"Not just someone," Kingsley corrected, eyes wide and concerned. "Dad's archenemy."

"Kids," I said, stashing the phone in my pocket. "I have to speak with your dad. Can you wait here for five minutes?"

"Hey." I clapped my hands to get the attention of the IT folks sitting in the back who had set up the feed for us. "Where's the closest bathroom?"

"Uhh." The long-haired guy looked clueless. "Not sure. Probably somewhere down the hall or maybe upstairs?"

I rolled my eyes then pointed at the kids. "Watch them." I glanced at my charges. "Kamie, Kingsley, please stay put."

I dashed out of the room and searched for the bathroom or some other private place where I could go ghost then magically teleport to Jay's side. No luck. By foot then.

I found my way to the stage exit, but Jay was long gone. The lobby wasn't far. My heels pounded the carpeted corridor. He wasn't there. I cut in front of a tourist and darted for the hotel help desk. "I'm looking for Jay Nichols. Did he pass through here?"

"Yes, miss," the concierge said; he wore a professional suit and a whimsical Santa hat. "Mr. Nichols got in his car a minute ago." He pointed toward the hotel entrance, the main drive visible from the desk.

"This may not be any of my business . . ." he continued. I glanced back at him. "But if you care about Mr. Nichols you should hurry. He seemed like he was in a bad way and people make bad decisions when they're vulnerable. No one is beyond help though. You just have to be persistent."

I stared at the concierge. Then the alert on my phone went off again. I stomped toward the main entrance, swiped away the notification on my phone, and dialed Jay's number. After two rings, he answered.

"Jay!" I exclaimed. "Listen, I know that news about Annie is

. . . horrible, but you have a responsibility to your kids. Celia isn't going to give you another chance like this if you ditch them. *They* may not give you another chance."

"I'm sorry, Frost. Tell them I'm sorry. I need some space right now." He breathed heavily. "Annie knows everything about me. If she is working for Farah, they'll bury me unless I do . . . something." A long pause ensued. "I have to think. Kingsley and Kamie can't see me like this. Get them home."

"I'm coming to talk to you in person as soon as I find a place to go ghost."

"You can't. I thought of that. I'm leaving the divider down in the car. Rocco and Lucas would see you if you tried."

"Jay—"

He hung up and I stared at my phone, completely flabbergasted. Suddenly it started ringing. The caller ID said Specter One. I picked up and struck first.

"I know, I know. I'm on it," I said curtly.

"Frost, you need to come back to the CCD," Specter One said, tone severe. "I need to talk with your team. Be here in one hour. For all your sakes, don't keep me waiting."

"Specter One—"

He also hung up on me.

Son of a snowman!

I stood motionless in the lobby. The world seemed big and blurry as tourists, families, and hotel staff passed around me. For the second time in the last hundred years, I felt like I was fading away. I felt genuinely afraid.

I leaned against the front door of Celia and Eddie's home after it closed behind me. It had been painful trying to explain to them what happened. The cab ride with Kamie and Kingsley had been awkward enough. I felt completely drained, but I had to rally.

I checked my watch. I had twenty minutes to get back to the CCD. Logic would indicate I should head there now. My soul told me to go after Jay. I didn't know if he was still around people—actively trying to avoid me—but I could check.

I concentrated my magic on finding him. My blue glow activated per usual. Suddenly my form flickered like a bad hologram. As I started to teleport, a heaviness similar to an anchor brought me back. My stomach clenched painfully as if I'd consumed cocoa with extremely expired dairy.

I took a moment to regroup and check my magic supply. The face of my watch glowed meekly—only 30% of my magic remained. This close to the Christmas Eve deadline, upticks in the Christmas Spirit of our Scrooges were supposed to sustain our powers. With Jay's recent downturn, my fuel was running out faster than I was used to. I was getting weaker.

"You can do this," I thought aloud. "Concentrate." With a deep breath I tried again, focusing on all the Christmassy things I could think of. *Pine trees, reindeer, Santa, cookies, candy canes, sleighs, snow . . .*

FLASH!

I appeared in the lobby of the old Orpheum theatre, now the Palace. At first I was surprised, then I remembered that Jay told me he used to come here as an escape when he was stressed.

Jay wasn't in the lobby, so I phased through the doors leading to the auditorium. It was dark inside; a Christmas movie played on the screen for an audience of maybe a hundred and fifty people. Thankfully Jay was seated in the back—no one else in his row or in the rows immediately behind him. Ghost me drifted down the aisle then took the seat beside him before becoming visible.

"So what are we watching? Aside from your pity party," I whispered, my eyes on the screen.

For once Jay didn't react with surprise or annoyance that I'd dropped in. It almost seemed like he'd been expecting me.

"It's a Christmas movie marathon," he replied distantly, keeping his eyes forward. "Your job only gets done if I have Christmas Spirit. I can't exactly do mine right if I'm miserable either. I thought this would help. It's hard to watch one of these and not feel some sense of hope for humanity."

"Is it working?" I asked.

He sighed. "Not really. I keep thinking how paradoxical it is that awful people can see these movies and have their hearts warmed just like you or me and yet, after the credits roll, they go back into the world unchanged. I mean, Farah loves *Home Alone*. That TV host Tiffany who threw me under the bus loves *Home Alone 2*. And do you know what Annie's favorite movie is? *It's a Wonderful Life*. A movie quintessentially about putting others first and showing goodwill toward others." He grunted. "Why are people so terrible?"

I leaned back in my chair with a sigh of my own. "Even monsters see movies, Jay. I can't tell you why some people are more affected by them than others. And I agree with you in a way; people can be terrible. But if Scrooging you has taught me anything, it's that maybe we shouldn't label people so presumptively—good or bad, redeemable or hopeless, optimist or cynic. In that spirit, maybe we shouldn't brand someone as completely terrible just because they let us down. I'm not saying Farah or any of the people who've wronged you are good, but you have worked with Annie for a year and while I don't like her, I don't know if I would call her a bad person."

I tucked some loose hair behind an ear then leaned forward, looking right at Jay though he wouldn't look at me. "We all have a tendency to ignore people's humanity—we flatten them in our minds and label them so it's easier to do what we want and treat them how we want. For example your kids, Celia, and your whole family may be thinking right now that you're a lousy father. But I know that you're not and that you really do care. Sometimes things get in the way of people being their best selves. Sometimes we forget what that's even supposed to look like."

Finally Jay turned his eyes to me. He released a deep, wary breath. "How bad was it?"

"Celia and Eddie were angry. Kamie and Kingsley were sad. If you don't repent soon, you'll lose them and will end up with that lonely future Midori and I warned you about."

"Maybe I should straight-up accept that future . . ." Jay said morosely. "Obviously I'd rather have my kids in my life, but if I can't even be the father they need for one day—on Christmas Eve no less—maybe it's better for all of us if we stop kidding ourselves. You chose to walk alone in life. Maybe I should do the same."

I put my hands on his arm. "Don't say that, Jay. Being alone isn't your path. If it were, I wouldn't be here. You need people. I don't mean in the egotistical way that applause validates you or votes propel you. You have people in your life who love you and vice versa. You're better because of them. They're meant to walk with you. But they can't do that if you convince yourself that you should stand alone. If you give up."

I checked my watch. "I have to go. I don't know what time I'll be back, but we still have to take one final trip to the future and, well, I still have to save you."

"*Can you?*" Jay asked sincerely.

I held his eyes. "Honestly, I don't know. But *I'm* not giving up on you."

The news was so awful that my brain couldn't fully process it. It was so surprising that my mouth couldn't formulate a response. And it was so frightening that for once in my hundred years as a ghost, I realized there were far worse things than my current fate.

"What do you mean, we'll expire?" Brandon exclaimed. Midori and I—next to the kid on the bench in Specter One's office—were equally shocked.

"As Santa explained to Frost earlier this month, your CCD forms are more fragile than you realize," Specter One said. "Souls aren't meant to be stopped in transit between life and death. Only strong magic allows you to stay here. Each season, that magic is replenished when you save a soul. The positive energy generated by that act is enough to keep the three of you going. But if you fail, then your souls won't be able to continue."

"What'll happen if we fail?" Brandon challenged. "Like, exactly? Expire is a vague word. We're already dead. How much worse can it get?"

"You'll be gone," Specter One responded somberly. "I can't explain more than that."

"Why not?" Brandon asked. "Hasn't it happened before?"

"Not to any souls that still exist . . ."

My team and I looked at each other.

Specter One cleared his throat. "When a ghost does not have the magic to continue, he or she ceases to exist. Ghosts are already dead, after all, so if they run out of our version of life energy, there is nowhere else to go. They just . . . vanish."

The possibility hung in the air like a supernatural noose.

At last, I spoke. "Specter One, I've always begrudgingly accepted that you and the Senior Specters, and even the Santas, have your secrets. But this is crossing a line. Our existence is in danger every season. This matters! Why didn't you tell us about this from the beginning? All the ghosts should be aware of what's at stake."

"The only thing that knowledge would do is spread fear," Specter One said. "Your souls are here because of your untapped ability to care about others and spread goodness. It's a little hard to do both when you're worried about vanishing from existence. It's the same reason why you're not supposed to be aware of your fragile nature. We only tell you if it becomes relevant."

"You don't think it would become relevant when we wake up one season and realize that ghosts we know, our friends, have disappeared?" Brandon countered. "What happens when people ask questions?"

"They never will," Specter One replied. "By vanishing from existence, all memory of you is gone too. Again, this isn't like dying. This will be like you never happened."

"That's not possible," I said.

"Isn't it?" Specter One looked at me sadly. "Frost let me ask you—how many ghosts were in your training class?"

I blinked. "Three. Me, Bill James, and Ty Watanabe."

"Are you sure?"

"Yes. The three of us are the only ones up for retirement this year because we started together. It's just us in all my memories . . ." My mind did a quick run though of the recent dreams I'd had of our trio—the first refreezing, our pre Scrooging pep talk with Santa when I met Kris, the day I woke up in that North Pole igloo and stepped out of my ice coffin . . .

Realization flashed before my eyes. *Four.*

"There were four ice capsules in the infirmary when I woke up for my first season!" I thought aloud with a gasp.

My boss nodded. "When souls vanish, memories of *them* are wiped clean, but the environment they affected may still leave clues that someone was there. Your training class had four ghosts.

One failed some time ago and as a result that whole Scrooging team ceased to exist."

I felt a tremor go down my spine. "But *you* know," I argued. "You know a member of my training class is missing and you told us this morning that the Scrooge success rate is 99.5%. Which means you're aware of who has failed and when. You didn't forget them."

"Yes and no," Specter One replied sadly. "I have no idea who those souls were who failed and we lost, but I do know how many there have been."

He used his magical desk keyboard and a wave of his hand to bring up a view of our realm-evator lobby like a security camera feed. My boss gestured at the three Christmas trees and their eerily beautiful baubles. "One of those crystal ornaments appears on the appropriate tree every time we lose a member of the CCD. Since Past, Present, and Future Ghost teams rely on the same Scrooge for their magic refuels, when they fail, new ornaments show up in batches of three."

The four of us sat quietly for a long, *painful* moment.

"What about me?" I said softly. "Jay was supposed to be my one hundredth soul. Doesn't that mean anything? How can someone do good deeds for so many years and have it amount to nothing if they mess up once?"

"I'm sorry, Frost. When you build a house of cards, it doesn't matter how many are positioned perfectly; one wrong move will cause the whole thing to fall apart. Saving a soul each year allows ghosts to go on. Saving one hundred souls in a row produces a powerful result that allows you to obtain new life. Fail in your first year or your last—the result is the same."

Specter One wiped away the screen with a wave and then leaned forward on his desk, hands folded. I'd never seen such remorse in anyone's expression. Though his tone remained even, his icy eyes sparkled with such empathy that they outshone his glittery cheeks.

"I am sorry that this is how it is. I didn't design our afterlife this way, and neither did any of the Santas. When the CCD was founded, that Claus did everything he could to create something wonderful and magical, but even powerful souls like ours can't fully control the universe; it sets its own rules and results. These are the ones we've been working with for centuries. All I can do now is warn you so that you go into your final hours of Christmas Eve fully aware of what you're dealing with. That is what the intervention alert on your phones means; it's when I have to step in to reveal the truth so the stakes are completely clear and you don't give up by any means. You *fight harder*."

Specter One pulled up Jay's analytics screen from the Merry Meter app. It floated beside the desk ominously, like a ghost haunting *us*.

"When Jay's spirit dropped this afternoon after his press conference, he sank below the danger line again. Since Frost's talk with him in the theater, it has leveled off a bit but it is not rising out of that zone. He's in serious jeopardy now, as are all of you. I let you proceed without my interference this morning, but not anymore. I'm ordering you to immediately re-strategize. Throw out what you were planning and do something more creative and daring. Funerals are traditionally the best closing move, but now is not the time for tradition. Be bold. Try the unexpected. Do something you've never done before." He looked at me directly. "Even if that scares you. Otherwise, by day's end, he will be lost . . . and all of you will be too."

Specter One walked us to the elevator. I felt more like a zombie than a ghost, drifting in the surreal state of these new circumstances.

The door opened and our trio stepped inside. Specter One kept the door from closing with his arm.

"Good luck, you three. I mean that as sincerely and deeply as possible." He gave us a pitying look, then cleared his throat and tilted up his chin—refocused with professionalism. "Remember, with Jay this far gone, the closer it gets to midnight, the more your powers will weaken. You must not let him sink any lower, or your magic and ability to remain present on Earth could falter completely, and then you may not be able to stay to finish the job. So please . . . tell me you all can handle this."

We stood in the elevator, silent. Then—

"The future has changed," Midori said. "There is still a way."

Brandon and I whipped our heads toward Midori. Specter One was so surprised that he took a step back and let go of the elevator door. It snicked shut in our stunned faces as we stared at our teammate.

24

"Hey, Frost!" Paul loudly answered my SpaceTime call. "Is Marley okay?"

"He's fine thanks to your dad," I said, sitting at my desk in my CCD office. "Where are you?"

"We're halfway through South America. Sorry if I'm yelling. There's a lot of wind tonight. What about you? It's getting close to five in California right now. Shouldn't you be prepping for your finale?"

"I'm headed there soon. Before I go though, just in case, I wanted to tell you and your dad something. Bismaad made me realize what a rotten friend I've been over the years. I'm sorry for that; I should have appreciated you all more and I want you to know I am really glad to have known you. Thank you for always being kind to me, for accepting me, and for trying to get me to change. I wish I hadn't fought it for so long."

"Frost." Paul's tone changed. "Are you sure you're okay?"

A lump welled in my throat. "Yes," I said. "I actually think I'm better than I have been in a while. I only hope that's enough to bring this home. Goodbye, Paul. Good luck with the rest of your night."

"Yeah . . . you too."

I hung up and checked Tinsel. Bismaad's feed showed a pic of her Scrooge hugging a young man. Snow fell in the background—the perfect Christmas touch, as always. I read the caption of her post.

"That's another one for the books. This Scrooge is saved and my team and I are done! Power on the cocoa machine, Wobbles. Work hard; play harder." #Scrooged #goodwill #ChristmasEve #secondchances

Second chances.

According to the time stamp of the post, Bismaad had probably been back at the CCD for hours. That was one of the benefits of being assigned a Scrooge in a time zone that was ahead; you finished early compared to everyone else.

"Wish me luck, Marley," I said, patting his head. "It's a big night in majorly different ways." My soul felt heavy as I drifted down the hall. I didn't know how my story with Jay was about to play out, but I'd been taken by surprise before.

I journeyed to the ballroom where our annual holiday party was held every Christmas Eve. There were already a couple dozen spirits there. Many of them greeted me amiably as I passed by. I greeted each of them too—a pat on the arm, a wave, a genuine smile. I spotted Bismaad by the cheese fountain, her back to me. She wore a forest green salwar and kameez combo (pleated trousers with a tight fit around the ankles paired with an intricately embroidered flowing top). A matching, embellished, scarf-like cloth hung off her left shoulder and draped to the floor. I think that was called a dupatta.

"Bismaad."

She turned around and frowned. Her double braids were interwoven with glimmering golden ribbon. "What do you want?"

"Just to say that you were right about me. And to apologize."

"I know I was right, and apologies are only words, Frost. Just because someone says them doesn't mean all the hurt gets undone."

"I understand that," I said. "But even if you don't forgive me, I want you to know that you've helped me in more ways than I ever appreciated. I finally heard you in my office, and I hope that I can use what I've learned to save Jay. It's not too late for his redemption, even if it is too late for mine."

Bismaad stared at me. The alarm on my phone began to sound off.

Five o'clock.

"Hey, Bismaad!" A group of ghosts waved her over to their table.

She regarded me with an unreadable expression. "I have to go."

My friend left me without another word. I wasn't surprised. I hadn't expected her to forgive me. I had been a total mistletool. Like I told her, I accepted that it was too late for me. At least in this afterlife.

I returned to my apartment in LA with a steady mind and eerily calm feeling. Outside the bay windows of my loft, the clouds were drenched in an orange creamsicle color that bled across my hardwood floors. Moving toward the kitchen, flecks of gold from the dying Christmas Eve sun hit my cold face. It was time to get ready for the most important party of my afterlife. I climbed into my Fa-La-La-La Fashion Pod for a final time.

I could feel my powers ebbing as I wrapped myself in ethereal blue energy, but my resolve held strong as I forced my weakened magic to teleport me to Jay.

Next thing I knew, my black pumps were sinking into soft grass. Trees, vast lawns, and innumerable headstones surrounded me. Many had been decorated for the holidays. Across the cemetery, families visited lost loved ones. Most were wrapping it up though, walking up the pathway toward the exit to outrun the falling darkness.

Not the gala I was expecting to find Jay at.

I glanced around. The place felt familiar. However, I'd visited a lot of graveyards during my Scrooging missions over the past century. I supposed they were getting jumbled in my memory.

I stepped behind a tree and turned visible. Wind swept the hair from my shoulders as I searched for Jay. I spotted him standing in front of a plot a bit downhill. His tuxedo's black sheen complemented the feathers of the three ravens eyeing him from nearby branches.

I walked toward him. My strapless gown flounced with each step. I lifted the hem of the bustled skirt as I descended stairs on the path. The dress's shimmering gold color was a stark contrast to my black silk gloves and the black ribbon in my hair. The wind began to blow more heavily. It was a lucky thing cold and I were close acquaintances otherwise I would've frozen in this outfit.

Jay glanced up, hearing me coming. His eyebrows rose. "You look great. I didn't know ghosts could dress up that nice."

"Well, I left my white sheet with holes for eyes back at the North Pole."

He smirked mildly. I came to stand next to my Scrooge and we beheld his father's gravestone together. Despite the growing shadows and wear-and-tear of time, Marlon Nichols's name was still legible.

"I don't know why I came here," Jay admitted. "It felt like something I had to do."

"You're at a crossroads," I responded knowingly. "It's not unusual to revisit the past when that happens. I think deep down you've heard everything my team and I have been telling you about your family. All that fronting you've done since then— including this afternoon—is you trying to run because you're scared. You're comfortable choosing distance because you're in control. If you are the one preemptively pushing others away, there is no chance that you will get hurt or taken by surprise. You made your bed and though it's lonely, you're fine lying in it because every crease and fold is by your design."

I shook my head. My bitterness was as biting as the wind had become.

"'No space of regret can make amends for one life's opportunity misused.'"

"Is that Dickens?" Jay asked.

I nodded. "*A Christmas Carol.*"

"Appropriate quote."

"In more ways than one." I took a breath. "Jay, this whole month I've wondered why I have felt so drawn to you, so motivated yet flustered by your case. I started to think it was for reasons regarding your personality, heart, and conscience. As we began to become friends, I thought surely that my caring about you was the main reason. However, while all these things contributed, now I know the truth. I'm invested in you because you're me. We are the same."

I realized I was scratching my nails against my palm and made myself stop. Instead I took a deep breath and spoke the truth.

"I pushed people away in life because being alone was familiar and safe. I thought choosing distance on my terms would protect me, and that I didn't need anyone to be happy. I lived my afterlife the exact same way. But this week, another friend helped me see reality. My boss helped me get there too, in his own weird way."

I sighed and shook my head. "I regret the choices I made, Jay. I see you making the same choices where your family is concerned and subconsciously, I think regret for my own missed chances made me want to save you because it felt like saving **me** too. Sadly, no amount of regret can make up for the mistakes I made. I can't live vicariously through you. I have to accept what I've done wrong in order to change and move forward in whatever kind of life I have left. All I can really do is warn you and advise you. Warn you that the road that is familiar is not necessarily less dangerous. And advise you what my friends have taught me. Truly caring about someone is the bravest thing a person can do."

The last rays of sun vanished behind the graveyard hill as my eyes held his. Then I turned and began to walk away.

"Frost," Jay called after me. "Are you going to the gala?"

I looked back over my shoulder. "I am. We have a future to face together, Jay."

I continued up the path another few steps then paused. I turned around slowly, taking in my surroundings and finally realizing why I recognized this place.

How appropriate.

My eyes searched the grounds and narrowed in on a path of weeping willow trees that swayed hauntingly in the wind. They led to an older part of the cemetery. I pivoted to Jay and pointed in that direction.

"Plot number 2137."

"What's there?" Jay asked cautiously.

"I am," I replied. And with that, I vanished.

I had not attended such an extravagant affair for years. Men in dapper suits and women in radiant gowns floated through the grand mansion. Expertly decorated Christmas trees filled every corner. Luscious garlands hugged the banisters. Waiters passed around crystal drinkware that twinkled in the glow of countless chandeliers.

Jay arrived a half hour after me. Although I kept an eye on my Scrooge, I decided to give him space and let him mingle with the affluent crowd for a while. Presently I was on the phone, watching him from the corner beside a tree decorated with a checker-pattern motif.

"Yes. I want it delivered now so he can find it later. Thank you. Merry Christmas to you too." When I hung up the phone, I saw the time. It was half past six. No more mingling for Jay. The moment had come for my team's closer move; our best shot; our finale. I fetched Midori, put her in position, and then went to collect the man of the hour.

"Jay," I gingerly touched my gloved hand to his arm as I approached from behind. He turned slowly. "It's time."

He didn't fight me. The two of us drifted up the magnificent staircase side by side in a state of shared requirement.

"I saw your grave," he said when we were halfway up. "It rattled me."

"I didn't react well the first time I saw it either."

We finished the ascension; then Jay hesitated at the top of the stairs and regarded me seriously. "Frost. I'm sorry."

"For what?"

"For your loss."

I paused. "Thank you," I said. "The dead don't often receive condolences."

"You're not dead to me."

We continued down the corridor until we arrived at my preselected room. It was dark inside except for the hearth of blue flames that palpitated in the fireplace to our right. Midori stood in front of the fireplace, her eyes housing the flames' reflection.

I shut the door. Midori extended her hand to Jay, beckoning him forward. The creases of wrinkles and veins on her arms looked more dramatic in the shadows.

Jay approached warily. I followed.

My Scrooge and I each gripped one of Midori's cold hands. She gave me a nod. This would work. It had to.

Powerful energy cycloned the room, fluttering the long white curtains and knocking bric-a-brac off the shelves. I felt strong vibrations in my soul to the point that my body trembled. We were going very far into the future, and it took a mighty use of magic to get us there.

A bright, almost heavenly light took over everything and when it faded, we were back in the cemetery. Night had totally fallen. Despite the touches of Christmas that families had left upon headstones, the thousands of plots were foreboding in the evening shadow, barely illuminated by the outdoor lamps.

Jay released Midori's hand. Like ours, his glowing spectral blue body stood out against the dark like the shine of Luke's first lightsaber.

Jay put his hands in his pockets and wandered out on the grass. After a moment, he pivoted to face us. "I don't mean to offend you both, but I am not exactly taken aback. I've seen plenty *A Christmas Carol* remakes. They always end with some sort of visit to the Scrooge's grave or his funeral. If you're trying to show me that I die without a lot of people around to mourn me, I can't say I'm shocked. Like you said, Frost, I made my bed. It's been made with a heavy, lonelier heart, but I'll lie in it." He released a sad, short breath. "I'm ready for that now. I accept it. Seeing my grave isn't going to break me at this point when I know what has to be done and accept the consequences."

I strode out on the grass and squared off with him. "You're right. A Scrooge's funeral and lonely headstone are usually the finale moves for a Ghost of Christmas Future. In fact, until this afternoon, we had a similar scenario planned because those scenes usually have the most impact. But not on you, Jay. You're different. And also, as of today, your future has changed."

I drifted along a path lined with dark trees. Dying leaves caught in the wind as they fell from gnarled branches and petered to the ground around us.

"You're wrong on two counts, you see," I said as Jay came to walk beside me, Midori pulling up the rear. "First—your funeral is not going to be an empty, sad affair like most Scrooges. As you've seen, on your current path you accomplish your greatest political ambitions. You become president. For two terms actually. And when you die, you get all the fixings that go along with that—the American flags, the military honor guard in full dress uniform, the assembly of important guests. Even your family shows up. After all, it would look bad if they didn't."

We ascended a final step before I changed our trajectory and took a path curving left.

"Okay, what's the other thing I'm wrong about?" Jay asked.

I pointed ahead. A figure had come into view. Cloaked in the night, his back was to us, his shadow streaming over the grass. We approached the man. He was lost in thought with head crooked down and hands in his pockets as he gazed at a plot. I stopped five feet from Jay and looked directly at my Scrooge.

"This is not your grave," I said. I tilted my chin toward the mysterious man. Midori and I kept our distance as Jay slowly made his way around to look at the man's face. When he did, Jay's expression warped with horror and shock—the expression that every Scrooge made before the big enlightenment finally set in. His fear and surprise made me glad; it meant we'd finally gotten through to him.

Jay took a heavy step back. *The man was him*—an older version of Jay, maybe in his early seventies. My Scrooge glanced at me. I gestured for him to look down at the gravemarker Old Jay was staring at. He moved to better see the headstone.

Kingsley Tarob Nichols
Beloved Husband, Father, Grandfather
2011–2094

Jay stood frozen.

"Keep looking," I said evenly, waving my hand at the surrounding plots.

In a frenzy, Jay started searching around. There were plenty of names he didn't recognize, but after a few moments, he came across Kamie's grave too.

"I don't understand," he said, whirling around. "How am I . . . how is *he* here?" Jay gestured at his older self. "How are Kingsley and Kamie dead and I'm still alive?"

"Jay!"

We turned as a guy in his mid-twenties with a man bun and a young girl maybe six came over to the plot. They couldn't see us; they'd been talking to Old Jay, who pivoted around.

"You shouldn't be here," said Man Bun. "I know it's hard. We all have a tendency to want to find those we left behind when we return home for the first time. But you're not supposed to use your magic for selfish purposes." He pointed at Old Jay's wrist.

Old Jay lifted his hand. When the sleeve of his suit drew back, we saw that his watch was blinking red.

"I had to find them," Old Jay said sadly, eyes glassy with regret. "I thought I could see them one last time. I can't believe they're already gone." He suddenly cringed like something had stung his face. He lifted his hand to his cheek and when he pulled it away, he held a small ice particle between his fingers.

"Wow, bro, I'm sorry," said Man Bun. "Ghosts can't usually produce tears. The pain you're feeling must be . . . something."

The young girl patted Old Jay's arm sympathetically. "Come

on. We better get back to base. Specter One will want to talk to you."

The trio linked hands, swirled with radiant energy, and vanished. Our Jay was speechless.

"There's one more part of this future we'd like you to see," I told him. I signaled Midori. She took his hand and mine and we were swept away to the refreezing chamber at the CCD. Like how Brandon could take us to different scenes within the same past Christmas, Midori could transport us to different scenes within the same future one.

Jay gazed at the dozens of ice capsules, the elves, and the frosty infrastructure with total bewilderment.

"I told you that in order to become a ghost like me, there are three requirements you must meet," I said steadily. "You need to have a large capacity to love that you didn't use on Earth. And there can't be anyone who truly matters to you *and* who you truly matter to."

"But my kids . . ." Jay became defensive. "No. This can't be. I love my kids. Even if I push them away. Even if we drift apart, I'll always love them. *Even if they don't love me.*"

"You overestimate yourself . . ." Midori's chilling voice—shockingly being used for the second time today—caused Jay and me to shiver. It was strong but soft, like a weighty whisper.

Midori drifted closer. "Without action, love is just a word, a memory, a ghost. Something that feels real but isn't anymore."

Goodness, Midori didn't speak often, but her words certainly held impact. Perhaps it was the lack of speaking constantly that allowed the thoughts she did choose to truly resonate with meaning.

"She's right, Jay." I turned to him. "After so many decades of distancing yourself from your family and making choices that put your career first, your kids no longer mattered in your life. You existed fine without them and you didn't feel the need to change that. Kamie and Kingsley eventually came to view you in the same way. A father in name, not action. And so, when you die, you end up like me, like us. A ghost doomed to serve humanity for a hundred years, watching people you knew grow old and die, and being alive for one month a year solely to help someone else who is ungrateful for life's most precious gift."

The elevator behind us dinged open. Old Jay and other ghosts entered the warehouse, approaching the area where elves in coveralls used cranes to move ice capsules from racks to ground level. Based on the deadpan acceptance on the ghosts' faces, I knew this was not their first time here. These were returning ghosts.

The lids of the latest round of lowered ice capsules opened, releasing purges of wintery mist. Old Jay and his colleagues began to climb in like vampires settling into their coffins. Our Jay stood over the frost tomb of his elder counterpart as if in a trance, staring down at the sadness etched into the wrinkles of Old Jay's face.

The lid of the capsule started to close. I nodded to Midori. Her magic mainly revolved around going to the future, but with extra effort and focus, she could manipulate the environment of the future momentarily too.

Midori's pupils illuminated with dense, dark energy; her irises were rings of lightning. Suddenly, our Jay's spirit was absorbed into his older form lying in the coffin. It took him a second and a half to realize what was happening. His eyes buggered and he tried to sit up. "Hey, what—"

But it was too late. The ice coffin snapped shut and locked. It started to glow. Through the icy lid, Midori and I could see Jay banging against the interior.

"No! NO!"

I stared down, unyielding and unforgiving, as his face warped with anger and alarm. That fearful urgency only escalated when he saw his hands begin to flicker, turning to blue energy.

He shouted desperately. Finally Midori placed one hand on the ice capsule and took my grip in hers. In an instant, the three of us were back in the room at the mansion where the gala was being held. Jay lay on the floor—on his back and writhing like an upside-down turtle.

"NO!" he hollered.

"Jay," I said.

It took him a moment to comprehend where we were. He gradually got up—blinking a lot and off balance. He seemed to be having difficulty reorienting himself.

"Hang tight. I'll be right back." I grabbed Midori and teleported her back to my loft.

"You did excellent!" I said, letting go of her hand. "Thank you for being better at your job this year than I was at mine. I think you just saved us."

"We are a team," Midori said. She gave a single, finite nod like a period at the end of a sentence. "Finish strong."

"Finish strong." I nodded in agreement. As Midori headed for my bathroom door, I flashed back to Jay's side. He was sitting on the edge of the bed, leaning forward and staring blankly at the wall with his hands clasped together.

"You look like you've just seen a ghost," I joked.

He didn't respond. He didn't even seem to hear me. I stood in front of him like a prosecutor waiting for a verdict.

"Jay?"

"Can you give me some time?" he asked, his eyes still wide.

"Of course," I replied. "As it happens, I have an errand to run. I'll be back."

I exited the room, closing the door behind me. By the time I returned, Jay should be ready for his grand revelation. I hustled through the hallway then down the stairs. One silk gloved hand gathered up some of my golden dress bustles, the other slid over the smooth dark wood of the banister. As I trotted outside the twinkling mansion and moved toward the valet, my phone rang in my gown's hidden pocket. I checked the caller ID and answered. "Yes, Specter One?"

"Frost, how did the trip to the future go? Jay's Merry Meter reading hasn't shifted yet."

"It went perfectly," I replied with confidence. "And that shift should happen any time now. He just needs a few minutes to let everything sink in."

All Scrooges got shell-shocked by a well-done finale. Once Jay came to, I had no doubt the line graph Specter One monitored would skyrocket and Jay would run to his family to make amends. Reuniting with them would reconnect him to his true self. Once that happened, he wouldn't slip back into the grip of those political taskmasters. His spirit would be too strong for that. Too whole. He'd be saved.

One of the valets signaled me. "Your car is here, Miss Mason!"

"Why are you getting in a car?" Specter One asked, hearing through the phone. "Frost, why aren't you with Jay?"

I waved at the cab to pull forward and bobbed around fancy guests. "Jay needs a bit more time. In an hour he has to be at the debate. After that, it'll be too late and he'll be swept up in his role beyond repair. I am going to delay the debate for as long as possible with as much magic as I have left."

"Hurry, Frost."

"I know. I know." I stashed the phone in my pocket and hopped in the back seat of the cab, giving the driver the address.

The traffic was thick, as expected, but thankfully we moved

quickly. On arrival at my destination, I asked the cabbie to park around the corner and keep the meter running. When his taillights were out of sight, I walked across the street. There it was: the auditorium where Jay's debate was scheduled to take place shortly.

The lights of the structure blared. Plenty of cars already circled the area.

I stood in the shadow of several trees, ensuring no one could see me. Then I turned over my magic charm bracelet. There were three charms left—a TV charm, a lightning bolt charm, and a snowflake charm from my original set. My watch showed only 25% of my magic remained. Given the scale of what I wanted to do, I'd only have enough power to make this final magic trick work. Hopefully that was all I needed. My plan—my team's plan—didn't go beyond this moment. If we'd done our jobs properly, by the time I returned to the gala, Jay would finally be at the helm of his great Christmas Spirit reawakening.

I concentrated enormous amounts of magic and focus on the lightning bolt charm and snapped my fingers. With all that oomph behind it, the charm erupted in a huge flare of glitter like a small firework coming off my wrist. I felt power surge through me until it leaked from my spirit like blue fire.

Electrical sparks shot from my skin and my whole form flickered—wavering from the amount I was draining it. I pushed through, and soon those sparks developed into full streaks of electricity. I pivoted and redirected my limbs like lightning rods. I aimed at the auditorium. Then I let all the magic rush out of me—unleashing the deadliest ode to Rice Krispies Treats ever.

SNAP!

A powerful electrical surge exploded around the roof of the auditorium.

CRACKLE!

The notable noise of generators shorting out sounded through the neighborhood.

POP!

Several telephone wires were shocked loose from their towers, flailing about wildly as they rained sparks.

The entire auditorium and half the surrounding block went dark.

I took a painful breath and clutched my stomach as my form flickered. *That* was a lot. Cringing, I breathed in deeply as my body solidified.

After a moment I stood upright, though my arms continued to blur. I checked my watch. Only 5% of my magic remained; it was the lowest my reserve had ever gotten. A decade ago I'd depleted myself down to 20%, but never anything like this. When using the lightning bolt charm I'd left myself *just enough* that I could continue to exist on Earth and not disappear. It was a dangerous situation, but it shouldn't matter much longer. The second Jay had his grand Scrooge awakening, my magic, as well as Midori's and Brandon's, would be restored.

With pride, confidence, and hope, I stared out at the damage I had done. This really ought to do it. Even with the money and resources of powerful political people, it would take hours to fix this. It was Christmas Eve, after all. The debate would be substantially delayed, maybe even cancelled, giving Jay enough time to come to his senses.

I returned to the cab and the driver whisked me across town. When I arrived back at the mansion, it was atwitter with news of the blackout.

I hastened up the stairs; Jay was no longer in the room where I'd left him. That wasn't shocking, but where would he go? I didn't have the privacy or the power left for a ghostly teleport to his side. I began searching on foot, poking my way through the crowds. Eventually, when I was walking through a library, I heard his voice coming from a connecting room. Other voices, deep and low, followed. I pressed myself close to the corner and peeked around the bend.

The neighboring office had a low ceiling and was both walled and floored with mahogany wood. All the seats were leather; all the lampshades were green glass. Jay sat in an armchair. Sitting across from him at an unnecessarily large desk was one of the older guys from Friedman's Election Consulting that Jay had dinner with last week—the overweight, overly smug guy in his sixties. The other two men from dinner were also there.

"You're compelling, Jay," the big guy mused. "Charismatic. Forceful. Ambitious. We've known you could go far since your profile crossed our desks. When you agreed to do things our way where your ex-wife was concerned and green lit our investigation of Farah it was promising, but things changed this morning when we heard about Annie. It makes us really wonder—can you be the man we hoped you would be, the man you told us you wanted to be?"

"I can," Jay said firmly.

"I don't know . . ." The big guy stroked his chin, then took a drink of the amber liquid in his crystal tumbler. "You've proven to be a little too righteous for my taste. Nothing gets in the way of a political career quite as much as unmoving principles. To play with us long term means you have to be willing to throw a curveball sometimes."

Jay leaned forward, eyes chilling. "Listen to me carefully. I am not a bad person. I will never compromise to the extent that this changes. That being said, I have seen where I can go if I follow a prudent man's path and I want to cement our partnership to get me there, like Annie intended. She knows how to win. She always did and I drove her away. Give me another chance. I can do this. I admit to being distracted this month with some personal issues, but that's over now. It won't happen again."

"I'm not sure if your confidence is enough to renew our faith, Jay," said Salt-and-Pepper Beard. "Losing Annie doesn't reflect well on you. I don't see why we should continue to back you if she doesn't. If we trust her opinion as a barometer, you don't have what it takes."

"I have *exactly* what it takes," Jay said. "I know that now. Most people are weak; they fear the future and waver as a result on their way to it. I finally know what I have to be to get where I want to go, and I accept that." He paused and nodded once. "I choose this. No matter the cost."

The men were silent for a moment. Then the big guy pushed back in his leather chair, came around the side of the desk, and moved in front of Jay. Jay stood and faced him. Then the big guy extended his hand.

"I'll hold you to that."

Jay shook his hand then I shouted with pain. It wasn't intentional, but I felt like I had been kicked in the stomach with a combat boot. I folded forward, wrapping both arms around myself as ache and agony throbbed my system.

Jay and the other men rushed around the corner.

"Miss, are you okay?" asked Salt-and-Pepper Beard as I tried to straighten up.

"Jay, is this the assistant Farah tried to scandalize?" the big guy said.

"Temporary assistant," Jay replied, torn between aloofness and concern. He tried to take my arm. "Frost, are you—"

I recoiled and shooed him away. "I'm . . . urgh." I leaned against the wall and forced myself erect, addressing the other three men. "There's a mansion full of rich people out there. Can you gentlemen find me a doctor please."

"Yes. Hold tight," said Salt-and-Pepper Beard. "Do you—"

"Go!" I barked.

The Friedman's creeps hurried out of the room just before I started to flicker.

"What's happening to you?" Jay asked in panic.

"Me? What's happening to *you*?" I replied angrily, my fury with him surpassing worry for myself. I gestured to the office. "What was that?"

Jay's face hardened. "That was me making a choice."

"The wrong choice."

"For who?"

"For you!" I exclaimed. With a deep breath, I moved for the doors and locked them. I was panting when I returned to Jay and staggered, grabbing the edge of a chair to steady myself.

"Jay . . ." I grunted and shook my head, suppressing the hurt. "Half of your spirit is in peril because of your career ambitions; the other half is rooted in struggles with your family. But the two are *linked*. If you make amends with your family and fill the voids in your life with them, you won't be as vulnerable to losing your spirit to people like the Three Stooges of Scrooges out there— *Argh!*"

A bolt of pain shot through my system. I flickered again— way more intensely and for a solid three seconds. Once more Jay attempted to come to my aid, but I put my hand up and pushed him away firmly.

"You've seen your future, Jay. On this path you're going to end up alone, die with no meaningful connection to anyone, and turn into a ghost for Kris Kringle's sake! You were supposed to realize the error of your ways and run from that fate, not *toward* it."

"But then I would die another way," he said sadly.

I frowned. "I don't understand."

"Exactly. And I think it's because of the connection you felt with me, Frost—the similarities between us. You said it yourself: half of my fate is tied to my struggle with family and the other half with my career hopes. But when you think about it, although you mixed it up with my present and future visits, all of our journeys to the past were focused on my family. You came to understand the pain, suffering, and resentment I'd built there, and focused on rejection where my relationships were concerned. But in doing so—in trying to save that part of me you related to—you overlooked the other part of me that's been hurting for decades. You didn't dig into the pain, suffering, and resentment created from a life's worth of rejection and failure where my ambitions are concerned."

My face twisted with confusion. "Jay, I know you lost dozens of elections throughout your life. I know until college you weren't victorious in obtaining any of the positions you strived for. But positions don't really matter in life. You're a good guy with genuinely good intentions; I know titles don't mean a lot to you. Not really. All you want is a chance to work hard for the things you care about."

"That's right," Jay said. "And you know what scares me the most, Frost? More than ghosts or even dying alone? The idea I will never get that chance."

He paced around the office brusquely. "My family damaged me. Losing so many times over so many years *broke me*. Not all at once, but bit by bit. It's a hurt I keep hidden beneath smiles and smothered under perseverance, but it's there. Constantly. Grating at me. Sacrificing the connection to my family is a hard thing to swallow, but since my odds of repairing things there are almost nonexistent, it's safer and smarter for me to move on. If I accept that, lean into it, then I can let go and do what needs to be done. I can be the man that wins governor, becomes president, and goes the distance."

I was dumbfounded. "Are you telling me that what you got out of this experience is that you should *choose* the path of a Scrooge because it satisfies your ambitions? That this part of you is worth more than trying to make reparations with your family?"

"My career ambitions aren't just a part of me, Frost; they are me. And like I said, I know a lost cause when I see one. Even if I could get the kids to forgive me for today, even if I could get Celia and Eddie to give me another chance, things like this will keep happening, especially if I focus on my campaign the way I'm supposed to. So rather than needlessly prolong the pain, I will do the honorable and easier thing for all of us and withdraw—stop trying to have the normal family that I clearly wasn't meant to have. And I will do the wiser thing for me and pick a path where I know I can control the outcome."

I blinked—processing—then full rage exploded from my chest. "That is the DUMBEST, most COWARDLY thing I have ever heard. So what if you haven't gotten a lot of the things you've wanted in life? So what if you've had a few doors slammed in your face? That can't be a strong enough motivator to choose career fulfillment over love and family."

Now Jay got upset; he loomed over me—brows low and jaw tight as he pointed a finger at my chest. "You don't know what it's like to try so hard to get someone, *anyone*, to give you a chance and for it to lead to nothing. I would kill to have doors slammed in my face, Frost, but for most of my life, no one even opened them in the first place. You don't understand what that does to a person, how worn out my heart is from hoping that maybe this time will be different, or the time after that, or the time after that."

I spread my arms wide. "I know exactly what that's like, Jay! You are the hundredth person I've tried to help. I've spent my afterlife giving second chances to people, and do you know how many have used them wisely? Like forty percent. That's a horrible thing to swallow—more than half the people I've poured my soul into gave up on themselves. Every time I set foot on Earth I am less motivated because my spirit has been broken by disappointment, but that's not . . ." I paused and blinked as realization sunk in.

"*That's no reason to give up, is it?*"

For a moment all my anger and frustration left, replaced by cleansing clarity.

The enlightenment that had eluded me for decades had finally dawned on me at the midnight hour of my afterlife. For the first time in a century, I wholeheartedly believed what Specter One—and so many ghosts, elves, and Santas—had tried to convince me of. Despite a high probability of failure, *there was a purpose for all of this.*

There was always a reason to give it your all, even if being hurt was a risk. Existence was a synonym for struggle, but also possibility. If you forgot that, you would end up living in fear and making choices to avoid pain rather than taking a gamble at happiness.

A loud banging came at the doors. The handles jiggled. "Jay? Miss Mason?"

"I'm sorry to let you down, Frost," Jay said solemnly, recapturing my attention. "But what's the point of being alive if you never get to live up to your potential? What's the point of life if no matter how hard you try or how good you are, you feel like you're dying a little bit every day? I choose this path. I hope you can forgive me."

My watch started blaring with red light; according to it, I only had 1% of my magic left. The phone in my pocket sounded with equal alarm.

Suddenly the ache that tremored though my soul escalated to a point that I couldn't contain it. My body painfully flickered in and out and this time it wouldn't stop. I held up my hands, gasping as they shimmered back and forth from solid to blue spectral energy.

"Frost . . ." Jay said, eyes wide.

I heard the door unlocking from the outside. Panicked, I ran. I phased through Jay and wall after wall until I tumbled out of the mansion into a garden, collapsing behind the cover of white rose bushes. My phone fell out of my pocket, flashing its doomsday message.

"*Extreme Danger: Scrooge Spirit Levels Unrecoverable – Return to CCD – Press Home Button for Emergency Teleport*"

I writhed in pain as every inch of me flickered like the damaged reel of an old movie. Parts of my body began dissolving to pure energy, making the phone slip through my fingers. I grasped at it desperately, hitting the home button the second my hand temporarily became solid.

Jay burst out of the mansion from a nearby door but he didn't see me. "Frost!"

Glittering magic swarmed from my phone and cocooned my body—wrapping me up like a damaged present and taking me home.

25

It was like standing at the edge of the world. Perhaps this was what ancient peoples imagined before Eratosthenes calculated the circumference of the Earth to prove it round.

I found myself on the flat roof of a two-story ice castle constructed entirely of bricks glowing with blue energy. Tiny snowflakes fell from the sky. A blanket of white covered the ground and every branch of the forest behind me—innumerable pines hugging so closely they practically created a wall. The main attraction was ahead though. Directly in front of the castle: a drop into splendid oblivion.

The Northern Lights playing above spilled down, down, down—my eyes traced the colors from the sky, over the edge of the castle, then past a cliff with no bottom. It was like a green, purple, and cobalt waterfall plunging for thousands of feet below until the colors pooled together in the cosmos. That's right; just past the edge of the castle, solid terrain ended. The universe and all its stars spread out beneath me as brightly as they did overhead. It was breathtaking, terrifying, inspiring, and mystifying all at the same time. I felt I could stare at it forever. Too bad I didn't have the time.

"It has been twenty-three years since new ornaments appeared on the trees in the realm-evator lobby," Specter One spoke from behind.

I turned. The coattails of his white tailored jacket fluttered in the wind as snowflakes gusted by. Midori and Brandon stood on the roof as well. We'd woken up here only a little while ago, each dressed in the clothes of our death time period. I wore an ankle-length, wine-colored dress with long sleeves that rustled as I moved toward my team.

"The last time they did, Santa and I began constructing this place." Our boss gestured at the winter castle. "It hasn't been tested yet, but our hope is that maybe the magic here can keep you all going."

"You can't just have the other ghosts donate some magic to each of us, pool their powers together?" Brandon asked.

"Unfortunately no," Specter One replied. "Staying alive isn't like teleporting or using a magic charm—it is defying the laws of the universe to make the dead undead. You need the powerful energy of a saved soul's Christmas Spirit to sustain full afterlife and wake up next season. Deducting anything more than a couple sparks from your fellow ghosts before their refreezing would be dangerous, and you would each need substantially more than that to continue. But while we can't risk the other ghosts' existence by draining them of significant magic, as I said, the cumulative magic of this place may prolong your afterlives for a while."

I gazed at the power of the sky.

"The Northern Lights are a coalesced cosmic view of all the Christmas Spirit that humans feel in their hearts," Specter One explained. "It powers this realm and the CCD, and is strongest here, at the edge of the North Pole. Santa, the Senior Specters, the elves, and I have been building this castle one brick at a time since the last ghosts vanished from existence. Each brick is infused with a spark of ghost magic."

"Our annual donations," I said blankly.

"Precisely. Between the small sparks of magic in each brick and the power pumping through the atmosphere, it may help extend your afterlives."

"For how long?" Brandon asked.

"We're not sure."

"Until next season?" Brandon pressed.

Specter One sighed. "Probably not. More likely a few months . . . half a year at best."

"What good will that do us?" I argued.

"*It's something,*" Specter One said sadly. "It is better than vanishing by the time the clock strikes midnight like you were all going to. Look what this place has already done for you. When the three of you got here you were all flickering out of existence because of Jay's tanked Christmas Spirit. Now your bodies have solidified. Each of you is back to 15% magic capacity."

"But this is just a bandage?" I clarified. "We're all still doomed?"

Specter One wrung his hands together. I did no such thing—no tremor, no shaking, no raking the nails of one hand against the palm of another. Right now my hands were steady as a sharpshooter's.

"What happens if we leave the castle?" I asked.

"I wouldn't advise it," Specter One said. "Staying here will keep your souls alive for as long as possible. The magic of this place is making you stable now, but the farther you get from here, the less magic there will be to sustain your forms and you'd start fading again."

"So what," I said flatly, "we live here now? You're just going to Rapunzel us in a tower until the magic can't hold us together anymore and we disappear anyway?"

"Technically, I think this is more of an Elsa from *Frozen* situation," Brandon piped in. "But either way, it's a no-go, bro," he said to Specter One.

"It's not as if I wanted this to happen!" our boss protested with more emotion than I'd ever heard in his voice. "All of your souls are in my care. My job may be to assign you to save other people, but I always hope that these experiences will help you save yourselves—teach you to love and learn and live more than you did when you were alive."

A beat passed.

"It did."

Specter One looked at me. I held his eyes with solemn gravity as resolute as my comment. His expression filled with empathy. "I wanted you to have another chance at life, Frost, not for your journey to end this way. I truly am sorry. I am sorry to all of you. All I can do now is try to extend your remaining time and make it as pleasant as possible."

On cue, we heard jingling bells; they were attached to the shoes of a trio of elves coming up the stairs to the roof. "Food and drink from the Christmas party have been set up downstairs, sir," said an elf in a purple hat.

Then a fourth elf rose to the roof and my spirit lifted a tiny amount. "Marley!"

The elf set down my wriggling dog and Marley scampered over. I pressed him against my chest like a therapy dog. Which, in retrospect, is what he had been for me all these years while I figured out how stupid and lonely I'd been.

"We'll bring your other things over later," Specter One said. "Once all the other ghosts have been resealed in their capsules."

"I don't want to die!" Brandon said suddenly. He sniffled, his eyes glassy. "I mean, I know I'm dead now, but I don't want to *end.*"

I looked down at him. For the first time since I'd known the bold, big-talking nine-year-old, I saw him for what he was . . . a little kid. A kid who didn't deserve this any more than he deserved to trade life for afterlife in the first place. I was about to console him when Midori wrapped her arms around his small frame. She held him close, gently stroking his back with one hand. He returned the embrace.

Specter One's face was riddled with pain of his own. Scared and upset as I was, I knew I couldn't direct my anger at him. This wasn't his fault. And I could only imagine how much pressure and responsibility he felt. He was our boss, but in reconsideration he was also our guardian, and in many ways the manager of mankind's spirit. This wasn't easy for him either.

"Go," I said simply. "The other ghosts will be wondering where you are."

Specter One nodded and pivoted away. Then he hesitated and turned back. "Frost, you and Jay formed a strong bond in the last month. I don't suppose you told him about what would happen to you if he didn't understand what your team was trying to show him?"

I shook my head. "We may have ended things at an impasse in terms of what is right and good, but I can honestly say we became friends through all of this. If he knew that his changing was tied to my survival, it could have influenced his choices. That wouldn't be right, and I don't believe it would count here anyway. He has to decide who he wants to be for himself. Otherwise, it's not real Christmas Spirit. And that wouldn't restore our magic or his soul."

"For someone who has broken the rules so frequently this season, I'm glad to know you still respect the important ones," Specter One mused sadly.

I forced a smile. "I did always tell you I was good at my job. I just stopped believing there was a point to it. Until now, anyway."

Specter One observed me with actual affection. "I'll be back. Stay put. It's dangerous for you out there."

Our boss disappeared down the stairs. The elves took

Brandon's hands, escorting him to the lower level of the castle as well with the promise of all his favorite foods. Midori touched my arm, then followed.

I stood alone on the roof with Marley. I set him down and wandered to the edge where the roof was rimmed with a waist-high balcony of ice bricks. Staring out at the waterfall of Northern Lights, I contemplated my existence and the churning brink of the world below.

"So what do you think they'll label this story as? Genre-wise, I mean."

I rotated at Specter One's voice. What was he doing back here? He strode over to stand next to me, staring into the wonder of color swirling over the stars.

I looked at him curiously. "What are you talking about?"

"You love movies and stories. I'm just trying to speak your language. Based on everything I've seen, there wasn't enough high-minded rhetoric and shady dealings for a political drama. But Christmas stories have happy endings and this one isn't solidified . . . yet."

He was speaking a bit strangely; the tone and turn of phrase didn't sound like him.

"Specter One, you don't need to baby me. What's happening to me, Brandon, and Midori isn't your fault. We'll deal with this just as we dealt with death. You can go. Really. We all face the end alone in one way or another. I need some space to process it."

"Oh, Frost, that's silly. Space is down there." He gestured at the cosmos. "You just spent the last week finally figuring out that's not what you want defining *your* universe."

I tilted my head at him.

Sorry?

"Tell me," he said. "If you could do anything right now, do

something to redeem all the time you've lost, what would you do?"

"It doesn't matter. I have no magic or time left."

"Humor me."

I sighed. Where to begin? Who hadn't I let down and pushed away?

"I would find Bismaad and show her how much she means to me with more than just words. I already apologized, but I'd prefer not to leave this lifetime without her knowing how I truly feel. I'd do the same for Nick and Paul. Then . . . I'd go back to Jay." I shook my head, thinking of the frustrating but undeniable friend. "I don't want him to go down this dark path. Not because I want to save myself, but because I want to save him. I really, really do. He can be so much more than what he thinks, and I don't want him to build a life based on fear, anger, and compromise. No one should live that way."

Specter One nodded knowingly. "So go."

I blinked. "You told us that we had to stay here for our spirits to remain alive as long as possible."

"But you don't feel *alive*, do you?" Specter One asked.

I stared at him.

He sort of chuckled. "*Alive*. Such a funny, full, frustrating, fascinating word. So many people on Earth take it for granted without living up to the wonders it holds and the possibilities it dares us with. Meanwhile, here we are on Christmas Eve at the edge of the world, and you finally understand what it means, but won't seize it."

"Specter One—"

"There are many ways to be alive, Frost. Even in death, our spirits can fill people with hope and happiness and inspiration. That's what we should all strive for. Because a life that has been worth living is never truly forgotten. And the people and purposes that help us feel alive should be held close, not written off when things get hard. Also . . . I am not Specter One."

The man in front of me started to morph. Within seconds his appearance altered a dozen times into a dozen different people of various ages and ethnicities. Some I didn't recognize right away, but others I did.

The brown-nosing ticket taker at the movie theater who'd been eating cookies. That annoying, handsome guy at the Christmas party with the glass of milk and unsolicited psychoanalysis. Rocco on the day he wore that Christmas tree patterned tie. The concierge with the Santa hat from the hotel this afternoon. Then finally . . .

"Kris!!!"

My *old*, old friend who I'd watched die and disappear over twenty years ago stood in front of me. He looked exactly as I remembered—dressed in full Santa attire with rosiness in his cheeks and a lustrous beard as white as snow.

"Apologies for the misrepresentation," he said, straightening his hat. "I thought I'd ease you into our reunion with a more familiar face. Specter One is a good form to take when I want to talk to ghosts who need a little extra care."

"I don't . . . I don't understand." I blinked, wide-eyed. "How are you here?"

"I am here because you needed me. I am Santa Claus, Frost. I am there when anyone with true Christmas Spirit in their hearts needs me. Just maybe not in the form you expect."

"Kris, I don't have a beating heart. I'm a ghost."

"You *have heart* though, Frost. I saw it in you the moment we met—that spark of life in your eyes, that wonder, that positive energy. It has gotten warped and damaged over the years, but you are still you as much as Jay is still Jay. All people—including the Scrooges we help who return to their old ways—are never truly lost. They have just forgotten themselves. They have forgotten that Christmas Spirit's hope, optimism, and desire to be better and spread goodwill must be actively worked on, and we must remind each other to do it. Without that attention, our potential to be good can melt as quickly as off-season snow. Humanity is a difficult endeavor and we weren't meant to endure it alone. We need each other to help keep us on track." He touched my shoulder. "Change, my dear friend, is hardly ever a solo activity."

I looked down. "I know that now. I shouldn't have given up my faith in people, or faith in myself. I wish I had time to undo the damage."

"We can't always undo the bad that's been done, but we can always add good to the world to counteract it."

Marley was sniffing Kris's pant leg curiously. My friend chuckled and bent down to pet him. "You just told me all the things you'd like to do, Frost. Go and do them."

Uncertainty rose inside me. "But my magic and my form are so weak. And midnight is only a few hours away. What if there isn't enough time? What if I don't make it? What if I disappear before I even get the chance?"

"What ifs," Kris mused. "The shackles of good intentions. 'Men's courses will foreshadow certain ends, to which, if persevered in, they must lead. But if the courses be departed from, the ends will change.' Do you know the quote?"

"Of course. A lot of Dickens's lines from *A Christmas Carol* have been haunting me lately."

"Well, rest your mind. This one should not haunt, but inspire. It means that while the paths we take will inevitably lead to certain outcomes, if you change course and break away from the pattern, then you can forge a new fate for yourself."

I didn't reply immediately so Kris gently put both his hands on my shoulders and looked into my eyes. "Frost, this is the bottom line. Do you want to give up, lay down and die again, and accept this fate—or do you want to try to change? Do you believe that you and other people *can* change?"

I paused and felt the full weight of the universe behind me. Then, with strength equal to the churning magical lights at my back, I responded. "I do."

"Then what are you waiting for?" he asked, drawing back. "The North Pole main city is a straight shot from here, and isn't far. Go now. It's never too late for a Christmas Miracle. And we all have the power to make those happen. The true magic of this holiday isn't found in flying reindeer and jolly men sliding down chimneys; it's right here." He pointed at my chest. "Magic is inside you year-round if you decide to use it."

His form started to fade—dissolving into ethereal golden glimmers.

"Kris!"

"It's okay, Frost. No one you love is ever truly gone. We're always alive . . . *in spirit*." He winked at me, then melted into magic.

I stood frozen for a second. Then, like a drumbeat getting louder at the climax of a movie, my soul pounded with urgency and I started to run.

"Marley, come!" I shouted. We sprinted across the icy roof and down the stairs. A Christmassy version of the *Chariots of Fire* theme played in my head.

"Frost? Where are you going?" Brandon asked, glancing around the twelve-stack of pancakes on the ice table as I sprinted past.

"To do my job!" I replied, not slowing down. "Protect Christmas Spirit!"

I burst through the castle's main doors. Brandon, Midori, and the elves hurried after me.

"But what about your life force?" Brandon protested, hesitant to go beyond the threshold of the castle.

"It will be wasted if I don't try my best," I called back.

I paused then and turned to look at my team and the elves standing in the doorway. "My magic may not last, my form may weaken, and maybe putting myself at risk will only backfire. But I can't just do nothing. Christmas Spirit hinges on people trying everything they can to be together and bring people together."

"Frost—"

"Don't worry about me, Brandon. I'm at peace. Finally at peace. Thank you for being my partner in this. It's been a privilege to know you and Midori."

I gave her a nod reminiscent of the deeply profound ones she gave me. Then I addressed them both. "If I don't see you again . . . Merry Christmas."

With that, Marley and I plunged into the forest—quest recommenced.

When my dog started to slow, I picked him up and kept running. After we cleared the trees the snowfall increased. I raised my free hand and shielded my eyes to look for signs of life. Nothing yet.

I trudged on, keeping focused on my mission and the steps I'd take to see it through. My form held firm, but I was very aware that this could change at any second and sadly, before I knew it, minutes turned into an hour.

Just as I began to fear my body would run out of steam in all this snow, I spotted the twinkling lights of the North Pole villages. Still pushing ahead, I put Marley down, pulled out my CCD phone, and selected Bismaad's number.

The cell rang three times. Thankfully she answered. "Frost, what is it?"

"Come to the North Pole."

"Frost, I'm not just going to—"

"PLEASE, Bismaad. If our time together meant anything to you at all, please come now and meet me at the realm-evators."

I hung up. Marley and I finished our trek and finally arrived at our destination. The empty lobby made my faith waver, but then one set of doors slid open and Bismaad stepped out.

"What is it?" she asked pouting, her arms crossed.

In three long strides I reached Bismaad and wrapped my arms around her. The first real hug I'd given in over a century. My friend stood still like a statue, but when I didn't step back right away, she returned the embrace.

When I eventually did pull away, she seemed confused and concerned. "Frost, what is going on?"

"What's going on is that I was wrong."

"We already established that."

"No, I wasn't just wrong about how I treated you, and how I approached my job, and how I chose to use my afterlife. I was wrong tonight when I told you that it was too late for my redemption. *It's never too late for redemption.* That's the whole purpose of what we do here. That's the whole purpose of every Christmas movie. To show people they should never give up on miracles, and goodness, and themselves."

I took a deep, cleansing breath. "You're not going to see me again after tonight, Bismaad. And it matters to me that you forgive me, and that you understand you meant something to me all these years. The best way I can think to show you how much is this."

I bent down and picked up Marley. I kissed his head lovingly, then handed him to Bismaad. "Marley isn't simply a dog or a toy. He has always filled the void where my heart should've been. I want you to have him to remember me when I'm gone."

Bismaad was in shock. "I . . . But you . . ."

"I love him and I love you. Thank you for being my friend, Bismaad. I don't know what comes next for me, but I know that if spirits really can stay connected even when they're apart, then yours will always be a part of me." I sighed. "And now I have to go."

I started to leave, but Bismaad stopped me. "Frost!" This time it was her turn to fling her arms around me. I returned the hug.

"You'll always be my friend, Frost," she said.

"And you mine."

We held hands for a moment, then I withdrew and delved back into the wintery world. My soul pulsed with energy—emotional adrenaline overpowering and suppressing sadness and fear. My next destination was in sight.

As I'd hoped, the reindeer stables were deserted of their usual elfin staff. That Christmas party at Santa's Workshop was too tempting to pass up. Even from this distance I could hear the music thumping, and strobe lights shot through the barn windows in erratic streaks.

I raced past the empty stalls where Santa's eight senior sleigh-pulling reindeer slept and turned into the teen reindeer section of the stables. Four dark brown flying reindeer and two white, currently visible reindeer were awake. Thinking through my sleigh driving lessons with Kris, Nick, and Paul over the years, I felt like I could pull this off.

"Okay, who wants to go on a road trip?"

I selected a white reindeer named Yogurt and a dark brown steed named Usain Bolt and attached their reins and harnesses. The magical creatures followed me to the storage closet where the practice mini sleighs were kept—each roughly the size of a motorcycle sidecar. They were relatively light, like sledding toboggans, so with some effort I was able to carry one while I led the reindeer by their reins to the realm-evator lobby.

Bismaad and Marley were gone. I guided my reindeer to the freight elevator at the back and pressed the down button.

"Okay, come on. In you go." The reindeer huffed, but eventually I got them, myself, and the toboggan-sized sleigh into the lift.

I pressed the button to Earth. Nothing happened. The scanner blinked and worry shot through me. I didn't have my ID badge! It was in my bag, and who knew where that was.

DING!

The realm-evator across from me opened. Allan Cantes stepped out—dressed in a dashing suit with a black wool coat and red scarf that made him look like a fancy East Coast lawyer. He had been texting but stopped when he looked up and saw me crammed into the elevator with a pair of teen reindeer and a small sleigh.

His jaw dropped.

"Uh, hey, Allan."

"Frost. What are you doing?"

I sighed and spoke the truth. "I am trying to save my Scrooge, but with it being so close to midnight and his spirit so low, I don't have the power to teleport across a city looking for him. I need a fast ride. I figure the elves can collect these reindeer from Earth if I don't make it back. Their collars have trackers."

"Oh ... I didn't know you were having such trouble with your Scrooge. And on your last year too. That's rough."

"So is life. And the afterlife apparently. Listen, I know you and I haven't been amicable in years, but in the name of Christmas Spirit, can you do me a favor and lend me your ID? I don't have mine on me."

Allan hesitated. Then he stowed his phone and took the ID from his coat pocket. I reached out, thinking he was going to give it to me, but instead he smushed himself into the freight elevator too.

"Allan. What are *you* doing?"

"You're stealing reindeer and a sleigh, Frost. Forgive me if I don't trust you to bring me back my badge if I lend it to you." Allan scanned his ID and we started plummeting toward Earth. The red and green flashing lights of the realm-evator reflected in the reindeers' eyes, but they didn't seem that impressed by the effects. In fact, they were shockingly chill. I guess if you could fly or make things invisible, a lightshow and speedy elevator ride didn't thrill you.

The elevator stopped. Like chimneys magically expanded for Santa, my LA bathroom door warped and stretched until we'd all piled out, then snapped back to normal size.

I grabbed my TV remote and switched on the news. Probably the dumbest show a person could watch at Christmastime—talk about programming that killed your spirit—but I needed an update. A serious brunette woman filled my screen. "Following the blackout, safety inspectors are in the process of approving the auditorium for use. Doors should open soon and the debate is set to begin at just past eleven o'clock."

My watch read 10:30 exactly. Not much time to work with. But enough time for a miracle. That *is* what I was going for. I turned off the TV and hurried to the kitchen while talking to Allan. "I'm actually glad you came with me," I said, whipping a piece of paper and a pen out of a drawer. "I need you to do me a favor."

"Another one?"

I ignored him and focused on the note, feelings rushing through me as I put my soul into every word. Once done, I folded it up, grabbed a ribbon from the drawer, and then pulled my special wooden box from under my bed.

Allan approached as I flipped the lid open. I took a final look at the contents inside and ran my hand through the collection of faded movie ticket stubs, cherishing the memories. When I lifted my hand out, I let them slip through my fingers like sand.

I picked up the toy submarine I had made for Kris all those years ago. I smiled at it fondly. Then I attached my note to the toy and put it back in the box.

I closed the lid and presented it to Allan. "I'm not coming back, Allan. I wish I could say more, but it's best if you don't know the details. I realize you don't owe me anything, but I would like you to give this to Santa and his son. They are dear friends of mine and since I can't say goodbye to them properly because they're flying across the world and I'm running out of time, it would mean a lot to me if you delivered this to them."

If I was successful in saving Jay and got to retire, Bismaad, Nick, and Paul now had the purest forms of my love and friendship to remember me by. If I failed . . . at least in this moment they would know how much I cared for them. And perhaps since the toy in this box wasn't mine to start with, and Marley was built by someone else, they would escape the universal eraser that would wipe me from existence, like that ice capsule belonging to the poor ghost whose name I'd never recall.

Allan accepted the box hesitantly, looking confused.

"Since we're on a farewell kick . . ." I continued. "I am sorry I was never as nice to you as I should've been, Allan. Fifty years is more than enough time to get to know someone. Maybe if I had, I would've found things we share in common and there could've been friendship between us, not friction. I get why you snipe at me and treat me with coldness. You really tried to include me and I was too stuck in my own world and troubles to appreciate the effort. I never tried to be friends with you or any of the other ghosts who extended olive branches. I only pushed you away, so you all have every reason to dislike me. I slept in the lonely bed

I made just like I accused my Scrooge of doing. And for that, I truly apologize."

Allan stared at me, rendered speechless as he processed the shock of me admitting I was wrong, and also asking for his forgiveness. I gave him a caring pat on the arm and a small smile, then headed toward the reindeer, who were chewing on my couch blankets.

"Frost," Allan said abruptly. "Do you have any magic charms left?"

Puzzled, I held up my wrist. "A TV charm and a snowflake charm. But I barely have enough magic left inside to sustain this body. I can't risk activating them."

Allan tucked my keepsake box under one arm and walked over to me. Then he took my wrist in his hand. His eyes flashed with our signature blue light. Energy in the same shade trickled down his arm and passed into mine. Suddenly I felt a tiny bit stronger.

"It's just a little burst," he said. "But it should be enough to use one of those charms. I'm not sure if that can help you save your Scrooge, but at least you can try. Sometimes all it takes is the smallest spark of magic to make a difference."

"Wow . . . Thank you, Allan."

"Yeah, yeah." He smirked a bit then walked back toward the realm-evator bathroom, turning at the last moment before stepping inside. "Merry Christmas, Frost."

"Merry Christmas, Allan."

With my fellow ghost gone, I grabbed the reindeer by their reins and pulled the sleigh with my other hand, dragging it across the wooden floor and out the door.

When I got to the stairwell of the building, I glanced around to make sure the coast was clear then set the sleigh in its proper position and kicked it down the stairs one flight at a time to speed things up. I guided the teen reindeer behind me. The dark brown one levitated off the ground a few times and the invisible one vanished twice, but I didn't let go of either.

When we made it to the street, my hands flickered for a moment. I gasped, but took a deep breath. After a second my form solidified. Allan's magic may have helped, but I was using a lot of physical effort and needed to be careful. Who knew just how stable I was or how long the energy reboot of the ice castle would hold.

Being out this late on Christmas Eve had one benefit— though cars still sped by on the streets, the sidewalks were far emptier. At this moment, by great fortune, my strip of curb was completely clear. I harnessed my steeds to the small sleigh and hopped in. Then with reins firmly in hand I snapped them with the Old West ferocity of John Wayne in his prime.

"Heeyah!"

The reindeer took off, leaping from the sidewalk and into the street, cutting off a minivan.

"Sorry!" I called back.

Caramel corn, I should've told them to activate their powers first.

"Usain Bolt, fly! Yogurt, shield!"

The teen reindeer did as I asked. Well, sort of. As the creatures weren't totally mature, their powers weren't fully developed and their focus wavered.

Usain Bolt shot upward. His magic spread over us enough to grant some lift, but not a ton. We rose off street level and maintained flight a few feet above the cars, however the flight was bumpy and now and then my sleigh or the reindeer's hooves scraped the roofs of vehicles. Yogurt only kept us invisible half the time. As a result we left more than a few surprised drivers in our wake. That was unfortunate. I brought Yogurt so that maybe my dramatic dash across the city would be more inconspicuous.

Aw, you know what, fudge it. Desperate times called for desperate measures. Hopefully anyone who saw a fancily dressed lady riding a flying reindeer sleigh wouldn't question their sanity, or their eyeglass prescription. It was Christmas, after all—the season of magical, ridiculous things. Speaking of ridiculous things, the situation became notably dicier when we merged onto the 101.

Ugh! Why are the freeways in LA always so busy?!

"Look out!" I jerked on the reins and Usain Bolt jolted up just in time to miss a transport truck. The back bumper of my sleigh bounced off the vehicle's roof. My reindeer abruptly veered left into the carpool lane before I could stop them, then swerved as a car cut us off.

Seriously?! Why don't these sleighs have horns?

Oh, wait. They do.

Disregarding inconspicuousness, I blasted the horn three times.

I glanced at my watch and gave the reindeer another "Heeyah!" We clambered over the roof of the sedan, flew between several semitrucks, then ducked low to avoid a bridge.

As time ticked on, the reindeer started to lose their concentration. Our flight height decreased more frequently and Yogurt held his invisibility for shorter periods. I was getting worried, then at last we arrived at our exit and I yanked on the reins to swerve right. We zoomed off the freeway and, to my good luck, Usain Bolt found a second wind and pulled us higher. Our caravan sailed over the surrounding streets, shaving off a ton of travel time. Finally I spotted the bright lights of the auditorium.

The press was going to be swarming the debate. I couldn't let them get a pair of plucky magic reindeer on camera.

"Come on, Yogurt! You can do it!" I called, cupping a hand to my mouth.

The reindeer made a *KERRUFFMPHAHA* then suddenly shone brighter, causing us to vanish as we descended. I let out a sigh of relief and we landed in the parking lot, neatly pulling into a space.

When I stepped out of the sleigh Yogurt's magic didn't affect me anymore, and it looked like nothing was there. However, if I kept my hand on any part of the convoy—the sleigh, the reins, the reindeer themselves—I could see them perfectly.

I tied the reins to a manicured tree growing from the parking lot median and held Yogurt by her face. "Stay invisible. *Stay.*" She made that crazy sound again, and I patted her head, then Usain Bolt's. When I let go of them and stepped away, I turned visible—and then flickered. I hurried across the parking lot, my entire body fading in and out several times.

Focus, Frost. Come on. Come on.

I willed my strength to solidify me as I approached the crowd that had formed outside the auditorium. I made it to the front doors, but when I attempted to enter, a wall of security guards blocked me.

"Only candidates and their personal staff are allowed in right now, miss. Media and the general audience will be permitted inside in ten minutes."

"I *am* personal staff. Frost Mason—Jay Nichols's personal assistant."

The two guards blocking my way looked me up and down. "Yeah, I recognize her from the newspapers," said one of them.

"Of course you do." I narrowed my glare. "Open the door, please."

They let me in. I hurried through the lobby and made my way down the corridors.

"Frost?" I turned at Annie's voice. She looked at me with raised eyebrows. "What are you wearing?"

I swished my long skirt. "I'm going for an old-fashioned Christmas look. And what about you?" I waved at her. "Is that pantsuit the latest in backstabbing fashion?"

She frowned. "I wasn't trying to hurt Jay, Frost. I did what I had to do for my career."

"*Oh, and that makes it okay?*" I rolled my eyes. "You know, over the years I've dealt with a lot of people like you, Annie. You're not a bad person, but you're so blinded by tunnel vision that you don't see how you're affecting people; you don't notice the consequences you leave in your wake. Once, just once, I wish you would widen your perspective. Because what's the point of winning, or money, or power, if the world around you is burning to a crisp? But you don't care. Doing good isn't a priority for you, and neither *is* caring. If you can't attach a dollar amount to it or add it as notch on your career belt, then no need to bother."

"Frost, I care. I just—"

"Lost your spirit? Never mind. I don't have time for this. Goodbye, Annie. And good luck. I hope you turn out to be the person you wanted to be as a child."

I continued my fast pace through the halls. Jay's dressing room was empty. The package I'd ordered before everything went south at the gala was on the table, unopened.

I kept looking, peeking through every window and into every room until I made it to the media viewing gallery and spotted Jay through the window on the door. He was sitting alone inside, facing the other way. Hastily I grabbed the handle and jiggled it, but the door was locked.

"Jay!"

I banged on the door. No reaction from my Scrooge. My eyes flicked to the far right of the room where the massive screen took up the entire wall. I glanced at my bracelet.

"Come on, magic; don't fail me now."

I snapped my fingers and focused on how I wanted the enchantment of my TV charm to take form. My body blurred, whirred, and wavered, but I glowed with power as the charm melted to glitter.

Thank you, Allan.

I dissolved and shot through free space. When I opened my eyes, I was gazing at Jay from the perspective of a giant. My Scrooge looked as small as a teacup poodle below me.

"JAY!"

He fell out of his chair from the startle.

Jay scrambled up from the carpeted floor, smoothing his jacket and tie as he approached the enormous screen where I had appeared. "Frost?"

The fluorescent light of the screen illuminated him like the ghost he was destined to be.

"Where did you go? I thought maybe you left because you were out of futures to show me and your job was done. Why are you here?"

"I went to the North Pole, where I figured some things out. And I am here for you—in all senses of the word." The screen flashed brilliantly then the entire background was consumed in blinding white light. I stepped out of the screen and onto solid ground, shrinking back to normal size. I went straight to Jay and took his hands in mine.

"You are making a mistake. It's that simple. Please don't. I know you think it's too late to mend things with your family, but I promise you it's not. I know you worry about breaking their hearts and having your own heart get broken if your dreams and ambitions don't work out. But there is no point to life if all your decisions are made to avoid pain rather than chase happiness."

"Frost . . . I appreciate your belief in me, but I am just doing the practical thing. A person can't be soft to make it as far as I want to go. Times have changed. The world is on fire and a person has to be steel to move through it."

"Oh, Jay." I shook my head and let go of his hands. "The world has been on fire for centuries. And Billy Joel was wrong; you *did* start it. People like you who aren't bad but make bad decisions, people who let anger trump forgiveness and fear overpower faith. I've seen it firsthand over and over again through the decades. For as long as time has flowed, the pressure to turn hard, forget your spirit, and disregard the responsibility to show goodwill toward others has been burning humanity alive. Every time the flames are quelled in one area, someone pours gas on another and the danger continues. It doesn't have to be this way though. People were given the tools from the beginning—compassion, hope, love. That's all any of you need to make it feel like Christmas all year round. That's all you need to make this work."

"To make what work?"

"*Being alive.*"

"CANDIDATES BACKSTAGE PLEASE," blared a voice on the auditorium-wide intercom. "Doors opening in one minute."

I locked eyes with Jay. "Don't sign away your soul. Don't live a passive life where you fall into choices you never thought you'd make and ride the consequences to whatever fate hands out. You remember when I told you that you should appreciate life's most precious gift? This is it; it's all around you." I waved at myself, then the general area.

"What, the present?" Jay said. "Isn't that reveal a bit . . . predictable? Most people have heard the saying: Yesterday is history, tomorrow is a mystery, and today is a gift—that is why it is called the present."

I shook my head. "No, Jay. You misunderstand. It's not about the present; it's about BEING present. The present doesn't matter if you don't actively participate in it—if you don't let your soul breathe and make choices that heed your heart, mind, and spirit. Without that, you may as well *be* a ghost—existing in a daze, having life happen to you, not contributing to or sharing in it."

A security guard unlocked the room and various staffers started filing in. From down the hall I heard the click-clacking and footfalls of more shoes headed this way.

"I don't know if I can . . ." Jay said, glancing between me and the incoming people. "Even if I hear what you're saying, Frost, I've been on this path for a while and you're done at midnight. I don't think I can change long-term on my own. You said yourself that a ton of Scrooges revert back once they're alone. Why should I be any different?"

"Because I figured out the secret," I replied. I stepped close and whispered in his ear. "We're not supposed to be alone. Change, like humanity, is a team sport. We *need* someone to help us and remind us to keep at it. Otherwise it can vanish . . ." I stepped back. "Go to your family, Jay. Love and support helps us stay on track. In order to keep your Christmas Spirit alive, you must stay close to those that help it shine the brightest. Even when times get tough."

Reporters started to come in. They got excited when they saw Jay, but Jay's bodyguard Lucas appeared and cut off the pack.

"Come on, sir. This way." Lucas nodded at me and guided us both through a back door into a connecting hall while cameras flashed and questions were shouted at our backs.

Once the door clicked shut, Lucas continued to escort Jay along, however I stayed behind. Jay noticed and glanced back, but didn't say anything. I didn't either. I raised one hand in wave and gave him a small smile as I watched him walk away.

I'd done all I could do.

Once Jay had gone, I wandered down the corridor by myself. My magic was at 2%. With every step, my form faded. I'd used everything I had to keep it together, and now it was dissolving like Jay's chance at redemption—disintegrating with every moment he drew closer to that podium and solidifying who he would be.

I pulsed with faint blue light and slowly evaporated until my footsteps became inaudible and my appearance ceased to cause a reflection in the glass of the paintings in the hall. I'd returned to my intangible, invisible state, though not by choice. White clusters of sparkling energy like enchanted eczema began to develop on my dress, arms, and hands.

I think . . . I think I was being erased from existence.

"PLEASE TAKE YOUR SEATS" boomed the auditorium intercom.

I turned a corner and recognized this hallway as the one that connected to the control room. Several people phased through me as they hurried down the corridor. Usually I didn't feel a thing when this happened, but now their passage made me cringe. It was as if their life making contact with my increasing lack thereof was a cosmic incompatibility.

In the control room, the intense vibe reminded me of Santa's Workshop in its final twenty-four hours before the Big Guy took off in his sleigh. The twelve TVs displayed assorted feeds of the main stage, audience, and backstage. Jay was the focus of one, standing behind thick cobalt curtains. Several crewmembers were talking to him, but he seemed on autopilot—eyes distant, only nodding occasionally.

Loud applause turned my attention to one of the audience screens. It was starting. The moderator for the debate, a tan woman with a Jackie Kennedy flipped bob hairstyle, sat down at a desk positioned in front of the stage. She spoke into the mic.

"Thank you for joining us for tonight's debate. I realize it's late and it's a holiday, but nothing is more important in these troubling times than ensuring we put the right people in office. They control our futures. So I think we can all agree that Christmas can wait in the name of confronting the big questions. Who are these people, are the rumors true, are they qualified? Let's get into the nitty-gritty of the hot-button topics we all care about. Without further ado, may I introduce Miss Farah Jaffrey and Mr. Jay Nichols."

Jay and Farah took the stage from opposite sides as the applause roared. Farah smiled grandly as she walked and waved. Jay smiled and waved too, but was more conservative about it. His mind seemed elsewhere.

It was dizzying to see so many changing viewpoints on the TVs in front of me. When Jay and Farah were stationed at their podiums, the moderator spoke again.

"In order to keep this as concise as possible, we are waiving opening statements and will be jumping right into questions. This first one is for you, Miss Jaffrey. Some have criticized your involvement with big business related to international markets. If elected, will these affiliations affect your decisions as governor?"

"Thank you for the question," Farah responded. She spoke into the mic while directing her gaze to different parts of the audience as if acknowledging each attendee individually.

"My interest for all business, regardless of type, is that people be allowed to work in a competitive market that pushes them to grow. I believe that evolving in a global market means infusing the influence of the proper partners. I have seen a lot of the world and have spent years moving in business and political arenas, so

I understand what this state needs in order to progress in the coming years.

She turned sharp eyes on Jay. "My opponent does not have these qualifications. He was raised in a small community and remains inexperienced in dealing with the bigger world and larger perspectives. He is severely untested, small-minded, and irresponsible. He cares more about capturing a title than doing the work and making the tough choices. And most of all, he is a man who has lost over fifty elections in his career. *Let that sink in.* If an elementary school fifth grade class, and a high school debate team, and a college philanthropy board didn't trust him to govern their affairs, why should you trust him to govern that of millions?"

The crowd clapped and the moderator pivoted. "Mr. Nichols, your response?"

I stared at the TV screen that zoomed into a close-up of Jay's face. It was so familiar to me now—every crease, every angle—that it bewildered me to think that those details, everything about him, would soon cease to exist in my mind. All my memories would fade with me like they never happened. No one in the control room could see it, but two thirds of body was now covered in white smudges of existential energy. I could feel myself slipping away and forgetting—Paul's face, Marley's bark, Bismaad's laugh, the twinkle in Nick's eyes . . .

"Mr. Nichols?"

My mind was fuzzy, but I realized Jay hadn't answered his question.

"Would you like to respond?"

Another beat passed. Jay blinked and stared out at the audience, then he shook his head and looked down.

"I'm sorry. I can't do this."

Murmurs erupted and the moderator readdressed him. "Come again, Mr. Nichols?"

He raised his head and gripped the sides of the podium, making eye contact with the audience and cameras. "I appreciate all of you being here tonight, and I appreciate everyone at home who took the time to tune in, but I disagree with our moderator's opening. Christmas can't wait. It shouldn't have to, and it was egotistical of Farah and me to believe that taking televised shots at one another was more important than spending time with the people we love on the one night a year that most people believe should prioritize thinking about others."

Farah scoffed. "Jay, it's just a holiday. There are much greater things at stake, and the fact that you don't see that says a lot about you."

"It's not about the holiday, Farah. It's the principle. And I hope that *does* say a lot about me. Our moderator claims that we control people's futures and that the public wants to sink their teeth into touchy topics on Christmas. I say that no one controls your future, and that people would rather focus on actual issues at the right time in the right way. *This* is pointless. There is so much bad blood between us that you and I would probably spend the next hour taking cheap shots at each other's character, not discussing anything that matters, because that's what these kinds of debates turn into. No one really wants to listen to that, let alone during a season when we should strive to be better. This time of year wasn't meant for cruelty or pettiness. Season aside, we shouldn't be constantly tearing people apart at *any* time of year. It causes us to look at the world through a more cynical, angry lens, and it distracts us from the *spirit* of why we are here, why we run for office . . . To help."

He nodded once to punctuate the thought.

"That's the best use of a soul—to selflessly go out and try

our best to make people's lives better, and at the very least give them the opportunity and inspiration to make positive change for themselves. A friend taught me that recently. I wish I'd appreciated the lesson sooner."

The auditorium stood still and quiet for a moment. Until Farah scoffed.

"How idealistic," she said. "Perhaps you should take up writing Christmas cards instead of politics."

Jay looked at her evenly. "Thanks for the tip, Farah. I'd offer a response, but to quote my daughter, Christmas is no time for political stuff or arguing with mean people who don't get it." He turned back to the audience, all the cameras in the control room on him.

"I really do hope you vote for me next year. I hope you give me a chance, focus on the issues, and listen to every side before making your decision. At my core has always been the desire to make the world better. Lately I've been straying from that path. I could say life got in the way, but that's a lousy excuse. Life is not something that gets in the way; we get in our own way. We need to be present and active participants in our own stories because being alive is a gift and we should treat it that way all year round, not just at Christmas."

He took a deep breath and made a fist that he drove onto the podium. "I believe that with hard work and positivity, anything is impossible. I believe that small communities are the heart of our country and that everything great starts as something small. And I believe that good intentions are meaningless without actions. So, on that note, I'm sorry again that I won't be helping you fill this time slot, but I have to go. If I am going to be a man good enough to govern, first I have to be a good man. Thank you."

He marched off the stage. Silence persisted for a moment and then—*APPLAUSE*. Roaring, vibrant, leap-to-your-feet applause filled the auditorium. Even the people in the control room stood and clapped.

All of a sudden, the white magic patches consuming me started to glow. I held up my hands; they were beaming like stars. I sped out of the room as that energy spread around my body. People ran through me to get to the control room or the stage to be a part of the grand occasion. I kept moving. As I hastened down the hall, I heard a thumping sound that felt like it was coming from my chest, but I assumed it was my feet becoming solid again.

A moment later, the power surging inside me was too strong and I faltered to my knees. A striking, single pulse of light burst from every part of my body like I was the center of a meteorite on fire. When I opened my eyes, golden sparkles rained around me.

Gradually I stood up. I felt whole again—stronger and more grounded, but slightly shaky. I didn't feel powerful and renewed like when my Scrooges were totally redeemed, but I wasn't fading out of existence anymore. I concentrated on my magic and tried to teleport.

"Jay Nichols."

My blue energy activated; unfortunately I only flickered in place. I was disappointed, though not shocked. I was saved, but hadn't been restored completely and I knew why. There was still the other half of Jay's soul to polish.

I dashed to his green room on foot. Lucas and Rocco were standing at the door when I arrived, stern and intimidating in the face of the producers and reporters who wanted to speak to Jay. I pushed through the crowd and looked up at the bodyguards.

"Please?"

Lucas nodded and let me in. Jay was hastily grabbing his things—phone, wallet, etc.

"Going somewhere?" I asked.

He turned. "I think you already know."

My face broke into a grin and I abandoned all protocol to race over and throw my arms around him for my third huge hug of the night. "I'm so proud of you."

He hugged me back. "Thanks. I just hope it's not too late like you said."

"Never." I looked at my watch. "But I don't think churches appreciate tardiness. If you're going to make it across the city to you kids' choir recital at midnight mass, we're going to have to hurry."

The door opened again and we were surprised to see Annie enter.

Jay's brow knitted. "What are you doing here, Annie?"

"I've never seen anything like that, Jay," she began. "What you did out there. The courage to be . . . yourself." She took a deep breath. "I'm sorry. I am truly sorry. It was cold and cruel of me to do what I did. You didn't deserve that. But I would like to make it up to you. I just told Farah's assistant that I quit. I'd like to come back and help you help other people. If you'll let me."

Jay sighed. "Annie, I don't know if I can trust you again. It wasn't healthy for me to be constantly pressured by you and Friedman's and those donors you both connected me with. I'm not sure if I'll always be able to keep my spirit where it is now, but I do know I'll have a better chance if I surround myself with the right people. So if you're coming back with Friedman's interests, I'll pass."

"This isn't about Friedman's. *Forget them*," Annie said passionately. "I am doing this for me. Frost said something to me that cut deeply, and after I heard you speak, well, I just . . . I want to try supporting someone who I believe in for a change, not someone who simply signs my checks. And I want to compete because of what can be accomplished if we win, not just for the sake of winning."

Jay glanced at me. "What do you think?"

I studied Annie, then pivoted toward Jay. "I think tonight I've come to understand the importance of second chances as much as anyone can. You're trying to change, Jay, and so am I. Maybe she deserves the same chance."

Jay nodded, took a breath, then readdressed Annie. "I'm closing the office next week as a thank you to everyone for their hard work. You can come back in the new year but this time, I call the shots. You can offer support and counsel when asked. You can work with me, but no trying to control me. We'll work out the details from there. Deal?"

Annie smiled. "Deal. Thank you, Jay."

"Now if you'll excuse us, Frost and I have somewhere to be. Merry Christmas, Annie."

I snagged the package on the table before we exited the room. The crowd surged forward to swarm Jay, but Lucas and Rocco held them back as my Scrooge and I bolted down the hall.

"How are we going to get there?" Jay asked as we ran.

I smirked deviously. "How are you with heights?"

Usain Bolt and Yogurt did better this time around as we flew through the city—staying airborne and invisible for longer stints. However, that did not calm Jay as we sat squished together in the jolting sleigh. I'd have been lying if I said I didn't laugh a couple times at his panicked expression or when he clung to me like a cat climbing a tree during a water gun fight.

When we pulled into the church parking lot, the last of the crowds were filing in. I let Jay get a head start as I tied the reindeer in place. It was ten to midnight. "Take this and go inside." I tossed him the package. "I need to secure the reindeer."

"What is it?"

"Just open it and then put it inside your jacket for the right moment."

He nodded and dashed off. After another minute, I finished my task and sped over the lot. I caught up with Jay inside the church. It was an old-fashioned cathedral with gold, purple, and white silks draped across the ceiling from exposed wooden beams. Dozens and dozens of lit candles twinkled on shelves, alters, candelabras, and inside of glass jars hanging from the large pine at the front of the church.

Jay stood just past the entrance, looking around. The venue was extremely crowded—formally dressed attendees, members of the church processional, children preparing to perform in the choir. The latter looked angelic in white tunics draped with shimmering golden sashes and sparkling braided cords.

"There!" I pointed. I spotted Kamie and Kingsley near the front of the church on the left. Eddie adjusted Kingsley's tie while Celia smoothed Kamie's sash. Jay's sisters stood nearby with their own kids dressed in choir attire. The rest of the family gathered around them—Ray Jr. laughed with Monica's husband Dion; Sandra and Raymond sat on the bench behind the group.

Jay stiffened as he took them in. He noticeably gulped.

"*Well* . . ." I nudged his shoulder with my own. "Do I really need to say there's no time like the present or don't you grasp that already?"

He took a deep breath. "Okay, okay. Can you come with me?"

"Fine, but at midnight, however this plays out, I have to go."

"What? No."

"Jay, you knew that was my cutoff."

"Yeah, but I just thought . . . I still don't know if I can do this without you."

"You have them. I know you can."

"What if I don't want to?" His eyes were full of caring. He released a sad sigh. "I wish you could stay."

I smiled at him and put a hand on his arm. "I do too. But this is *your* Christmas story. Now go."

He still seemed reluctant, but journeyed up the aisle to reach his family. I followed at a moderate distance—close enough for support, far enough to respect that this was his moment.

Felicia spotted him first. "*Jay?*"

His entire family turned. Jay gave a self-conscious wave as he came to a stop in front of them. "Um, hi."

"Hi," Felicia said.

"Who's that?" one of her kids asked, pulling on her dress.

"This is your uncle Jay." Felicia gave Jay a sassy, pointed look. "You've never met him before."

"Jay, baby, what's going on with you?" Sandra asked, standing with some effort. Ray Jr. helped her. "We watched your political talk on one of the kid's phones. What's gotten into you?"

He did an awkward smirk-shrug. "Would you believe the Christmas Spirit?"

Monica slapped him upside the head.

"Ow! Monica!"

"Hey, you deserve it. You really think you can make some sort of life-loving, humble speech and everyone will accept that you've changed and forgive you for being a total sh—"

"Kids present, babe." Dion put a hand on her shoulder.

Monica took a deep breath. "You've been distant a long time, Jay. You've missed birthdays, holidays, weddings; you don't respond to emails or phone calls—I don't know what kind of Ebenezer Scrooge metamorphosis you're supposedly going through, but it doesn't erase how you've hurt your siblings, your kids, and our mother and Celia in particular. Do you know how many times I've had to console Mom over the years when she's depressed about how you shut her out? And that horrible move earlier in the week throwing Celia under the bus by disparaging her past? I'd like to make a crude Dickens pun right now, but since kids are present I'll just say this. *You're the worst.*"

Jay gulped again. Thankfully he didn't back away. "You're right. You're one hundred percent right. I have been so angry and resentful for so long it turned me into a terrible brother, son, and father. It hit me all at once, and it hit me hard. I can't say I don't want to lose any of you because I know I did that a while ago, but I would like it if you could give me a chance to find my way back."

He looked at his sisters. "Monica and Felicia, I abandoned you. I thought we had to choose sides when Mom and Dad got divorced and I let that drive a wedge between us." He turned to Ray Jr. "I held such a grudge about what happened with my parents I barely acknowledged you growing up, and that was a messed-up thing to do."

Jay stepped forward and addressed Eddie and Raymond. "I hated you both because I thought you were replacing me and replacing someone I loved. I know that was wrong now. Raymond, you didn't force my dad away; his bitterness did. He had the relationship with us that he chose. Eddie, I've painted you as this obstacle between me and my kids, but I've been my own obstacle. My anger and my belief that I was better off choosing distance rather than risk getting forgotten or letting people down kept me away, not you. And, kids . . ."

He knelt down in front of Kamie and Kingsley. "My job and career are important, but nothing is more important to me than the job of being your father. That's not even the right word for it because it's a privilege. I love you so much, and I don't ever want you to forget that or forget me. I want to be in your lives no matter what it takes, and I hope you can forgive me for not trying to do better before."

Jay stood and then slowly, humbly went to his mother. "I don't have the words, Mom. There aren't any strong enough to convey an apology that's so overdue. I was angry with you for too long and it had everything to do with me and not you. I should have listened. I should have tried. I should have seen you for the strong, loving person who always tried to bring me home, not as the reason Dad left. It was unfair of me to blame you for that. And it was stupid."

Jay took a deep breath and lastly walked over to his ex-wife.

"Celia, for years now you have asked me to accept your amends. But the truth is that you don't need anything from me. You've only become a stronger woman and better mother over the years, whereas I have become a worse parent and person. I would like to offer you *my* amends. For everything. I only hope you can accept them."

Jay reached into his jacket pocket and pulled out the item I'd had sent to his green room earlier with my purest hope that we would get to this moment. In his hand, Jay held a beautiful Christmas Rose, which he offered to Celia with utter respect.

The scene between Jay and his family held perfectly still amid the surrounding hustle and bustle of the church for a moment. Then Celia took the flower, wrapped her free hand around the back of Jay's neck, and brought him in for an embrace.

It was beautiful.

Kamie and Kingsley joined in, hugging their parents from the side. Jay and Celia welcomed them in the squeeze.

Once the group finished hugging, Eddie shook Jay's hand.

Raymond stood and offered the same gesture. More hugs were exchanged, culminating in one from Sandra.

When Jay's mom pulled back after the embrace, she grabbed Jay's face between both her hands and brought him down for a kiss on the forehead. Tears glistened on her cheeks. "Don't go losing yourself again, you hear me? My heart can't take it."

"Don't worry, mom. Neither can mine." The pair looked into each other's eyes affectionately before Monica smacked Jay on the arm—lighter this time.

"What's with nineteen-hundreds Nancy over there?" she pointed at me.

"That's Frost!" Kingsley declared. "Dad's assistant. She's cool. Pun intended."

The family regarded me. "Hi there," I said, drawing closer.

"She's cute," Felicia commented.

"When she's not scaring me," Jay replied, winking at me. "She is actually the one who helped me realize what a jerk I've been."

"Then she's welcome with us any time," Monica said. "In fact, maybe we should get your cell number on speed dial, Frost, in case this fool screws up again."

"Monica," Sandra interjected. "Leave the poor girl alone." She came up to me and took my arm, leading me to the bench. "Would you like to sit with us, dear?"

"Oh, I would love to," I said, stopping. "But I have to go. I only came to give Jay moral support and make sure he reunited with you okay."

From the stage, the choir director, dressed in robes that matched the children's, clapped his hands. "Places, everyone! Places!"

Kamie gave her father one more leap-into-his-arms hug. He kissed her head. He also hugged Kingsley again before sending him off. The majestic clock at the back of the church showed the time as two minutes to twelve.

"I'll walk Frost out and be right back," Jay said to his family.

"We'll save you a seat, baby," Sandra said.

As the choir assembled on stage, and the church's congregation flocked to their seats, Jay and I walked side by side in silence. At the main doors, we gazed out at the picturesque holiday assembly, then at each other.

With no words we exchanged a final hug. When we pulled apart, he held onto my hand a little longer before my fingers slipped through his and I stepped away.

"Merry Christmas, Jay."

"Merry Christmas, Frost."

I turned and didn't look back. I exited the church and jogged down the steps just as the angelic voices of the children's choir rang through the air. Out in the deserted parking lot, I could still hear their voices through the open windows of the church—hauntingly beautiful, just like my last year as a ghost.

The clock outside the church struck midnight. The chime reverberated through me and echoed across the block as my entire body flared with spectral blue energy. With this final piece of the puzzle, Jay's full Christmas Spirit radiantly refilled me with magic. He was redeemed. He was saved. He was Scrooged.

My entire body sang with power now. Jay had completed his journey. As a result, I had completed mine. I checked my watch; my power was totally restored. I was saved, which meant Midori and Brandon were saved too.

I gazed up at the church and smiled. Now all that was left was the finishing touch. With 100% power, I could spare a tiny flex of magic muscle. I held up my wrist and looked at the snowflake charm, the last magical trick up my sleeve.

"What, the current finale wasn't dramatic enough for you?"

I spun around to find Bismaad standing behind me, holding Marley. She set the dog on the ground and he bounded over to me. I bent and rubbed his ears.

"Bismaad—how? What are you doing here?"

"When you left the North Pole and risked vanishing from existence, Specter One decided to tell me what was happening with you. I spoke to Allan too, after he delivered your package to Paul and Santa. I am so proud of you."

"There's a lot of that going around tonight," I replied. "I am glad to see you again."

"Back atcha ten times over," Bismaad replied. "Now seriously, I'm guessing you want to add a frosty final cinematic touch to this Christmas moment?" She pointed at my charm bracelet.

"Why not? I have one charm left and fully restored powers. I may need the bulk of that magic for my upcoming reincarnation, but I think I can spare a little to make it snow over this church and give this Christmas story, and Jay, the ending they deserve."

"That's a good idea," Bismaad said. "But I say go big or go home. If you're open to the help, of course . . ."

All of a sudden dozens and dozens of human-sized blue light flashes went off across the parking lot. All the ghosts—not just my Present colleagues, but Midori and the Ghosts of Christmas Future, and Brandon and the Ghosts of Christmas Past—appeared in the lot. They strode closer together, forming one circle with Bismaad and me.

I grinned in disbelief. Brandon ran to my side and gave me a hug. I returned it then stood and patted his ginger head. "What's going on? What are you all doing here?"

"It's like we've been trying to tell you for a century, Frost," Bismaad said. "You are not alone." She began to glow with modest blue light. "If we all share a spark, we can create something far more spectacular, don't you think?"

Brandon offered me his hand. "On your lead, Frost."

He started to glow, as did all the other spirits in the circle who began taking each other's hands, linking us all together.

My soul enlivened with appreciation, warmth, and joy. Once again, I felt like I heard some sort of thudding nearby, but everyone was standing still so I didn't know where it was coming from.

I snapped my fingers and the snowflake charm on my wrist disintegrated. As those golden glimmers sprinkled away, I linked hands with Brandon on one side and Bismaad on the other. They clasped onto the ghosts beside them and our massive circle was complete; we were all connected.

Our bodies glowed and a small waft of blue energy drifted away from each of us, cumulating together to form a swirling ring of light above our congregation like a grand halo. It rose higher and higher into the sky until it burst with a shimmering flash—transforming into golden clouds that spread out over the church and the entire city. The clouds shifted to normal gray as they extended through the heavens—blending with the sky.

Then . . . snow began to fall.

On my own, with the restriction of needing to conserve my magic, I could've only covered this church with snow. With the help of all the ghosts, the whole of Southern California was suddenly dumbfounded as flecks of winter purity rained down.

The ghosts and I gazed up at the falling flakes—standing with one another in spirit literally and figuratively. My lips curved into a smile.

After a moment, I drew my phone from my pocket, opening the Tinsel app.

Bismaad looked at me curiously. "What are you doing?"

"Updating my status." I snapped a picture of the scene and typed as I grinned mischievously. Then I showed her my post.

"Sleighed it!"

#neveralone

Bismaad laughed. We enjoyed the moment arm in arm, all of us taking in the cold, calming wonder. After a minute the other ghosts waved and began to teleport away. As the last of them departed, a new soul appeared.

"Specter One!" I exclaimed.

"Frost. Let's talk."

I bid Bismaad to give me a moment and strolled across the parking lot with my boss. Snow was already starting to thoroughly coat the cars.

"It's time for your reward," he said. "You fulfilled your mission—one hundred years of saved souls. I am genuinely as happy as anyone could be to offer this opportunity to you, Frost. You did good. *In more ways than one.* So tell me—are you ready for your new life?"

I sighed. "I guess so. It's funny, I was just getting used to this one."

"Well, would you like it?"

"What do you mean?"

We paused in front of a sports car with frosted windows.

"The magic you've accumulated will grant you new life, Frost. All the ghosts who've ever made it to retirement have chosen a new life in the form of rebirth, so that's what I pitch it as when I meet with spirits who are up for their hundredth. But if you are happy here—in the present, as it were—that magic can be used to make you human again as you are right now."

"Seriously?!"

He nodded. "I think your spirit knew it too. You don't seem very dead anymore, Frost. If I'm not mistaken, I think I can even detect a previously frozen heart beating in there." Spector One pointed at me and smiled. "I suppose you melted it."

I held my hand to my chest. He was right! That was the thudding I'd been hearing. I could feel an actual heartbeat for the first time in a hundred years.

Emotion welled in my throat but I tried to keep composed. "I suppose I did."

"So what do you say?"

I glanced at Bismaad and Marley. I looked over at the cathedral and listened to the sweet choir voices in the air. Snow continued to fall like a miracle.

With firm decision, I faced Specter One with my answer.

"I'm happy in the present."

He put a hand on my shoulder. "I'm glad to finally hear it."

"All right, I think you're set. Dog—check. Phone—check. Beating heart—hang on!" Paul jokingly pulled a toy stethoscope from the present sack in the sleigh and listened to my chest. "Check."

I playfully swatted him away. "Thanks for changing your route to see me off," I told him and Nick, standing beside me.

We'd parked on the snow-covered roof of a cute two-story house in a suburban nook of Los Angeles. Everything for miles was coated in the most graceful blanket of white Christmas promise. The miraculous flakes hadn't stopped falling since midnight, but now they came down much lighter—trickling from the heavens as we made our farewells.

People had gone nuts about it—news cameras, social media explosion, folks running and frolicking and making snow angels in the streets—the whole nine yards. But now, at half past one in the morning, a still calm had settled over the city.

I could relate. The same peaceful sensation had settled over me as well.

Bismaad, Brandon, and Midori were riding in the back seat

of the sleigh—squished with the magical sack of presents but content nonetheless. I was glad all my friends had come to say goodbye.

"Hey, we deliver a lot of stuffed animals, technological gadgets, and dolls," Nick replied, patting the sleigh. "It's not every day that we drop off a friend as a gift."

I hugged him and then Paul. "Come visit," I said when I pulled away. "Not just in December. I've never seen you guys in the off-season."

"And that's a tragedy in itself," Paul said. "I look awesome in a bathing suit." He smacked his abs.

"I've gotten mixed reviews," Nick said, slapping his belly, which jiggled like a bowl full of jelly. We laughed.

"And you feel free to visit us whenever you want, too," Nick continued, drawing a set of Beaming Bells from his pocket. He gestured to Brandon and the kid handed Nick a lumpy tote bag. Nick put the bells inside the bag as he spoke.

"We also put your keepsake box in here, along with my father's submarine toy. Now that you're not going to be erased from existence, I know he'd be glad we are giving it back to you. There are also keys to your loft downtown—Specter One has taken care of it—and your CCD ID badge. Your former spirit boss says you're welcome in our realms any time. He'd even like to talk to you about taking on a consulting job or teaching a seminar next season. Every ghost who's ever made it to retirement has gone with the rebirth option, which means no memories of all this Christmas Carol magic. You're special. A successfully retired ghost turned human can provide valuable insight, I'm sure."

"Sounds fun," I said. "I think next season I'd also like to start getting to know the other ghosts. I've put it off too long, and there are probably plenty of awesome friends just waiting to be made. Maybe I can arrange movie nights at the CCD next

December when you all wake up. That's valuable knowledge too, you know." I glanced at Bismaad, Midori, and Brandon. "What do you think?"

Bismaad grinned. "I'll bring the popcorn."

"I'll bring the pancakes," Brandon seconded.

Midori gave me a thumbs-up and an actual smile—no teeth, but super sincere.

My dog kicked up some snow on the rooftop. I looked back to Bismaad and put my hands on the rail of the sleigh beside her. "Are you sure you don't want to keep Marley with you? I love him, but I love you and I can't think of a better gift to show how much. If you're giving him back because you think I need him, I promise you I am done with crutches."

She put her hand over mine. "I know, Frost. And I love the gift and that you've changed. But he'd be happier with you versus in his sleep mode for eleven months of the year while I'm frozen. How about shared custody? Next winter our furry friend can see the world with me."

"Deal." I smiled and we exchanged a side hug. Then I tilted my chin at the tote in Paul's hands. "Anything else in there I should know about?"

"Just an old friend." Paul drew out my copy of *A Christmas Carol*. I smiled as he put it back, then handed me the bag.

"Thank you." I glanced at the street below and took a deep breath. "Well, I guess this is it. Merry Christmas, everyone."

Nick activated his sensational Santa magic, and Marley and I floated off the roof in a swirl of glistening splendor, descending to the snowy streets. Now that I was human, I didn't have my magic anymore. I'd have to get used to traveling on foot. I'd have to get a driver's license. I chuckled at the thought.

Once released from Nick's magic, I waited. Then came the unmistakable clacking of reindeer hooves against the rooftop and the scraping of the sleigh before it lifted off. I watched Santa's sleigh fly away—the Big Guy, his son, and my three favorite ghosts waving. I waved back and watched them disappear into the clouds.

With a great sense of peace and possibility, I flipped open my phone and selected Jay's number. He answered after two rings. Laughing and music filled the background.

"Frost?"

"Hi, Jay."

"Frost!"

"Sorry to interrupt your family time, but can you come outside your mom's house for a minute?"

"Yeah, sure. One second."

I hung up the phone and snapped for Marley's attention. He was currently sticking his face in the snow.

"Come on, boy."

He yapped and trotted after me as we made our way across the road. The pure white of the snow-draped streets, driveways, and lawns provided incredible contrast to the black sky. It was such a striking composition. For arguably the first time in Los Angeles, there wasn't a single car on the road or the slightest sound of traffic. Pure peace.

The majority of homes on the block were still lit up by Christmas lights, but the windows were dark—the neighborhood residents already lost in a slumber of the sweetest sugar plum visions no doubt. All except the home directly ahead. Sandra's house glowed.

Jay opened the front door of his mother's house and the warm radiance from within spilled out. Then he looked up, saw me, and forgot to close the door.

"Frost!" He raced over and halted a couple feet away. "You're back."

"I'm retired," I said. "As a ghost I mean. You were my hundredth Scrooge. My reward for saving you was another chance at life. I'm human now. Listen."

I grabbed his hand like we were Tarzan and Jane and held it to my chest so he could feel my heart beating. He cracked a smile and I let him go.

"What?" I said.

"I just . . . I'm just so glad to see you. Are you staying in LA?"

"I am. It was my home once. I'd like it to be my home again. *And* it is the heart and soul of the movie industry so—spoiler alert—on my days off from working on your political campaign, I'm going to be buying *a lot* of popcorn, if you catch my drift."

"You still want to work with me?"

"Just as long as you promise to mellow out in the new year. You run kind of uptight, you know?"

He smiled widely. The snowflakes fell delicately, each an unspoken thought or feeling passing between us.

"So, now what?" Jay asked.

"Well, I have a job, a home, and a dog . . . I guess now I just need to find a family."

Jay glanced over his shoulder at the boisterous, radiant house. "I have one. It may be loud, messy, and complicated, but you're more than welcome to try it on for size. I mean, if you want . . ." His kind eyes held mine, and he offered me his hand.

It hovered outstretched in front of me.

A particularly big snowflake fell on my nose and shivered my skin. I felt . . . cold. What an extraordinary feeling. The icy contrast reminded me how alive and full of warmth I was.

My favorite quote from *A Christmas Carol* came to mind—the same one Kris had said to me earlier this evening.

"'Men's courses will foreshadow certain ends, to which, if

persevered in, they must lead. But if the courses be departed from, the ends will change.'"

Jay tilted his head. "What's that from?"

"A great story," I replied thoughtfully. "But I think I'm finally ready to write my own. No more dwelling on the past and no more fear of the future. Just me, you, and the present."

I took his hand and we exchanged a smile.

Then we walked toward the house together.

the End

About the Author

Geanna Culbertson is the award-winning author of *The Crisanta Knight Series*. The series has been featured in *Girls Life Magazine* as recommended reading for preteen and teen girls, and is an ongoing supporter of *Girls on the Run, Read to a Child,* and *Girl Scouts of the USA*. In the last few years Culbertson has been a regular speaker at schools across the country for an array of age groups (from elementary schools to major universities).

Culbertson is a proud alumna of the University of Southern California where she earned her B.A. in Public Relations and triple minor degrees in Marketing, Cinematic Arts, and Critical Approaches to Leadership. She is a part of only 1.3% of her graduating class to earn the double distinction of Renaissance Scholar and Discovery Scholar. Her Discovery Scholar thesis

"Beauty & the Badass: Origins of the Hero-Princess Archetype" earned her acclaim in the School of Cinematic Arts and helped fuel her female protagonist writing passions.

When she is not writing, Culbertson enjoys pursuing tasty foods, working out, and adventure. Outside of authoring, Culbertson has excelled as a marketing and branding manager for various companies, earned her black belt, taught karate to kids, learned the piano, and graduated as a certified sushi chef.

Culbertson wishes to thank all fans, allies, and supporters of her work. She is excited about continuing to thrill readers of all ages by expanding her rich, magical, and morally-driven content with the Crisanta Knight world, and other series and standalone books on the way! Keep an eye out for the first book in her new guardian angel series in 2022, as well as her Crisanta Knight finale!